TOP FANTASY

This one's for Richard, brother and friend

TOP FANTASY
The Authors' Choice

*Selected and introduced by
the authors themselves*

Compiled and edited by
Josh Pachter

J.M. Dent & Sons Ltd
London and Melbourne

First published in paperback 1986
First published in Great Britain 1985
© Introduction and selection Josh Pachter and Loeb, uitgevers BV, Amsterdam,
1985

This book is set by
The Word Factory, Rossendale, Lancs
Printed in Great Britain by
Guernsey Press Co. Ltd, Guernsey C.I., for
J. M. Dent & Sons Ltd
Aldine House, 33 Welbeck Street, London W1M 8LX

British Library Cataloguing in Publication Data

Top fantasy : the authors' choice.
  1. Fantastic fiction, English   2. English
fiction——20th century
I. Pachter, Josh
823'.01'0815 [FS]   PR1309.F3

ISBN 0-460-02467-1

Contents

Acknowledgments

It took half a year to fit the pieces of this jigsaw puzzle together, and during that time I received much invaluable cooperation, encouragement and support from an assortment of men and women. I'd like to take this opportunity to acknowledge them and to thank them for their participation. First and foremost, my thanks to the authors represented in these pages, who selected and introduced the stories you are about to read. A number of agents provided important assistance, especially Virginia Kidd, Leslie Flood (of the E.J. Carnell Literary Agency), Russell Galen (of Scott Meredith) and Don Congdon (of Don Congdon Associates). Ed Hoch and Peter Pautz helped me to locate the addresses of the 100+ authors I originally contacted, and offered many useful suggestions as well. Thanks also to John Bunch, Dennis Puisto and Frank Williams of the Bahrain School, for many kindnesses. And finally, my gratitude and love to Vicki and Martha Jones, whose friendship transformed this challenging project into a joyous experience.

Introduction

This is not an ordinary book.

In an ordinary book, a boy meets a girl and either wins her or loses her. In an ordinary book, a company of tough and determined heroes fights the bad guys and either beats them or doesn't beat them. In an ordinary book, intrepid explorers travel uncharted lands and either make it home alive or die.

Actually, a boy meets a girl in *this* book, too, and in point of fact they lose her. Wait a minute, you ask yourself, did I say 'they' lose her? Yes, I did, that's exactly what I said. Because this is not an ordinary book, you see, even though a boy meets a girl in it. In *this* book, the boy who meets the girl has two heads, although the girl they meet and lose has only one.

There are heroes and villains in this book as well – although, since this is not an ordinary book, the heroes are elves and the villains are trolls, and the baddest bad guys of all are . . . well, that would be telling.

When it comes right down to it, you'll even find intrepid explorers and uncharted lands in these pages. Remember, though, that this is no ordinary book, and don't be surprised when the travellers turn out to have two dozen legs apiece and the territory they cover bristles with Eaters and Destroyers and Skimmers and Interceders.

Unlike most ordinary books – which tell of real or realistic people, real or realistic events, real or realistic places – this is a book of fantasy. It is populated by dragons and dragonboys, by werewolves and sea monsters, by talking cats and mysterious butterflies, by a man who walks on air and a man who collects Poe and a man who has terrible trouble with water. In these pages, you will learn what happened when the Magician-Lord Subyrus purchased a blue vase of ghosts for seven thousand golden vaimii. You will hear of the Sun Kings' struggle with Arawn, the spectral Black Rider, and of the immortal Kane's encounter with the dread Grey Lord. You will visit the State Institution for the Criminal Incurably Insane, and a marvellous little bookshop in New York's Greenwich Village – yes, one of *those* marvellous little bookshops! – and an incredible cemetery whose location is much less important than its size.

I warn you, dear reader, that this is no ordinary book. It is the third volume in the *Authors' Choice* series of anthologies – a companion to *Top Crime* and *Top Science Fiction* – and, as such, it is a collection of some of the very best contemporary fantasy stories, as selected and introduced by the authors themselves.

Thus, if I may say so myself, it is an *extra*ordinary book, and I hope you enjoy reading it as much as I have enjoyed compiling it for you. But beware: once you have savoured the 24 tales which follow, you may never settle for an *ordinary* book again. . . .

Josh Pachter
September, 1984

THE MAN WHO WALKED ON AIR
Michael Avallone

I finally cracked Weird Tales, *after years of trying, with 'The Man Who Walked on Air'. It is perhaps the finest fantasy I ever conceived – and it all came to me in a supermarket, where I was trapped between hordes of housewives with their shopping carts on the one hand, and counters overloaded with bargain sales on the other. Wistfully, I wished I could walk on air to escape the madness. When I got back to my furnished room in the West Eighties of mad Manhattan, the full story surged in an unbroken narrative line from my typewriter.*

The slicks ignored the tale, but fabled Dorothy McIlwraith of Weird Tales *loved it. And so did I – so much so that, twenty years later, I incorporated it into my Ed Noon novel,* The Moon Maiden.

Let me tell you about the man who walked on air. John Henry could have told you but John Henry is dead. That leaves just me. You've heard of me. Lester Borne, the great American showman. Of course, someone else could have told you, too. The man who walked on air had a wife—

But I'm getting ahead of a story that really began one day in my office. Tomlin's Three-Ring Circus was in town and I, Lester Borne, its manager and sole owner, was thinking rather regretfully of how little I had to offer a public that ate peanuts and adored death-defying thrills.

Certainly, I had clowns, bareback riders and a whole ring full of wild animal acts. Even the Benzo Brother, who gleefully and fearlessly submitted to being shot from the cannon's mouth once every performance at quite a chunk of dough per season. But nothing really new. Or different. Possibly, this explains my willingness to see the man whose card preceded him into my Fifth Avenue office.

It was quite a strange card:

1

PINKERTON FLY
THE MAN WHO WALKS ON AIR
NO ROPES NO NETS NO WIRES

When my secretary ushered him in, I was skeptical. He was a small, undersized man. A sallow complexion, skimpy build, and a curious attitude of listening in the way he cocked his angular, almost bald head. He didn't look anything at all the way a Big Tent performer should look.

I wasted no time with the usual preambles. I'd been consoling myself with Martinis and wondered later if this had anything to do with what I was about to see.

'Show me,' I scoffed.

He did.

Without comment, he performed one of those things Nijinsky was so famous for. I don't know what they call it, but Pinkerton Fly sprang high into the air, crossed his feet about fifteen times with small scissor-kicks — and here he went the great Russian ballet artist one better. He *stayed* up there. He didn't come *down*. Just stood there and stared down at me intently, looking for all the world as if he were standing on the floor.

I blinked at him. He regarded me with that odd, listening expression. Then I stared at the half-empty glass near my outstretched hand. I am a practical man. I buzzed Miss Evans on the office intercom. 'Miss Evans, come in for a moment, please.'

Miss Evans appeared, took one look at my suspended visitor, gave a low moan and stood stock-still, clutching her steno pad and pencil, as if they were weapons.

'Tell me what you see,' I barked, conscious of tiny pinpricks at the base of my scalp. Miss Evans didn't answer. Her mouth was a thin, pinched line. Her eyes were glued on my visitor.

'Well?' I rasped harshly. 'Is he standing up there or isn't he?'

All this time Pinkerton Fly just remained where he was, regarding us with that peculiar listening air about him.

Miss Evans lowered her gaze. Her secretarial calm was in ruins. I could see that. Her voice forced its way out of her tightly locked lips.

'I see it — but it's a trick — Mr. Borne — it can't be — it's not possible—'

'That will be all, Miss Evans. Go out and draw up a contract. I'll call you when I need you.'

She flung a last look at Pinkerton Fly, but his great height from the floor only seemed to mock her reason and sanity still more. With a low scream, she fled through the door, leaving it ajar. I came around the desk, closed the portal softly and went back to my chair. I took a great deal of time lighting up a cigar, taking an elaborate delay stoking it up properly. I leaned back in my swivel and brought my eyes slowly up from room level to Pinkerton Fly. He was still *there*. Standing serenely, defying the law of gravity, waiting expectantly for me to say something.

'Well—' I got my courage up. 'Walk on *air*. Go ahead. That's what your card says. Show me. The Showman is asking you to show him something.'

Wordlessly, Pinkerton Fly *walked* around the room. Somewhere about four feet above my head. Normally, naturally, as if he was taking a stroll about any room in the whole wide world. My wall paintings were at his foot level; his waspish bald head was nearly scraping the ceiling. Then he threw the topper in. He did a handstand in mid air. Until you've seen a man do a handstand in mid air with his two hands braced against nothingness as though it were the most substantial of hand-holds, you haven't seen anything.

I had another drink. A tall, stiff one. I waved my free hand at him feebly. 'Turn it off,' I hoarsed. 'Whatever it is. Come on down. Fast. That's enough.'

He did. It was as if a fast elevator brought him down to the floor. He landed with a light thud, softly and deftly on his toes. Then he spoke for the first time. I was a little surprised to find he had one of the most normal, nasal voices in the world.

'Then you believe I can do it, Mister Borne? You are convinced?'

I was past argument. 'I'm convinced it will be one of the greatest stunts ever seen in any circus, anywhere.' My mind was flying. 'The house is packed. High above the crowd, in the lighted arena – you walking across the air. No tight-wire, no ropes, no nets. No nothing. People will refuse to believe. They'll claim I've run some invisible wire across the space between the two poles. But – they'll pay to see it. Pay plenty.'

Suddenly, he sighed. 'That is good. Zelma will be pleased.'

'Zelma? What does she do – the same thing? Say, a double would be even better—'

'You don't understand.' He smiled at me. His smile was like a weak candle lighting up his yellow face. 'Zelma is my wife. She has taught me how to walk on air.'

We were back to that again. My reasoning mind had been giving me a bad time about it.

'You really did it, didn't you? You didn't trick me – you didn't hypnotize me or anything like that? No, of course not. I did see you do it. I'm not blind but—'

As if in answer, he Nijinskyed up into the air again, scissored his legs and stood on solid nothing for a full minute, then came down again. I noticed the listening business once more. He'd cock his head forward as if to catch something that was being said. His head remained in that position all the time he was aloft.

I shook myself dumbly. It was unbelievable. Any way you look at it.

'You sure you didn't escape from the Moon or something? Are you a citizen?'

The candle lighted his sallow complexion. 'I am a native New Yorker, Mister Borne.'

I fiddled with my cigar. 'How do you do it?'

The candle went out in his face. 'I can't tell you. Zelma wouldn't like it. John Henry could have told you. But John Henry is dead. He was Zelma's first husband.'

This of course was pure Greek to me. But handling circus people for thirty years has convinced me they have to talk a little differently from other people. Anybody that risks their necks every day for a couple of bucks is entitled to talk different, don't you think? What the hell – if Pinkerton Fly had developed a method to walk on air without any visible aids – it was his secret and his business. I never argue with a sure-fire act.

'Okay, that's it. You'll start immediately. Tomorrow's performance. Center ring. I'll squeeze you in between the bareback rider and the animal act of Dan Burley.' I let out a big laugh. 'Are you going to open a lot of eyes and fill that old box office with the coin of the realm! This will be the biggest act since Barnum was a pup. THE MAN WHO WALKS ON AIR – THE GREATEST SHOW *OFF* EARTH!'

It was.

The audience was stunned into unthinking silence. I didn't even give Pinkerton Fly an eye-catching costume. Just threw a terrific spotlight on him, standing on the small scaffold shelving off from the thin, towering pole. It had the effect I had hoped for. A small, undernourished figure in a shabby, meaningless gray suit ambling off the platform high above the ground and strolling serenely across space to the opposite pole.

Just like I said. Lights all over the place to show them there were no ropes, pulleys or trick wiring to suspend him as he walked. If anything, the very naturalness of his ambling gait precluded any idea of wiring of some kind. You just had to believe your own eyes. Here was a skinny little guy walking on air. Walking on nothing.

I had some qualms though. Maybe I had been drunk in the office. So as a part of that first time he went on, I had a standby crew of roustabouts at convenient positions with a net in case he needed it. But, if anything, it lent something rather than detracted from the performance. It was a little funny to watch the big, burly crew circle warily beneath him, high up in the air, moving steadily with him on the trip across utter space.

The audience reaction was electric. The Great Fly, The Man Who Walked On Air captured the imagination. I wish I could show you the attendance receipts from the first month of business. Capacity every performance. The Benzo Brothers had been my star act and Dan Burley's sensational act with the lions had always been reliable crowd-getters. But they couldn't compare with the Great Fly. He was unbeatable.

Funny thing though. I kept wondering when the Great Fly was going to come down. An act that's always up in the air has to come down sometime. It was sooner than I expected.

I was coming back to go over an added clause in Pinkerton Fly's contract when I heard a big argument going on inside Lola's dressing room. Lola is the best bareback rider Tomlin's Three Ring ever had. Also, the loveliest.

I pushed into the little room to find Lola, still in her skimpy costume, pushing between a very belligerent Dan Burley and a very frightened Pinkerton Fly. Dan looked plenty sore about something and besides being a terrific animal trainer, he was one of the brawniest customers you'd ever want to see. Bad blood among the performers can kill any circus, so I cut in.

'What's going on here – a rodeo or something? The show's been over a full fifteen minutes!'

'Oh, yeah?' Burley's expression was ugly. 'Fly doesn't think so. Fly thinks Lola needs some help changing her dress.'

'That's a lie!' Pinkerton Fly, for his size, was actually standing up to the giant.

Lola's sensuous face told me plenty, the way she smiled at Pinkerton and glowered at Burley.

'Mr. Borne,' she appealed to me, 'I've had about all I can stand of this muscle-bound cat trainer! I asked the Fly in here. Burley has no right to dictate to me.'

'Haven't I?' The animal trainer seized her wrist in a vise. 'You forget a lot of things, Lola. Like—'

She flung away from him, picked up one of her riding crops that was dangling from a straprack and before any of us could stop her, slashed him full across the mouth with it. Dan stopped, the sudden welt across his strong face making his expression even uglier.

With that, he pushed past me out of the dressing room.

'Lola, you shouldn't have done that!' I stormed.

Her glance was contemptuous of my opinion. 'There's nothing in my contract that says I have to cater to Dan Burley. If I like Pinkerton, that's my business.'

Pinkerton Fly's sallow face smiled at her words. I put my oar in, playing what I thought was a trump card.

'But he's a married man, Lola. Aren't you, Pinkerton?'

He leered at me. 'What Zelma doesn't know won't hurt her.'

I was dumbfounded. First, because I couldn't see what Lola saw in him. Secondly, because I had thought he wasn't the type. But I guess with someone as breathtaking as Lola anyone was the type. As for her, men were just toys who were discarded after she tired of them. I threw up my hands.

'I hope you two know what you're doing,' I concluded meekly.

Lola winked. It made her dazzling. 'We'll be all right, Mr. Borne. Won't we, Pinky?'

Well, that finished any arguments I might have had. When Lola started calling him Pinky, I could see he was finished.

It went on being 'Pinky' for four weeks.

It was something like the 65th day of capacity business. The receipts were as high as Mount Everest. The Man Who Walked On Air – Who Didn't Need A Net – Who Never Fell – was packing them in. Tomlin's Three Ring was having its biggest season under my direction. But I wasn't kidding myself. Without Fly, it wouldn't have been a case of There'$ No Bu$ine$$ Like $how Bu$ine$$.

So I was feeling pretty good when word came that Pinkerton Fly wanted to see me. The Lola business was out of my hands anyway and Dan Burley had restricted himself to his tigers so everything had been pretty calm.

But the Fly certainly got into my ointment in a hurry.

'It's too little, Mister Borne,' he said, ignoring my outstretched hand.

'What is, Pinkerton?' I was feeling too good to notice his breach of etiquette.

'My salary.'

'Your salary?' I echoed. 'Two thousand a week isn't sawdust, Pinkerton. For a First-of-May in the circus game, it's unheard of. Not that you don't deserve it, of course—'

'That's just it, Mister Borne.' His tiny skull shone under the overheads. His small eyes held a new glint of avarice. Something that didn't quite jibe with his undersized build. 'I do deserve it. I do deserve more.'

I took a long time lighting one of my favorite cigars. After all, he *was* my biggest act on the card.

'Ten thousand dollars,' he said.

My teeth came down hard on the end of the cigar.

'You're crazy, Pinkerton!'

'Am I?' His eyes gleamed brighter. 'It's either that or the Man Who Walks On Air—'

'—doesn't walk,' I concluded wearily. 'Pinkerton, this is pretty close to blackmail. I could hold you to your contract.'

'You could,' he admitted, surprisingly enough, 'but I'd still be on the ground. Doing nothing. Even a court of law couldn't make me walk on air.'

I could see his point. I shook my head.

'Pinkerton, Lola put you up to this. It figures. She wants a fur coat, or a Cadillac. That's it, isn't it?'

He ignored my question and asked one of his own. The same one. 'Ten thousand, Mister Borne?'

Suddenly, I hated his nasal voice, his utter blindness to the ways of man-eaters like Lola.

'All right. Ten thousand. We're agreed. I'll have a new contract drawn up tomorrow.'

He licked his lips, abruptly looking surprised at himself for pulling it off. He gave a nervous little giggle, whirled and left the tent.

I stared after him for a long time before I went back to my office, cursing Fly and the circus business in general.

I had company. Company I had never expected. Zelma Fly. Mrs. Zelma Fly.

I was amazed at her appearance. She was – well, beautiful. An exotic woman, tall, well-made, with the oddest eyes I have ever seen. They were deep blue, striking, and you found yourself slightly overcome with their overpowering levelness of direction. It seemed an eternity before she blinked. An eon before she got down to the reason for her visit.

She seemed troubled. There had been rumours, some talk about Pinkerton and Lola. Naturally, she scarcely credited them but—

Getting control of a queer feeling of uncertainty, I explained the whole thing as well as I could, going as easy as possible on Pinkerton Fly. In a way I was glad she had come. I was just curious enough to find out more about this walking-on-air business.

'So that's the whole thing, Mrs. Fly. Harmless enough, I guess. It's just that Lola is bad for any man. You'll understand what I mean when I say she could lead a thirsty horse away from water.'

She stirred slightly. It was as if a soft wind had wafted over her. Her eyes were fathomless.

'Thank you, Mr. Borne. It is well that you told me. I am glad.'

Suddenly, I thought less of the idea. Something about Zelma Fly said it wasn't all right, shouted to the rooftops that Pinkerton Fly had been very, very stupid to trifle with her affections.

I tried to laugh.

'So that's it – all I can suggest is that you pay more attention to your husband. Come and see him work. Maybe he'd straighten out if you came to see him perform. Say, that's an idea. I'll reserve a seat for you. Might make all the difference in the world.'

She waited a long time before answering. In the interim, I mixed myself a drink. There was an air about Zelma Fly that made me extremely uneasy. I felt like I was giving a baby a lighted match to play with.

'Yes, Mr. Borne,' she purred in a manner that was more cat than woman. 'It is a fine idea. Tonight I will come at your kind invitation. As you say, Pinkerton has been dazzled by this Lola person. Yes, perhaps you are right. It is settled. I'll be there.'

I saw her to the door, still sensing the monumental proportions of an error that hadn't matured yet.

'Tell me, Mrs. Fly.' I couldn't resist the question. 'You are responsible for your husband's fantastic ability to walk on air. At least, that's what he told me. Tell me – how does he do it?'

She turned as if I had uttered an improper remark. Then her stiffened back relaxed and her smile was a slow, somehow deadly thing.

'It is so very easy, Mr. Borne. I simply tell him that he *can* walk on air. That is the simple truth of it. Pinkerton walks on air because I told him that I *believe* he can.'

I laughed, partly to appreciate a joke I didn't understand, more so to relieve a tension that was clutching my insides like a wet clammy hand.

As soon as the door closed behind her, I had another drink. And another one.

I suddenly felt that I had pulled a lid off a garbage can that I should never have gone near. I opened the windows wide and thought for a long time.

All day it bothered me and when Tomlin's Three Ring band beat up its first sounds of overture that night, I was as confused as ever.

The whole thing was so curious. Now I was thinking of Pinkerton Fly walking on air and how fantastic it really was. Hell, a man just couldn't do that, when you got right down to it. It was a trick. It had to be. Mass hypnosis or the power of suggestion. I remembered the letters I had received wanting explanations. The University, the Magicians' Union—

Well, before I knew it, the Benzo Brothers had cannoned into space, the Ringmaster had put Lola through her paces on beautiful white Nellie and Dan Burley had tamed lions and tigers for a solid half hour. And then – the Great Fly was on.

I hurried to the grandstand. I wanted to watch the Fly walk on air with his wife as company.

She seemed pleased to see me. Cold and distant but still pleased.

'Mr. Borne. I'm glad you joined me.'

'Pleasure,' I lied. 'You'll get a good view from here.'

'So will you, Mr. Borne. An eyeful, as you Americans say.' I had somehow always known there was a touch of European in her.

A fanfare skied to the tent-top with a burst of musical noise.

'Well, here he is – the Great Fly.'

'Yes,' she echoed, sounding like the knell of doom. 'Here he is.'

The fanfare died and the spotlight picked him out, standing idly on the tiny shelf that jutted from the towering thinness of the big pole. Still in his shabby, meaningless gray suit, his sickly build. Even from where I sat, I could see the curious, cocked position of his head. Still in that listening attitude.

The crowd hushed as the drum roll started up, waited in that heart beat of eternity for Fly's feet to step off the shelf onto nothing. The drummers came down on a loud bassoon that always made everybody jump with its unexpected interruption . . . and the Great Fly walked casually off his tiny platform.

It was amazing really. Some seventy-five feet separated one towering shaft from another and until you've seen a man bridge that distance by walking on nothing but air, you haven't seen a thing. You could have heard a watch being wound as Fly's feet struck forth and gobbled up yards of airy ground.

Slowly, carefully, yet completely naturally, he ambled across a thousand memories.

I broke my eyes away from Pinkerton's brand of magic and looked at Zelma Fly.

I was hardly prepared for what I saw.

Her head was flung back, her mouth distended and the muscles in her throat had leaped into focus. Alarmed, I reached for her. Thousands of eyes were levelled skyward on the Great Fly.

But abruptly, sound rushed from her throat, blending into a leaping, sarcastic burst of laughter that reverberated across the hushed arena with the volume of a cannonade.

That laugh lingers in my ears to this day. And its effect. The peal of rippling sarcasm filled the vast amphitheatre, hung poised like a deadly python.

I forced my eyes upward, to where Pinkerton Fly was.

It was uncanny. He had halted, was standing stock-still up there on his floor of air.

He stared down at us, toward the source of the condemning laughter and I could see the utter surprise and consternation written in every line of him. His meaningless form had taken on meaning now. New, terrible meaning with the accent on terror.

Suddenly he clawed convulsively at walls that weren't there, pawed frantically for hand-holds that didn't exist. A hoarse shout escaped him. And still Zelma Fly laughed. Long, loud, incessantly.

Then it happened. A mammoth roar of fear went up. Shock ripped from ten thousand throats.

A long scream trailed off into the night and Pinkerton Fly plummeted to earth like a heavy rock dropped into a well. Down he came, his terror welling out of him, sirening his way deathward. The thud of his body against the hard-packed floor of the arena was a crunch of sound no one who was there will ever forget.

Dan Burley and the clowns reached him first and wisely threw a spangled robe over him. The crowd was rooted to their seats as the band, snapping out of its trance, struck up a cover-up medley that was louder than music from hell. And Zelma Fly's long laugh had broken into fitful sobbing. Lola fainted and Burley slung her over his shoulder and pushed through the mob that had gathered.

There was nothing I could do really. The show was far from over – it was going on. I turned to Zelma Fly. She had relaxed in her chair, suddenly limp and spent.

I had a hard time finding my voice, finding the right words with which to condemn her.

'You – did it,' I panted. 'As if you'd shot him in cold blood, as if you'd run him over – that laugh—.'

The face she turned towards me was no longer beautiful. Just naked and terrible. Just deep, hidden emotion suddenly exposed to the light.

'No, Mr. Borne,' she barely breathed the words. 'He knew I no longer believed he *could* walk on air. My laugh merely told him that.'

'But it's murder!' I shouted. 'You killed him. Just as you—' I found myself saying it as if I'd known it all the time—'killed John Henry, your first husband.'

'Yes,' she hissed. 'Exactly like that. Only that was the Paris Circus. And her name was Yvonne.'

I got away from her fast. Back to my office, back to reality.

That's all there is to the story. Except one thing more.

Dan Burley quit the show, quit cold. Quit Lola, quit everything. I still have his telegram somewhere in my drawer:

GETTING MARRIED TO ZELMA FLY – NO MORE ANIMALS FOR ME – WISH ME LUCK
Stop. . . .

REPORT ON AN UNIDENTIFIED SPACE STATION
J.G. Ballard

'Report on an Unidentified Space Station' is one of the very few
stories that I have written to be set in that happy hunting ground of
traditional science fiction – outer space. Out of some hundred or
more of my short stories, which fill some ten volumes, this is only the
third to take place in deep space. Perhaps the silence of those infinite
spaces, which so terrified Pascal, has at last begun to get through to
me. However, readers of the story will see that this is, after all, a
special kind of space, far closer to terra firma than it might seem at
first, and even perhaps to inner space itself.

  The story is also one of the very few of mine to be directly inspired
by a dream – in this case, a nightmare of extreme anguish, though I
like to think that the mood of the story is one of serenity and peace,
part of the difference, it may be, between dream and imagination.

Survey Report 1

By good luck we have been able to make an emergency landing on
this uninhabited space station. There have been no casualties. We all
count ourselves fortunate to have found safe haven at a moment
when the expedition was clearly set on disaster.

  The station carries no identification markings and is too small to
appear on our charts. Although of elderly construction it is soundly
designed and in good working order, and seems to have been used in
recent times as a transit depot for travellers resting at mid-point in
their journeys. Its interior consists of a series of open passenger
concourses, with comfortably equipped lounges and waiting rooms.
As yet we have not been able to locate the bridge or control centre. We
assume that the station was one of many satellite drogues surrounding
a larger command unit, and was abandoned when a decline in traffic
left it surplus to the needs of the parent transit system.

  A curious feature of the station is its powerful gravitational field, far stronger than would be suggested by its small mass. However, this probably represents a faulty reading by our instruments. We hope shortly to complete our repairs and are grateful to have found shelter on this relic of the now forgotten migrations of the past.

Estimated diameter of the station: 500 metres.

Survey Report 2

Our repairs are taking longer than we first estimated. Certain pieces of equipment will have to be reconstructed from scratch, and to shorten this task we are carrying out a search of our temporary home.

To our surprise we find that the station is far larger than we guessed. A thin local atmosphere surrounds the station, composed of interstellar dust attracted by its unusually high gravity. This fine vapour obscured the substantial bulk of the station and led us to assume that it was no more than a few hundred metres in diameter.

We began by setting out across the central passenger concourse that separates the two hemispheres of the station. This wide deck is furnished with thousands of tables and chairs. But on reaching the high partition doors 200 metres away we discovered that the restaurant deck is only a modest annexe to a far larger concourse. An immense roof three storeys high extends across an open expanse of lounges and promenades. We explored several of the imposing staircases, each equipped with a substantial mezzanine, and found that they lead to identical concourses above and below.

The space station has clearly been used as a vast transit facility, comfortably accommodating many thousands of passengers. There are no crew quarters or crowd control posts. The absence of even a single cabin indicates that this army of passengers spent only a brief time here before being moved on, and must have been remarkably self-disciplined or under powerful restraint.

Estimated diameter: 1 mile.

Survey Report 3

A period of growing confusion. Two of our number set out 48 hours ago to explore the lower decks of the station, and have so far failed to return. We have carried out an extensive search and fear that a tragic accident has taken place. None of the hundreds of elevators is in working order, but our companions may have entered an un-anchored cabin and fallen to their deaths. We managed to force open one of the heavy doors and gazed with awe down the immense shaft.

Many of the elevators within the station could comfortably carry a thousand passengers. We hurled several pieces of furniture down the shaft, hoping to time the interval before their impact, but not a sound returned to us. Our voices echoed away into a bottomless pit.

Perhaps our companions are marooned far from us on the lower levels? Given the likely size of the station, the hope remains that a maintenance staff occupies the crew quarters on some remote upper deck, unaware of our presence here. As soon as we contact them they will help us to rescue our companions.

Estimated diameter: 10 miles.

Survey Report 4

Once again our estimate of the station's size has been substantially revised. The station clearly has the dimensions of a large asteroid or even a small planet. Our instruments indicate that there are thousands of decks, each extending for miles across an undifferentiated terrain of passenger concourses, lounges and restaurant terraces. As before there is no sign of any crew or supervisory staff. Yet somehow a vast passenger complement was moved through this planetary waiting room.

While resting in the armchairs beneath the unvarying light we have all noticed how our sense of direction soon vanishes. Each of us sits at a point in space that at the same time seems to have no precise location but could be anywhere within these endless vistas of tables and armchairs. We can only assume that the passengers moving along these decks possessed some instinctive homing device, a mental model of the station that allowed them to make their way within it.

In order to establish the exact dimensions of the station and, if possible, rescue our companions we have decided to abandon our repair work and set out on an unlimited survey, however far this may take us.

Estimated diameter: 500 miles.

Survey Report 5

No trace of our companions. The silent interior spaces of the station have begun to affect our sense of time. We have been travelling in a straight line across one of the central decks for what seems an unaccountable period. The same pedestrian concourses, the same mezzanines attached to the stairways, and the same passenger lounges stretch for miles under an unchanging light. The energy needed to maintain this degree of illumination suggests that the operators of the station were used to a full passenger complement. However, there are unmistakable signs that no one has been here since the remote past. Clearly, whoever designed the station based the transit system within on a timetable of gigantic dimensions.

We press on, following the same aisle that separates two adjacent lounge concourses. We rest briefly at fixed intervals, but despite our steady passage we sense that we are not moving at all, and may well be trapped within a small waiting room whose apparently infinite dimensions we circle like ants on a sphere. Paradoxically, our instruments confirm that we are penetrating a structure of rapidly increasing mass.

Is the entire universe no more than an infinitely vast space terminal?

Estimated diameter: 5,000 miles.

Survey Report 6

We have just made a remarkable discovery! Our instruments have detected that a slight but perceptible curvature is built into the floors of the station. The ceilings recede behind us and dip fractionally towards the decks below, while the disappearing floors form a distinct horizon.

So the station is a curvilinear structure of finite form! There must be meridians that mark out its contours, and an equator that will return us to our original starting point. We all feel an immediate surge of hope. Already we may have stumbled on an equatorial line, and despite the huge length of our journey we may in fact be going home.

Estimated diameter: 50,000 miles.

Survey Report 7

Our hopes have proved to be short-lived. Excited by the thought that we had mastered the station, and cast a net around its invisible bulk, we were pressing on with renewed confidence. However, we now know that although these curvatures exist, they extend in all directions. Each of the walls curves away from its neighbours, the floors from the ceilings. The station, in fact, is an expanding structure whose size appears to increase exponentially. The longer the journey undertaken by a passenger, the greater the incremental distance he will have to travel. The virtually unlimited facilities of the station suggest that its passengers were embarked on extremely long, if not infinite, journeys.

Needless to say, the complex architecture of the station has ominous implications for us. We realise that the size of the station is a measure, not of the number of passengers embarked – though this must have been vast – but of the length of the journeys that must be undertaken within it. Indeed, there should ideally be only one passenger. A solitary voyager embarked on an infinite journey would require an infinity of transit lounges. As there are, fortunately, more than one of us we can assume that the station is a finite structure with the appearance of an infinite one. The degree to which it approaches an infinite size is merely a measure of the will and ambition of its passengers.

Estimated diameter: 1 million miles.

Survey Report 8

Just when our spirits were at their lowest ebb we have made a small but significant finding. We were moving across one of the limitless passenger decks, a prey to all fears and speculations, when we noticed the signs of recent habitation. A party of travellers has paused here in the recent past. The chairs in the central concourse have been disturbed, an elevator door has been forced, and there are the unmistakable traces left by weary voyagers. Without doubt there were more than two of them, so we must regretfully exclude our lost companions.

But there are others in the station, perhaps embarked on a journey as endless as our own!

We have also noticed slight variations in the decor of the station, in the design of light fittings and floor tiles. These may seem trivial, but multiplying them by the virtually infinite size of the station we can envisage a gradual evolution in its architecture. Somewhere in the station there may well be populated enclaves, even entire cities, surrounded by empty passenger decks that stretch on forever like free space. Perhaps there are nation-states whose civilisations rose and declined as their peoples paused in their endless migrations across the station.

Where were they going? And what force propelled them on their meaningless journeys? We can only hope that they were driven forward by the greatest of all instincts, the need to establish the station's size.

Estimated diameter: 5 light years.

Survey Report 9

We are jubilant! A growing euphoria has come over us as we move across these great concourses. We have seen no further trace of our fellow passengers, and it now seems likely that we were following one of the inbuilt curvatures of the station and had crossed our own tracks.

But this small setback counts for nothing now. We have accepted the limitless size of the station, and this awareness fills us with feelings that are almost religious. Our instruments confirm what we have long suspected, that the empty space across which we travelled from our own solar system in fact lies within the interior of the station, one of the many vast lacunae set in its endlessly curving walls. Our solar system and its planets, the millions of other solar systems that constitute our galaxy, and the island universes themselves all lie within the boundaries of the station. The station is coeval with the cosmos, and constitutes the cosmos. Our duty is to travel across it on a journey whose departure point we have already begun to forget, and whose destination is the station itself, every floor and concourse within it.

So we move on, sustained by our faith in the station, aware that every step we take thereby allows us to reach a small part of that destination. By its existence the station sustains us, and gives our lives their only meaning. We are glad that in return we have begun to worship the station.

Estimated diameter: 15,000 light years.

'Report on an Unidentified Space Station', by J. G. Ballard © 1982, published in *Lands of Never* (Allen and Unwin). Reprinted by permission of the author and his agent, Margaret Hanbury.

THE SHIP OF DISASTER
Barrington J. Bayley

I once had a particular method of generating stories. I would sit down and write evocative openings, a few paragraphs long, with little or no idea as to what would happen next. Sometimes these seeds would germinate into stories; more often, not.

'The Ship of Disaster' started out that way, and was written in the early 1960s. At the time, I was coming under new influences. Formerly I had been interested only in straight science fiction, but now I was being introduced to another aspect of other-worldliness – the genre that was loosely termed 'fantasy' – largely by Michael Moorcock, a close friend. Moorcock was writing his tales of the 'proud prince of ruins', Elric the albino, and I enjoyed his almost self-mocking descriptions of disdainful elves, with 'eyes staring into infinity'. I felt I would like to try my hand at writing something of the kind myself. And it was just this type of image that I chose for the elf-lord, Elen-Gelith. (I had of course already read Tolkien's Lord of the Rings; I cannot now remember whether I had at the time read Poul Anderson's glorious The Broken Sword, with its great war between elves and trolls on an Earth coextensive with our own but invisible to human senses.)

What makes the story memorable for me is that I think I may have succeeded in creating the characteristic atmosphere for this style of fantasy. I set my war between the two races, not in an invisible present but in the distant past. It is a war neither side can win, for both *sides are doomed to be replaced*.

That situation is more than just a fictional one, of course. The sight of a proud, inflexible culture confronted with a newer, more capable one that it can neither emulate nor withstand is, in recent times, a familiar one.

The great *Ship of Disaster* rolled tirelessly over the deep and endless ocean. Long she was, strong and golden, and the somber waters like oil beneath her prow. Yet a ship of disaster she truly was: vapors obscured the air about her, and nowhere could a horizon be seen. Her crew knew not where to find land, and already her hasty provisions ran low.

For it was by disaster that this ship lived. Disaster had struck the yards that built her, and now disaster had run its full course upon the elf-nation that had equipped her for war.

On a high seat in her poop languished Elen-Gelith, elf-lord of the Earth's younger days when men had not yet come into their own. 'Disaster,' he promised to himself, 'shall come upon any accursed enemy that I find!' His hands, like thin wax laid on bone, rested negligently, yet there was power in them, as ever there was in an elf's grace. His pale and beautiful features were calm for all his anger; but his eyes, large and black, gazed at nothing but his own dark reflections. For it did not suit an elf to see his people defeated in battle, their cities reduced and their navies scattered.

And as he brooded his dark and pointed thoughts, a cry came from the look-out. A ship to port! The elf-lord's prayer was answered! Swiftly the *Ship of Disaster* heeled about, seeking surcease for her injured pride. Her war-gear had long been prepared, her warriors hungry for vengeance.

Drawing closer, a hint of disappointment showed on Elen-Gelith's face. This was no enemy's ship, for they were easily recognizable, as huge hulking beasts of the sea which wallowed with its drift. This was a ship built by men, a wretched craft compared to the elf-lord's shining war-galley, for men had none of the elves' science in ship-building. Nevertheless it was rumored that they had traded with trolls in times past, and apart from any other consideration Elen-Gelith's temper was far from good. Cold and sharp, his silvery voice rang out.

'Ram them broadside!'

The second officer echoed the command. With a series of rhythmic thuds the oars turned the ship about, and poised for a bare second.

The water, on which the two ships stood like a king's mansion beside a peasant's hut, was covered with a fine mist. The oars dipped and drove. The *Ship of Disaster*, carried forward by the labors of troll galley-slaves, smashed the defenseless vessel with her underwater beak.

Elen-Gelith, still not stirring from his sheltered chair in the poop, laughed with the full flavor of malice. He gave a fresh command, and his sailors were quick to do his bidding, pouring slick green oil upon the sea where human survivors struggled to stay afloat. A lighted brand followed, and lo, the elf galley floated unharmed upon a sea of fire! The specially treated wood of her own tall hull was proof against the flame she used to such deadly purpose.

Yet there was one who survived even that peril. As the galley's bow fell upon his vessel, he had leaped upwards to cling to her carved and painted woodwork. Now, as the blistering heat of the blazing ocean billowed over him, he pulled himself up the ship's side and dropped into her slave-pits.

He did not stay there long. The burning wreck, the searing ocean, were scant yards astern when he was dragged before Elen-Gelith. The elf looked disdainfully on his prisoner. To him, a man was little more than a brute beast.

'Speak, animal, if you have the wit to do it,' he said. 'What do they call you in that coarse grunting you use for talk?'

The man answered in the merchant's tongue, a low-class derivation of elf-language crudely known the world over. 'Ours was a trading ship!' the man protested angrily. 'You had no call to attack us. As for my name, I have no obligation to tell it.'

'Ho, ho!' The elf-lord was amused. 'This is an animal not yet fully domesticated! That was ever the pity among men, so I hear.' A harder glint came into the elf's eyes. 'Well, animals can be tamed.'

He signaled, with one finger. A cruel lash descended, twice, on the man's back. 'Your name?' Elen-Gelith demanded, distantly.

The man spat impotently. 'Kelgynn of Borrod, son of Jofbine, whom you have just sent to the bottom of the ocean.'

'Such terrible dangers these sailors meet!' taunted the elf. 'Well, Kelgynn of Borrod, we have lost one of our trolls. Alas for the poor fellow, he fell sick and had to be thrown overboard. I fear you have no troll's muscles, but you will have to do.'

By now the elf-lord was no longer looking at him. He gazed over his head, towards the prow, as if already he was returning to deeper problems.

'To the bench with him,' he ordered absently.

With surprising elfin strength slender hands yanked at Kelgynn and threw him to a vacant place at the rear of the oar-benches. Dazed, he submitted to being chained with the light, clinking metal elves used, reputedly stronger than the finest iron.

At first he refused to work. But gradually, partly by the punishment meted out to him, partly by the indifference of the elf hortator, he was persuaded to grasp the oar's handle and learn the stroke.

It was almost more than he could bear. The oar was made for trolls, not men. Like a great unwieldy stanchion, it was so big that his hands could hardly get purchase. Before and behind him, the great beveled oars kept up their inexorable sweep, forcing him to keep pace until his body cried out for rest.

After endless hours the trolls were fed, and he heard their snorts and grunts of satisfaction. A chunk of putrid meat was thrown down at him. He turned his head away in nausea. Even had the meat been fresh, it was from an animal that to him was utterly uneatable. He retched as the foul odor entered his throat and nostrils, and, seeing his distaste, the elf took it up again. A few minutes later a small cake of bread was handed to him.

Despite his misfortune, Kelgynn grinned. It was elf-bread, worth half a fortune in his home town, for few humans ever tasted elves' food. As he bit into the tiny loaf the bread dissolved in his mouth, nothing of it reaching his stomach. Immediately its vivifying effects ran through him like a woman's touch, but he knew that it would not sustain him properly, as it would a finer-bodied elf.

Scarcely had he taken his hands from the oar when a lash touched his back as a signal to resume rowing. The bull-like trolls rumbled mournfully, throwing up waves of indescribable perspiration. Head drooping with weariness, Kelgynn pulled on his oar, trying beyond hope to keep up with the aloof pounding of the hortator's drum.

On and on rowed the *Ship of Disaster*. Elen-Gelith stared eternally ahead from his position in the poop of the steady-driving vessel. The fit of temper which had gained him a rower availed him of no real pleasure. He was not one to feel triumph in petty victories. But elves are constant creatures, and the icy rage which blew through him at the thought of his people's defeat would not soon, if ever, abate.

Elen-Gelith knew not where they were bound. They were hopelessly lost in this strange mist. His sole hope for salvation – if an elf can be said to harbour hope in his heart – was that if they continued on without changing direction, sooner or later they must strike land. So, patient but tense, he waited.

In this manner six days passed, and despite the vast distance covered the look-out remained silent. The sea stayed placid, gleaming with strange dull colors and lifting with a regular mechanical swell. Hanging in cold curtains, the vapors cut off the world fifty yards away, creating the illusion that the ship made absolutely no progress.

On board, the situation had reached danger point. The galley's provisions, already scanty by reason of her urgent departure and the failure of the crops the year before, were all but gone.

Yet there appeared to be little that could be done. Casting about for some small action, Elen-Gelith had his officers bring the man to him. The new prisoner had not been much use as a rower. For one thing, it had proved impossible to keep him awake for more than three days, whereas trolls, like elves, could, if need be, live indefinitely without sleep. True, trolls achieved this only at the cost of hideous daydreams, fearful ancestral memories which rose before their eyes and plagued all their waking hours with suffering and terror . . . but this little concerned their elf masters. And after a while the trolls were grateful for the whips which kept them awake. For without goading now, they fell despite their most desperate efforts into an even worse slumber, a sleep of which they lived in perpetual horror, in which they were assailed by nightmares a hundred times more unbearable.

So Kelgynn, who slumped in an envied sleep of exhaustion across his oar, was called for. He was dull-eyed for some time after they dragged him from his bench, but after the elf-lord had generously allowed him a mouthful of wine, he recovered sufficiently to speak.

'Animal,' Elen-Gelith told him, 'we have nothing to feed you with, unless you care after all for trolls' food.'

'Elf bread suits me well enough,' Kelgynn answered wearily, 'though I find it somewhat thin.' Then, as his senses awoke, he suddenly understood the elf's meaning.

'So,' he said wonderingly, 'you have nothing to eat, either.'

After a brief hesitation, Elen-Gelith nodded.

Yet already his interest in the conversation seemed to have waned, and he gazed with an abstracted expression over Kelgynn's head. Not knowing his purpose, Kelgynn waited, surmising that perhaps he would be sent back to the bench.

Abruptly the elf pricked up his pointed ears and leaned forward to look more closely at him.

'Tell me,' he said in a confidential tone, 'are you acquainted with these waters?'

Slowly Kelgynn shook his head. 'None of us knew of it. We were trying to find a new passage to Posadoras.'

'Posadoras?' The elf raised his eyebrows. 'You were truly off course.'

'As well we knew. We had almost despaired of seeing land again, when you sighted us.'

The elf leaned back, becoming meditative. 'A sad idea for a sailor to have.'

Kelgynn shrugged.

Elen-Gelith sighed resignedly, gazing blandly across the warship's deck, into the sea and mist. The mist, hanging and eddying, drifted abstractedly, placing a vague pearly layer over all surfaces, even here under the lord's awning.

Kelgynn was truly amazed at how much more amiable Elen-Gelith had become. The sudden change of mood was inexplicable by the simple standards of his own folk.

'Without doubt this is an uncommon region,' the elf went on in a friendly tone, 'and I have never seen the like. I confess to you, human, this sea lies outside my knowledge of the oceans also. I do not know where we are, and hardly more do I know how we got here.'

Then he leaned towards Kelgynn again, and his voice became more commanding. 'Now you will tell me how *you* came to enter the Misty Sea.'

'I already have told you. We were seeking a route to Posadoras.'

'And that is all?'

Kelgynn hesitated.

'Speak on,' Elen-Gelith urged. 'You have somewhat to say?'

'Perhaps it is of interest,' Kelgynn said at last, 'so I will speak of it. Our shamans performed a sacrifice before we sailed. No sooner had the magic sticks been dipped in the blood than the sky was covered from east to west with a single flash of lighting. One shaman said it was a good omen, another bad. Well, good or bad, we put to sea. Fifteen days into strange waters, there was another lightning flash. From then on the ocean began to change. We sailed for another twenty days before . . . you came upon us.'

'And how do you account for this lightning?'

'By the skill of our shamans in sacrifice.'

Kelgynn glanced apprehensively at the elf, to see whether his boast would evoke jealousy in his haughty, acute countenance. Elen-Gelith laughed mockingly. 'Semi-sentient humans speak of *magic*,' he said. 'We elves have *science*. But pray continue with your tale.'

'There is nothing else to tell,' Kelgynn answered. 'Did you, also,' he ventured, 'see lightning?'

Inwardly Elen-Gelith snorted. Why, no – and if there had been any, how would he have noticed it amidst the uproar of the giant sea-battle? Torment take the animal! Would he have him tell of the earth-shaking Armageddon when the *Ship of Disaster*, like many other remnants, had fled to save herself? Yet if he were to tell the truth, he must admit that there had been a sense of weirdness aboard the vessel in those last stages, when they had been caught in a sudden rolling gust of mist, and had pulled hard into its friendly cover, escaping the furious black troll-fire and the pursuit of the enemy's barges.

Just the same, he could not accept the human's attempt to put a supernatural turn on events. This sea was a part of the world's geography, he was certain of that.

'I saw nothing,' he answered flippantly, 'but here is a marvel for you. The trolls have devised a fire which burns black, and nothing withstands it. What think you of that?'

Kelgynn smiled. He was cheered by the elf's admission that he was lost. Making up his mind, he decided there was no point in deference.

'The tricks of neither elves nor trolls impress me,' he said flatly.

Elen-Gelith's unpupiled eyes glowed luminously. It was fortunate for the animal that he had no true mind, and his words were not significant. . . .

But Kelgynn had made a stand. 'I see nothing in elves except conceit. Nothing in trolls except brute force. Shortly the world will see the end of both.'

Elen-Gelith waved a hand negligently, aware that even in the animal kingdom men were an insignificant breed. His prisoner had little comprehension of the great war being waged by the only two truly intelligent races of the world.

An age ago elf savants had casually observed men appear from random mutations among lower animals. Thus they sprang from quite different sources than did either elves or trolls. Why, elves had maintained their beauteous civilization for as long as record persisted! The whole Earth was but their playing ground. The man's pathetic attempts to claim magical abilities for his people could be taken as a sign of a dim awareness of his own inferiority.

Elves had no animal heritage at all. It was recorded that they had come into being as an act of self-creation. Springing into existence perfectly formed, of their own will, they were destined to be Earth's fairest flower.

Kelgynn pressed his point. 'Listen,' he said, maliciously earnest, 'is it not true that your crops have been failing? Stories reach us. Your stores of elf-bread dwindle. In a few years you face starvation!'

A dangerous mood flickered involuntarily across Elen-Gelith's face. 'That is due to the trolls.'

Kelgynn pulled a small pouch from among the folds of his

clothing. Opening its neck, he poured some of the contents into the palm of his hand. Tiny grains of a dull gold color glittered there.

'Look, *we* have food. Too coarse for elves, too fine for trolls, but food for men. We call it wheat.'

Elen-Gelith stared at the grains. For no accountable reason something so terrible stirred in him that he could barely contain his emotion. With an effort at indifference he said: 'What of it? And how easily you slander the masters of the world, whose skills and science none can match.'

'For what do you use your science, besides your own gratification?' Kelgynn countered quickly. 'Do you ever give thought to anything that does not further your own pleasure?'

The elf-lord started forward, startling Kelgynn with the cold flash of his visage. 'You are too perspicacious, human. Learn to guard your tongue or it will be cut out.'

For some seconds Kelgynn was intimidated. 'They say elves had grace once,' he murmured, half to himself, 'yet look at this one – from the first meeting a murderer.' As he said this, he glanced up again at Elen-Gelith.

Suddenly recovering his humor, the elf-lord enjoyed the frightened, white defiance of the young man's expression. 'If you were an intelligent being,' he said, 'for those words you would have been tortured as only elves can torture. You being human, it is of no consequence. It only remains to decide whether we throw you overboard or keep you as food for our trolls, who soon will be growing hungry.'

Kelgynn let the wheat grains fall to the deck.

'Tell me,' Elen-Gelith continued after a pause, 'what do men do when they run out of food at sea?'

'We carry little food in any case. We fish.'

'You do what? Catch fishes?'

'Yes. The sea is bountiful.'

Elen-Gelith reflected. 'Could elves eat fishes, do you think?'

'I do not know. There are many kinds of fish in the sea.'

'If you help me, Kelgynn of Borrod, I may set you free when we strike land.'

Kelgynn laughed unpleasantly. 'You think I would trust an elf's mercy! Just the same, I will fish for you, if only to fill my own stomach while I live. Give me a hook and line.'

While the tackle was being prepared Kelgynn took his first close look at the *Ship of Disaster*, seeing in detail the long, high sweep of the decks, the beautiful abstract carvings which adorned the woodwork. A vessel of great size and mass, the ship depended for motive power solely upon troll rowers. The decks were inlaid with silver and mother-of-pearl designs depicting elf-lore. Everywhere, in fact, was proof of untold wealth and craftsmanship, making a gleaming setting for the battle equipment which studded about.

Only one thing marred the effect. One side of the golden hull bore a long charcoal-black scorch-mark, the result of a badly aimed gout of troll-fire.

Everything came sharply to Kelgynn's eye. The lines of the ship, the enveloping vapor, the oily sea. His gaze lifted and lingered on the lonely elf commander. Kelgynn did not think he was wrong when he discerned behind the noble, aloof posture a spirit of overwhelming dejection.

Yes, she was a wondrous creation, this foreign war-galley. Wondrous, powerful, dutifully-functioning. But for all her beauty she carried the flavor of all elves: self-contained arrogance. Elf civilization was materialistic, inbred.

As for trolls, their character might be different; but the same errors lay ingrained in their being.

Elen-Gelith gave an order for the rowers to ship their oars. The trolls bellowed in wild despair, pulling at their chains and begging to be given no respite. But the elf masters seemed not to hear, and perforce the wretched slaves gave themselves up willy-nilly to the all-dreaded sleep.

Deprived of motive power the *Ship of Disaster* coasted a short distance before giving herself up to the regular swell of the ocean. Kelgynn cast his line into an undisturbed sea.

Elen-Gelith returned to his thoughts.

For many hours he lounged in his high seat, his mind still, calm, but all-encompassing and brooding. No amount of intellectual detachment – and elves had plenty of that – could make elves emotionally dispassionate. One look at their physical forms, their sharp glowing faces, their light, nerve-burning bodies, would have assured any creatures of that. Elen-Gelith would retain his steady-burning elf emotions, would remain cruel, egotistical and unremitting, even though his mind ranged to the far reaches of the universe and found that all existence cried out against his ways. Of all other inquiries he might make, he would never question his own nature.

Even so, the constant creature suffers more than the flighty one; Elen-Gelith found no solace for himself, nor sought any. Not one moment came to salve the torment of his hot unwavering mind.

Bending, he picked up two of the grains the human had dropped, inspecting them curiously. The man had been right in his information, inadvertently reminding Elen-Gelith of the root cause of his fury. The trolls had evidently found a way to poison the crops, for year after year the downy harvest refused to blossom.

And at this very moment the same mighty enemy was laying waste the finest, as well as the most self-dependent, civilization that could ever exist from the beginning to the end of time.

Meanwhile, instead of returning to succor the elf-nation, the warship under Elen-Gelith's command was hopelessly, inexplicably lost.

This fact also gave him cause for much anguish.

He tossed the two grains aside. Unnoticed by him, they fell overboard.

'What?' he muttered to himself. 'Will trolls rule the world?'

Eventually he rose and retreated back into the shadow of his awning. Here, on a small table, was a jug of wine and a bowl; also various small trinkets and figurines, such as any elf commander might carry with him to remind him of absent companions. He fingered one, smiling gently. Imt-Tagar, valiant soldier, burning with his ship in billowing black fire!

Elen-Gelith poured himself a bowl of wine.

Then a shout came from outside, and he stepped onto the open deck to see that the man was struggling with his tackle. Where the cord met the sea the water thrashed and swayed. Quickly the elf-lord motioned a sailor to help.

Suddenly the sea welled up and streamed from an enormous flat head fully five feet across.

Kelgynn gazed in fascination at the sea-beast which his fishing had so unexpectedly provoked. The hide seemed wrought in hammered copper. Strength and solidity gleamed from every scabrous knob, and Kelgynn stared into a partly-opened mouth which could have swallowed him whole.

The focus of his eyes shifted slightly; then he gasped in outraged horror. The beast was *looking* at him, with eyes revealing an intelligence which was unrefined, primeval, yet greater than his own.

Kelgynn's whole consciousness became fixed on the unknown space behind those staring eyes. A shiver of terrified delight vibrated through him. He seemed to have been sucked away from the immediate presence of the world.

Fantastic notions formed in his brain. The beast clearly stared at something more than just him. The eyes seemed to reflect something beyond his ability to perceive. '*Future*,' they glinted. '*Future*.'

In the beast's eye, Kelgynn fancied he saw the motion of the unfolding future.

The experience was over in a second. He staggered back. At the same time the iron-snouted head disappeared into the sea.

Moments later he realized that the line was still pulled. He hauled feebly until a stronger-nerved elf came to his side, and together they heaved a fish over the side.

Once on the deck the fish ceased to struggle and lay still, giving Kelgynn and the elves time for a leisurely study. It was nearly the size of a man. Its skin had a pearly pallor, delicately tinged with pink. Its back was a broad expanse, carrying a shallow superstructure of pink sea-shell, built up into elaborate decorations and whorls. Along the sides, dipping slightly in towards the curve of the belly, ran twin rows of fluted orifices. The thinly-ribbed fins and tail glistened in all colors, translucent, shining.

The mouth lay open, showing creamy white flesh torn by the metal hook. The eyes were closed – to Kelgynn's surprise, for he had never seen a fish's eyes close before. Long, curved eyelashes rested on the soft skin.

The effect was that of a sleeping babe.

Then, through the fluted orifices which Kelgynn had taken to be gills, air sighed, building up to a mewling, distressed cry. Kelgynn even thought he detected half-coherent words, voiced in helpless protest. It was exactly like the cry of a distressed child.

Unlike Kelgynn, the elves seemed unaffected. A pause descended on the *Ship of Disaster*, during which Elen-Gelith came forward, his cloak falling into listless shapes about his spare body, bending to inspect Kelgynn's catch.

He looked up and caught Kelgynn's eye with an interrogative glance.

Cold sweat broke out in the palms of Kelgynn's hands. What did the elf commander intend to do with this – monster?

'Quite so,' the elf said, quietly thoughtful. He motioned to his sailors. 'Dispose of it.'

While the corpse was being heaved over the side he turned to Kelgynn. 'Now cast your line again.'

'Have you not seen enough?' Kelgynn muttered, his eyes on the deck.

'Enough? Enough for what?' The elf's voice was supercilious and threatening. 'Keep to your bargain or the penalty is quick and final.'

Kelgynn dared a brief look into Elen-Gelith's unblinking eyes. Did the elf not sense the potency in this deep sea? Something wakeful, implacable, reducing all purpose to vanity.

The elf-lord regained his awning and disposed himself leisurely on his seat. 'Make your choice,' he said casually, looking the other way.

Kelgynn vacillated for a moment, trying not to shiver. 'I would not care to fish here again,' he said in a subdued voice, 'but I'll risk it elsewhere.'

The elf nodded absently.

With a great concerted groan of relief the trolls awakened from their noisy, horrid slumber, pleading mournful gratitude to the lashes of their keepers. Soon the oars were unshipped, and the great vessel was under way.

Then all was silent aboard the elf ship save for the slow beating of the hortator's drum, the thud and creak of the oars, the desultory wash of water as the blades lifted from the sea. Since boarding the *Ship of Disaster* Kelgynn had felt no hope for himself, but until now he had not cared unduly. Now a dark shadow came over his mind. He felt an immeasurable foreboding.

He sank so deep into himself that at first he failed to notice the stir of interest that suddenly rustled through the crew of the ship. When he did finally turn his attention to the cause of the interest, all he saw at first was a vague movement and color in the distance.

But as they drew closer definite forms appeared, claiming his attention with a still, soundless lure.

They were more like pictures than real objects. Shapes, blocks, sights and scenes projected themselves up from the deep, spilling over the face of the sea. They were ever-changing, rising up, displaying, falling and transforming like the turning pages of a book. Unimaginable buildings, streets and bridges spread themselves over the water. It was a scene of silent, deliberate activity.

Kelgynn blinked. He could not make up his mind at first if he really saw what he saw. It was like a film of memory occluding what lay before the eyes. Or like a vivid dream which persists in the mind's eye, overlaying the real world, for several seconds after a man has forcibly awoken.

But even this impression did not take away the color, the clarity, the senses of presence. If it was a phantom, it was an external phantom, not a derangement of the mind – unless this whole impossible sea was such a derangement.

No comment was made on the decks. The trolls' muscles bore them steadily onwards into the region of the strange visions, and

Kelgynn looked to left and right. Then they were in the midst of a fantastic city. Broad avenues, vast boulevards, giant buildings and throngs of people debouched onto the sea, and lingered, to be replaced by others. Rectilinear shafts of towers soared skywards. He craned his neck, up and up, but the summits simply disappeared into the mist.

'What is this we see?' wondered Elen-Gelith to himself. Yet in fact he already half knew, for he also had looked into the sea-beast's eyes. He saw images of future ages.

The thought brought into motion a deeper, frightful knowledge which he fought to quell, for as they passed he had been inspecting closely the phantom inhabitants of this phantom city. Now they came to another part of it, which after a while he realized must be a harbor. The realization took time, for it was by no means immediately that he was able to recognize the huge shapes resting there as . . . ships. They were such gigantic ships as made his own *Ship of Disaster* seem no more than a boat.

The elf craft bore down on one such floating mountain, and within seconds they had passed through the dull gray hull and were rowing through a cavernous interior. The visions hung around them, floating like thoughts in the mind. Unfamiliar contrivances lay about, tended by . . . men.

Where were the elf overseers who should have been supervising these animals? There were none. There had been none in any of the scenes in the city; and the men did not wear the expressions of slaves.

The elf-lord looked sharply this way and that, shifting uncomfortably. Then, despite all his efforts at self-control, a shudder passed right through him.

Kelgynn, who had moved closer, noticed this and laughed cruelly.

Kelgynn himself did not know it, but this was the sea of the Earth's imagination. Here the Earth dreamed and thought to herself, planning the clothing with which she would adorn herself in future. But the talk of the shamans came easily to him, and now he cast aside all caution and spoke up again.

Breaking through the opposite side of the metal hull, the ship came into the open sea. Behind them, the fantastic visions died away like spoken words.

'Does this prove what I said?' he cried. 'The world has finished with elves! You think the Earth is just dead matter with which you can do what you will. But it is the *Earth* that created us, for her own pleasure. You elves have taken all the pleasure for yourselves and ceased to be of use to her.'

Elen-Gelith said softly: 'You were not given permission to speak, animal.'

Kelgynn tossed his head. 'Arrogance still blinds you. You do not realize that you are completely in the power of the world in which you exist. If it cuts off its support, you perish.'

Earnestly he continued: 'Listen. You think the trolls poisoned your crops – but the truth is that they believe the same of you. Their herds of three-horns and long-necks are no longer breeding, and for this they blame the elves.'

Elen-Gelith glared at him, for the first time in his centuries-long existence faced with a completely new fact.

'It is the Earth herself who has denied you food,' Kelgynn told him. 'For hundreds of years you have robbed her without giving anything in return. Inevitably, she has withheld her bounty; for you, the soil no longer works. And while you still pride yourself on your science, your knowledge decays steadily.'

Impudent worm! All that mattered in the whole universe was that elves lived and ruled.

Elen-Gelith was silent.

Presently he stirred, and spoke to his officers in a silvery tone.

'Bring me one of those sluggards on the benches,' he demanded. 'The brightest, if there be any bright ones among them.'

A troll was led onto the deck, a bull-shouldered brute wearing an expression of woe-begone melancholy, dull-eyed from long years on the bench. He blinked, and skirted nervously round the inlaid pictures of elf mythology, snorting with superstitious fear. Kelgynn allowed himself to feel a trace of pity for the creature's degraded condition.

'Tell me, fellow,' the elf-lord said sharply, 'what do you understand by what you have seen?'

The troll's short, curved horns waggled; he seemed incapable of answering. To Kelgynn it was clear that he thought nothing of what he had seen. His slavery had broken his spirit, and unlike the penetrating elf, he took little interest in things new. He thought of nothing but home, where earthy, strong-smelling trolls huffed in carousal, sometimes sad, sometimes ebullient, and cow-like troll maidens made the floors quiver with their tread.

'Away with this moron!' Elen-Gelith said after a moment. 'Over the side with him!'

Lowing in ineffectual protest, the troll was herded to the side of the ship and brought up against the railing, where he cowered miserably. A few seconds afterwards there was a heavy splash.

Elen-Gelith called a halt.

'Will this place do?'

'Eh?' Kelgynn growled.

'Fish!'

'Fish be damned! I'll do no more for an extinct species.'

Elen-Gelith half rose in his seat. Kelgynn fell back, gasping with shock. He had never seen such emotion. As he gazed, spellbound, he saw that behind elfin loftiness lay a gloom more intense, more hopeless of cessation, than the merely human frame could have borne.

The elf-lord made a gesture, of whose meaning his servants were well conversant. Kelgynn was hurled over the plush railing of the ship and hit the ocean with a quiet, soon-forgotten splash.

This time he made no attempt to climb the hull. The sea was cold and slick as it closed over his head, lacking in salt. Kelgynn sank, waiting for the few seconds to pass before he must draw that oily, painful water into his body.

Then he became aware of salt on his lips, and sea-sounds in his ears. A surging wave dashed against his head to cover him in spray.

When he breathed in, tangy air filled his lungs. He opened his eyes. The elf ship, the alien ocean, were gone. He saw an azure sky and a warm sun, beneath which a living ocean swelled and sparkled. Not far off, he saw a white line of foam and a yellow beach, and tall trees.

'Thanks, elf-lord,' he thought. 'You said you would spare my life.'

He struck out towards the shore.

Elen-Gelith seated himself again. 'Forward!' he called in his high, yelping voice.

He sat in the poop, alert, intelligent, utterly despondent. Provisioned only with despair, the *Ship of Disaster* drove steadily on, occasionally veering in vain attempts to find a direction, landless, futureless, but ever vengeful.

COLLABORATING
Michael Bishop

The idea for this story – the existential dilemma of two distinct intellects sharing the same body – grabbed me one night while I lay in bed and would not let go. I knew when I got up the next morning that I would have to write the story, would have to submerge my own identity in the personalities of the two brothers – James and Robert Self – for as long as it took to illuminate their predicament.

To the outside world, of course, they would be an 'it', a 'monster', a 'freak' – no matter how sensitive, intelligent, or spiritually independent the minds of each of them. And, of course, they would even come to regard the body that they shared as a stranger to themselves, terming it with a kind of melancholy facetiousness, or facetious bitterness, 'The Monster' – just as they themselves are perceived as a single monstrous entity by the world at large. A marriage of minds? A union of quintessential estranging intimacy? I have seldom felt so deeply for my characters as I felt for James and Robert Self while telling their story, and likewise for the young woman who tries to overcome the self-hatred of one of the brothers by declaring her love to both.

This story has offended or repulsed some readers, but – although it is of course tactless, déclassé and egotistical to bring negative judgments to bear on those who find fault with one's own work – such a response strikes me as tantamount to being offended or repulsed by a persistent aspect of the human condition itself, namely, the universal quest for some external validation of our self-worth, and the concomitant fear that we are, perhaps, unworthy.

Is that too grandiose an interpretation to place on a story about two men with the same body?

Maybe it is.

Is this story a fantasy?

Well, yes and no. You see, I believe it is one of the saddest and most realistic pieces of 'fiction' I have ever written.

And that is all I am going to say about it.

How does it feel to be a two-headed man? Better, how does it feel to be two men with one body? Maybe we can tell you. We're writing this – though it's I, Robert, who am up at the moment – because we've been commissioned to tell you what it's like living inside the same skin another human being inhabits and because we have to have our say.

I'm Robert. My brother's name is James. Our adoptive surname is Self – without contrivance on our part, even if this name seems to mock the circumstances of our life. James and I call our body The Monster. Who owns The Monster is a question that has occupied a good deal of our time, by virtue of a straitjacketing necessity. On more than one occasion The Monster has nearly killed us, but now we have pretty much domesticated it.

James Self. Robert Self. And The Monster.

It's quite late. James, who sits on the right side of our shoulders, has long since nodded away, giving control to me. My brother has subdued The Monster more effectively than I, however. When he's up, we move with a catlike agility I can never manage. Although our muscle tone and stamina are excellent, when I'm up The Monster shudders under my steering, and shambles, and shifts anatomical gears I didn't even know we possessed. At six foot three I am a hulking man, whereas James at six foot four – he's taller through the temples than I – is a graceful one. And we share the same body.

As a result, James often overmasters me during the day: I feel, then, like a sharp-witted invalid going the rounds in the arms of a kindly quarterback. Late at night, though, with James down in sleep and The Monster arranged propitiatingly on a leather lounge chair, even I can savour the animal potential of our limbs, the warmth of a good wine in our maw, the tingle of a privately resolvable sexual stirring. The Monster can be lived with.

But I'm leaping ahead. Let me tell you how we got this way, and what we look forward to, and why we persevere.

James and I were born in a southeastern state in 1951. (Gemini is our birth sign, though neither of us credits astrology.) A breech delivery, we've been told. I suppose we aligned ourselves buttocks first because we didn't know how to determine precedence at the opposite end. We were taken with forceps, and the emergence of James and Robert together, two perfect infant heads groggy from the general anesthetic they'd given our mother, made the obstetrics team draw back into a white huddle from which it regarded us with fear, scepticism, awe, incredulity. How could anyone have expected this?

A two-headed infant has only one heartbeat to measure, and there'd been no X-rays.

We were spirited away from the delivery room before our mother could recover and ask about us. The presiding physician, Dr Larimer Self, then decreed that she would be told her child was stillborn. Self destroyed hospital records of the birth, swore his staff to silence, and gave my biological father, an itinerant labourer following the peach and cotton crops, a recommendation for a job in Texas. Thus, our obstetrician became our father. And our real parents were lost to us for ever.

Larimer Self was an autocrat – but a sentimental one. He raised James and me in virtual isolation in a small community seventeen miles from the tri-county hospital where we'd been born. He gave us into the daytime care of a black woman named Velma Bymer. We grew up in a two-storey house surrounded by holly bushes, crape myrtle, nandin, and pecan trees. Two or three months ago, after attaining a notoriety or infamy you may already be aware of, we severed all connections with the outside world and returned to this big, eighty-year-old house. Neither James nor I know when we will choose to leave it again; it's the only real home we've ever had.

Velma was too old to wet-nurse us, and a bachelor woman besides, but she bottle-fed us in her arms, careful to alternate feedings between James's head and mine since we could not both take formula at once. She was forty-six when we came into her care, and from the beginning she looked upon us not as a snakish curse for her own barrenness, but as a holy charge. A guerdon for her piety. My memories of her focus on her raw-boned, purple hands and a voice like sweet water flowing over rocks. James says he remembers her instead for a smell like damp cotton mixed up with the odour of slowly baking bran rolls. Today Velma drives to Wilson and Cathet's for her groceries in a little blue Fiat and sits evenings in her tiny one-room house with the Bible open on her lap. She won't move from that house – but she does come over on Thursday afternoons to play checkers with James.

Larimer Self taught us how to read, do mathematics, and reconcile our disagreements through rapid, on-the-spot bargaining. Now and again he took a strop to The Monster.

Most children have no real concept of 'sharing' until well after three. James and I, with help from our stepfather, reached an earlier accommodation. We had to. If we wanted The Monster to work for us at all we had to subordinate self and co-operate in the manipulation of legs, arms, hands. Otherwise we did a Vitus dance, or spasmed like an epileptic, or crumpled into trembling stillness. Although I wrote earlier that James often 'overmasters' me, I didn't mean to imply that his motor control is stronger than mine, merely better, and that I sometimes voluntarily give him my up time for activities like walking, lifting, toting, anything primarily physical. As children we were the same. We could neutralise each other's strengths, but we couldn't – except in rare instances of fatigue or inattention – impose our will on the other. And so at six or seven months, maybe even earlier, we began to learn how to share our first toy: the baby animal under our necks. We became that organisational anomaly, a team with two captains.

Let me emphasise this: James and I don't have a psychic link, or a telepathic hookup, or even a wholly trustworthy line to each other's emotions. It's true that when I'm depressed James is frequently depressed, too; that when I'm exhilarated or euphoric James is the same. And why not? A number of feelings have biochemical determinants as well as psychological ones, and the biochemical state of Robert Self is pretty much the biochemical state of James Self. When James drinks, I get drunk. When I take smoke into our lungs, after a moment's delay James may well do the coughing. But we can't read each other's thoughts, and my brother – as I believe he could well say of me, too – can be as unpredictable as an utter stranger. By design or necessity we share many things, but our personalities and our thoughts are our own.

It's probably a little like being married, even down to the matter of sex. Usually our purely physical urges coincide, but one can put himself in a mental frame either welcoming or denying the satisfaction of that urge, whereupon, like husband and wife, James and Robert must negotiate. Of course, in our case the matter can be incredibly more complex than this. Legislation before congress, I suppose you could call some of our floor fights. But on this subject I yield to James, whose province the complexities are.

All right. What does being 'up' mean if neither James nor I happen to be strong enough to seize The Monster's instrument panel and march it around to a goose step of our own? It means that whoever's up has almost absolute motor control, that whoever's down has willingly relinquished this power. Both James and I can give up motor control and remain fully aware of the world; we can – and do – engage in cognitive activity and, since our speech centres aren't affected, communicate our ideas. This ability has something Eastern and yogic about it, I'm sure, but we have developed it without recourse to gurus or meditation.

How, then, do we decide who's to be up, who's to be down? Well, it's a 'you first, Alphonse'/'after you, Gaston' matter, I'm afraid, and the only thing to be said in its favour is that it works. Finally, if either of us is sleeping, the other is automatically up.* The Monster gets only three or four hours of uninterrupted rest a night, but that, we have decided, is the price a monster must pay to preserve the sanity of its masters.

Of course there are always those who think that James and I are the monster. Many feel this way. Except for nearly two years in the national limelight, when we didn't know what the hell we were doing, we have spent our life trying to prove these people wrong. We are human beings, James and I, despite the unconscionable trick played on us in our mother's womb, and we want everybody to know it.

Come, Monster. Come under my hand. Goodbrother's asleep, it's seven o'clock in the a.m., and you've had at least three long hours of shut-eye, all four lids fluttering like window shades in gusty May! Three hours! So come under my hand, Monster, and let's see what we can add to this.

There are those who think that James and I are the monster.

O considerate brother, stopping where I can take off with a tail wind, even if The Monster is a little sluggish on the runway this morning. Robert is the man to be up, though; he's the one who taps this tipritter with the most authority, even if I am the high-hurdle man on our team. (He certainly wouldn't be mixing metaphors like this, goodbrother Robert.) Our editor wants both of us to contribute, however, and dissecting our monsterhood might be a good place for James to begin. Just let Robert snooze while you take my dictation, Monster, that's all I ask.

Yes. Many do see us as a monster. And somewhere in his introductory notes my goodbrother puts his hand to his mouth and whispers in an aside, "James is taller than me." Well, that's true – I am. You see, Robert and I aren't identical twins. (I'm better looking than Robert.) (And taller.) This means that a different genetic template was responsible for each goodbrother's face and features,

---

* This state can be complicated, however. James dreams with such intensity that The Monster thrashes out with barely restrainable, subterranean vehemence. Not always, but often enough.

and, in the words of a local shopkeeper, "That Just Don't Happen." The chromosomes must have got twisted, the genes multiplied and scrambled, and a monster set loose on the helical stairway of the nucleotides. What we are, I'm afraid, is a sort of double mutant. . . . That's right, you hear me clearly: a mutant.

M.U.T.A.N.T.

I hope you haven't panicked and run off to Bolivia. Mutants are scary, yes – but usually because they don't work very well or fit together like they ought. A lot of mutations, whether fruit flies or sheep, are stillborn, dead to begin with. Others die later. The odds don't favour creatures with abbreviated limbs and heads without skull caps. Should your code get bollixed, about the best you can hope for is an aristocratic sixth finger, one more pinky to lift away from your tea cup. And everybody's seen those movies where radiation has turned picnicking ants or happy-go-lucky grasshoppers into ogres as big as frigates. Those are *mutants*, you know.

And two-headed men?

Well, in the popular media they're usually a step below your bona fide mutant, surgical freaks skulking through swamps, axe at the ready, both bottom lips adrool. Or, if the culprit *is* radiation – an after-the-bomb comeuppance for mankind's vanity – one of the heads is a lump capable only of going 'la la, la la' and repeating whatever the supposedly normal head says. Or else the two heads are equally dumb and carry on like an Abbott and Costello comedy team, bumping noggins and singing duets. Capital crimes, all these gambits. Ha ha.

No one identifies with a two-headed man.

If you dare suggest that the subject has its serious side, bingo, the word they drop on you is – 'morbid'. Others in the avoidance arsenal? Try: 'Grotesque.' 'Diseased.' 'Gruesome.' 'Pathological.' 'Perverse.' Or even this: '*Poly*perverse.' But 'morbid' is the mortar shell they lob in to break off serious discussion and the fragments corkscrew through you until even you are aghast at your depravity. People wonder why you don't kill yourselves at first awareness of your hideousness. And you can only wince and slink away, a morbid silver trail behind you. Like snail slime.

Can you imagine, then, what it's like being a (so-called) two-headed man in Monocephalic America? Robert and I may well be the ultimate minority. Robert and I and The Monster, the three of us together.

Last year in St Augustine, Florida, at the Ripley museum, on tour with an Atlanta publicist, my brother and I saw a two-headed calf.

Stuffed. One head blind and misshapen, lolling away from the sighted head. A mutant, preserved for the delight and edification of tourists to the Oldest City in the USA. Huzza huzza.

In the crowded display room in front of this specimen our party halted. Silence snapped down like a guillotine blade. What were the Selfs going to do now, everyone wondered. Do you suppose we've offended them? Aw, don't worry about it, they knew what they were getting into. Yeah, but—

Sez I to brother, 'This is a Bolshevik calf, Robert. The calf is undoubtedly no marcher in the procession of natural creatures. It's a Soviet sew-up. They did it to Man's Best Friend and now they've done it to a potential bearer of Nature's Most Perfect Food. Here's the proof of it, goodbrother, right here in America's Oldest City.'

'Tsk, tsk,' sez Robert. He sez that rather well.

'And how many Social Security numbers do you suppose our officialdom gave this calf before it succumbed? How many times did they let this moo-cow manqué inscribe in the local voting register?'

'This *commie* calf?'

'Affirmative.'

'Oh, two, certainly. If it's a Soviet sew-up, James, it probably weaselled its rights from both the Social Security apparatus and the voting registrar. Whereas we—'

'Upright American citizens.'

'Aye,' sez Robert. 'Whereas we are but a single person in the eyes of the State.'

'Except for purposes of taxation,' sez I.

'Except for purposes of taxation,' Robert echoes. 'Though it is given to us to file a joint return.'

We can do Abbott and Costello, too, you see. Larry Blackman, the writer, publicist, and 'talent handler', wheezed significantly, moved in, and herded our party to a glass case full of partially addressed envelopes that – believe it or not – had nevertheless been delivered to the Ripley museum. One envelope had arrived safely with only a rip (!) in its cover as a clue to its intended destination.

'From rip to Zip,' sez I, 'and service has gotten worse.'

Blackman coughed, chuckled, and tried to keep Robert from glancing over our shoulder at that goddamn calf. I still don't know if he ever understood just how bad he'd screwed up.

That night in our motel room Robert hung his head forward and wept. We were wracked with sobs. Pretty soon The Monster had ole smartass Jamebo doing it, too, just as if we were nine years old again and crying for Velma after burning a strawberry on our knobbly knee. James and Robert Self, in a Howard Johnson's outside St Augustine, sobbing in an anvil chorus of bafflement . . . I only bring this up because the episode occurred toward the end of our association with Blackman and because our editor wanted a bit of 'psychology' in this collaborative effort.

There it is, then: a little psychology. Make of it what you will.

Up, Monster! Get ye from this desk without awakening Robert and I'll feed ye cold peaches from the Frigidaire. Upon our shared life and my own particular palate, I will.

People wonder why you didn't kill yourselves at first awareness of your hideousness.

(James is reading over our chest as I write, happy that I've begun by quoting him. Quid pro quo, I say: tit for tat.)

Sex and death. Death and sex. Our contract calls upon us to write about these things, but James has merely touched on the one while altogether avoiding the other. Maybe he wishes to leave the harvesting of morbidities to me. Could that possibly be it?

('You've seen right through me, goodbrother,' replies James.)

Leaving aside the weighty matter of taxes, then, let's talk about death and sex . . . No, let's narrow our subject to death. I still have hopes that James will spare me a recounting of a side of our life I've allowed him, by default, to direct. James?

('Okay, Robert. Done.')

Very well. The case is this: When James dies, I will die. When I die, James will die. Coronary thrombosis. Cancer of the lungs. Starvation. Food poisoning. Electrocution. Snakebite. Defenestration. Anything fatally injurious to the body does us both in – two personalities are blotted out at one blow. The Monster dies, taking us with it. The last convulsion, the final laugh, belongs to the creature we will have spent our lives training to our wills. Well, maybe we owe it that much.

You may, however, be wondering: isn't it possible that James or Robert could suffer a lethal blow without causing his brother's death? A tumor? An embolism? An aneurysm? A bullet wound? Yes, that might happen. But the physical shock to The Monster, the poisoning of our bloodstream, the emotional and psychological repercussions for the surviving Self would probably bring about the other's death as a matter of course. We are not Siamese twins, James and I, to be separated with a scalpel or a medical laser and then sent on our individual ways, each of us less a man than before. Our ways have never been separate, and never will be, and yet we don't find ourselves hideous simply because the fact of our interdependence has been cast in an inescapable anatomical metaphor. Just the opposite, perhaps.

At the beginning of our assault on the World of Entertainment two years ago (and, yes, we still receive daily inquiries from carnivals and circuses, both American and European), we made an appearance on the *Midnight Chatter*. This was Blackman's doing, a means of introducing us to the public without resorting to loudspeakers and illustrated posters. We were very lucky to get the booking, he told us, and it was easy to see that Blackman felt he'd pulled off a major show-business coup.

James and I came on at the tail end of a Wednesday's evening show, behind segments featuring the psychologist Dr Irving Brothers, the playwright Kentucky Mann, and the actress Victoria Pate. When we finally came out from the backstage dressing rooms, to no musical accompaniment at all, the audience boggled and then timidly began to applaud. (James says he heard someone exclaim 'Holy cow!' over the less than robust clapping, but I can't confirm this.) *Midnight Chatter*'s host, Tommy Carver, greeted us with boyish innocence, as if we were the Pope.

'I know you must, uh, turn heads where you go, Mr Self,' he began, gulping theatrically and tapping an unsharpened pencil on his desk. 'Uh, *Misters* Self, that is. But what is it – I mean, what question really disturbs you the most, turns you off to the attention you must attract?'

'That one,' James said. 'That's the one.'

The audience boggled again, not so much at this lame witticism as at the fact that we'd actually spoken. A woman in the front row snickered.

'Okay,' Carver said, doing a shaking-off-the-roundhouse bit with his head, 'I deserved that. What's your biggest personal worry, then? I mean, is it something common to all of us or something, uh, peculiar to just you?' That *peculiar* drew a few more snickers.

'My biggest worry,' James said, 'is that Robert will try to murder me by committing suicide.'

The audience, catching on, laughed at this. Carver was looking amused and startled at once – the studio monitor had him isolated in a close-up and he kept throwing coy glances at the camera.

'Why would Robert here — that's not a criminal face, after all — want to murder you?'

'He thinks I've been beating his time with his girl.'

Over renewed studio laughter Carver continued to play his straight-man's role. 'Now is *that* true, Robert?' I must have been looking fidgety or distraught — he wanted to pull me into the exchange.

'Of course it isn't,' James said. 'If he's got a date, I keep my eyes closed. I don't want to embarrass anybody.'

It went like that right up to a commercial for dog food. Larry Blackman had written the routine for us, and James had practised it so that he could drop in the laugh-lines even if the right questions weren't asked. It was all a matter, said Blackman, of manipulating the material. The *Midnight Chatter*'s booking agent had expected us to be a 'people guest' rather than a performer — one whose appeal lies in what he is rather than the image he projects. But Blackman said we could be both, James the comedian, me the sincere human expert on our predicament. Blackman's casting was adequate, I suppose; it was the script that was at heart gangrenous. Each head a half. The audience liked the half it had seen.

('He's coming back to the subject now, folks,' James says. 'See if he doesn't.')

After the English sheepdog had wolfed down his rations, I said, 'Earlier James told you he was afraid I'd murder him by committing suicide—'

'Yeah. That took us all back a bit.'

'Well, the truth is, James and I *have* discussed killing ourselves.'

'Seriously?' Carver leaned back in his chair and opened his jacket.

'Very seriously. Because it's impossible for us to operate independently of each other. If I were to take an overdose of amphetamines, for instance, it would be *our* stomach they pumped.'

Carver gazed over his desk at our midsection. 'Yeah. I see what you mean.'

'Or if James grew despondent and took advantage of his up time to slash our wrists, it would be both of us who bled to death. One's suicide is the other's murder, you see.'

'The perfect crime,' offered Victoria Pate.

'No,' I replied, 'because the act is its own punishment. James and I understand that very well. That's why we've made a pact to the effect that neither of us will attempt suicide until we've made a pact to do it together.'

'You've made a pact to make a suicide pact?'

'Right,' James said. 'We're blood brothers that way. And that's how we expect to die.'

Carver buttoned his jacket and ran a finger around the inside of his collar. 'Not terribly soon, I hope. I don't believe this crowd is up for that sort of *Midnight Chatter* first.'

'Oh, no,' I assured him. 'We're not expecting to take any action for several more years yet. But who knows? Circumstances will certainly dictate what we do, eventually.'

Afterwards viewers inundated the studio switchboard with calls. Negative reaction to our remarks on suicide ran higher than questions about how the cameramen had 'done it'. Although Blackman congratulated us both heartily, The Monster didn't sleep very well that night.

'He thinks I've been beating his time with his girl.'

Well, strange types scuttled after us while Blackman was running interference for Robert and James Self. The Monster devoured them, just as if they were dog food. When it wasn't exhausted. We gave them stereophonic sweet nothings and the nightmares they couldn't have by themselves. Robert, for my and The Monster's sakes, didn't say nay. He indulged us. He never carped. Which has led to resentments on both sides, the right and the left. We've talked about these.

Before leaving town for parts north, west, and glittering, Robert and I were briefly engaged to be married. And not to each other. She was four years older than us. She worked in the front office of the local power company, at a desk you could reach only by weaving through a staggered lot of electric ranges, dishwashers, and hot-water heaters, most of them white, a few avocado.

We usually mail in our bill payments, or ask Velma to take them if she's going uptown – but this time, since our monthly charges had been fluctuating unpredictably and we couldn't ring through on the phone, I drove us across the two-lane into our business district. (Robert doesn't have a licence.) Our future fiancée – I'm going to call her X – was patiently explaining to a group of housewives and day labourers the rate hike recently approved by the Public Service Commission, the consumer rebates ordered by the PSC for the previous year's disallowed fuel tax, and the summer rates soon to go into effect. Her voice was quavering a little. Through the door behind her desk we could see two grown men huddling out of harm's way, the storeroom light off.

(Robert wants to know, 'Are you going to turn this into a How-We-Rescued-the-Maiden-from-the-Dragon story?')

('Fuck off,' I tell him.)

(Robert would probably like The Monster to shrug his indifference to my rebuke – but I'm the one who's up now and I'm going to finish this blood-sucking reminiscence.)

Our appearance in the power company office had its usual impact. We, uh, turned heads. Three or four people moved away from the payments desk, a couple of others pretended – not very successfully – that we weren't there at all, and an old man in overalls stared. A woman we'd met once in Wilson & Cathet's said, 'Good morning, Mr Self,' and dragged a child of indeterminate sex into the street behind her.

X pushed herself up from her chair and stood at her desk with her head hanging between her rigid supporting arms. 'Oh, shit,' she whispered. 'This is too much.'

'We'll come back when you're feeling better,' a biddy in curlers said stiffly. The whole crew ambled out, even the man in overalls, his cheeks a shiny knot because of the chewing tobacco hidden there. Nobody used the aisle we were standing in to exit by.

The telephone rang. X took it off the hook, hefted it as if it were a truncheon, and looked at Robert and me without a jot of surprise.

'This number isn't working,' she said into the receiver. 'It's out of order.' And she hung up.

On her desk beside the telephone I saw a battered paperback copy of *The Thorn Birds*. But X hadn't been able to read much that morning.

'Don't be alarmed,' I said. X didn't look alarmed. 'We're a lion tamer,' I went on. 'That's the head I stick into their mouths.'

'Ha ha,' Robert said.

A beginning. The game didn't last long, though. After we first invited her, X came over to Larimer Self's old house – *our* old house – nearly every night for a month, and she proved to be interested in us, both Robert and me, in ways that our little freakshow groupies never had any conception of. They came later, though, and maybe Robert and I didn't then recognise what an uncommon woman this hip and straightforward X really was. She regarded us as people, X did.

We would sit in our candle-lit living room listening to the Incredible String Band sing 'Douglas Traherne Harding', among others, and talking about old movies. (The candles weren't for romance; they were to spite, with X's full approval, the power company.) In the kitchen, The Monster, mindless, baked for us chocolate-chip cookies and gave its burned fingers to Robert or me to suck. Back in the living room, all of us chewing cookies, we talked like a cage of gibbering monkeys, and laughed giddily, and finally ended up getting serious enough to discuss serious things like jobs and goals and long-dreamt-of tomorrows. But Robert and I let X do most of the talking and watched her in rapt mystification and surrender.

One evening, aware of our silence, she suddenly stopped and came over to us and kissed us both on our foreheads. Then, having led The Monster gently up the stairs, she showed it how to co-ordinate its untutored mechanical rhythms with those of a different but complementary sort of creature. Until then, it had been a virgin.

And the sentient Selfs? Well, Robert, as he put it, was 'charmed, really charmed'. Me, I was glazed over and strung out with a whole complex of feelings that most people regard as symptomatic of romantic love. How the hell could Robert be merely – I think I'm going to be sick – 'charmed'?

('The bitterness again?')

('Well, goodbrother, we knew it would happen. Didn't we?')

We discussed X, rationally and otherwise. She was from Ohio, and she had come to our town by way of a coastal resort where she had worked as a night-clerk in a motel. The Arab oil embargo had taken that job away from her, she figured, but she had come inland with true resilience and captured another with our power company – on the basis of a college diploma, a folder of recommendations, and the snow job she'd done on old Grey Bates, her boss. She flattered Robert and me, though, by telling us that we were the only people in town she could be herself with. I think she meant it, too, and I'm pretty certain that Robert also believed her. If he's changed his mind of late, it's only because he has to justify his own subsequent vacillation and sabotage.

('James, damn you — !')

('All right. All right.')

About two weeks after X first started coming to our house in the evenings Robert and I reached an argument. We asked her to marry us. Both of us. All three of us. There was no other way.

She didn't say yes. She didn't say no. She said she'd have to think about it, and both Robert and I backed off from crowding her. Later, after we'd somehow managed to get past the awkwardness of the marriage proposal, X leaned forward and asked us how we supported ourselves. It was something we'd never talked about before.

'Why do you ask?' Robert snapped. He began to grind his molars – that kind of sound gets conducted through bones.

'It's Larimer's money,' I interjected. 'So much a month from the bank. And the house and grounds are paid for.'

'Why do you ask?' Robert again demanded.

'I'm worried about you,' X said. 'Is Larimer's money going to last forever? Because you two don't *do* anything that I'm aware of, and I've always been uptight about people who don't make their own way. I've always supported myself, you see, and that's how I am. And I don't want to be uptight about my — well, my husbands.'

Robert had flushed. It was affecting me, too – I could feel the heat rising in my face. 'No,' Robert said. 'Larimer's legacy to us won't last forever.'

X was wearing flowered shorts and a halter. She had her clean bare feet on the dirty upholstery of our divan. The flesh around her navel was pleated enticingly.

'Do you think I want your money, Rob? I don't want your money. I'm just afraid you may be regarding marriage to me as a panacea for all your problems. It's not, you know. There's a world that has to be lived in. You have to make your way in it for yourselves, married or not. Otherwise it's impossible to be happy. Don't you see? Marriage isn't just a string of party evenings, fellows.'

'We know,' I said.

'I suppose you do,' X acknowledged readily enough. 'Well, I do, too. I was married in Dayton. For six years.'

'That doesn't matter to us. Does it, goodbrother?'

Robert swallowed. It was pretty clear he wished that business about Dayton had come out before, if only between the clicks of our record changer. 'No,' he said gamely. 'It doesn't matter.'

'*One light*,' the Incredible String Band sang: '*the light that is one though the lamps be many.*'

'Listen,' X said earnestly. 'If you have any idea what I'm talking about, maybe I *will* marry you. And I'll go anywhere you want to go to find the other keys to your happiness. I just need a little time to think.'

I forget who was up then, Robert or me. Maybe neither of us. Who cares? The Monster trucked across the room with the clear intention of devouring X on the dirty divan. The moment seemed sweet, even if

46

the setting wasn't, and I was close to tears thinking that Robert and I were practically *engaged* to this decent and compassionate woman.

But The Monster failed us that night. Even though X received the three of us as her lover, The Monster wasn't able to perform and I knew with absolute certainty that its failure was Robert's fault.

'I'll marry you,' X whispered consolingly. 'There'll be other nights, other times. Sometimes this happens.'

We *were* engaged! This fact, that evening, didn't rouse The Monster to a fever pitch of gentle passion – but me, at least, it greatly comforted. And on several successive evenings, as Robert apparently tried to acquiesce in our mutual good fortune, The Monster was as good as new again: I began to envision a home in the country, a job as a power company lineman, and, God help me, children in whose childish features it might be possible to see something of all three of us.

('A bevy of bicephalic urchins? Or were you going to shoot for a Cerberus at every single birth?')

('Robert, damn you, *shut up!*')

And then, without warning, Robert once again began sabotaging The Monster's poignant attempts to make it with X. Although capable of regarding its malfunctioning as a temporary phenomenon, X was also smart enough to realise that something serious underlay it. Sex? For the last week that Robert and I knew her, there wasn't any. I didn't mind that. What I minded was the knowledge that my own brother was using his power – a purely *negative* sort of power – to betray the both of us. I don't really believe that I've gotten over his betrayal yet. Maybe I never will.

So that's the sex part, goodbrother. As far as I'm concerned, that's the sex part. You did the death. I did the sex. And we were both undone by what you did and didn't do in both arenas. At least that's how I see it . . . I had intended to finish this – but to hell with it, Robert. You finish it. It's your baby. Take it.

All right. We've engaged in so many recriminations over this matter that our every argument and counterargument is annotated. That we didn't marry X is probably my fault. Put aside the wisdom or the folly of our even hoping to marry – for in the end we didn't. We haven't. And the fault is mine.

You can strike that 'probably' I use up there.

James once joked – he hasn't joked much about this affair – that I got 'cold foot'. After all, he was willing, The Monster was amenable, it was only goodbrother Robert who was weak. Perhaps, I only know that after our proposal I could never summon up the same enthusiasm for X's visits as I had before. I can remember her saying, 'You two don't *do* anything that I'm aware of, and I've always been uptight about people who don't make their own way.' I'll always believe there was something smug and condescending – not to say downright insensitive – in this observation. And, in her desire to know how we had managed to support ourselves, something grasping and feral. She had a surface frankness under which her ulteriority bobbed like a tethered mine, and James never could see the danger.

('Bullshit. Utter Bullshit.')

('Do you want this back, Mr Self? It's yours if you want it.')

(James stares out of the window at our Japanese yew.)

X was alerted to my disenchantment by The Monster's failure to perform. Even though she persevered for a time in the apparent hope that James would eventually win me over, she was as alert as a finch. She knew that I had gone sour on our relationship. Our conversations began to turn on questions like 'Want another drink?' and 'How'd it go today?' The Monster sweated.

Finally, on the last evening, X looked at me and said: 'You don't really want us to marry, do you, Robert? You're afraid of what might happen. Even in the cause of your own possible happiness, and you don't want to take any risks.'

It was put up or shut up. 'No,' I told her: 'I don't want us to marry. And the only thing I'm afraid of is what you might do to James and me by trying to impose your inequitable love on us in an opportunistic marriage.'

'*Opportunistic?*' She made her voice sound properly disbelieving.

'James and I are going to make a great deal of money. We don't have to depend on Larimer's legacy. And you knew that the moment you saw us, didn't you?'

X shook her head. 'Do you really think, Rob, that I'd marry' – here she chose her words very carefully – 'two-men-with-one-body in order to improve my own financial situation?'

'People have undergone sex changes for no better reason.'

'That's speculation,' she said. 'I don't believe it.'

James, his head averted from mine, was absolutely silent. I couldn't even hear him breathing.

X shifted on the divan. She looked at me piercingly, as if conspicuous directness would persuade me of her sincerity: 'Rob, aren't you simply afraid that somehow I'll come between you and James?'

'That's impossible,' I answered.

'I know it is. That's why you're being unreasonable to even assume it could happen.'

'Who assumed such a thing?' I demanded. 'But I do know this – you'll never be able to love us both equally, will you? You'll never be able to bestow your heart's affection on me as you bestow it on James.'

She looked at the ceiling, exhaled showily, then stood up and crossed to the chair in which The Monster was sitting. She kissed me on the bridge of my nose, turned immediately to James and favoured him with a similar benediction.

'I would have tried,' she said. 'Bye, fellas.'

James kept his head averted, and The Monster shook with a vehemence that would have bewildered me had I not understood how sorely I had disappointed my brother – even in attempting to save us both from a situation that had very nearly exploded in our faces.

X didn't come back again, and I wouldn't let James phone her. Three days after our final goodbye, clouds rolled in from the Gulf and it rained as if in memory of Noah. During the thunderstorm our electricity went out. It didn't come back on all that day. A day later it was still out. The freezer compartment in our refrigerator began to defrost.

James called the power company. X wasn't there, much to my relief. Bates told us that she had given her notice the day before and walked out into the rain without her paycheck. He couldn't understand why our power should be off if we had paid our bills as conscientiously as we said. Never mind, though, he'd see to it that we got our lights back. The whole episode was tangible confirmation of X's pettiness.

It wasn't long after she had left that I finally persuaded James to let me write to Larry Blackman in Atlanta. We came out of seclusion. As X might have cattily put it, we finally got around to *doing* something. With a hokey comedy routine and the magic of our inborn uniqueness we threw ourselves into the national spotlight and made money hand over fist. James was so clever and co-operative that I allowed him to feed The Monster whenever the opportunity arose, and there were times, I have to admit, when I thought that neither it nor James was capable of being sated. But not once did I fail to indulge them. Not once—

All right. That's enough, goodbrother. I know you have some feelings. I saw you in that Howard Johnson's in St Augustine. I remember how you cried when Charles Laughton fell off the cathedral of Notre Dame. And when King Kong plummeted from the Empire State Building. And when the creature from 20,000 fathoms was electrocuted under the roller coaster on Coney Island. And when I suggested to you at the end of our last road tour that maybe it was time to make the pact that we had so long ago agreed to make one day. You weren't ready, you said. And I am unable by the rules of both love and decency to make that pact and carry out its articles without your approval. Have I unilaterally rejected your veto? No. No, I haven't.

So have a little pity.

Midnight. James has long since nodded away, giving control to me. Velma called this afternoon. She says she'll be over tomorrow afternoon for checkers. That seemed to perk James up a little. But I'm hoping to get him back on the road before this month is out. Activity's the best thing for him now – the best thing for both of us. I'm sure he'll eventually realise that.

Lights out.

I brush my lips against my brother's sleeping cheek.

'Collaborating' by Michael Bishop, copyright © 1979 by Lee Harding. Reprinted by permission of the author and the author's agent, Virginia Kidd.

THE MAN WHO COLLECTED POE
Robert Bloch

I have always had a special fondness for 'The Man Who Collected Poe'. It was the only story I ever submitted to Famous Fantastic Mysteries, and its appearance there led to some gratifying results.

It was read by Poe scholar Thomas O. Mabbott, who at that time happened to be compiling a collection of Poe's work for college students. In the course of his research, Professor Mabbott had come across a copy of Poe's final and uncompleted tale, 'The Light-House'. It occurred to him, after reading my pastiche, that I might be interested in completing the story, and he sent it to me for my consideration.

Naturally, I accepted the challenge. Virtually all of us who work in the fantasy genre acknowledge our debt to Edgar Allan Poe and admire his work. It had been this admiration which inspired 'The Man Who Collected Poe' in the first place, and knowledgeable readers will detect that I deliberately incorporated portions of 'The Fall of the House of Usher' into my story, verbatim, as a homage.

Thus the idea of actually emulating Poe's style in a story of his own intrigued me, as did the idea of trying to guess how he would have developed the material and contriving an ending. I did so, and the result has defied a generation of readers, who have been unable to determine where Poe left off and I took over.

So I'm grateful to 'The Man Who Collected Poe' for affording me the opportunity to collaborate, as it were, with an acknowledged master of the fantasy field.

If you're not familiar with it already, I suggest you read 'The Fall of the House of Usher' first, and then proceed to my story. While I make no pretensions of rivalling Poe's prose, you may find it amusing to see just how I contrived my own tale from the elements present in his.

And I trust you will realize the basis of my fondness for 'The Man Who Collected Poe'. Writing it was truly a labor of love.

During the whole of a dull, dark and soundless day in the autumn of the year, when the clouds hung oppressively low in the heavens, I had been passing alone, by automobile, through a singularly dreary tract of country; and at length found myself, as the shades of the evening drew on, within view of my destination.

I looked upon the scene before me – upon the mere house and the simple landscape features of the domain, upon the bleak walls, upon the vacant eyelike windows, upon a few rank sedges, and upon a few white trunks of decayed trees – with a feeling of utter confusion commingled with dismay. For it seemed to me as though I had visited this scene once before, or read of it, perhaps, in some frequently rescanned tale. And yet assuredly it could not be, for only three days had passed since I had made the acquaintance of Launcelot Canning and received an invitation to visit him at his Maryland residence.

The circumstances under which I met Canning were simple; I happened to attend a bibliophilic meeting in Washington and was introduced to him by a mutual friend. Casual conversation gave place to absorbed and interested discussion when he discovered my preoccupation with works of fantasy. Upon learning that I was traveling upon a vacation with no set itinerary, Canning urged me to become his guest for a day and to examine, at my leisure, his unusual display of *memorabilia*.

'I feel, from our conversation, that we have much in common,' he told me. 'For you see, sir, in my love of fantasy I bow to no man. It is a taste I have perhaps inherited from my father and from his father before him, together with their considerable acquisitions in the genre. No doubt you would be gratified with what I am prepared to show you, for in all due modesty I beg to style myself the world's leading collector of the works of Edgar Allan Poe.'

I confess that his invitation as such did not enthrall me, for I hold no brief for the literary hero-worshipper or the scholarly collector as a type. I own to a more than passing interest in the tales of Poe, but my interest does not extend to the point of ferreting out the exact date upon which Mr. Poe first decided to raise a mustache, nor would I be unduly intrigued by the opportunity to examine several hairs preserved from that hirsute appendage.

So it was rather the person and personality of Launcelot Canning himself which caused me to accept his proffered hospitality. For the man who proposed to become my host might have himself stepped from the pages of a Poe tale. His speech, as I have endeavored to indicate, was characterized by a courtly *rodomontade* so often exemplified in Poe's heroes – and beyond certainty, his appearance bore out the resemblance.

Launcelot Canning had the cadaverousness of complexion, the large, liquid, luminous eyes, the thin, curved lips, the delicately modeled nose, finely molded chin, and dark, weblike hair of a typical Poe protagonist.

It was this phenomenon which prompted my acceptance and led me to journey to his Maryland estate which, as I now perceived, in itself manifested a Poe-etic quality of its own, intrinsic in the images of the gray sedge, the ghastly tree stems, and the vacant and eyelike windows of the mansion of gloom. All that was lacking was a tarn and a moat – and as I prepared to enter the dwelling I half expected to encounter therein the carved ceilings, the somber tapestries, the ebon floors and the phantasmagoric armorial trophies so vividly described by the author of *Tales of the Grotesque and Arabesque*.

Nor, upon entering Launcelot Canning's home, was I too greatly disappointed in my expectations. True to both the atmospheric quality of the decrepit mansion and to my own fanciful presentiments, the door was opened in response to my knock by a valet who conducted me, in silence, through dark and intricate passages to the study of his master.

The room in which I found myself was very large and lofty. The windows were long, narrow and pointed, and at so vast a distance from the black oaken floor as to be altogether inaccessible from within. Feeble gleams of encrimsoned light made their way through the trellised panes and served to render sufficiently distinct the more prominent objects around; the eye, however, struggled in vain to reach the remoter angles of the chamber or the recesses of the vaulted and fretted ceiling. Dark draperies hung upon the walls. The general furniture was profuse, comfortless, antique and tattered. Many books and musical instruments lay scattered about, but they failed to give any vitality to the scene.

Instead, they rendered more distinct that peculiar quality of quasi-recollection; it was as though I found myself once again, after a protracted absence, in a familiar setting. I had read, I had imagined, I had dreamed, or I had actually beheld this setting before.

Upon my entrance, Launcelot Canning arose from a sofa on which he had been lying at full length and greeted me with a vivacious warmth which had much in it, I at first thought, of an overdone cordiality.

Yet his tone, as he spoke of the object of my visit, of his earnest desire to see me, of the solace he expected me to afford him in a mutual discussion of our interests, soon alleviated my initial misapprehension.

Launcelot Canning welcomed me with the rapt enthusiasm of the born collector – and I came to realize that he was indeed just that. For the Poe collection he shortly proposed to unveil before me was actually his birthright.

The nucleus of the present accumulation, he disclosed, had begun with his grandfather, Christopher Canning, a respected merchant of Baltimore. Almost eighty years ago he had been one of the leading patrons of the arts in his community and as such was partially instrumental in arranging for the removal of Poe's body to the southeastern corner of the Presbyterian Cemetery at Fayette and Green Streets, where a suitable monument might be erected. This event occurred in the year 1875, and it was a few years prior to that time that Canning laid the foundation of the Poe collection.

'Thanks to his zeal,' his grandson informed me, 'I am today the fortunate possessor of a copy of virtually every existing specimen of Poe's published works. If you will step over here,' – and he led me to a remote corner of the vaulted study, past the dark draperies, to a bookshelf which rose remotely to the shadowy ceiling – 'I shall be pleased to corroborate that claim. Here is a copy of *Al Aaraaf, Tamerlane and other Poems* in the 1829 edition, and here is the still earlier *Tamerlane and other Poems* of 1827. The Boston edition, which, as you doubtless know, is valued today at $15,000. I can assure you that Grandfather Canning parted with no such sum in order to gain possession of this rarity.'

He displayed the volumes with an air of commingled pride and cupidity which is ofttimes characteristic of the collector and is by no means to be confused with either literary snobbery or ordinary greed. Realizing this, I remained patient as he exhibited further treasures – copies of the *Philadelphia Saturday Courier* containing early tales, bound volumes of *The Messenger* during the period of Poe's editorship, *Graham's Magazine*, editions of the *New York Sun* and the *New York Mirror* boasting, respectively, of *The Balloon Hoax* and *The Raven*, and files of *The Gentleman's Magazine*. Ascending a short library ladder, he handed down to me the Lea and Blanchard edition of *Tales of the Grotesque and Arabesque*, the *Conchologist's First Book*, the Putnam *Eureka*, and, finally, the little paper booklet, published in 1843 and sold for 12½¢, entitled *The Prose Romances of Edgar A. Poe* – an insignificant trifle containing two tales which is valued by present-day collectors at $50,000.

Canning informed me of this last fact and, indeed, kept up a running commentary upon each item he presented. There was no doubt but that he was a Poe scholar as well as a Poe collector, and his words informed tattered specimens of the *Broadway Journal* and *Godey's Lady's Book* with a singular fascination not necessarily inherent in the flimsy sheets or their contents.

'I owe a great debt to Grandfather Canning's obsession,' he observed, descending the ladder and joining me before the bookshelves. 'It is not altogether a breach of confidence to admit that his interest in Poe did reach the point of an obsession, and perhaps eventually of an absolute mania. The knowledge, alas, is public property, I fear.

'In the early seventies he built this house, and I am quite sure that you have been observant enough to note that it in itself is almost a replica of a typical Poesque mansion. This was his study, and it was here that he was wont to pore over the books, the letters and the numerous mementos of Poe's life.

'What prompted a retired merchant to devote himself so fanatically to the pursuit of a hobby, I cannot say. Let it suffice that he virtually withdrew from the world and from all other normal interests. He conducted a voluminous and lengthy correspondence with aging men and women who had known Poe in their lifetime – made pilgrimages to Fordham, sent his agents to West Point, to England and Scotland, to virtually every locale in which Poe had set foot during his lifetime. He acquired letters and souvenirs as gifts, he bought them and – I fear – stole them, if no other means of acquisition proved feasible.'

Launcelot Canning smiled and nodded. 'Does all this sound strange to you? I confess that once I too found it almost incredible, a fragment of romance. Now, after years spent amidst these surroundings, I have lost my own objectivity.'

'Yes, it is strange,' I replied. 'But are you quite sure that there was not some obscure personal reason for your grandfather's interest? Had he met Poe as a boy, or been closely associated with one of his friends? Was there, perhaps, a distant, undisclosed relationship?'

At the mention of the last word, Canning started visibly, and a tremor of agitation overspread his countenance.

'Ah!' he exclaimed. 'There you voice my own inmost conviction. A relationship – assuredly there must have been – I am morally, instinctively certain that Grandfather Canning felt or knew himself to be linked to Edgar Poe by ties of blood. Nothing else could account for his strong initial interest, his continuing defense of Poe in the literary controversies of the day, his final melancholy lapse into a world of delusion and illusion.

'Yet he never voiced a statement or put an allegation upon paper – and I have searched the collection of letters in vain for the slightest clue.

'It is curious that you so promptly divine a suspicion held not only by myself but by my father. He was only a child at the time of my Grandfather Canning's death, but the attendant circumstances left a profound impression upon his sensitive nature. Although he was immediately removed from this house to the home of his mother's people in Baltimore, he lost no time in returning upon assuming his inheritance in early manhood.

'Fortunately being in possession of a considerable income, he was able to devote his entire lifetime to further research. The name of Arthur Canning is still well known in the world of literary criticism, but for some reason he preferred to pursue his scholarly examination of Poe's career in privacy. I believe this preference was dictated by an inner sensibility; that he was endeavoring to unearth some information which would prove his father's, his, and for that matter, my own, kinship to Edgar Poe.'

'You say your father was also a collector?' I prompted.

'A statement I am prepared to substantiate,' replied my host, as he led me to yet another corner of the shadow-shrouded study. 'But first, if you would accept a glass of wine?'

He filled, not glasses, but veritable beakers from a large carafe, and we toasted one another in silent appreciation. It is perhaps unnecessary for me to observe that the wine was a fine old Amontillado.

'Now, then,' said Launcelot Canning. 'My father's special province in Poe research consisted of the accumulation and study of letters.'

Opening a series of large trays or drawers beneath the bookshelves, he drew out file after file of glassined folios, and for the space of the next half hour I examined Edgar Poe's correspondence – letters to Henry Herring, to Doctor Snodgrass, Sarah Shelton, James P. Moss, Elizabeth Poe; missives to Mrs. Rockwood, Helen Whitman, Anne Lynch, John Pendleton Kennedy; notes to Mrs. Richmond, to John Allan, to Annie, to his brother, Henry – a profusion of documents, a veritable epistolary cornucopia.

During the course of my perusal my host took occasion to refill our beakers with wine, and the heady draught began to take effect – for we had not eaten, and I own I gave no thought to food, so absorbed was I in the yellowed pages illumining Poe's past.

Here was wit, erudition, literary criticism; here were the muddled, maudlin outpourings of a mind gone in drink and despair; here was the draft of a projected story, the fragments of a poem; here was a pitiful cry for deliverance and a paean to living beauty; here was dignified response to a dunning letter and an auctorial *pronunciamento* to an admirer; here was love, hate, pride, anger, celestial serenity, abject penitence, authority, wonder, resolution, indecision, joy, and soul-sickening melancholia.

Here was the gifted elocutionist, the stammering drunkard, the adoring husband, the frantic lover, the proud editor, the indigent pauper, the grandiose dreamer, the shabby realist, the scientific inquirer, the gullible metaphysician, the dependent stepson, the free and untrammeled spirit, the hack, the poet, the enigma that was Edgar Allan Poe.

Again the beakers were filled and emptied. I drank deeply with my lips, and with my eyes more deeply still.

For the first time the true enthusiasm of Launcelot Canning was communicated to my own sensibilities – I divined the eternal fascination found in a consideration of Poe the writer and Poe the man; he who wrote Tragedy, lived Tragedy, was Tragedy; he who penned Mystery, lived and died in Mystery, and who today looms on the literary scene as Mystery incarnate.

And Mystery Poe remained, despite Arthur Canning's careful study of the letters. 'My father learned nothing,' my host confided, 'even though he assembled, as you see here, a collection to delight the heart of a Mabbott or a Quinn. So his search ranged further. By this time I was old enough to share both his interest and his inquiries. Come,' and he led me to an ornate chest which rested beneath the windows against the west wall of the study.

Kneeling, he unlocked the repository, and then drew forth, in rapid and marvelous succession, a series of objects, each of which boasted of intimate connection with Poe's life.

There were souvenirs of his youth and his schooling abroad; a book he had used during his sojourn at West Point; mementoes of his days as a theatrical critic in the form of playbills; a pen used during his editorial period; a fan once owned by his girl-wife, Virginia; a brooch of Mrs. Clemm's – a profusion of objects including such diverse articles as a cravat and, curiously enough, Poe's battered and tarnished flute.

Again we drank, and I own the wine was potent. Canning's countenance remained cadaverously wan but, moreover, there was a species of mad hilarity in his eyes – an evident restrained hysteria in his whole demeanor. At length, from the scattered heap of *curiosa*, I happened to draw forth and examine a little box of no remarkable character, whereupon I was constrained to inquire its history and what part it had played in the life of Poe.

'In the *life* of Poe?' A visible tremor convulsed the features of my host, then rapidly passed in transformation to a grimace, a rictus of amusement. 'This little box – and you will note how, by some fateful design or contrived coincidence it bears a resemblance to the box he himself conceived of and described in his tale, *Berenice* – this little box is concerned with his death rather than his life. It is, in fact, the selfsame box my grandfather Christopher Canning clutched to his bosom when they found him down there.'

Again the tremor, again the grimace. 'But stay, I have not yet told you of the details. Perhaps you would be interested in seeing the spot where Christopher Canning was stricken; I have already told you of his madness, but I did no more than hint at the character of his delusions. You have been patient with me, and more than patient. Your understanding shall be rewarded, for I perceive you can be fully entrusted with the facts.'

What further revelations Canning was prepared to make I could not say, but his manner was such as to inspire a vague disquiet and trepidation in my breast.

Upon perceiving my unease he laughed shortly and laid a hand upon my shoulder. 'Come, this should interest you as an aficionado of fantasy,' he said. 'But first, another drink to speed our journey.'

He poured, we drank, and then he led the way from that vaulted chamber, down the silent halls, down the staircase, and into the lowest recesses of the building until we reached what resembled a dungeon, its floor and the interior of a long archway carefully sheathed in copper. We paused before a door of massive iron. Again I felt in the aspect of this scene an element evocative of recognition or recollection.

Canning's intoxication was such that he misinterpreted, or chose to misinterpret, my reaction.

'You need not be afraid,' he assured me. 'Nothing has happened down here since that day, almost seventy years ago, when his servants discovered him stretched out before this door, the little box clutched to his bosom; collapsed, and in a state of delirium from which he never emerged. For six months he lingered, a hopeless maniac – raving as wildly from the very moment of his discovery as at the moment he died – babbling his visions of the giant horse, the fissured house collapsing into the tarn, the black cat, the pit, the pendulum, the raven on the pallid bust, the beating heart, the pearly teeth, and the nearly liquid mass of loathsome – of detestable putridity from which a voice emanated.

'Nor was that all he babbled,' Canning confided, and here his voice sank to a whisper that reverberated through the copper-sheathed hall and against the iron door. 'He hinted other things far worse than fantasy – of a ghastly reality surpassing the phantasms of Poe.

'For the first time my father and the servants learned the purpose of the room he had built beyond this iron door, and learned too what Christopher Canning had done to establish his title as the world's foremost collector of Poe.

'For he babbled again of Poe's death, thirty years earlier, in 1849 – of the burial in the Presbyterian Cemetery and of the removal of the coffin in 1875 to the corner where the monument was raised. As I told you, and as was known then, my grandfather had played a public part in instigating that removal. But now we learned of the private part – learned that there was a monument and a grave, but no coffin in the earth beneath Poe's alleged resting place. The coffin now rested in the secret room at the end of this passage. That is why the room, the house itself, had been built.

'I tell you, he had stolen the body of Edgar Allan Poe – and as he shrieked aloud in his final madness, did not this indeed make him the greatest collector of Poe?

'His ultimate intent was never divined, but my father made one significant discovery – the little box clutched to Christopher Canning's bosom contained a portion of the crumbled bones, the veritable dust that was all that remained of Poe's corpse.'

My host shuddered and turned away. He led me back along that hall of horror, up the stairs, into the study. Silently, he filled our beakers, and I drank as hastily, as deeply, as desperately as he.

'What could my father do? To own the truth was to create a public scandal. He chose instead to keep silence, to devote his own life to study in retirement.

'Naturally, the shock affected him profoundly; to my knowledge he never entered the room beyond the iron door and, indeed, I did not know of the room or its contents until the hour of his death – and it was not until some years later that I myself found the key amongst his effects.

'But find the key I did, and the story was immediately and completely corroborated. Today I am the greatest collector of Poe – for he lies in the keep below, my eternal trophy!'

This time I poured the wine. As I did so, I noted for the first time the imminence of a storm – the impetuous fury of its gusts shaking the casements and the echoes of its thunder rolling and rumbling down the time-corroded corridors of the old house.

The wild, overstrained vivacity with which my host hearkened, or apparently hearkened, to these sounds did nothing to reassure me – for his recent revelation led me to suspect his sanity.

That the body of Edgar Allan Poe had been stolen; that this mansion had been built to house it; that it was indeed enshrined in a crypt below; that grandsire, son and grandson had dwelt here alone, apart, enslaved to a sepulchral secret – was beyond sane belief or tolerance.

And yet, surrounded now by the night and the storm, in a setting torn from Poe's own frenzied fancies, I could not be sure. Here the past was still alive, the very spirit of Poe's tales breathed forth its corruption upon the scene.

As thunder boomed, Launcelot Canning took up Poe's flute, and, whether in defiance of the storm without or as a mocking accompaniment, he played; blowing upon it with drunken persistence, with eerie atonality, with nerve-shattering shrillness. To the shrieking of that infernal instrument the thunder added a braying counterpoint.

Uneasy, uncertain and unnerved, I retreated into the shadows of the bookshelves at the further end of the room and idly scanned the titles of a row of ancient tomes. Here was the *Chiromancy* of Robert Flud; the *Directorium Inquisitorum*, a rare and curious book in quarto Gothic that was the manual of a forgotten church; and betwixt and between the volumes of pseudo-scientific inquiry, theological speculation and sundry incunabula I found titles that arrested and appalled me. *De Vermis Mysteriis* and the *Liber Eibon*, treatises on demonology, on witchcraft, on sorcery, moldered in crumbling bindings. The books were old, the books were tattered and torn, but the books were not dusty. They had been read—

'Read them?' It was as though Canning divined my inmost thoughts. He had put aside his flute and now approached me, tittering as though in continued drunken defiance of the storm. Odd echoes and boomings now sounded through the long halls of the house, and curious grating sounds threatened to drown out his words and his laughter.

'Read them?' said Canning. 'I study them. Yes, I have gone beyond Grandfather, and Father, too. It was I who procured the books that held the key, and it was I who found the key. A key more difficult to discover, and more important, than the key to the vaults below. I often wonder if Poe himself had access to these selfsame tomes, knew the selfsame secrets. The secrets of the grave and what lies beyond, and what can be summoned forth if one but holds the key.'

He stumbled away and returned with wine. 'Drink,' he said. 'Drink to the night and the storm.'

I brushed the proffered glass aside. 'Enough,' I said. 'I must be on my way.'

Was it fancy, or did I find fear frozen on his features? Canning clutched my arm and cried, 'No, stay with me! This is no night on which to be alone; I swear I cannot abide the thought of being alone. You must not, cannot leave me here alone; I can bear to be alone no more!'

His incoherent babble mingled with the thunder and the echoes; I drew back and confronted him. 'Control yourself,' I counseled. 'Confess that this is a hoax, an elaborate imposture arranged to please your fancy.'

'Hoax? Imposture? Stay, and I shall prove to you beyond all doubt—' And so saying, Launcelot Canning stooped and opened a small drawer set in the wall beneath and beside the bookshelves. 'This should repay you for your interest in my story, and in Poe,' he murmured. 'Know that you are the first other than myself to glimpse these treasures.'

He handed me a sheaf of manuscripts on plain white paper — documents written in ink curiously similar to that I had noted while perusing Poe's letters. Pages were clipped together in groups, and for a moment I scanned titles alone.

'*The Worm of Midnight, by Edgar Poe,*' I read, aloud. '*The Crypt,*' I breathed. And here, '*The Further Adventures of Arthur Gordon Pym.*' In my agitation I came close to dropping the precious pages. 'Are these what they appear to be — the unpublished tales of Poe?'

My host bowed. 'Unpublished, undiscovered, unknown, save to me — and to you.'

'But this cannot be,' I protested. 'Surely there would have been a mention of them somewhere, in Poe's own letters or those of his contemporaries. There would have been a clue, an indication – somewhere, someplace, somehow.'

Thunder mingled with my words, and thunder echoed in Canning's shouted reply.

'You dare to presume an imposture? Then compare!' He stooped again and brought out a glassined folio of letters. 'Here – is this not the veritable script of Edgar Poe? Look at the calligraphy of the letters, then at the manuscripts. Can you say they are not penned by the selfsame hand?'

I looked at the handwriting, wondered at the possibilities of a monomaniac's forgery. Could Launcelot Canning, a victim of mental disorder, thus painstakingly simulate Poe's hand?

'Read, then!' Canning screamed through the thunder. 'Read, and dare to say that these tales were written by any other than Edgar Poe, whose genius defies the corruption of Time and the Conqueror Worm!'

I read but a line or two, holding the topmost manuscript close to eyes that strained beneath wavering candlelight; but even in the flickering illumination I noted that which told me the only, the incontestable truth. For the paper, the curiously *unyellowed* paper, bore a visible watermark; the name of a firm of modern stationers and the date – 1949.

Putting the sheaf aside, I endeavored to compose myself as I moved away from Launcelot Canning. For now I knew the truth; knew that, one hundred years after Poe's death, a semblance of his spirit still lived in the distorted and disordered soul of Canning. Incarnation, reincarnation, call it what you will; Canning was, in his own irrational mind, Edgar Allan Poe.

Stifled and dull echoes of thunder from a remote portion of the mansion now commingled with the soundless seething of my own inner turmoil, as I turned and rashly addressed my host.

'Confess!' I cried. 'Is it not true that you have written these tales, fancying yourself the embodiment of Poe? Is it not true that you suffer from a singular delusion born of solitude and everlasting brooding upon the past; that you have reached a stage characterized by the conviction that Poe still lives on in your own person?'

A strong shudder came over him, and a sickly smile quivered about his lips as he replied. 'Fool! I say to you that I have spoken the truth. Can you doubt the evidence of your senses? This house is real, the Poe collection exists, and the stories exist – exist, I swear, as truly as the body in the crypt below!'

I took up the little box from the table and removed the lid. 'Not so,' I answered. 'You said your grandfather was found with this box clutched to his breast, before the door of the vault, and that it contained Poe's dust. Yet you cannot escape the fact that the box is empty.' I faced him furiously. 'Admit it, the story is a fabrication, a romance. Poe's body does not lie beneath this house, nor are these his unpublished works, written during his lifetime and concealed.'

'True enough.' Canning's smile was ghastly beyond belief. 'The dust is gone because I took it and used it – because in the works of wizardry I found the formulae, the arcana whereby I could raise the flesh, recreate the body from the essential salts of the grave. Poe does not *lie* beneath this house – he *lives*! And the tales are *his posthumous works*!'

Accented by thunder, his words crashed against my consciousness.

'That was the be-all and end-all of my planning, of my studies, of my work, of my life! To raise, by sorcery, the veritable spirit of Edgar Poe from the grave – reclothed and animate in flesh – and set him to dwell and dream and do his work again in the private chambers I built in the vaults below – and this I have done! To steal a corpse is but a ghoulish prank; mine is the achievement of true genius!'

The distinct, hollow, metallic and clangorous, yet apparently muffled, reverberation accompanying his words caused him to turn in his seat and face the door of the study, so that I could not see the workings of his countenance – nor could he read my reaction to his ravings.

His words came but faintly to my ears through the thunder that now shook the house in a relentless grip; the wind rattling the casements and flickering the candle flame from the great silver candelabra sent a soaring sighing in anguished accompaniment to his speech.

'I would show him to you, but I dare not; for he hates me as he hates life. I have locked him in the vault, alone, for the resurrected have no need of food or drink. And he sits there, pen moving over paper, endlessly moving, endlessly pouring out the evil essence of all he guessed and hinted at in life and which he learned in death.

'Do you not see the tragic pity of my plight? I sought to raise his spirit from the dead, to give the world anew of his genius – and yet these tales, these works, are filled and fraught with a terror not to be endured. They cannot be shown to the world, he cannot be shown to the world; in bringing back the dead I have brought back the fruits of death!'

Echoes sounded anew as I moved toward the door – moved, I confess, to flee this accursed house and its accursed owner.

Canning clutched my hand, my arm, my shoulder. 'You cannot go!' he shouted above the storm. 'I spoke of his escaping, but did you not guess? Did you not hear it through the thunder – the grating of the door?'

I pushed him aside and he blundered backward, upsetting the candelabra, so that flames licked now across the carpeting.

'Wait!' he cried. 'Have you not heard his footstep on the stair? MADMAN, I TELL YOU THAT HE NOW STANDS WITHOUT THE DOOR!'

A rush of wind, a roar of flame, a shroud of smoke rose all about us. Throwing open the huge antique panels to which Canning pointed, I staggered into the hall.

I speak of wind, of flame, of smoke – enough to obscure all vision. I speak of Canning's screams, and of thunder loud enough to drown all sound. I speak of terror born of loathing and of desperation enough to shatter all sanity.

Despite these things, I can never erase from my consciousness that which I beheld as I fled past the doorway and down the hall.

There without the doors there *did* stand a lofty and enshrouded figure; a figure all too familiar, with pallid features, high, domed forehead, mustache set above a mouth. My glimpse lasted but an instant, an instant during which the man – the corpse, the apparition, the hallucination, call it what you will – moved forward into the chamber and clasped Canning to its breast in an unbreakable embrace. Together, the two figures tottered toward the flames, which now rose to blot out vision forevermore.

From that chamber, and from that mansion, I fled aghast. The storm was still abroad in all its wrath, and now fire came to claim the house of Canning for its own.

Suddenly there shot along the path before me a wild light, and I turned to see whence a gleam so unusual could have issued – but it was only the flames, rising in supernatural splendor to consume the mansion, and the secrets, of the man who collected Poe.

THE FOG HORN
Ray Bradbury

This is one of my favourite stories, for a variety of reasons.

First, it allowed me, through a fanciful metaphor, to trap a lot of Shakespearean and Biblical poetry wandering around in my subconscious and get it on paper.

Then there was the moment of conception itself – walking the beach one night with my wife and coming upon the bones of the old Venice pier and the skeleton of the roller coaster lying there being covered over by the tides of water and sand. What is this dinosaur doing lying here dead on the beach? *I asked my wife, myself. And had the answer several nights later when the fog horn in the Bay wakened me with its cries and I sat up, thinking:* Yes! That's it! The fog horn called the sea beast in! *I leaped from bed to write the story.*

And finally, this story, read by John Huston, caused him to guess at the Melvillean ghost hidden in my bones. He hired me soon after, to write the screenplay for Moby Dick.

Out there in the cold water, far from land, we waited every night for the coming of the fog, and it came, and we oiled the brass machinery and lit the fog light up in the stone tower. Feeling like two birds in the gray sky, McDunn and I sent the light touching out, red, then white, then red again, to eye the lonely ships. And if they did not see our light, then there was always our Voice, the great deep cry of our Fog Horn shuddering through the rags of mist to startle the gulls away like decks of scattered cards and make the waves turn high and foam.

'It's a lonely life, but you're used to it now, aren't you?' asked McDunn.

'Yes,' I said. 'You're a good talker, thank the Lord.'

'Well, it's your turn on land tomorrow,' he said, smiling, 'to dance the ladies and drink gin.'

'What do you think, McDunn, when I leave you out here alone?'

'On the mysteries of the sea.' McDunn lit his pipe. It was a quarter past seven of a cold November evening, the heat on, the light switching its tail in two hundred directions, the Fog Horn bumbling in the high throat of the tower. There wasn't a town for a hundred miles down the coast, just a road which came lonely through dead country to the sea, with few cars on it, a stretch of two miles of cold water out to our rock, and rare few ships.

'The mysteries of the sea,' said McDunn thoughtfully. 'You know, the ocean's the biggest damned snowflake ever? It rolls and swells a thousand shapes and colors, no two alike. Strange. One night, years ago, I was here alone, when all of the fish of the sea surfaced out there. Something made them swim in and lie in the bay, sort of trembling and staring up at the tower light going red, white, red, white across them so I could see their funny eyes. I turned cold. They were like a big peacock's tail, moving out there until midnight. Then, without so much as a sound, they slipped away, the million of them was gone. I kind of think maybe, in some sort of way, they came all those miles to worship. Strange. But think how the tower must look to them, standing seventy feet above the water, the God-light flashing out from it, and the tower declaring itself with a monster voice. They never came back, those fish, but don't you think for a while they thought they were in the Presence?'

I shivered. I looked out at the long gray lawn of the sea stretching away into nothing and nowhere.

'Oh, the sea's full.' McDunn puffed his pipe nervously, blinking. He had been nervous all day and hadn't said why. 'For all our engines and so-called submarines, it'll be ten thousand centuries before we set foot on the real bottom of the sunken lands, in the fairy kingdoms there, and know *real* terror. Think of it, it's still the year 300,000 Before Christ down under there. While we've paraded around with trumpets, lopping off each other's countries and heads, they have been living beneath the sea twelve miles deep and cold in a time as old as the beard of a comet.'

'Yes, it's an old world.'

'Come on. I got something special I been saving up to tell you.'

We ascended the eighty steps, talking and taking our time. At the top, McDunn switched off the room lights so there'd be no reflection in the plate glass. The great eye of the light was humming, turning easily in its oiled socket. The Fog Horn was blowing steadily, once every fifteen seconds.

'Sounds like an animal, don't it?' McDunn nodded to himself. 'A big lonely animal crying in the night. Sitting here on the edge of ten billion years calling out to the Deeps, I'm here, I'm here, I'm here. And the Deeps *do* answer, yes, they do. You been here now for three months, Johnny, so I better prepare you. About this time of year,' he said, studying the murk and fog, 'something comes to visit the lighthouse.'

'The swarms of fish like you said?'

'No, this is something else. I've put off telling you because you might think I'm daft. But tonight's the latest I can put it off, for if my calendar's marked right from last year, tonight's the night it comes. I won't go into detail, you'll have to see it yourself. Just sit down there. If you want, tomorrow you can pack your duffel and take the motorboat in to land and get your car parked there at the dinghy pier on the cape and drive on back to some little inland town and keep your lights burning nights, I won't question or blame you. It's happened three years now, and this is the only time anyone's been here with me to verify it. You wait and watch.'

Half an hour passed with only a few whispers between us. When we grew tired waiting, McDunn began describing some of his ideas to me. He had some theories about the Fog Horn itself.

'One day many years ago a man walked along and stood in the sound of the ocean on a cold sunless shore and said, "We need a voice to call across the water, to warn ships; I'll make one. I'll make a voice like all of time and all of the fog that ever was; I'll make a voice that is like an empty bed beside you all night long, and like an empty house when you open the door, and like trees in autumn with no leaves. A sound like the birds flying south, crying, and a sound like November wind and the sea on the hard, cold shore. I'll make a sound that's so alone that no one can miss it, that whoever hears it will weep in their souls, and hearths will seem warmer, and being inside will seem better to all who hear it in the distant towns. I'll make me a sound and an apparatus and they'll call it a Fog Horn and whoever hears it will know the sadness of eternity and the briefness of life."'

The Fog Horn blew.

'I made up that story,' said McDunn quietly, 'to try to explain why this thing keeps coming back to the lighthouse every year. The Fog Horn calls it, I think, and it comes. . . .'

'But—' I said.

'Sssst!' said McDunn. 'There!' He nodded out to the Deeps.

Something was swimming toward the lighthouse tower.

It was a cold night, as I have said; the high tower was cold, the light coming and going, and the Fog Horn calling and calling through the raveling mist. You couldn't see far and you couldn't see plain, but there was the deep sea moving on its way about the night earth, flat and quiet, the color of gray mud, and here were the two of us alone in the high tower, and there, far out at first, was a ripple, followed by a wave, a rising, a bubble, a bit of froth. And then, from the surface of the cold sea came a head, a large head, dark-colored, with immense eyes, and then a neck. And then – not a body – but more neck and more! The head rose a full forty feet above the water on a slender and beautiful dark neck. Only then did the body, like a little island of black coral and shells and crayfish, drip up from the subterranean. There was a flicker of tail. In all, from head to tip of tail, I estimated the monster at ninety or a hundred feet.

I don't know what I said. I said something.

'Steady, boy, steady,' whispered McDunn.

'It's impossible!' I said.

'No, Johnny, *we're* impossible. *It's* like it always was ten million years ago. *It* hasn't changed. It's *us* and the land that've changed, become impossible. *Us!*'

It swam slowly and with a great dark majesty out in the icy waters, far away. The fog came and went about it, momentarily erasing its shape. One of the monster eyes caught and held and flashed back our immense light, red, white, red, white, like a disk held high and sending a message in primeval code. It was as silent as the fog through which it swam.

'It's a dinosaur of some sort!' I crouched down, holding to the stair rail.

'Yes, one of the tribe.'

'But they died out!'

'No, only hid away in the Deeps. Deep, deep down in the deepest Deeps. Isn't *that* a word now, Johnny, a real word, it says so much: the Deeps. There's all the coldness and darkness and deepness in the world in a word like that.'

'What'll we do?'

'Do? We got our job, we can't leave. Besides, we're safer here than in any boat trying to get to land. That thing's as big as a destroyer and almost as swift.'

'But here, why does it come *here*?'

The next moment I had my answer.

The Fog Horn blew.

And the monster answered.

A cry came across a million years of water and mist. A cry so anguished and alone that it shuddered in my head and my body. The monster cried out at the tower. The Fog Horn blew. The monster roared again. The Fog Horn blew. The monster opened its great toothed mouth and the sound that came from it was the sound of the Fog Horn itself. Lonely and vast and far away. The sound of isolation, a viewless sea, a cold night, apartness. That was the sound.

'Now,' whispered McDunn, 'do you know why it comes here?'

I nodded.

'All year long, Johnny, that poor monster there lying far out, a thousand miles at sea, and twenty miles deep maybe, biding its time, perhaps it's a million years old, this one creature. Think of it, waiting a million years; could *you* wait that long? Maybe it's the last of its kind. I sort of think that's true. Anyway, here come men on land and build this lighthouse, five years ago. And set up their Fog Horn and sound it and sound it, out toward the place where you bury yourself in sleep and sea memories of a world where there were thousands like yourself, but now you're alone, all alone in a world not made for you, a world where you have to hide.

'But the sound of the Fog Horn comes and goes, comes and goes, and you stir from the muddy bottom of the Deeps, and your eyes open like the lenses of two-foot cameras and you move, slow, slow, for you have the ocean sea on your shoulders, heavy. But that Fog Horn comes through a thousand miles of water, faint and familiar, and the furnace in your belly stokes up, and you begin to rise, slow, slow. You feed yourself on great slakes of cod and minnow, on rivers of jellyfish, and you rise slow through the autumn months, through September when the fogs started, through October with more fog and the horn still calling you on, and then, late in November, after pressurizing yourself day by day, a few feet higher every hour, you are near the surface and still alive. You've got to go slow; if you surfaced all at once you'd explode. So it takes you all of three months to surface, and then a number of days to swim through the cold waters to the lighthouse. And there you are, out there, in the night, Johnny, the biggest damn monster in creation. And here's the lighthouse calling to you, with a long neck like your neck sticking way up out of the water, and a body like your body, and, most important of all, a voice like your voice. Do you understand now, Johnny, do you understand?'

The Fog Horn blew.

The monster answered.

I saw it all, I knew it all – the million years of waiting alone, for someone to come back who never came back. The million years of isolation at the bottom of the sea, the insanity of time there, while the skies cleared of reptile-birds, the swamps dried on the continental lands, the sloths and saber-tooths had their day and sank in tar pits, and men ran like white ants upon the hills.

The Fog Horn blew.

'Last year,' said McDunn, 'that creature swam round and round, round and round, all night. Not coming too near, puzzled, I'd say. Afraid, maybe. And a bit angry after coming all this way. But the next day, unexpectedly, the fog lifted, the sun came out fresh, the sky was as blue as a painting. And the monster swam off away from the heat and the silence and didn't come back. I suppose it's been brooding on it for a year now, thinking it over from every which way.'

The monster was only a hundred yards off now, it and the Fog Horn crying at each other. As the lights hit them, the monster's eyes were fire and ice, fire and ice.

'That's life for you,' said McDunn. 'Someone always waiting for someone who never comes home. Always someone loving some thing more than that thing loves them. And after a while you want to destroy whatever that thing is, so it can't hurt you no more.'

The monster was rushing at the lighthouse.

The Fog Horn blew.

'Let's see what happens,' said McDunn.

He switched the Fog Horn off.

The ensuing minute of silence was so intense that we could hear our hearts pounding in the glassed area of the tower, could hear the slow greased turn of the light.

The monster stopped and froze. Its great lantern eyes blinked. Its mouth gaped. It gave a sort of rumble, like a volcano. It twitched its head this way and that, as if to seek the sounds now dwindled off into the fog. It peered at the lighthouse. It rumbled again. Then its eyes caught fire. It reared up, threshed the water, and rushed at the tower, its eyes filled with angry torment.

'McDunn!' I cried. 'Switch on the horn!'

McDunn fumbled with the switch. But even as he flicked it on, the monster was rearing up. I had a glimpse of its gigantic paws, fishskin glittering in webs between the fingerlike projections, clawing at the tower. The huge eye on the right side of its anguished head glittered before me like a caldron into which I might drop, screaming. The tower shook. The Fog Horn cried; the monster cried. It seized the tower and gnashed at the glass, which shattered in upon us.

McDunn seized my arm. 'Downstairs!'

The tower rocked, trembled, and started to give. The Fog Horn and the monster roared. We stumbled and half fell down the stairs. 'Quick!'

We reached the bottom as the tower buckled down toward us. We ducked under the stairs into the small stone cellar. There were a thousand concussions as the rocks rained down; the Fog Horn stopped abruptly. The monster crashed upon the tower. The tower fell. We knelt together, McDunn and I, holding tight, while our world exploded.

Then it was over, and there was nothing but darkness and the wash of the sea on the raw stones.

That and the other sound.

'Listen,' said McDunn quietly. 'Listen.'

We waited a moment. And then I began to hear it. First a great vacuumed sucking of air, and then the lament, the bewilderment, the loneliness of the great monster, folded over and upon us, above us, so that the sickening reek of its body filled the air, a stone's thickness away from our cellar. The monster gasped and cried. The tower was gone. The light was gone. The thing that had called it across a million years was gone. And the monster was opening its mouth and sending out great sounds. The sounds of a Fog Horn, again and again. And ships far at sea, not finding the light, not seeing anything, but passing and hearing late that night, must've thought: There it is, the lonely sound, the Lonesome Bay horn. All's well. We've rounded the cape.

And so it went for the rest of that night.

The sun was hot and yellow the next afternoon when the rescuers came out to dig us from our stoned-under cellar.

'It fell apart, is all,' said Mr. McDunn gravely. 'We had a few bad knocks from the waves and it just crumbled.' He pinched my arm.

There was nothing to see. The ocean was calm, the sky blue. The only thing was a great algaic stink from the green matter that covered the fallen tower stones and the shore rocks. Flies buzzed about. The ocean washed empty on the shore.

The next year they built a new lighthouse, but by this time I had a job in the little town and a wife and a good small warm house that glowed yellow on autumn nights, the doors locked, the chimney puffing smoke. As for McDunn, he was master of the new lighthouse, built to his own specifications, out of steel-reinforced concrete. 'Just in case,' he said.

The new lighthouse was ready in November. I drove down alone one evening late and parked my car and looked across the gray waters and listened to the new horn sounding, once, twice, three, four times a minute far out there, by itself.

The monster?

It never came back.

'It's gone away,' said McDunn. 'It's gone back to the Deeps. It's learned you can't love anything too much in this world. It's gone into the deepest Deeps to wait another million years. Ah, the poor thing! Waiting out there, and waiting out there, while man comes and goes on this pitiful little planet. Waiting and waiting.'

I sat in my car, listening. I couldn't see the lighthouse or the light standing out in Lonesome Bay. I could only hear the Horn, the Horn, the Horn. It sounded like the monster calling.

I sat there wishing there was something I could say.

THE DAY OF THE BUTTERFLIES
Marion Zimmer Bradley

I have always been interested in the nature of reality. Everything one reads tends to indicate that our only knowledge of what is real comes through the conduit of our five (or more) senses; we have no other way of knowing what is 'out there'. Some writers have even suggested that what we know as matter, space and time do not in or of themselves exist *– that the 'real world' is not only stranger than we know, but stranger than we* can *know. Space and time, at least, are simply an attempt of the linear human brain to make sense out of that which it cannot comprehend in any other way. We accept 'our' reality because it is the consensus of what we hear other people saying, defining, accepting. What we define as 'reality' and 'objective fact' is actually a series of* agreements. *We accept what 'is' because everybody agrees, for instance, that a flower is a flower and a table is solid, that fire will burn us and water drown us.*

But are those agreements objective fact – are they always and everywhere realities? Growing up in Bali, for instance, a young girl learns that, under certain circumstances, fire will not *burn her – when she does the sacred firewalking dance, for example. Is her reality less real to her, when she walks the fire and remains un-burned, than it is to the skeptical missionary who thinks it is all a trick and is seriously hurt while trying to imitate her feat?*

'The Day of the Butterflies' was written during the Summer of Love in Haight-Ashbury, or shortly thereafter; its primary image stemmed from a remark by Don Wollheim, that if I wished to see men walking like robots or zombies, I should go down into the financial district of New York City any working day around noon. I did, and I was horrified by the inhuman look of those men, to whom the concrete sidewalks, the skyscraper canyons and the blind rush for business was their only reality. Suppose they had, like the protagonist of this story, a glimpse of another *reality – and were sufficiently convinced of it to build up a new set of agreements?*

This is a romantic story. It arises out of a romantic premise. And yet I still wish it were true: that, before this world becomes one big concrete parking lot, we might feel the stamp of the hoof of Pan, and see violets bursting up through splitting sidewalks and flowers growing in the canyons of the city.

Diana was a city girl, had always been a city girl and liked it that way.

She came through the revolving doors at half-past-five, pulling kid gloves over her hands. The soft kid insulated her hands from the rough touch of wall and door, as her stilt heels tapping in bright rhythm insulated her feet from the hard and filthy concrete pavement. Her eyes burned with the smog, but to her senses it was fresh air, a normal sunshiny day in the city. She bought a paper from a street vendor without looking at him or it, and turned for the brisk three block walk to the subway which was her daily constitutional.

And then – what happened exactly? She never knew. There was a tiny queer lurch as if the sidewalk had shifted very slightly either this way or that, and. . . .

. . . the sun was golden and honeywarm and the green light filtered through a soft leaf canopy, lying like silk on her bare shoulders. Soft-scented wind rustled grass and caressed her bare feet, and suddenly she was dancing, a joyous ecstatic whirl of dance, in a cloud of crimson and yellow butterflies, circling like sparks around the tossing strands of her hair. She flung out her hands to trap them, pressed cold turgid grass blades underfoot, the chilly scent of hyacinths refreshed her nose, and as the butterflies flowed away from her fingertips she was. . . .

. . . slipping down the first step of the subway, so violently that she turned her foot over hard and had to grab at the railing. A fat garlic-smelling woman shoved by, muttering 'Whynya look whereya going?' Diana shut her eyes, opened them again with a sort of shudder. The sooty light of the subway struck her with almost a physical pain; it's very strange, she thought with confused detachment, that I never realized before quite how *ugly* a subway staircase is, how grimy and dark . . . and then the jolt, delayed, hit her.

My goodness, she thought, there must be something wrong with my mind! Because I was *there*, for just a minute, *dancing*! I didn't just smell it, or feel it, or see it, I smelled it *and* felt it *and* saw it, and tasted it and walked on it and touched it! It was a hallucination, of course. A thought pinked her cheek with tingles, did I really *dance* here on Lexington Avenue? Automatically she thrust her token into the subway turnstile.

A golden butterfly fluttered from her hand.

Diana let the man behind shove her through the turnstile. She looked up, dazed, as the brilliant flicker of gold danced up through the noisy dismal stench and was gone. A tiny child squealed, 'Oh, lookit the butterfly!' but none of the grim faces pouring through the maw of the subway station faltered or looked up.

Diana wedged herself into the train and grabbed, dazed, at a strap. The rattle and jolt under her feet was acutely painful, though she had never noticed it before. Her toes wriggled, craving the cold of grass; she breathed, trying to recapture the hyacinth, and choked on garlic, sweaty bodies fetid with chemical deodorants, hairspray, cheap perfume and soot.

But what happened? She thought wildly that she wasn't the kind of person things like that ever happened to! No, I dreamed it, butterfly and all, or there's something wrong with my eyes.

And so, as a child of the twentieth century, who never had believed anything she could not see, and in these days of TV and camera dynamation and special effects, only about half of what she did see, she managed to close her mind against this incredible opening of the door.

Until the next time.

The next time she was in the hurly burly of Penn Station, midmorning of a busy Saturday. Bodies pushed, shouted, stared anxiously at some destination known only to themselves. The public address system made cryptic noises distorted into impossible sounds. Diana hurried along, her gloved hands resting firmly on Pete's serge arm, her heels racing to keep pace with his stride. It was not that they were in any particular hurry, but all the surroundings screamed at them to hurryhurryhurry, and obediently they hurryhurried.

It was as rapid as a thought, the fading of the thick noisy air, the descent of silence . . . except for the gently rustling wind in the long grass at her feet. She was running, dancing in a whirl of the jewelled butterflies, tossing her arms in wild abandon, the play of chilly winds against her bare legs and feet. . . .

. . . she was *not*. The air was thick and harsh in her lungs, and she literally gasped at the impact of noise in the moment before she felt Pete stop in his tracks and watch her with a frown.

'Something the matter, Di?'

She felt like saying 'Yes, everything. This horrible place, I've just realized just how horrible it is . . .' but she didn't. That would be to give reality, to give preference even to that . . . that dream or hallucination or whatever it was. She moved her feet inside the tight shoes, sighing a little.

'No, nothing. I felt – it's a little hot and stuffy in here and I felt a little absent-minded.'

Absent-minded is right. My body was here – or Pete would have noticed – but my mind went off on a leave of absence, heaven knows *where* my mind was. She asked 'Why did you ask, Pete? What did I do?'

'Well, you sort of stopped in your tracks, and I couldn't see what you were looking at,' said Pete the practical, 'and you sort of lurched a little like you turned your ankle. You all right?'

'Of course,' she said, responding to the tenderness in his voice. Oh, she loved him, he wasn't just another date, he was the right one, the one she wanted to spend her life with, and yet, was anything *here* ever really right, after all?

No, thinking like that gave all this reality . . . that hallucination . . .

'Got something on your foot? Chewing gum, dog mess?'

'No,' said Diana, scraped her foot backward and it was true. Who would see or believe a crushed blade of grass here in the noise of Penn Station?

'Then let's hurry and get our train,' he urged.

'Is there really any hurry?' she asked in sudden rebellion, 'except, maybe, to hurry up and get out of this ugly filthy station? Did you ever stop and think how *ugly* most of the city is?'

'Wouldn't live anywhere else,' Pete said promptly, 'and neither would you! Or are you getting homesick for the cornfed hills of Iowa or something like that?'

'Pete, you nut, you know I was born in Queens!' It isn't even nostalgia for some faraway and lovely childhood! But what is it, then? How can I be – homesick? – for something I never saw, never even *dreamed*? Maybe I've just had a little too much of a good thing. Surely the city is a good thing, everything man ever wanted is here, culture, progress, companionship, even beauty, and Pete. . . .

'Pete,' she said, 'do we have to finish this shopping right now?'

'No, certainly not. You're the one was in a hurry to pick out towels and skillets and things and put them away for the day when we find that apartment and get that license. But what shall we do instead, then?'

And all too accurately she foresaw the astonishment in his face when she said 'Let's go walk in the park – under the trees – and look at some flowers.' But she knew he would say yes, and he did. It wasn't much. But it helped. A little.

And now she never knew, when she blinked her eyes, whether she would open them to the noise and roar of the city – or to the green and dancing world of the butterfly glade. In some part of herself she *knew* it was hallucination, aberration of eyes and mind, but . . . why did she, now and then, find herself clasping a butterfly, a flower, a blade of grass? But she did not deceive herself about why she put off, again and again, her promised visit to a doctor – or an optician – or a psychiatrist. Next time, she told herself, next time for sure. But she knew why it was always next time and never this.

If it's a hallucination a doctor would make it go away.

And I don't want it to go away!

She flattered herself that no one knew, and yet one day she emerged from a maenad dance to the sound of distant Pan pipes, her disheveled hair hot and sweaty on her bare neck – and then with the shock and jerk, feeling the pins taut in the French knot at her neck, her hands just touching the keys of her office Selectric, and the girl at the next desk staring.

'What's *with* you, Diana? I've spoken to you three times.'

She raised her hands from the keyboard, unwilling to let it go this time, aware that she had lost the thread of the document she was copying. '. . . comprising that particular tract of land being the Western half of a section beginning at the point of intersection between the Northern line of 48th Street and the Eastern line of Raymond Street, formerly called Beaver Street, as said streets are shown on the map and hereinafter referred to as Lots 13, 14 and 15 of . . .'

What absolute, utter rubbish! she thought, cradling in her hand the cool softness of the tiny blue blossom, her fingers cherishing the tiny petals. She concealed it inside her palm from the other girl's eyes and knew that her voice sounded strange as she said 'I'm sorry, Jessie. A – a kind of daydream, I guess.'

'It must have been a real doozy,' Jessie said, 'you looked all sort of soft and radiant. Who was the guy? Michael Sarrazin, or somebody? Or just Pete? If he turns you on *that* much, you're one lucky woman!'

Diana laughed softly. 'If it was anybody, it would be Pete. No, I just—' She found the words hard to form. 'I was daydreaming about a – a wood. A kind of grove full of flowers and butterflies.'

She had expected a flippant comment from the other woman, but it did not come. Instead Jessie's round face took on a remembering look. 'Funny. That sounds like what I did the other day. I went to see my Aunt Marge in Staten Island, and I took the ferryboat, and I thought, all of a sudden, that I was running on a beach picking up shells. It seemed so *real*. I could hear the gulls, and smell the salt, and I even thought there was sand under my feet – *bare* feet, that is. Only the only beach I ever been to is Coney Island, you know, so it wasn't that, this was a beach like in the movies, you know.' She laughed, embarrassed. 'Funny thing happened later.'

'Yes?' Diana felt a choking lump in her throat and her upper arms prickled goose flesh.

'You won't believe me,' Jessie said, 'but when I got home, I took off my shoes – I always take my shoes off first thing when I get home, and—'

'Yes—?'

'You won't believe it. But there was sand in my shoes.'

'Sand?'

'Sand. White sand. Like it was all over my *rug*.'

'You're right,' Diana said, 'I won't believe it.'

If I did, what else would I have to believe?

She might have written it off as frustration – for she was very much a child of the Freudian age, and repressions and frustrations were as much a part of her vocabulary as computers and typewriters, but there was nothing either of repression or frustration in the surroundings next time, for she and Pete were curled up together on the big sofa in her apartment, the lights were low and the music soft, but Pete was quiet, abstracted; she thought for a moment he had dropped off to sleep, and moved ever so gently to extricate her arm, but he murmured, not opening his eyes, 'Golly, that wood smoke smells great—' and the implication electrified her, so that she jerked upright as if an electric current had jolted them apart.

'Pete – *you too?*'

He sat up, with the look she knew had been so often on her own face, but to his murmured disclaimer she charged, 'Where were you this time? Pete, it's happened to me too, only with me it's a wood, a wood with butterflies and grass ... Pete, what's happening to people? I thought it was only me, but a girl in my office . . . and now you . . .'

'Here, here, hold on!' His hands seized, calmed her. 'But it's happened to me – oh, maybe a dozen times; suddenly I'm *somewhere else*, I know it's a dream, but it smells so damned real . . .' He looked thoughtful. 'What's real anyhow? Maybe this is only *one* reality, or maybe our reality has something wrong with it. *Look* at us . . . all packed together like in a hive . . . fine for bees, sure, but people? Is this the way a million years of Nature evolved man to live?'

Diana felt curious choked excitement; but felt compelled to cling to logic. 'And you a city boy? You always said the city was the end result of man's progress, social evolution—'

'I said too many damfool things. Yeah, end result, all right. *Dead* end.'

'Oh, yes,' she sighed, 'I hate it so now. Maybe I've always hated it and didn't know.'

'And maybe there's nothing . . . nothing abnormal about this day-dream, or hallucination, or whatever it is. Maybe it's just our sub-conscious minds warning us that we've had enough city, that we've got to get out if we want to stay sane.'

'Maybe,' she said, unconvinced, and shifted weight as he changed position, bending to retrieve what fell from his lap.

It was a tiny brown-scented pinecone, no longer than her thumbnail. She held it out to him, her throat tight with excitement.

'Pete – what's *real*?'

Pete turned the small cone tenderly between his fingers. He said at last, 'Suppose – suppose experiences are only a form of *agreements*? Even the scientists are saying, now, that space and matter, and above all, time, are not what the material physicists have always thought. Did you ever hear that all the solid matter in a planet the size of our Earth could be compressed into a sphere the size of a tennis ball – that all the rest of it is the space between the atoms and the electrons and their nuclei? Maybe we only see the material universe *this* way—' he gestured at the room around them, 'because this is the way we *learned* to see it. And now humanity is so overcrowded and our senses so bombarded with stimuli that the – the texture of the *agreements* is breaking down, and those little spaces between the electrons are changing to conform to a new set of agreements? So that we find that ice isn't necessarily cold, and fire doesn't *necessarily* burn, and the chemical elements of smog might be butterflies in the oxygen—'

'But what would *make* that set of – of agreements break down, Pete?'

'God knows,' he said slowly, and she knew he was not swearing. 'Sensory deprivation can drive a man's sense receptors to pick up very funny things – five hours in a deprivation tank, they found out, was the most a man could take without going raving mad. Maybe sensory overload could do the same thing. Maybe—'

But she did not hear the rest, for the world dissolved in a green swirl, and she ran, dancing, through the green glade. Only this time Pete was there, too. . . .

From that day she began to look for signs. Her boss paused at her desk to ask for a legal document she was typing, but before Diana could pull it out of her typewriter he cocked his head to one side and she heard, briefly, the twittering of a distant bird, and he shivered a little, snapped, 'I'll talk to you later about it,' and she saw him, dazedly, heading downstairs for a drink. In a sudden rainstorm she managed to be first in the crush for a taxi – and a soft, curling green oakleaf lay on the seat.

Is it happening everywhere, then? And does everybody it happens to, think he or she is the only one?

She found herself scanning newspapers, for strange happenings, felt a curiously confirmatory thrill the night a news correspondent, straight from wherever the 'front' was this year, came on the air, sounding dazed, with a story he tried to refer to, flippantly, as 'the gremlins getting out of hand again'. It seemed that eight Army tanks had vanished without trace, before the eyes of an entire regiment. Sabotage was suggested, but then who had bothered to plant half a dozen beds of tulips in their place? A practical joke of enormous proportions?

But Diana was beyond surprise. Her own hands were filled with flowers she had gathered . . . somewhere. . . .

It made the cover of *Time*, next week, when after a lengthy manhunt, a criminal serving a sentence for armed robbery was found only a mile from the prison. Questioned, he said, 'I just got into a mood where I forgot the prison was there, and walked out,' while the guards on the walls swore repeatedly – and lie detectors confirmed – that no one had gone in or out, not even the usual laundry truck. And the man might have rifled a supermarket – only there weren't any in the locality – for his arms were filled with exotic tropical fruits.

All Pete said to this, when the story was shown to him, was, 'The fabric of *this* reality is getting thinner and thinner. I bet a day will come when every morning more of the cells in that prison will be empty, and they'll never find most of the ones who walk out. After all, *their* reality is a lot more unbearable than most.'

He frowned, staring into space. She thought he had gone away again, but he only mused, 'It's getting pretty thin. I wonder how long it will last, and where it will rip all the way across?'

She clung to him in terror. 'Oh, Pete, I don't want to lose you! Suppose it does – tear all the way across – and we lose each other, or one of us can't get back?'

'Hey, hey, hey!' He held her, comfortingly. 'I've got a feeling that whatever it is between you and me, it's part of a reality that's maybe realer than this. We might have to find each other again, but if what we have is real, it'll last through whatever form reality takes.' He looked somewhat abashed as he added, 'I know it sounds corny in this day and age, but I love you, Diana, and if love isn't real, I don't know what is.'

She was hardly surprised when, though his arms were still around her, she felt the cool grass beneath them, saw the green light through the trees. She whispered, against the singing winds, 'Let's never go back!'

But they did.

But the fabric thinned for Diana daily. Shopping in the East Village for beads to back up an advertising display, she was struck by the look of blank-faced ecstasy, the impression of being *elsewhere*, on the soft preoccupied faces of bearded boys and long-haired barefoot girls. *They can't all be on drugs*, she thought. *This is something else. And I think I know what.*

A delicate wispy girl, in a long faded dress, her hair waistlength, looked up at Diana; and Diana was conscious of her own elaborately twisted hair, her heels forced high on fashionable platforms, her legs itchingly imprisoned in nylon; thought wistfully of green forest light and gleaming butterflies, bare feet racing through the glades . . . *no. No. I'm here in the city, and I have to live with it. They seem to be living elsewhere . . .*

The hippie girl smiled gently up at Diana and gave her a flower. Diana would have sworn she had not been carrying flowers. She whispered, 'You *know*, don't you? Do your thing while you can, if it's really your thing. It won't be long.' And in her eyes Diana saw strange skies reflected, heard the distant roll of breakers and a faraway cry of gulls from . . . somewhere? Jessie's beach? She murmured, 'I know where *you* are.'

The sound of breakers died. 'Oh, no,' the girl said sadly, 'but you know where we ought to be. It won't be long now, though. They're trying to pave it all over, you know. Make it into one big parking lot. But it won't work. Even if they covered over the whole planet with concrete, one day it would just *happen*. The Great God Pan would step down off that statue in Central Park – the *real* one – and stamp his hoof down through the concrete, and then . . . then violets would spring up through the dead land. . . .'

Her voice trailed into silence; she smiled and wandered away, her bare feet treading the filthy pavement as if she already wandered on the prophecied violets. Diana wanted to run after her, into that place where she so obviously spent so much of her time now, but she forced her feet on her own errand. She and the girl were in different layers of time, almost in different layers of space, and only by some curious magic had they come within speaking distance; like passing ships drifting through fog just within hail, or two falling leaves just touching as they fell from separate trees. She saw the street through a blur of tears, and for the first time tried, deliberately, to breach the veil, to reach for that other world which broke through into this so unpredictably, and never when you wanted it. . . .

Even as a city girl, Diana had never liked Wall Street. At high noon it is chaos, noise and robotlike humans all alike and all perpetually rushing nowhere; a human ant hill populated by mimic creatures, in suits and ties of a pattern so rigid that they seem to have grown on the semihuman forms. The rush and pandemonium assaulted her senses so violently that she stopped dead, letting the insectlike mimics – surely they could *not* be human – divide their flow around her, as if she were a rock in their stream.

Ugliness! Noise everywhere! Horror! She thought wildly, this world is *wrong*, a huge cosmic mistake, a planetary practical joke! If everyone who *knew*, everyone who's seen the *real* world, would somehow just say NO to all this, would just reach out all together, say, *This is too much, we don't, we won't, we can't stand* . . . then maybe those ugly skyscrapers would just dissolve, violets spring up . . .

Oh, *listen*, she implored, her whole body and mind and senses all one strained hunger, *listen*! If they'd only stop and see all this the way it *really* is, see what's happening to people who think it's real and think they have to live in it!

Time and space are only this way because we have made them this way, and we've made them all wrong! Let's start all over again and do it right this time!

She never knew how long she stood there, because for her the accidents of time and space had stopped. She only knew that everything she was and ever had been had poured itself into the one, anguished passionate plea, *listen*! And then she became aware that hers was only one voice in a vast, swelling choral song. As perception slowly came back to her overloaded senses, she saw first one, then another and another of the rigidly suited forms stop, fling away umbrella and briefcase, then split like an insect shedding his· chitinous shell and burst into humanity again. The veil of illusion shredded from top to bottom, skyscrapers thinned to transparency, melted and vanished, and the great, towering, *real* trees could be seen through their wavering outlines. Through the dead and splitting concrete, a shy blade of grass poked up its head, wavered slightly, then erupted in a joyous riot of green, swiftly blotting out the concrete.

Great green lawns expanded from horizon to horizon, as the sky quickly cleared to a delicious blue. Silence descended, threaded with tracery of birdsong; one lonely, bewildered taxi horn lingered, questioning and frantic, before it died away forever; in the canyons of Manhattan, the *real* Manhattan breaking through, men and women ran naked on the grass, flowers in their hands and garlands in their hair, as the jeweled butterflies flashed upward, flaming and gleaming in the sun.

Diana, sobbing with joy, ran into the throng, knowing that Pete was there somewhere, and Jessie, and the hippie girl, and children and prisoners and everyone for whom illusion had vanished. She ran on, shedding butterflies at every step, and wondered, once and never again, if the other world, the one that wasn't real, was still there for *anybody*. But she didn't really care . . . it wasn't there for *her* anymore, and Pete was waiting for her here. She knew she would find him, and of course she did.

THE DEPTHS
Ramsey Campbell

There was a point at which I thought of calling this story 'Where Do You Get Your Ideas?' – in tribute to that most popular of questions. Where do I get my ideas? From the air and from the everyday, from passing thoughts and trains of them – and the only trick is to have a notebook always handy. Ideas aren't my problem, believe me; the hard part, generally, is developing them and telling their stories and finding the titles that fit. Sometimes ideas wait for years to be used – my first novel used one I'd abandoned thirteen years earlier – and sometimes they wait for another idea to marry. I suspect that one of my literary legacies will be notebooks scattered with the many ideas I never used.

Occasionally, I have an idea I think is original. So it was with the idea for 'The Depths', which is why I included the story in my New Terrors anthology. At least, I planned to include it, until Andrew Offutt – or, rather, andrew offutt – sent me his story, 'Symbiote', which was uncannily, not to say dismayingly, similar to mine. This wasn't the first time I'd had such an experience – many years ago I wrote a Henry Kuttner story, almost scene for scene, which I had not and could not then have read – but considering that both offutt's story and mine had ominous suggestions to make about the sources of fiction, this occurrence was particularly disconcerting. I withdrew my story and used offutt's, as was only proper, and 'The Depths' eventually saw print in my best collection, Dark Companions. Meanwhile, the theme had stayed with me, and it became central to my novel, Incarnate.

One reason 'The Depths' is a favorite of mine is that I believe it has something important to say, even if metaphorically. I'm always suspicious of the notion of fantasy as escapism: in my opinion, only bad fantasy is. I also distrust the convention of fantasy (and of horror fiction, of course) by which evil is always external, something to be fought by the hero and never a part of him. I find that attitude unjustifiably reassuring, and I try not to be in the business of reassurance.

Judge for yourselves. . . .

As Miles emerged, a woman and a pink-eyed dog stumped by. She glanced at the house; then, humming tunelessly, she aimed the same contemptuous look at Miles. As if the lead was a remote control, the dog began to growl. They thought Miles was the same as the house.

He almost wished that were true; at least it would have been a kind of contact. He strolled through West Derby village and groped in his mind for ideas. Pastels drained from the evening sky. Wood pigeons paraded in a tree-lined close. A mother was crying, 'Don't you dare go out of this garden again.' A woman was brushing her driveway and singing that she was glad she was Bugs Bunny. Beyond a brace of cars, in a living-room that displayed a bar complete with beer-pumps, a couple listened to Beethoven's Greatest Hits.

Miles sat drinking beer at a table behind the Crown, at the edge of the bowling green. Apart from the click of bowls the summer evening seemed as blank as his mind. Yet the idea had promised to be exactly what he and his publisher needed: no more days of drinking tea until his head swam, of glaring at the sheet of paper in the typewriter while it glared an unanswerable challenge back at him. He hadn't realized until now how untrustworthy inspirations were.

Perhaps he ought to have foreseen the problem. The owners had told him that there was nothing wrong with the house – nothing except the aloofness and silent disgust of their neighbours. If they had known what had happened there they would never have bought the house; why should they be treated as though by living there they had taken on the guilt?

Still, that was no more unreasonable than the crime itself. The previous owner had been a bank manager, as relaxed as a man could be in his job; his wife had owned a small boutique. They'd seemed entirely at peace with each other. Nobody who had known could believe what he had done to her. Everyone Miles approached had refused to discuss it, as though by keeping quiet about it they might prevent it from having taken place at all.

The deserted green was smudged with darkness. 'We're closing now,' the barmaid said, surprised that anyone was still outside. Miles lifted the faint sketch of a tankard and gulped a throatful of beer, grimacing. The more he researched the book, the weaker it seemed to be.

To make things worse, he'd told the television interviewer that it was near completion. At least the programme wouldn't be broadcast for months, by which time he might be well into a book about the locations of murder – but it wasn't the book he had promised his publisher, and he wasn't sure that it would have the same appeal.

Long dark houses slumbered beyond an archway between cottages, lit windows hovered in the arch. A signboard reserved a weedy patch of ground for a library. A grey figure was caged by the pillars of the village cross. On the roof of a pub extension gargoyles began barking, for they were dogs. A cottage claimed to be a sawmill, but the smell seemed to be of manure. Though his brain was taking notes, it wouldn't stop nagging.

He gazed across Lord Sefton's estate towards the tower blocks of Cantril Farm. Their windows were broken ranks of small bright perforations in the night. For a moment, as his mind wobbled on the edge of exhaustion, the unstable patterns of light seemed a code which he needed to break to solve his problems. But how could they have anything to do with it? Such a murder in Cantril Farm, in the concrete barracks among which Liverpool communities had been scattered, he might have understood; here in West Derby it didn't make sense.

As he entered the deserted close, he heard movements beneath the eaves. It must be nesting birds, but it was as though the sedate house had secret thoughts. He was grinning as he pushed open his gate, until his hand recoiled. The white gate was stickily red.

It was paint. Someone had written SADIST in an ungainly dripping scrawl. The neighbours could erase that – he wouldn't be here much longer. He let himself into the house.

For a moment he hesitated, listening to the dark. Nothing fled as he switched on the lights. The hall was just a hall, surmounted by a concertina of stairs; the metal and vinyl of the kitchen gleamed like an Ideal Home display; the corduroy suite sat plump and smug on the dark green pelt of the living-room. He felt as though he was lodging in a show house, without even the company of a shelf of his books.

Yet it was here, from the kitchen to the living-room, that everything had happened – here that the bank manager had systematically rendered his wife unrecognizable as a human being. Miles stood in the empty room and tried to imagine the scene. Had her mind collapsed, or had she been unable to withdraw from what was being done to her? Had her husband known what he was doing, right up to the moment when he'd dug the carving-knife into his throat and run headlong at the wall?

It was no good: here at the scene of the crime, Miles found the whole thing literally unimaginable. For an uneasy moment he suspected that might have been true of the killer and his victim. As

Miles went upstairs, he was planning the compromise to offer his publisher: *Murderers' Houses? Dark Places of the World?* Perhaps it mightn't be such a bad book, after all.

When he switched off the lights, darkness came upstairs from the hall. He lay in bed and watched the shadows of the curtains furling and unfurling above him. He was touching the gate, which felt like flesh: it split open, and his hand plunged in. Though the image was unpleasant it seemed remote, drawing him down into sleep.

The room appeared to have grown much darker when he woke in the grip of utter panic.

He didn't dare move, not until he knew what was wrong. The shadows were frozen above him, the curtains hung like sheets of lead. His mouth tasted metallic, and made him think of blood. He was sure that he wasn't alone in the dark. The worst of it was that there was something he mustn't do – but he had no idea what it was.

He'd begun to search his mind desperately when he realized that was exactly what he ought not to have done. The threat had been waiting in his mind. The thought which welled up was so atrocious that his head began to shudder. He was trying to shake out the thought, to deny that it was his. He grabbed the light-cord, to scare it back into the dark.

Was the light failing? The room looked steeped in dimness, a grimy fluid whose sediment clung to his eyes. If anything the light had made him worse, for another thought came welling up like bile, and another. They were worse than the atrocities which the house had seen. He had to get out of the house.

He slammed his suitcase – thank God he'd lived out of it, rather than use the wardrobe – and dragged it onto the landing. He was halfway down, and the thuds of the case on the stairs were making his scalp crawl, when he realized that he'd left a notebook in the living-room.

He faltered in the hallway. He mustn't be fully awake: the carpet felt moist underfoot. His skull felt soft and porous, no protection at all for his mind. He had to have the notebook. Shouldering the door aside, he strode blindly into the room.

The light which dangled spider-like from the central plaster flower showed him the notebook on a fat armchair. Had the chairs soaked up all that had been done here? If he touched them, what might well up? But there was worse in his head, which was seething. He grabbed the notebook and ran into the hall, gasping for air.

His car sounded harsh as a saw among the sleeping houses. He felt as though the neat hygienic façades had cast him out. At least he had to concentrate on his driving, and was deaf to the rest of his mind. The road through Liverpool was unnaturally bright as a playing-field. When the Mersey Tunnel closed overhead he felt that an insubstantial but suffocating burden had settled on his scalp. At last he emerged, only to plunge into darkness.

Though his sleep was free of nightmares, they were waiting whenever he jerked awake. It was as if he kept struggling out of a dark pit, having repeatedly forgotten what was at the top. Sunlight blazed through the curtains as though they were tissue paper, but couldn't reach inside his head. Eventually, when he couldn't bear another such awakening, he stumbled to the bathroom.

When he'd washed and shaved he still felt grimy. It must be the lack of sleep. He sat gazing over his desk. The pebbledashed houses of Neston blazed like the cloudless sky; their outlines were knife-edged. Next door's drain sounded like someone bubbling the last of a drink through a straw. All this was less vivid than his thoughts – but wasn't that as it should be?

An hour later he still hadn't written a word. The nightmares were crowding everything else out of his mind. Even to think required an effort that made his skin feel infested, swarming.

A random insight saved him. Mightn't it solve both his problems if he wrote the nightmares down? Since he'd had them in the house in West Derby – since he felt they had somehow been produced by the house – couldn't he discuss them in his book?

He scribbled them out until his tired eyes closed. When he reread what he'd written he grew feverishly ashamed. How could he im-agine such things? If anything was obscene, they were. Nothing could have made him write down the idea which he'd left until last. Though he was tempted to tear up the notebook, he stuffed it out of sight at the back of a drawer and hurried out to forget.

He sat on the edge of the promenade and gazed across the Dee marshes. Heat-haze made the Welsh hills look like piles of smoke. Families strolled as though this were still a watering-place; children played carefully, inhibited by parents. The children seemed wary of Miles; perhaps they sensed his tension, saw how his fingers were digging into his thighs. He must write the book soon, to prove that he could.

Ranks of pebbledashed houses, street after street of identical Siamese twins, marched him home. They reminded him of cells in a single organism. He wouldn't starve if he didn't write – not for a while, at any rate – but he felt uneasy whenever he had to dip into his savings; their unobtrusive growth was reassuring, a talisman of success. He missed his street and had to walk back. Even then he had to peer twice at the street name before he was sure it was his.

He sat in the living-room, too exhausted to make himself dinner. Van Gogh landscapes, frozen in the instant before they became unbearably intense, throbbed on the walls. Shelves of Miles's novels reminded him of how he'd lost momentum. The last nightmare was still demanding to be written, unless he forced it into the depths of his mind. He would rather have no ideas than that.

When he woke, the nightmare had left him. He felt enervated but clean. He lit up his watch and found he'd slept for hours. It was time for the Book Programme. He'd switched on the television and was turning on the light when he heard his voice at the far end of the room, in the dark.

He was on television, but that was hardly reassuring; his one television interview wasn't due to be broadcast for months. It was as though he'd slept that time away. His face floated up from the grey of the screen as he sat down, cursing. By the time his book was published, nobody would remember this interview.

The linkman and the editing had invoked another writer now. Good God, was that all they were using of Miles? He remembered the cameras following him into the West Derby house, the neighbours glaring, shaking their heads. It was as though they'd managed to censor him, after all.

No, here he was again. 'Jonathan Miles is a crime novelist who feels he can no longer rely on his imagination. Desperate for new ideas, he lived for several weeks in a house where, last year, a murder was committed.' Miles was already losing his temper, but there was worse to come: they'd used none of his observations about the creative process, only the sequence in which he ushered the camera about the house like Hitchcock in the *Psycho* trailer. 'Viewers who find this distasteful,' the linkman said unctuously, 'may be reassured to hear that the murder in question is not so topical or popular as Mr Miles seems to think.'

Miles glared at the screen while the programme came to an end, while an announcer explained that *Where Do You Get Your Ideas?* had been broadcast ahead of schedule because of an industrial dispute. And now here was the news, all of it as bad as Miles felt. A child had been murdered, said a headline; a Chief Constable had described it as the worst case of his career. Miles felt guiltily resentful; no doubt it would help distract people from his book.

Then he sat forward, gaping. Surely he must have misheard; perhaps his insomnia was talking. The newsreader looked unreal as a talking bust, but his voice went on, measured, concerned, inexorable. 'The baby was found in a microwave oven. Neighbours broke into the house on hearing the cries, but were unable to locate it in time.' Even worse than the scene he was describing was the fact that it was the last of Miles's nightmares, the one he had refused to write down.

Couldn't it have been a coincidence? Coincidence, coincidence, the train chattered, and seemed likely to do so all the way to London. If he had somehow been able to predict what was going to happen, he didn't want to know – especially not now, when he could sense new nightmares forming.

He suppressed them before they grew clear. He needed to keep his mind uncluttered for the meeting with his publisher; he gazed out of the window to relax. Trees turned as they passed, unravelling beneath foliage. On a platform a chorus line of commuters bent to their luggage, one by one. The train drew the sun after it through clouds, like a balloon.

Once out of Euston Station and its random patterns of swarming, he strolled to the publishers. Buildings glared like blocks of salt, which seemed to have drained all moisture from the air. He felt hot and grimy, anxious both to face the worst and to delay. Hugo Burgess had been ominously casual: 'If you happen to be in London soon we might have a chat about things . . .'

A receptionist on a dais that overlooked the foyer kept Miles waiting until he began to sweat. Eventually a lift produced Hugo, smiling apologetically. Was he apologizing in advance for what he had to say? 'I suppose you saw yourself on television,' he said when they reached his office.

'Yes, I'm afraid so.'

'I shouldn't give it another thought. The telly people are envious buggers. They begrudge every second they give to discussing books. Sometimes I think they resent the competition and get their own back by being patronizing.' He was pawing through the heaps of books and papers on his desk, apparently in search of the phone. 'It did occur to me that it would be nice to publish fairly soon,' he murmured.

Miles hadn't realized that sweat could break out in so many places at once. 'I've run into some problems.'

Burgess was peering at items he had rediscovered in the heaps. 'Yes?' he said without looking up.

Miles summarized his new idea clumsily. Should he have written to Burgess in advance? 'I found there simply wasn't enough material in the West Derby case,' he pleaded.

'Well, we certainly don't want padding.' When Burgess eventually glanced up he looked encouraging. 'The more facts we can offer the better. I think the public is outgrowing fantasy, now that we're well and truly in the scientific age. People want to feel informed. Writing needs to be as accurate as any other science, don't you think?' He hauled a glossy pamphlet out of one of the piles. 'Yes, here it is. I'd call this the last gasp of fantasy.'

It was a painting, lovingly detailed and photographically realistic, of a girl who was being simultaneously mutilated and raped. It proved to be the cover of a new magazine, *Ghastly*. Within the pamphlet the editor promised 'a quarterly that will wipe out the old horror pulps – everything they didn't dare to be'.

'It won't last,' Burgess said. 'Most people are embarrassed to admit to reading fantasy now, and that will only make them more so. The book you're planning is more what they want – something they know is true. That way they don't feel they're indulging themselves.' He disinterred the phone at last. 'Just let me call a car and we'll go into the West End for lunch.'

Afterwards they continued drinking in Hugo's club. Miles thought Hugo was trying to midwife the book. Later he dined alone, then lingered for a while in the hotel bar; his spotlessly impersonal room made him feel isolated. Over the incessant trickle of muzak he kept hearing Burgess: 'I wonder how soon you'll be able to let me have sample chapters . . .'

Next morning he was surprised how refreshed he felt, especially once he'd taken a shower. Over lunch he unburdened himself to his agent. 'I just don't know when I'll be able to deliver the book. I don't know how much research may be involved.'

'Now look, you mustn't worry about Hugo. I'll speak to him. I know he won't mind waiting if he knows it's for the good of the book.' Susie Barker patted his hand; her bangles sounded like silver castanets. 'Now here's an idea for you. Why don't you do up a sample chapter or two on the West Derby case? That way we'll keep Hugo happy, and I'll do my best to sell it as an article.'

When they'd kissed goodbye Miles strolled along the Charing Cross Road, composing the chapter in his head and looking for himself in bookshop displays. Miles, Miles, books said in a window stacked with crime novels. NIGHT OF ATROCITIES, headlines cried on an adjacent newspaper stand.

He dodged into Foyles. That was better: he occupied half a shelf, though his earliest titles looked faded and dusty. When he emerged he was content to drift with the rush-hour crowds — until a newsvendor's placard stopped him. BRITAIN'S NIGHT OF HORROR, it said.

It didn't matter, it had nothing to do with him. In that case, why couldn't he find out what had happened? He didn't need to buy a paper, he could read the report as the newsvendor snatched the top copy to reveal the same beneath. 'Last night was Britain's worst night of murders in living memory . . .'

Before he'd read halfway down the column the noise of the crowd seemed to close in, to grow incomprehensible and menacing. The newsprint was snatched away again and again like a macabre card trick. He sidled away from the news-stand as though from the scene of a crime, but already he'd recognized every detail. If he hadn't repressed them on the way to London he could have written the reports himself. He even knew what the newspaper had omitted to report: that one of the victims had been forced to eat parts of herself.

Weeks later the newspapers were still in an uproar. Though the moderates pointed out that the murders had been unrelated and unmotivated, committed by people with no previous history of violence or of any kind of crime, for most of the papers that only made it worse. They used the most unpleasant photographs of the criminals that they could find, and presented the crimes as evidence of the impotence of the law, of a total collapse of standards. Opinion polls declared that the majority was in favour of an immediate return of the death penalty. 'MEN LIKE THESE MUST NOT GO UNPUNISHED,' a headline said, pretending it was quoting. Miles grew hot with frustration and guilt — for he felt he could have prevented the crimes.

All too soon after he'd come back from London, the nightmares had returned. His mind had already felt raw from brooding, and he had been unable to resist; he'd known only that he must get rid of them somehow. They were worse than the others: more urgent, more appalling.

He'd scribbled them out as though he was inspired, then he'd glared blindly at the blackened page. It hadn't been enough. The seething in his head, the crawling of his scalp, had not been relieved even slightly. This time he had to develop the ideas, imagine them fully, or they would cling and fester in his mind.

He'd spent the day and half the night writing, drinking tea until he hardly knew what he was doing. He'd invented character after character, building them like Frankenstein out of fragments of people, only to subject them to gloatingly prolonged atrocities, both the victims and the perpetrators.

When he'd finished, his head felt like an empty rusty can. He might have vomited if he had been able to stand. His gaze had fallen on a paragraph he'd written, and he'd swept the pages onto the floor, snarling with disgust. 'Next morning he couldn't remember what he'd done – but when he reached in his pocket and touched the soft object his hand came out covered with blood . . .'

He'd stumbled across the landing to his bedroom, desperate to forget his ravings. When he'd woken next morning he had been astonished to find that he'd fallen asleep as soon as he had gone to bed. As he'd lain there, feeling purged, an insight so powerful it was impossible to doubt had seized him. If he hadn't written out these things they would have happened in reality.

But he had written them out: they were no longer part of him. In fact they had never been so, however they had felt. That made him feel cleaner, absolved him of responsibility. He stuffed the sloganeering newspapers into the waste-basket and arranged his desk for work.

By God, there was nothing so enjoyable as feeling ready to write. While a pot of tea brewed he strolled about the house and revelled in the sunlight, his release from the nightmares, his surge of energy. Next door a man with a beard of shaving foam dodged out of sight, like a timid Santa Claus.

Miles had composed the first paragraph before he sat down to write, a trick that always helped him write more fluently – but a week later he was still struggling to get the chapter into publishable shape. All that he found crucial about his research – the idea that by staying in the West Derby house he had tapped a source of utter madness, which had probably caused the original murder – he'd had to suppress. Why, if he said any of that in print they would think he was mad himself. Indeed, once he'd thought of writing it, it no longer seemed convincing.

When he could no longer bear the sight of the article, he typed a fresh copy and sent it to Susie. She called the following day, which seemed encouragingly quick. Had he been so aware of what he was failing to write that he hadn't noticed what he'd achieved?

'Well, Jonathan, I have to say this,' she said as soon as she'd greeted him. 'It isn't up to your standard. Frankly, I think you ought to scrap it and start again.'

'Oh.' After a considerable pause he could think of nothing to say except, 'All right.'

'You sound exhausted. Perhaps that's the trouble.' When he didn't answer she said, 'You listen to your Auntie Susie. Forget the whole thing for a fortnight and go away on holiday. You've been driving yourself too hard – you looked tired the last time I saw you. I'll explain to Hugo, and I'll see if I can't talk up the article you're going to write when you come back.'

She chatted reassuringly for a while, then left him staring at the phone. He was realizing how much he'd counted on selling the article. Apart from royalties, which never amounted to as much as he expected, when had he last had the reassurance of a cheque? He couldn't go on holiday, for he would feel he hadn't earned it; if he spent the time worrying about the extravagance, that would be no holiday at all.

But wasn't he being unfair to himself? Weren't there stories he could sell?

He turned the idea over gingerly in his mind, as though something might crawl out from beneath – but really, he could see no arguments against it. Writing out the nightmares had drained them of power; they were just stories now. As he dialled Hugo's number, to ask him for the address of the magazine, he was already thinking up a pseudonym for himself.

For a fortnight he walked around Anglesey. Everything was hallucinatorily intense: beyond cracks in the island's grassy coastline, the sea glittered as though crystallizing and shattering; across the sea, Welsh hills and mist appeared to be creating each other. Beaches were composed of rocks like brown crusty loaves decorated with shells. Anemones unfurled deep in glassy pools. When night fell he lay on a slab of rock and watched the stars begin to swarm.

As he strolled he was improving the chapters in his mind, now that the first version had clarified his themes. He wrote the article in three days, and was sure it was publishable. Not only was it the fullest description yet of the murder, but he'd managed to explain the way the neighbours had behaved: they'd needed to dramatize their repudiation of all that had been done in the house, they'd used him as a scapegoat to cast out, to proclaim that it had nothing to do with them.

When he'd sent the manuscript to Susie he felt pleasantly tired. The houses of Neston grew silver in the evening, the horizon was turning to ash. Once the room was so dark that he couldn't read, he went to bed. As he drifted towards sleep he heard next door's drain bubbling to itself.

But what was causing bubbles to form in the greyish substance that resembled fluid less than flesh? They were slower and thicker than tar, and took longer to form. Their source was rushing upward to confront him face to face. The surface was quivering, ready to erupt, when he awoke.

He felt hot and grimy, and somehow ashamed. The dream had been a distortion of the last thing he'd heard, that was all; surely it wouldn't prevent him from sleeping. A moment later he was clinging to it desperately; its dreaminess was comforting, and it was preferable by far to the ideas that were crowding into his mind. He knew now why he felt grimy.

He couldn't lose himself in sleep; the nightmares were embedded there, minute, precise and appalling. When he switched on the light it seemed to isolate him. Night had bricked up all the windows. He couldn't bear to be alone with the nightmares – but there was only one way to be rid of them.

The following night he woke, having fallen asleep at his desk. His last line met his eyes: 'Hours later he sat back on his haunches, still chewing doggedly . . .' When he gulped the lukewarm tea it tasted rusty as blood. His surroundings seemed remote, and he could regain them only by purging his mind. His task wasn't even half finished. His eyes felt like dusty pebbles. The pen jerked in his hand, spattering the page.

Next morning Susie rang, wrenching him awake at his desk. 'Your article is tremendous. I'm sure we'll do well with it. Now I wonder if you can let me have a chapter breakdown of the rest of the book to show Hugo?'

Miles was fully awake now, and appalled by what had happened in his mind while he had been sleeping. 'No,' he muttered.

'Are there any problems you'd like to tell me about?'

If only he could! But he couldn't tell her that while he had been asleep, having nearly discharged his task, a new crowd of nightmares had gathered in his mind and were clamouring to be written. Perhaps now they would never end.

'Come and see me if it would help,' Susie said.

How could he, when his mind was screaming to be purged? But if he didn't force himself to leave his desk, perhaps he never would. 'All right,' he said dully. 'I'll come down tomorrow.'

When tomorrow came it meant only that he could switch off his desk-lamp; he was nowhere near finishing. He barely managed to find a seat on the train, which was crowded with football fans. Opened beercans spat; the air grew rusty with the smell of beer. The train emerged roaring from a tunnel, but Miles was still in his own, which was far darker and more oppressive. Around him they were chanting football songs, which sounded distant as a waveband buried in static. He wrote under cover of his briefcase, so that nobody would glimpse what he was writing.

Though he still hadn't finished when he reached London, he no longer cared. The chatter of the wheels, the incessant chanting, the pounding of blood and nightmares in his skull had numbed him. He sat for a while in Euston. The white tiles glared like ice, a huge voice loomed above him.

As soon as she saw him Susie demanded, 'Have you seen a doctor?'

Even a psychiatrist couldn't help him. 'I'll be all right,' he said, hiding behind a bright false smile.

'I've thought of some possibilities for your book,' she said over lunch. 'What about that house in Edinburgh where almost the same murder was committed twice, fifty years apart? The man who did the second always said he hadn't known about the first . . .'

She obviously hoped to revive him with ideas – but the nightmare which was replaying itself, endless as a loop of film, would let nothing else into his skull. The victim had managed to tear one hand free and was trying to protect herself.

'And isn't there the lady in Sutton who collected bricks from the scenes of crimes? She was meaning to use them to build a miniature Black Museum. She ought to be worth tracing,' Susie said as the man seized the flailing hand by its wrist. 'And then if you want to extend the scope of the book there's the mother of the Meathook Murder victims, who still gets letters pretending to be from her children.'

The man had captured the wrist now. Slowly and deliberately, with a grin that looked pale as a crack in clay, he – Miles was barely able to swallow; his head, and every sound in the restaurant, was pounding. 'They sound like good ideas,' he mumbled, to shut Susie up.

Back at her office, a royalty fee had arrived. She wrote him a cheque at once, as though that might cure him. As he slipped it into his briefcase, she caught sight of the notebooks in which he'd written on the train. 'Are they something I can look at?' she said.

His surge of guilt was so intense that it was panic. 'No, it's nothing, it's just something, no,' he stammered.

Hours later he was walking. Men loitered behind boys playing pinball; the machines flashed like fireworks, splashing the men's masks. Addicts were gathering outside the all-night chemist's on Piccadilly; in the subterranean Gents', a starved youth washed blood from a syringe. Off Regent Street, Soho glared like an amusement arcade. On Oxford Street figures in expensive dresses, their bald heads gleaming, gestured broken-wristed in windows.

He had no idea why he was walking. Was he hoping the crowds would distract him? Was that why he peered at their faces, more and more desperately? Nobody looked at all reassuring. Women were perfect as corpses, men seemed to glow with concealed aggression; some were dragons, their mouths full of smoke.

He'd walked past the girl before he reacted. Gasping, he struggled through a knot of people on the corner of Dean Street and dashed across, against the lights. In the moments before she realized that he'd dodged ahead of her and was staring, he saw her bright quick eyes, the delicate web of veins beneath them, the freckles that peppered the bridge of her nose, the pulsing of blood in her neck. She was so intensely present to him that it was appalling.

Then she stepped aside, annoyed by him, whatever he was. He reached out, but couldn't quite seize her arm. He had to stop her somehow. 'Don't,' he cried.

At that, she fled. He'd started after her when two policemen blocked his path. Perhaps they hadn't noticed him, perhaps they wouldn't grab him – but it was too late; she was lost in the Oxford Street crowd. He turned and ran, fleeing the police, fleeing back to his hotel.

As soon as he reached his room he began writing. His head felt stuffed with hot ash. He was scribbling so fast that he hardly knew what he was saying. How much time did he have? His hand was cramped and shaking, his writing was surrounded by a spittle of ink.

He was halfway through a sentence when, quite without warning, his mind went blank. His pen was clawing spasmodically at the page, but the urgency had gone; the nightmare had left him. He lay in the anonymous bed in the dark, hoping he was wrong.

In the morning he went down to the lobby as late as he could bear. The face of the girl he'd seen in Oxford Street stared up at him from a newspaper. In the photograph her eyes looked dull and reproachful, though perhaps they seemed so only to him. He fled upstairs without reading the report. He already knew more than the newspaper would have been able to tell.

Eventually he went home to Neston. It didn't matter where he went; the nightmares would find him. He was an outcast from surrounding reality. He was focused inward on his raw wound of a mind, waiting for the next outbreak of horrors to infest him.

Next day he sat at his desk. The sunlit houses opposite glared back like empty pages. Even to think of writing made his skin prickle. He went walking, but it was no good: beyond the marshes, factories coughed into the sky; grass-blades whipped the air like razors; birds swooped, shrieking knives with wings. The sunlight seemed violent and pitiless, vampirizing the landscape.

There seemed no reason why the nightmares should ever stop. Either he would be forced to write them out, to involve himself more and more deeply in them, or they would be acted out in reality. In any case he was at their mercy; there was nothing he could do.

But wasn't he avoiding the truth? It hadn't been coincidence that had given him the chance he'd missed in Oxford Street. Perhaps he had been capable of intervention all along, if he had only known. However dismaying the responsibility was, surely it was preferable to helplessness. His glimpse in Oxford Street had made all the victims unbearably human.

He sat waiting. Pale waves snaked across the surface of the grass; in the heat-haze they looked as though water was welling up from the marshes. His scalp felt shrunken, but that was only nervousness and the storm that was clotting overhead. When eventually the clouds moved on, unbroken, they left a sediment of twilight that clung to him as he trudged home.

No, it was more than that. His skin felt grimy, unclean. The nightmares were close. He hurried to let his car out of the garage. Then he sat like a private detective in the driver's seat outside his house. His hands clenched on the steering wheel. His head began to crawl, to swarm.

He mustn't be trapped into self-disgust. He reminded himself that the nightmares weren't coming from him, and forced his mind to grasp them, to be guided by them. Shame made him feel coated in hot grease. When at last the car coasted forward, was it acting out of his urge to flee? Should he follow that street sign, or that one?

Just as the signs grew meaningless because he'd stared too long, he knew which way to go. His instincts had been waiting to take hold, and they were urgent now. He drove through the lampless streets, where lit curtains cut rectangles from the night, and out into the larger dark.

He found he was heading for Chester. Trees beside the road were giant scarecrows, brandishing tattered foliage. Grey clouds crawled grub-like across the sky; he could hardly distinguish them from the crawling in his skull. He was desperate to purge his mind.

Roman walls loomed between the timber buildings of Chester, which were black and white as the moon. A few couples were window-shopping along the enclosed rows above the streets. On the bridge that crossed the main street, a clock perched like a moon-faced bird. Miles remembered a day when he'd walked by the river, boats passing slowly as clouds, a brass band on a small bandstand playing 'Blow the Wind Southerly'. How could the nightmare take place here?

It could, for it was urging him deeper into the city. He was driving so fast through the spotless streets that he almost missed the police station. Its blue sign drew him aside. That was where he must go. Somehow he had to persuade them that he knew where a crime was taking place.

He was still yards away from the police station when his foot faltered on the accelerator. The car shuddered and tried to jerk forward, but that was no use. The nearer he came to the police station, the weaker his instinct became. Was it being suppressed by his nervousness? Whatever the reason, he could guide nobody except himself.

As soon as he turned the car the urgency seized him. It was agonizing now. It rushed him out of the centre of Chester, into streets of small houses and shops that looked dusty as furniture shoved out of sight in an attic. They were deserted except for a man in an ankle-length overcoat, who limped by like a sack with a head.

Miles stamped on the brake as the car passed the mouth of an alley. Snatching the keys, he slammed the door and ran into the alley, between two shops whose posters looked ancient and faded as Victorian photographs. The walls of the alley were chunks of spiky darkness above which cramped windows peered, but he didn't need to see to know where he was going.

He was shocked to find how slowly he had to run, how out of condition he was. His lungs seemed to be filling with lumps of rust, his throat was scraped raw. He was less running than staggering forward. Amid the uproar of his senses, it took him a while to feel that he was too late.

He halted as best he could. His feet slithered on the uneven flagstones, his hands clawed at the walls. As soon as he began to listen he wished he had not. Ahead in the dark, there was a faint incessant shriek that seemed to be trying to emerge from more than one mouth. He knew there was only one victim.

Before long he made out a dark object farther down the alley. In fact it was two objects, one of which lay on the flagstones while the other rose to its feet, a dull gleam in its hand. A moment later the figure with the gleam was fleeing, its footsteps flapping like wings between the close walls.

The shrieking had stopped. The dark object lay still. Miles forced himself forward, to see what he'd failed to prevent. As soon as he'd glimpsed it he staggered away, choking back a scream.

He'd achieved nothing except to delay writing out the rest of the horrors. They were breeding faster in his skull, which felt as though it was cracking. He drove home blindly. The hedgerows and the night had merged into a dark mass that spilled towards the road, smudging its edges. Perhaps he might crash – but he wasn't allowed that relief, for the nightmares were herding him back to his desk.

The scratching of his pen, and a low half-articulate moaning which he recognized sometimes as his voice, kept him company. Next day the snap of the letter-box made him drop his pen; otherwise he might not have been able to force himself away from the desk.

The package contained the first issue of *Ghastly*. 'Hope you like it,' the editor gushed. 'It's already been banned in some areas, which has helped sales no end. You'll see we announce your stories as coming attractions, and we look forward to publishing them.' On the cover the girl was still writhing, but the contents were far worse. Miles had read only a paragraph when he tore the glossy pages into shreds.

How could anyone enjoy reading that? The pebbledashed houses of Neston gleamed innocently back at him. Who knew what his neighbours read behind their locked doors? Perhaps in time some of them would gloat over his pornographic horrors, reassuring themselves that this was only horror fiction, not pornography at all: just as he'd reassured himself that they were only stories now, nothing to do with reality – certainly nothing to do with him, the pseudonym said so –

The Neston houses gazed back at him, self-confident and bland: they looked as convinced of their innocence as he was trying to feel – and all at once he knew where the nightmares were coming from.

He couldn't see how that would help him. Before he'd begun to suffer from his writer's block, there had been occasions when a story had surged up from his unconscious and demanded to be written. Those stories had been products of his own mind, yet he couldn't shake them off except by writing – but now he was suffering nightmares on behalf of the world.

No wonder they were so terrible, or that they were growing worse. If material repressed into the unconscious was bound to erupt in some less manageable form, how much more powerful that must be when the unconscious was collective! Precisely because people were unable to come to terms with the crimes, repudiated them as utterly inhuman or simply unimaginable, the horrors would reappear in a worse form and possess whoever they pleased. He remembered thinking that the patterns of life in the tower blocks had something to do with the West Derby murder. They had, of course. Everything had.

And now the repressions were focused in him. There was no reason why they should ever leave him; on the contrary, they seemed likely to grow more numerous and more peremptory. Was he releasing them by writing them out, or was the writing another form of repudiation?

One was still left in his brain. It felt like a boil in his skull. Suddenly he knew that he wasn't equal to writing it out, whatever else might happen. Had his imagination burned out at last? He would be content never to write another word. It occurred to him that the book he'd discussed with Hugo was just another form of rejection: knowing you were reading about real people reassured you they were other than yourself.

He slumped at his desk. He was a burden of flesh that felt encrusted with grit. Nothing moved except the festering nightmare in his head. Unless he got rid of it somehow, it felt as though it would never go away. He'd failed twice to intervene in reality, but need he fail again? If he succeeded, was it possible that might change things for good?

He was at the front door when the phone rang. Was it Susie? If she knew what was filling in his head, she would never want to speak to him again. He left the phone ringing in the dark house and fled to his car.

The pain in his skull urged him through the dimming fields and villages to Birkenhead, where it seemed to abandon him. Not that it had faded – his mind felt like an abscessed tooth – but it was no longer able to guide him. Was something anxious to prevent him from reaching his goal?

The bare streets of warehouses and factories and terraces went on for miles, brick-red slabs pierced far too seldom by windows. At the peak hour the town centre grew black with swarms of people, the Mersey Tunnel drew in endless sluggish segments of cars. He drove jerkily, staring at faces.

Eventually he left the car in Hamilton Square, overlooked by insurance offices caged by railings, and trudged towards the docks. Except for his footsteps, the streets were deserted. Perhaps the agony would be cured before he arrived wherever he was going. He was beyond caring what that implied.

It was dark now. At the end of rows of houses whose doors opened onto cracked pavement he saw docked ships, glaring metal mansions. Beneath the iron mesh of swing bridges, a scum of neon light floated on the oily water. Sunken rails snagged his feet. In pubs on street corners he heard tribes of dockers, a sullen wordless roar that sounded like a warning. Out here the moan of a ship on the Irish Sea was the only voice he heard.

When at last he halted, he had no idea where he was. The pavement on which he was walking was eaten away by rubbly ground; he could smell collapsed buildings. A roofless house stood like a rotten tooth, lit by a single street lamp harsh as lightning. Streets still led from the opposite pavement, and despite the ache – which had aborted nearly all his thoughts – he knew that the street directly opposite was where he must go.

There was silence. Everything was yet to happen. The lull seemed to give him a brief chance to think. Suppose he managed to prevent it? Repressing the ideas of the crimes only made them erupt in a worse form – how much worse might it be to repress the crimes themselves?

Nevertheless he stepped foward. Something had to cure him of his agony. He stayed on the treaterous pavement of the side street, for the road way was skinless, a mass of bricks and mud. Houses pressed close to him, almost forcing him into the road. Where their doors and windows ought to be were patches of new brick. The far end of the street was impenetrably dark.

When he reached it, he saw why. A wall at least ten feet high was built flush against the last houses. Peering upward, he made out the glint of broken glass. He was closed in by the wall and the plugged houses, in the midst of desolation.

Without warning quite irrelevantly, it seemed – he remembered something he'd read about years ago while researching a novel: the Mosaic ritual of the Day of Atonement. They'd driven out the scapegoat, burdened with all the sins of the people, into the wilderness. Another goat had been sacrificed. The images chafed together in his head; he couldn't grasp their meaning – and then he realized why there was so much room for them in his mind. The aching nightmare was fading.

At once he was unable to turn away from the wall, for he was atrociously afraid. He knew why this nightmare could not have been acted out without him. Along the bricked-up street he heard footsteps approaching.

When he risked a glance over his shoulder, he saw that there were two figures. Their faces were blacked out by the darkness, but the glints in their hands were sharp. He was trying to claw his way up the wall, though already his lungs were labouring. Everything was over – the sleepless nights, the poison in his brain, the nightmare of responsibility – but he knew that while he would soon not be able to scream, it would take him much longer to die.

TOUCHSTONE

Terry Carr

My first published story, 'Who Sups With the Devil', was a fantasy, and so were most of my early stories. But I soon realized that – at that time, in the early 1960s – there wasn't a wide market for fantasy. Weird Tales *had folded, as had* Fantasy Fiction, Beyond, Fantastic Universe, Famous Fantastic Mysteries, *and most of the magazines that had carried the fantasy banner in the '50s. The only ones left were* The Magazine of Fantasy & Science Fiction *and* Fantastic – *and the latter was paying minuscule rates. I sold most of my stories to* F&SF, *but one good market isn't enough to support a free-lance writer and, before long, Avram Davidson took me aside and advised me to find additional markets, because he couldn't publish an infinite number of Terry Carr stories.*

I put a pen name ('Carl Brandon') on one story for F&SF, *but that was a stop-gap measure. I soon began writing more science fiction, so that I could sell to* If, Galaxy, *and other sf markets. They usually paid more, anyway, so I got into the habit of writing science fiction instead of fantasy.*

'Touchstone' was one of the last fantasies I wrote, and it was the one that pleased me most. When I finished it, I felt very satisfied with the story: it seemed to me that I had gone beyond simply ringing a new change on an old plot, and had managed to touch on a theme that was important to everyone – the need for caring among people. As I rolled the last page out of the typewriter I thought, 'This is my best story'.

Its setting was drawn from experience. In 1961 and 1962 I lived in the western section of New York City's Greenwich Village, then still untouched by such civic pollutants as pizza stands, discount record stores, and shops selling picture postcards of Washington Square. Instead, there were neighborhood delicatessens, Chinese laundries, and dim little bookstores in which one might find . . . anything. I had fallen in love with the area, and though rising rents had forced my wife Carol and me to move to Brooklyn Heights in 1963, I was still so infused with the mystique of the West Village that I conceived a story beginning in one of those timeless bookshops.

I sent the story to Avram Davidson, and a few days later he called me to say he wanted to buy it, but that he wanted to make an alteration in one line: I had referred to something as being 'as ugly and malformed as a human foetus', but Avram suggested that the mot juste here was 'unformed'. I agreed completely, and he made the change.

It was only after he'd hung up that I remembered Avram's wife was pregnant.

For thirty-two years, during which he watched with growing perplexity and horror the ways of the world and the dull gropings of men reaching for love and security, Randolph Helgar had told himself that there was a simple answer to all of it – somehow it was possible to get a handhold on life, to hold it close and cherish it without fear. And on a Saturday morning in early March when the clouds had disappeared and the sun came forth pale in the sky he found what he had been looking for.

The snow had been gone from the streets of Greenwich Village for over a week, leaving behind only the crispness on the sidewalks. Everyone still walked with a tentative step, like sailors on shore leave. Randolph Helgar was out of his apartment by ten, heading west. His straight, sandy hair was ruffled by an easterly wind, giving him the superficial appearance of hurrying, but his quick grey eyes and the faint smile that so often came to his mouth dispelled that. Randolph was busier looking around than walking.

The best thing about the Village, as far as he was concerned, was that you could never chart all of it. As soon as you thought you knew every street, every sandal shop, every hot dog or pizza stand, one day you'd look up and there'd be something new there, where you'd never looked before. A peculiar blindness comes over people who walk through the streets of the Village; they see only where they're going.

The day before, on the bus coming home from work at the travel agency on West 4th, he had looked out the window and seen a bookstore whose dirty windows calmly testified to the length of time it had been there. So of course this morning he was looking for that bookstore. He had written down the address, but there was no need now for him to take the slip of paper from his wallet to look at it; the act of writing it had fixed it in his memory.

The store was just opening when he got there. A large, heavy-shouldered man with thick black hair and prominent veins in the backs of his hands was setting out the bargain table in the front of the store. Randolph glanced at the table, filled with the sun-faded spines of anonymous pocketbooks, and nodded at the man. He went inside.

The books were piled high around the walls; here and there were handlettered signs saying MUSIC, HISTORY, PSYCHOLOGY, but they must have been put there years ago, because the books in those sections bore no relation to the signs. Near the front was an old cupboard, mottled with the light which came through the dirty window; a sign on one of its shelves said $10. Next to it was a small round table which revolved on its base, but there was no price on this.

The owner had come back into the store now, and he stood just inside the door looking at Randolph. After a moment he said, 'You want anything special?'

Randolph shook his head, dislodging the shock of hair which fell over his eyes. He ran his fingers through it, combing it back, and turned to one of the piles of books.

'I think maybe you'd be interested in this section,' said the owner, walking heavily over the bending floorboards to stand beside Randolph. He raised a large hand and ran it along one shelf. A sign said MAGIC, WITCHCRAFT.

Randolph glanced at it. 'No,' he said.

'None of those books are for sale,' the man said. 'That section is strictly lending-library.'

Randolph raised his eyes to meet those of the older man. The man gazed back calmly, waiting.

'Not for sale?' Randolph said.

'No, they're part of my own collection,' the man said. 'But I lend them out at 10¢ a day, if anybody wants to read them, or . . .'

'Who takes them out?'

The heavy man shrugged, with the faint touch of a smile about his thick lips. 'People. People come in, they see the books and think they might like to read them. They always bring them back.'

Randolph glanced at the books on the shelves. The spines were crisp and hard, the lettering on them like new. 'Do you think they read them?' he asked.

'Of course. So many of them come back and buy other things.'

'Other books?'

The man shrugged again, and turned away. He walked slowly to the back of the store. 'I sell other things. It's impossible to make a living selling books in this day and age.'

Randolph followed him into the darkness in back. 'What other things do you sell?'

'Perhaps you should read some of the books first,' the man said, watching him beneath his eyebrows.

'Do you sell . . . love potions? Dried bat's blood? Snake's entrails?'

'No,' said the man. 'I'm afraid you'd have to search the tobacconist's shop for such things as that. I sell only imperishables.'

'Magic charms?' Randolph said.

'Yes,' the man said slowly. 'Some are real, some are not.'

'And I suppose the real ones are more expensive.'

'They are all roughly the same price. It's up to you to decide which ones are real.'

The man had stooped to reach into a drawer of his desk, and now he brought out a box from which he lifted the lid. He set the open box on the top of his desk and reached up to turn on a naked lightbulb which hung from the shadowed ceiling.

The box contained an assortment of amulets, stones, dried insects encased in glass, carved pieces of wood, and other things. They were all tumbled into the box haphazardly. Randolph stirred the contents with two fingers.

'I don't believe in magic,' he said.

The heavy man smiled faintly 'I don't suppose I do either. But some of these things are quite interesting. Some are of authentic South American workmanship, and others are from Europe and the East. They're worth money, all right.'

'What's this?' Randolph asked, picking up a black stone which just fit into the palm of his hand. The configurations of the stone twisted around and in upon themselves, like a lump of baker's dough.

'That's a touchstone. Run your fingers over it.'

'It's perfectly smooth,' Randolph said.

'It's supposed to have magical powers to make people feel contented. Hold it in your hand.'

Randolph closed his fingers around the stone. Perhaps it was the power of suggestion, but the stone did feel very good. So smooth, like skin . . .

'The man who gave it to me said it was an ancient Indian piece. It embodies Yin and Yang, the opposites that complement and give

107

harmony to the world. You can see a little of the symbol in the way the stone looks.' He smiled slowly. 'It's also supposed to encase a human soul, like an egg.'

'More likely a fossil,' Randolph said. He wondered what kind of stone it was.

'It will cost five dollars,' the man said.

Randolph hefted the stone in his hand. It settled back into his palm comfortably, like a cat going to sleep. 'All right,' he said.

He took a bill from his wallet, and noticed the paper on which he'd written the store's address the day before. 'If I come back here a week from now,' he said, 'will this store still be here? Or will it have disappeared, like magic shops are supposed to do?'

The man didn't smile. 'This isn't that kind of store. I'd go out of business if I kept moving my location.'

'Well, then,' Randolph said, looking at the black stone in his hand. 'When I was young I used to pick up stones at the beach and carry them around for weeks, just because I loved them. I suppose this stone has some of that sort of magic, anyway.'

'If you decide you don't want it, bring it back,' said the man.

When he got back to the apartment Margo was just getting up. Bobby, seven years old, was apparently up and out already. Randolph put yesterday's pot of coffee on the burner to heat and sat at the kitchen table to wait for it. He took the touchstone out of his pocket and ran his fingers over it.

Strange . . . It was just a black rock, worn smooth probably by water and then maybe by the rubbing of fingers over centuries. Despite what the man at the store had said about an Indian symbol, it had no particular shape.

Yet it did have a peculiar calming effect on him. Maybe, he thought, it's just that people have to have something to do with their hands while they think. It's the hands, the opposable thumb, that has made men what they are, or so the anthropologists say. The hands give men the ability to work with things around them, to make, to do. And we all have a feeling that we've got to be using our hands all the time or somehow we're not living up to our birthright.

That's why so many people smoke. That's why they fidget and rub their chins and drum their fingers on tables. But the touchstone relaxes the hands.

A simple form of magic.

Margo came into the kitchen, combing her long hair back over her shoulders. She hadn't put on any makeup, and her full mouth seemed as pale as clouds. She set out coffee cups and poured, then sat down across the table.

'Did you get the paint?'

'Paint?'

'You were going to paint the kitchen today. The old paint is cracking and falling off.'

Randolph looked up at the walls, rubbing the stone in his fingers. They didn't look bad, he decided. They could go for another six months without being redone. After all, it was no calamity if the plaster showed through above the stove.

'I don't think I'll do it today,' he said.

Margo didn't say anything. She picked up a book from the chair beside her and found her place in it.

Randolph fingered the touchstone and thought about the beach when he had been a boy.

There was a party that night at Gene Blake's apartment on the floor below, but for once Randolph didn't feel like going down. Blake was four years younger than him, and suddenly today the difference seemed insuperable; Blake told off-center jokes about integration in the South, talked about writers Randolph knew only by the reviews in the Sunday *Times*, and was given to drinking Scotch and milk. No, not tonight, he told Margo.

After dinner Randolph settled in front of the television set and, as the washing of dishes sounded from the kitchen and Bobby read a comic book in the corner, watched a rerun of the top comedy show of three seasons past. When the second commercial came on he dug the touchstone from his pocket and rubbed it idly with his thumb. All it takes, he told himself, is to ignore the commercials.

'Have you ever seen a frog?' Bobby asked him. He looked up and saw the boy standing next to his chair, breathing quickly as boys do when they have something to say.

'Sure,' he said.

'Did you ever see a black one? A dead one?'

Randolph thought a minute. He didn't suppose he had. 'No,' he said.

'Wait a minute!' Bobby said, and bounded out of the room. Randolph turned back to the television screen, and saw that the wife had a horse in the living-room and was trying to coax it to go upstairs before the husband came home. The horse seemed bored.

'Here!' said Bobby, and dropped the dead frog in his lap.

Randolph looked at it for two seconds before he realized what it was. One leg and part of the frog's side had been crushed, probably by a car's wheel, and the wide mouth was open. It was grey, not black.

Randolph shook it off him onto the floor. 'You'd better throw it away,' he said. 'It's going to smell bad.'

'But I paid sixty marbles for him!' Bobby said. 'And I only had twenty-five, and you got to get me some more.'

Randolph sighed, and shifted the touchstone from one hand to the other. 'All right,' he said. 'Monday. Keep him in your room.'

He turned back to the screen, where everyone had got behind the horse and was trying to push him up the stairs.

'Don't you like him?' Bobby asked.

Randolph looked blankly at him.

'My frog,' Bobby said.

Randolph thought about it for a moment. 'I think you'd better throw him away,' he said. 'He's going to stink.'

Bobby's face fell. 'Can I ask Mom?'

Randolph didn't answer, and he supposed Bobby went away. There was another commercial on now, and he was toying idly with the thought of a commercial for touchstones. 'For two thousand years mankind has searched for the answer to underarm odor, halitosis, regularity. Now at last . . .'

'*Bobby!*' said his wife in the kitchen. Randolph looked up, surprised. 'Take that out in the hall and put it in the garbage *right now* ! Not another word!'

In a moment Bobby came trudging through the room, his chin on his chest. But tiny eyes looked at Randolph with a trace of hope.

'She's gonna make me throw him away.'

Randolph shrugged. 'It would smell up the place,' he said.

'Well, I thought *you'd* like it anyway,' Bobby said. 'You always keep telling me how *you* were a boy, and *she* wasn't.' He stopped for a moment, waiting for Randolph to answer, and when he didn't the boy abruptly ran out with the grey, crushed frog in his hand.

Margo came into the living-room, drying her hands on a towel. 'Ran, why didn't you put your foot down in the first place?'

'What?'

'You know things like that make me sick. I won't be able to eat for two days.'

'I was watching the program,' he said.

'You've seen that one twice before. What's the matter with you?'

'Take some aspirin if you're upset,' he said. He squeezed the stone in the palm of his hand until she shook her head and went away.

A few minutes later a news program came on with a report on some people who had picketed a military base, protesting bombs and fallout. A university professor's face came on the screen and gravely he pointed to a chart. 'The Atomic Energy Commission admits—'

Randolph sighed and shut the set off.

He went to bed early that night. When he woke up the next day he went and got a book and brought it back to bed with him. He picked up the touchstone from the chair next to the bed and turned it over in his hand a few times. It was really a very plain kind of stone. Black, smooth, softly curving . . . What was it about the rock that could make everything seem so unimportant, so commonplace?

Well, of course a rock is one of the most common things in the world, he thought. You find them everywhere – even in the streets of the city, where everything is man-made, you'll find rocks. They're part of the ground underneath the pavement, part of the world we live on. They're part of home.

He held the touchstone in one hand while he read.

Margo had been up for several hours when he finished the book. When he set it down she came in and stood in the doorway, watching him silently.

After a few minutes she asked, 'Do you love me?'

He looked up, faintly surprised. 'Yes, of course.'

'I wasn't sure.'

'Why not? Is anything wrong?'

She came over and sat on the bed next to him in her terry-cloth robe. 'It's just that you've hardly spoken to me since yesterday. I thought maybe you were angry about something.'

Randolph smiled. 'No. Why should I be angry?'

'I don't know. It just seemed that . . .' She shrugged.

He reached out and touched her face with his free hand. 'Don't worry about it.'

She lay down beside him, resting her head on his arm. 'And you do love me? Everything's all right?'

He turned the stone over in his right hand. 'Of course everything's all right,' he said softly.

She pressed against him. 'I want to kiss you.'

'All right.' He turned to her and brushed his lips across her forehead and nose. Then she held him tightly while she kissed his mouth.

When she had finished he lay back against the pillow and looked up at the ceiling. 'Is it sunny out today?' he asked. 'It's been dark in here all day.'

'I want to kiss you some more,' she said. 'If that's all right with you.'

Randolph was noticing the warmth of the touchstone in his hand. Rocks aren't warm, he thought; it's only my hand that gives it warmth. Strange.

'Of course it's all right,' he said, and turned to let her kiss him again.

Bobby stayed in his room most of the day; Randolph supposed he was doing something. Margo, after that one time, didn't try to talk to him. Randolph stayed in bed fingering the touchstone and thinking, though whenever he tried to remember what he'd been thinking about he drew a blank.

Around five-thirty his friend Blake appeared at the door. Randolph heard him say something to Margo, and then he came into the bedroom.

'Hey, are you all right? You weren't at the party last night.'

Randolph shrugged. 'Sure. I just felt like lounging around this weekend.'

Blake's weathered face cleared. 'Well, that's good. Listen, I've got a problem.'

'A problem,' Randolph said. He settled down in the bed, looking idly at the stone in his hand.

Blake paused. 'You sure everything's all right? Nothing wrong with Margo? She didn't look too good when I came in.'

'We're both fine.'

'Well, okay. Look, Ran, you know you're the only close friend I've got, don't you? I mean, there's a lot of people in the world, but you're the only one I can really count on when the chips are down. Some people I joke with, but with you I can talk. You listen. You know?'

Randolph nodded. He supposed Blake was right.

'Well . . . I guess you heard the commotion last night. A couple guys drank too much, and there was a fight.'

'I went to bed early.'

'I'm surprised you slept through it. It developed into quite a brawl there for awhile; the cops came later on. They broke three windows and somebody pushed over the refrigerator. Smashed everything all to hell. One of the doors is off the hinges.'

'No, I didn't hear it.'

'Wow. Well, look, Ran . . . the super is on my neck. He's going to sue me, he's going to kick me out. You know that guy. I've got to get ahold of some money fast, to fix things up.'

Randolph didn't say anything. He had found a place on the stone where his right thumb fit perfectly, as though the stone had been molded around it. He switched the stone to his left hand, but it didn't quite fit that thumb.

Blake was nervous. 'Look, I know it's short notice. I wouldn't ask you, but I'm stuck. Can you lend me about a hundred?'

'A hundred dollars?'

'I might be able to get by with eighty, but I figured a bribe to the super . . .'

'All right. It doesn't make any difference.'

Blake paused again, looking at him. 'You can do it?'

'Sure.'

'Which, eighty or a hundred?'

'A hundred if you want.'

'You're sure it won't . . . bother you, make you short? I mean, I could look around somewhere else . . .'

'I'll write you a check,' Randolph said. He got up slowly and took his checkbook from the dresser. 'How do you spell your first name?'

'G-E-N-E.' Blake stood nervously, indecisive. 'You're sure it's no trouble? I don't want to pressure you.'

'No.' Randolph signed the check, tore it out and handed it to him.

'You're a friend,' Blake said. 'A real one.'

Randolph shrugged. 'What the hell.'

Blake stood for a few seconds more, apparently wanting to say something. But then he thanked him again and hurried out. Margo came and stood in the doorway and looked at him silently for a moment, then went away.

'Are you going to get me the marbles tomorrow?' Bobby said that evening over supper.

'Marbles?'

'I told you. I still have to pay that guy for the frog you made me throw away.'

'Oh. How many?'

'Thirty-five of them. I owed him sixty, and I only had twenty-five.'

Bobby was silent, picking at his corn. He speared three kernels carefully with his fork and slid them off the fork with his teeth.

'I'll bet you forget.'

Margo looked up from where she had been silently eating. 'Bobby!'

'I'm finished with my dinner,' Bobby said quickly, standing up. He threw a quick glance at Randolph. 'I'll bet he does forget,' he said, and ran out.

After five minutes of silence between them Margo stood up and started clearing away the dishes. Randolph was rubbing the touch-stone against the bridge of his nose.

'I'd like to sleep with you tonight,' she said.

'Of course,' he said, a bit surprised.

She stopped beside him and touched his arm. 'I don't mean just sleep. I want you to love me.'

He nodded. 'All right.'

But when the time came she turned away and lay silently in the dark. He went to sleep with one arm lying carelessly across her hips.

When the telephone rang he came out of sleep slowly. It was ringing for the fifth time when he answered it.

It was Howard, at the agency. 'Are you all right?' he asked.

'Yes, I'm all right,' Randolph said.

'It's past ten. We thought maybe you were sick and couldn't call.'

'Past ten?' For a moment he didn't know what that meant. Then Margo appeared in the doorway from the kitchen, holding the alarm clock in her hand, and he remembered it was Monday.

'I'll be there in an hour or so,' he said quickly. 'It's all right; Margo wasn't feeling too good, but she's all right now.'

Margo, her face expressionless, put the clock down on the chair next to the bed and looked at him for a moment before leaving the room.

'Nothing serious, I hope,' said Howard.

'No, it's all right. I'll see you in a while.' He hung up.

He sat on the edge of the bed and tried to remember what had happened. The past two days were a blur. He had lost something, hadn't he? Something he'd been holding.

'I tried to wake you three times,' Margo said quietly. She had come back into the room and was standing with her hands folded under her breasts. Her voice was level, controlled. 'But you wouldn't pay any attention.'

Randolph was slowly remembering. He'd had the touchstone in

his hand last night, but it must have slipped out while he was asleep. He began to search among the covers.

'Did you see the stone?' he asked her.

'What?'

'The stone. I've dropped it.'

There was a short silence. 'I don't know. Is it so important right now?'

'I paid five dollars for it,' he said, still rummaging through the bed.

'For a rock?'

He stopped suddenly. Yes, five dollars for a rock, he thought. It didn't sound right.

'Ran, what's the matter with you lately? Gene Blake was up here this morning. He gave back your check and said to apologize to you. He was really upset. He said he didn't think you really wanted to loan him the money.'

But it wasn't just a rock, Randolph thought. It was a black, smooth touchstone.

'Is something worrying you?' she asked him.

The back of his neck was suddenly cold. Worrying me? he thought. No, nothing's been worrying me. That's just the trouble.

He looked up. 'It may be cold out today. Can you find my gloves?'

She looked at him for a moment and then went to the hall closet. Randolph got up and started dressing. In a few minutes she returned with the gloves. He put them on. 'It's a little cold in here right now,' he said.

When she had gone back into the kitchen he started looking through the bed again, this time coldly and carefully. He found the touchstone under his pillow, and without looking at it he slipped it into a paper bag. He put the bag into his coat pocket.

When he got to the agency he made his excuses as glibly as possible, but he was sure they all knew that he had simply overslept. Well, it wasn't that important . . . once.

He stopped off at the store on his way home that night. It was just as he remembered it, and the same man was inside. He raised his thick eyebrows when he saw Randolph.

'You came back quickly.'

'I want to return the touchstone,' Randolph said.

'I'm not surprised. So many people return my magic pieces. Sometimes I think I am only lending them too, like the books.'

'Will you buy it back?'

'Not at the full price. I have to stay in business.'

'What price?' Randolph asked.

'A dollar only,' the man said. 'Or you could keep it, if that's not enough.'

Randolph thought for a moment. He certainly didn't intend to keep the stone, but a dollar wasn't much. He could throw the stone away. . . .

But then someone would probably pick it up.

'Do you have a hammer here?' he asked. 'I think it would be better to break the stone.'

'Of course I have a hammer,' the man said. He reached into one of the lower drawers of his desk and brought one out, old and brown with rust.

He held it out. 'The hammer rents for a dollar,' he said.

Randolph glanced sharply at the man, and then decided that that wasn't really surprising. He had to stay in business, yes. 'All right.' He took the hammer. 'I wonder if the veins of the rock are as smooth as the outside.'

'Perhaps we'll see the fossilized soul,' said the man. 'I never know about the things I sell.'

Randolph knelt and dropped the touchstone from its bag onto the floor. It rolled in a wobbling circle and then lay still.

'I knew quite a bit about rocks when I was young,' he said. 'I used to pick them up at the beach.'

He brought the hammer down on the touchstone and it shattered into three pieces which skittered across the floor and bounced to a stop. The largest one was next to Randolph's foot.

He picked it up and the owner of the store turned on the overhead lightbulb. Together they examined the rock's fragment.

There was a fossile, but Randolph couldn't tell what it was. It was small and not very distinct, but looking at it he felt a chill strike out at him. It was as ugly and unformed as a human foetus, but it was something older, a kind of life that had died in the world's mud before anything like a man had been born.

LET US QUICKLY HASTEN TO THE GATE OF IVORY

Thomas M. Disch

At gut level, most of us do not believe in death. Though we know, intellectually, that the grave is everyone's final destination, that knowledge rarely stops us in our tracks the way you might suppose it would if we were to give serious thought to the proposition: All men are mortal.

This ability to look in the other emotional direction from the brute fact of death is never more needful or welcome than at those times and in those places where death stands directly before us. The pomp of funerals is a kind of cape we can use to divert the attention of a grief that otherwise might gore us. The pastoral fantasy of cemeteries is likewise calculated to direct our thoughts away from the particulars under the sod to dwell on the generalities of a landscaped garden, where Nature is represented in her most benign aspect.

All this is a rather roundabout route to the commonplace perception that cemeteries are intrinsically fascinating places. (Fascinating, I would suggest, because of their ambiguous nature.) Whenever I have been a tourist in a foreign city long enough to have taken in the basic four-star attractions, I like to set aside an afternoon to picnic and be generally elegiac at that city's chief cemetery. Were there but world enough and time, I would like some day to produce a guidebook to the world's greatest cemeteries. Among my personal favorites I would include Forest Lawn in Los Angeles (so unjustly mocked by both Huxley and Waugh), Highgate Cemetery in London (a delectable ruin where lush ivy overwhelms the tumbledown graves of Victorian celebrities), the staid and tiny Protestant cemetery outside Rome (where Keats is buried), and the superb cemetery across the Bosphorus from Istanbul that was the inspiration (though not the setting) for the following tale.

When I visited this particular Turkish cemetery, in 1968, it seemed to me that it struck just the right balance between the manicured neatness of Forest Lawn and the higgledy-piggledy desuetude of Highgate. In some areas, the turbanned headstones had lost all sense *of perpendicularity, but the cypresses that solemnized the horizon preserved a general sense of funerary decorum.*

I had been walking about for a couple of hours with my brand-new Voigtlander, snapping pictures of the more picturesque vistas, when a sense came over me that I was lost. I told myself not to panic: no cemetery could be so large that one could get lost in it.

Why, that would be impossible, wouldn't it?

The cemetery lay at some distance outside the city, but in such fine weather it was a pleasure to be able to escape into the country. The blue of the sky was emphasized by a few scattered clouds which obligingly kept well away from the sun. The morning warmth touched, but did not penetrate, the surfaces of the scene, the fields, the winding road, the muddy trenches on either side and the tall weeds. In such a landscape, on such a day, they (Mickey and Louise) figured only as decoration: one shepherd, one shepherdess. Louise, in her best pastoral mood, smiled and allowed her hair to be ruffled by the wind.

They parked the Volkswagen in a large lot of matt-black asphalt enlivened by the herringbone pattern of whitewash and authoritative traffic arrows, which (since the lot was empty) they ignored. She took the bouquet from the back seat, two dozen white and red roses. Three times during the drive out here Mickey had asked her how much she had paid for the flowers. Mickey wasted not and did not want.

'Aren't you taking your sweater?' he asked.

'On such a nice day?'

Mickey, the father now of two children, a man of responsibilities, frowned. 'You never know.'

'True, true.' She took her sweater, draped it over her shoulder, stretched.

'Did you lock the door on your side?'

'I don't know.'

Mickey went back and locked the right-hand door. Then he unlocked it, rolled up the window, and locked it again.

Just inside the brick gate, beside a bed of tulips, was a rack of flower vases – all of them, like so many empty milkbottles, of the same squat shape and tinny green color. Mickey paused a moment to select one.

FROM THEIR LABOR
NOW THEY REST

118

The grounds of the cemetery swelled and dipped agreeably. The young leaves and the grass insisted, this early in the year, rather too much on their color, and even the pines had been caught up in this naive enthusiasm: their branches were tipped with that same vivid lime.

'I hope you know the way.'

'Pretty well,' Mickey said. 'We go over that high hill there—' Pointing west. 'From the top you can see a second little hill beyond, and it's on the other side of that, about halfway down. Between two fir trees.'

'Is it very big?'

'Not very. About up to my knees. Mom chose it herself.'

They started up the path. Louise was very conscious of the crunch of her heels on the gravel.

'Have you been here a lot?'

'No. Not since the funeral, in fact. We've had a rugged winter. And Joyce gets too depressed.'

'I suppose it would be depressing in the fall, but it's lovely now. More like a golf course than a cemetery.'

At these words the memory of their summer evening trespasses on the golf course returned to both of them and they exchanged shy smiles of complicity. In the winters they had gone sledding on those same illicit slopes.

With his smile as her sanction Louise caught hold of Mickey's free hand. Obediently his fingers curled around hers, but with the same gesture his smile vanished.

'Oh, we can, you know,' she assured him. 'Holding hands *is* permitted between brother and sister.'

'It's just that . . . well, it's been so long.'

> SACRED
> to the Memory of
> CECELIA HAKE
> Aug 15 1892-Dec 2 1955

'And that's the pleasure of it. Do you think Joyce would be jealous?'

'Probably, but she wouldn't dare admit it. Joyce is a great believer in family bonds. Do you like her?'

'I might learn to. But I think *I'm* too jealous still. I haven't been able to have you to myself for one minute. This is nice.'

'You don't have to leave tomorrow.'

'Ah, but that's just it — I *do* have to.'

Near the top of the hill the path became steeper. Ahead the tiers of markers and monuments caught the full dazzle of the morning light. Louise had to squint as she climbed on.

From the top one could see a wide wavering line of hills that graphed, against the blue sky, some very temperate recurrence. An artificial stream reemphasized the cemetery's resemblance to a golf course. Perhaps one would be able to find a hard white ball in unclipped grass at the base of a tree or by the stream's edge. Uncertain how much whimsy her brother would be willing to tolerate in the circumstances, she said nothing.

Behind them the VW was still alone in the parking lot.

The path branched right and left, and Mickey seemed in doubt which to take. 'I think it's that hill,' he said. She had to follow behind, for the path had narrowed.

'So many,' she said. 'I had not thought death had undone so many.'

INTO THY HANDS O LORD

'Oh, it's not bad, really,' Mickey said. 'The real trouble will be in twenty, thirty years' time. . . . It *will* be getting cramped then. There was an article in the paper about it. The population problem.'

'Oh, I didn't mean to say it was crowded – just so very *big*. I mean, there was a time when they could fit everyone into a churchyard.'

'Doesn't sound sanitary,' he observed.

'It wasn't. That's why they had to start building big cemeteries like this. The ground used to rise up outside of the church until it came right up to the windows. Really.'

'Where'd you ever pick up a story like that?'

'From Lesley. He was full of morbid knowledge.'

'Oh.' Mickey quickened his pace to avoid any larger response. Louise's divorce was still a sore point with the Mangans, staunch Catholics all, though (as she had pointed out to her other, less-favored brother, Lawrence) her marriage could not have counted for much in the eyes of Mother Church, having never been consummated. Neither Louise nor four years of psychoanalysis had been of much benefit to Lesley.

'Oh, dear,' Louise said. 'It *won't* be a perfect day.'

Mickey turned around. 'Why?'

'The sun's gone under. Look.'

In
Loving Memory
of

MARJORIE EDNA
NOYES

who fell asleep May 6, 1911
Aged 5 years.
Also of Clement Hoffman
Uncle of the Above
who died Jan 24, 1923, aged 41 years

'Are you sure it's this hill?' Louise asked. 'Didn't you say between two *fir* trees? These are all pines.'

'To tell the truth, I'm not sure of anything now. It all looks so much alike. It never occurred to me how hard it would be to find again. Maybe it was the hill farther to the right.'

'That one? Or would it be farther back by now? You'll have to keep playing Virgil, I'm afraid. You know me – I can get lost on my way to the Laundromat.'

'Let's try it, anyhow. It's easier than going back to square one. Or would you rather rest for a moment?'

'Rest? I'm good for hours yet. Though I am glad I wore low heels. What does it look like, exactly, the stone?'

'Just a plain slab, like most of these, a rectangle with the edges rough and the face polished. Granite. Marble would have cost twice as much, and it doesn't last so well.'

'Did you use his initials – or his full name?'

'Mom gave them the whole works – Edward Augustus Mangan. I argued with her about it. He never liked people to know his name, but she felt it wouldn't be Christian, just the initials. She's down as Patricia, Wife of the Above.'

'It sums her up nicely.'

Mickey always remained neutral in Louise's quarrels with her mother, and so (was it not the special purpose of this day that these misunderstandings should be patched up once and for all?) he steered the conversation toward safe pieties:

'Why *didn't* you come, Louise? If it had been only a question of money, I'd have been glad to pay for your ticket.'

Louise saw no reason to express any doubt of this very doubtful statement. Ever since high school, Mickey had been touchy on the

subject of his stinginess. She replied in
the same slightly unctuous spirit of
reunion, 'I wanted to, of course, but it was so soon after the divorce,
and I was only inches away from a breakdown. Besides,' she went on,
unable to repress her legitimate grievance, 'except for the announcement, none of you had written to me. And in Dad's case, you know, I
didn't even receive the announcement. It was almost by accident that
I ever did find out.'

'HE GIVETH
HIS BELOVED SLEEP'

'I'm sure we sent one. Perhaps it got lost in the mail. That was the
time you were in England, or one of those places.'

'Well, it doesn't matter – I'm here now. Let's hope *they* are.'

At the base of the hill the path branched once more, both forks
going off, by Mickey's calculations, in wrong ways. They left it and
walked on the trim grass toward a row of newly planted poplars.
Bouquets of spring flowers, some withered, some still fresh, decorated the gravestones, which in this part of the cemetery seemed rather
statelier and (she observed) older. She didn't point this out to
Mickey, who was now visibly irritated at his failure to find their
parents' grave. It would hardly do to tell him that it made no
difference to her, that she'd come for his sake, not theirs.

Beyond the poplars there was an unexpected dip in the ground.
Pink hawthorn filled the small valley from end to end. The shaded
blossoms gave off a pallid glow, and
she remembered how, only five days
ago, the plane had risen above the
cloudbanks into such a sudden pink
luminescence as this.

STEPHEN BLYTHE
MARY BLYTHE

'Damn all!' Mickey said. It was an
admission of defeat: they were lost.

'Oh, darling, what does it matter that we've come a bit out of
the way? If we hadn't we would have never seen this. And it's
lovely!'

Mickey looked at Louise strangely. 'Darling' had possibly been the
wrong thing to say: it exceeded the limits he assigned to a sisterly
affection.

'We can't just turn our backs on this, you know. We *have* to go
down there. It won't take five minutes.'

Mickey looked at his watch. 'We shouldn't be late for lunch.'

'Just a sniff of those flowers. Then we'll go back to that first hill
and start fresh.'

'They are pretty, aren't they?' he conceded.

'It must be an accident. Cemeteries aren't supposed to be as pretty as all that. Who would bother going to heaven?'

That was rather overdoing it, she thought, but it seemed to work, for Mickey grinned and offered her his hand, quite voluntarily, as they stumbled down the slope zig-zagging between the marble angels and the elegant sarcophagi.

In Dear & Honored Memory of
GERALDINE
Cherished Wife of Martin Sweiger
who Departed this Life
February 4, 1887
Aged 54 years
'I am the Resurrection and the Life.'

The view northward across level ground terminated at the distance of about a mile in a violet haze; in all other directions extended a depthless continuum of hills as tall as or taller than this on which they stood. Nowhere were roads or buildings to be seen, only the green hills pocked with white, the stands of pine and poplar, fir and willow. No other persons, and no sound but their own heavy breathing and, now and again, the caucusing of unseen jays.

'It's impossible,' Mickey said in the same matter-of-fact tone in which he might have spoken of an unbalanced equation in one of his students' exam papers.

'It's silly,' Louise agreed. 'It's perfectly silly.'

'Cemeteries just aren't this *big*.'

'Of course not.'

'Joyce is going to be furious.'

'Won't she though? Imagine trying to explain to her that we got *lost* in a cemetery. It's impossible.'

This seemed to exhaust the possibilities of the topic. Once anything is firmly established in the category of the impossible it eludes further discussion or analysis. They had abandoned any pretense of looking for Mr. and Mrs. Mangan's gravestone an hour ago, though Louise still clung to their commemorative bouquet as to some fragment, a Miraculous Medal or a scapular, of a discarded faith. The wax-paper wrapping had frayed, and she had to be careful not to be pricked by the thorny stems. And the flowers themselves. . . .

MIZPAH

With a grimace she threw them away, as earlier, in his first fit of temper, Mickey had thrown away the squat tin vase.

Initially they had conceived of their project as finding their way back to the parking lot, simply that; now they were just trying to get out, by any exit, in any direction.

'There's no one here, have you noticed that?' Louise asked. 'I mean, there aren't even gardeners around. *Someone* has to cut the grass. And someone comes around with these flowers. We keep seeing fresh flowers everywhere.'

'Mm, yes.'

Mickey's eyes avoided hers. Perhaps the same point had already occurred to him, but he had not spoken out of a sense of delicacy. He knew her too little to be able to gauge her susceptibility to panic. She, for her part, could not gauge his. The consequence was that they both remained remarkably cool.

'It would be all right, you know, if this were a *wood*. People do get lost in woods, brothers and sisters especially. But not in cemeteries!' She essayed a careful laugh, conscious, bounded, calm.

'Well, which way do you think?' he asked.

'For plunging on? East, I suppose. I'm still convinced that that's where the car should be. But which way is east?'

Mickey regarded the sun, now at its zenith, and consulted his wristwatch. 'It's twelve-thirty, and we're on Daylight Saving Time. So I'd say *that* would be east, give or take fifteen degrees either way.' He pointed to the crest of the highest hill that they could see, behind which gray clouds had begun massing.

'The question is – should we climb it or follow the low ground? It's a bit higher than this hill, we might see farther.'

'Not another hill, Mickey, please! I really am a bit bushed. Not to speak of being hungry. I wish now that I could eat those farmhouse breakfasts that you do.'

'Yeah. Jesus.'

At the mention of food the thought of Joyce returned more vividly to both of them, the dismal thought of the explanations that would have to be made, of the failure of those explanations.

TO DEAR
FLORRIE
FROM HER MOM
SEPT 18 1960

The moment they reached the bottom of the hill the quiet of the day was broken by a mechanical roar that seemed to come from all the hills at once. *A truck!* she thought. The highway! Then she recognized the sound and looked up. A jet flew past westward. It was unusually low. She wondered if the pilot could have seen them down here. Perhaps just barely, if he'd known where to look. She pictured herself stripped to her brassiere, waving her white blouse at the airplane: it would never do.

'Flying that low, he must be coming in for a landing,' Mickey said. 'But I didn't think the airport was so close. In any case, he should be flying east.'

'Maybe he's taking off.'

The jet passed out of sight, leaving behind only its white, precise tail that slowly feathered out into the blue.

Louise giggled.

'Something amusing?'

'I was thinking – wouldn't it be funny if they sent out a rescue party for us? It would be in all the papers.'

'Jesus!' Mickey said. 'Don't make jokes like that.'

S. † P.

EUSTACHY TUSTANOWSKI

DOKTOR MEDYCYNY

18.5.1837–8.12.1918

The sprinkler revolved and jets of water arched up in two opposing spirals, fell with the sheen of dull silver.

They broke into a run down the grassy incline. Mickey tripped and it was Louise who reached the sprinkler first. Grasping the brass tube she drank avidly at the pencil-thin stream of water. She had scarcely wet her clothes.

When she looked up, mouth numbed with cold, Mickey was still sitting where he had fallen.

'Oh, it tastes wonderful! I didn't realize how thirsty – What's wrong, darling?'

Mickey was swearing, with great seriousness and small invention. Louise dashed away from the sprinkler, which resumed its duties, and went to her brother. 'What *is* it?'

He began to pull grass up around the half-submerged marker over which he'd tripped. The marker read, simply:

CLAESZ

'It's this son of a bitch that's the matter. He tripped me. I think I've sprained something, and it hurts like the devil.'

'Shouldn't you try to walk on it now – before it starts to swell?'

Mickey stood up, swearing, and hobbled toward the sprinkler. Before he could catch hold of the revolving brass arm he had been drenched. When he'd had his fill he turned the sprinkler upside down in the grass.

'You know what I want to do?' he said, seating himself on the nearest gravestone and removing his right shoe and sock. 'I want to smash something. I'd like to take a big sledgehammer and start smashing in all these goddamn tombs.'

TO OUR
DARLING
MOTHER
AND FATHER
'IN GOD'S KEEPING'

'Mickey, it can't be *very* much farther to one of the gates. We've been walking for miles, I'm sure we have. It's three o'clock by my watch. *Miles!*'

'I'll bet we've been walking in circles. People are supposed to do that when they're lost in the snow. It's the only explanation.'

'But we took our direction from the sun,' Louise objected.

'The sun! And what direction would that be? There *is* no sun.' And indeed the light now issued from the clouds with such perfect uniformity that this was not any longer a viable strategy. There were a few areas of somewhat more intense brightness, but these seemed to be distributed at random through the prevailing gray.

'Do you know what it's going to do? It's going to start raining, *that's* what it's going to do!' He smiled, a melancholy but triumphant prophet. The sprained ankle had triggered the latent melodramatist in Mickey, whose talents usually had no larger scope than family bickering and the bloodless victories of the classroom. Now, like Lear, he had all nature ranged against him.

'We'll wait it out under a pine tree if it does.'

'Wait it out! Jesus, Louise! It's three o'clock. Joyce has probably telephoned everyone we know, asking for us. Maybe she'll even drive out here and see the car parked in the lot.'

'Fine. Then someone can start looking for us.'

'You don't think they're going to believe us when we tell them we were lost, do you? Lost – in a cemetery!'

'What *will* they think, then?' Louise asked angrily. She knew he wouldn't dare put it into so many words, and he didn't.

'Jesus,' he said.

'Besides, your ankle is a perfect alibi. Anyone can get lost in a cemetery for a *little* while. We got lost, and then you sprained your

126

ankle and couldn't walk. I'll tell you what – I'll go on ahead and find the way out and then I'll come back here for you. I'll be very careful to memorize the way, I'll blaze a trail. What is it you have to do – drop breadcrumbs, or something like that? And with luck I'll find someone to help you back. How's that?'

Mickey nodded glumly.

She set off up the nearest hill to take her bearings. In this part of the cemetery there seemed to be no paths at all, and the lawn was not so well cared for. Though someone, surely, had set that sprinkler going – and not too long ago, either, or the ground about it would have been muddy. Really, they had been behaving quite irrationally about the whole thing.

Every ten or twelve yards she would glance back at Mickey, who was resting his face in his hands. His pose reminded her vaguely of some painting she had seen. Her year in Europe with Lesley had melted into a single conglomerate blur of churches and paintings and heavy meals. All afternoon, as her hunger had grown, she had chattered on compulsively about restaurants in Paris, in Amsterdam, in Genoa; German sausages, curried chicken, English puddings, the sweet heavy wines of Spain, and the hopeless inadequacy of all European coffees.

GARDENS OF MEMORY AND PEACE

At the top of the hill she rested, out of breath, against a tall oak. The close horizon of placid, swelling lawns, this endless unvarying cyclorama, filled her now with a subdued, almost meditative, horror. The ring of hills seemed to tighten more closely around her with each new prospect.

No, she would not be able to journey off into that blankness alone. Through the unacknowledged panic of the afternoon it had been Mickey's presence that had buoyed her up, and even in this brief moment away from him, not even out of his sight, she could sense the encroachment of those thoughts she had so far been able to evade. Even if they could not be evaded much longer, she did not want to have to face them on her own.

'Nothing?' he asked when she returned.

'Nothing. Those hills – they were the same hills we've seen all day. And I just couldn't . . . not by myself.'

'You don't have to explain. I was feeling much the same thing as soon as you left. It was like . . . I don't know, like being left alone in the dark.'

She squeezed his hand, grateful for his understanding. He no longer seemed embarrassed at her touch.

'It's so absurd, isn't it?'

'Absurd? It's supernatural, kid.'

She had to laugh at that.

'Oh, Jesus, it's starting to rain.'

'Let me help you as far as that pine. We'll be dry there.'

They waited out the rainstorm under the pine, telling each other stories about Europe and the high school where Mickey taught physics and algebra and coached the basketball team, about the whole sick mess with Lesley and about Joyce's hundreds of spiteful, sponging relations. It was the best talk they'd managed to have since Louise had come to town.

And after the rain the sky began to clear, though because of the wind that had sprung up the day remained, permanently, chillier.

ALDRIDGE

LOUIS	ANN	JAMES
1868–	1882–	1905–
1927	1939	

'To live in the hearts of those
we love is not to die.'

After so many hours of silence the birds came as a relief. They arrived in a great whirling flock that passed beyond the westward slopes, returning a minute later from the north to settle in the elms on both sides of the hollow. Their clamor had the reassuring quality that can sometimes be found in a noisy bar or a busy street, a pledge of the continuity of exterior event.

During their talk under the pine, Mickey's right foot had swollen so badly that he could no longer squeeze into his shoe, which now dangled by its laces from his belt. He walked with the help of a branch stripped from the same accommodating pine.

They did not talk, for what could they have spoken of but their improbable dilemma? There comes a point when analysis, a too-conscious awareness, becomes a liability and hindrance to action, and Louise feared that they had overstepped that point already. Their talk had suggested to her, at least, the central problem in this business of being lost: whether it had its source in the nature of the woods or in the nature of the orphans lost in those woods? In other words, could they be in any sense, perhaps without their knowing it, malingering? Each sequent hour seemed to argue for this hypothesis.

SUFFER LITTLE CHILDREN TO COME UNTO ME

The alternative – that the cemetery itself was responsible for their plight, that it was quite as big as it seemed to be – was intolerable and, in the most literal sense, unthinkable. Therefore (because it was unthinkable) they would not speak of it.

When they came upon the brook, it was a complete surprise. Had they been walking at a faster pace they might have tumbled right into it. The longer grass concealed the brink, just as the chattering of the birds had masked the sound.

'The stream!' Mickey said.

They looked up with one accord, as though expecting to see the parking lot just a few yards on. The brook curved out of sight around the base of a hill.

'It can't be much farther on,' Louise argued. 'The *only* time we saw the stream today was from that first hill.'

'Oh, Jesus,' Mickey said with relief.

'And it proves one thing – it proves we haven't been walking in circles, not entirely.'

Mickey put his hand in the water. 'It's flowing that way.' He nodded to the east-lying hill, where tesserae of marble and granite flared in the afternoon's declining light. 'Do we follow it upstream or downstream? What do you think? Louise, are you listening?'

This problem had occurred to Louise at the first sight of the brook, and she had been staring in the other direction, against the sun, while Mickey spoke.

'Look,' she said.

A crumpled mass of green paper was floating toward them. She stooped and picked it dripping from the water. She smoothed it on the grass.

'Is it the same?' he asked.

'I'm sure it is. See, where the stems have torn it. Do you believe in portents, Mickey?'

'I don't follow you.'

'The trouble is, even if one believes in them, how are they to be interpreted?'

'Hey, let's get into gear, sister dear. Which way – upstream or down?'

'Downstream? I'm not a very experienced druid.'

'Then downstream it is.'

They followed the winding course of the brook for an hour. Louise figured that in the space of an hour they could not accomplish more than a mile at Mickey's best pace.

Though they both believed they had found the thread that would lead them from the labyrinth, they remained chary of talk. Only once did Mickey break the hopeful silence:

'You know, Joyce will be talking about this for the rest of her life.'

Louise smiled. 'She won't be the only one.'

The brook emptied into a small pool that drained into two culverts. The culverts took their course thence under a hill. They climbed the hill, from which they were able to see other hills. The western horizon was an intense violet, veined with pink. The sun had set.

'I think I'm going to scream,' Louise said.

Instead, she sat down and began to cry. Mickey put his arm around her, but he couldn't think of anything reassuring to say.

They stayed on the hilltop until it was quite dark, hoping to see electric lights or at least the nimbus that would hover above a large congregation of lights, but they saw only the stars and the blackness behind the stars. When the mosquitoes discoverd them, they started off once again, following the probable course of the culverts.

At night the cemetery reminded them even more of the golf course of their youth. They held hands as they walked along, and sang, together, all the songs they could remember from *Oklahoma* and *The King and I*.

Here lies
the mortal body
of

LT. JOHN FRANCIS KNYE

only son of
FELIX & LORRAINE KNYE
Who was killed in action
Aug. 7, 1943, Aged 20 years.

'Taken to his Eternal Home'

Because the grounds were so well kept up, it was hard to gather an adequate supply of dry wood. Mickey built up the fire while Louise scouted about the neighboring slopes, foraging. As long as she kept in sight of the flames she didn't feel uneasy. On her third excursion she came upon a veritable windfall – two large fir branches that had come down in a storm some time before and were fairly dry by now, the fir tree itself having acted as an umbrella during subsequent downpours. They were so heavy she had to make a separate trip for each branch. With these broken up and stockpiled they decided they were well ahead of the game.

'With any luck,' Mickey said, 'someone will notice the glow of the fire and report it. I'm sure fires are illegal in a cemetery.'

'Oh, I'm sure.'

'I've reached the point where I'd be happy to be arrested. Anything to get out of this place.'

'Ditto me. Though let's hope they don't come *too* soon – I'd hate to think I'd gathered all this wood to no purpose. It's a nice fire.'

REQUIESCAT
IN PACE

'The day hasn't been an entire loss, I guess. We've managed to have our family reunion after all. Though it may have cost you an extra day.'

'As long as I have an excuse that satisfies my conscience, I don't mind the time lost. It's your ankle I worry about. How is it now?'

'All right if I keep still.'

'I keep having the funny feeling that the parking lot is probably only a hundred yards away, just out of sight.'

'I've had that feeling all day. Warm?'

'The front of me is toasting to a crisp, but my back is a little chilly. What saint was it said, "I'm done on this side – you can turn me over"?'

'St. Lawrence.'

'Lawrence, of course. I'll bet Joyce has been phoning him all day. My God, the thought of facing them . . .'

Most of the time they watched the fire in silence. Mickey lay on his left side, so that he could prop his bad foot on a low marker. Louise sat with her arms about her legs, her chin resting on her knees. Whenever the fire grew low she added another branch and the flames would leap up to double or treble their height until the brittle foliage had been consumed. At regular intervals white moths would flutter into the flames to achieve a final metamorphosis.

'The one thing I *don't* understand,' Mickey said, resuming the talk they had begun under the pine tree, 'is why you married him in the first place. You can't blame him for deceiving you.'

'Well, he *was* handsome. And very personable. Everyone agreed that we would make a dazzling couple, and they were right, in a way. Then, I suppose a woman likes to think that she can *redeem* that kind of man.'

'It doesn't sound as though he wanted redeeming.'

GOD IS LOVE

'Oh, he did and he didn't. In his own way he was quite fond of me. Besides, you forget – he was famous. In the set we moved in, most women would have done the same dumb thing. It's a different world.'

'And you say that you knew from the first how it would turn out.'

'When I thought about it. Perhaps *that* was the determining reason. Maybe it was just the kind of marriage I wanted, a kind of pantomime. It was the kind *he* wanted. Please, let's not talk about it now?'

'I'm sorry. I didn't want to upset you.'

'Oh, I'm very hard to upset. Today has proved that. I'm just tired. Mickey, do you still know the names of all the stars?'

'Some. I've forgotten a lot.'

'Teach me.'

Mickey pointed out the brighter constellations that could be seen despite the glare from the fire. Afterwards she laid her head in his lap to see if she could sleep. Untended, the fire began to die out, but they were resigned to this. Eventually they would have used up all the wood in any case. Where their bodies touched they kept warm.

'Mickey? Are you awake?'

'Yes. I didn't think you were.'

'When you told me, this morning, to take my sweater – how could you possibly have *known*?'

'Strange, isn't it? I was thinking almost the same thing a little while ago.'

Sometimes she stared up at the constellations, murmuring drowsily their renascent names; sometimes her eyes were closed. Mickey's hand was twined comfortingly in her hair.

Tomorrow she would have to fly back and it would all return to the way it had been. Mickey would write, once or twice, letters about his children's health, the terrible winters, his basketball team. And she would eat expensive lunches at hotels, and talk, for hours, with the same people, or with new people who would too quickly become the same people. She would go to their parties, their shows . . .

UNTIL
THE DAY BREAK

Tomorrow.

No. That was over. Tomorrow would find them in the cemetery still. They would walk across the same perpetual lawns. They were lost. They would continue to be lost. The cemetery would stretch on and on like – what had he said before? – like a Moebius strip. The same hills speckled with white rectangles of stone, striped with gravel paths. The same blue sky. In an almost perfect silence they would walk through the cemetery, lost. They would learn to eat tubers and roots and pine nuts. Perhaps they would find a way to catch small birds. Quite possibly. She fell asleep in her brother's arms, smiling: it was just like old times.

In Remembrance of
EDWARD AUGUSTUS MANGAN
1886 – 1967

and of
PATRICIA, Wife of the Above
1900 – 1968

'Let us quickly hasten to the Gate of Ivory'

TROUBLE WITH WATER
Horace L. Gold

*It's 1938, I'm twenty-four, and I'm walking in dismal rain towards
John Campbell's office for a story conference, me without a single
idea in my head . . . except worried subvocalization of an old song
about walking (running?) between the raindrops. Sudden elation:
'Hey, how about a man whom water will not touch?'*

*I tell John about experiment going blooey and inverted ionization
– and he, unbelievably, tells me to have something like a* water
gnome put a *curse* on *the protagonist! 'But you're putting out*
Astounding Science Fiction, *and that's fantasy!' I protest. 'Water
gnome . . . curse,' he repeats. 'Now go home and write it.'*

*I leave in complete confoundment. Months later, after suffering all
of my hero's humiliations and degradations while writing the tale,
John hands me a copy of the magazine fresh off the presses and sits
back smugly, watching my face. I flip through, look at the illus-
tration and am handing it back to him when he yells, 'The logo!
Look at the logo!' 'What's a logo?' I ask, innocently. 'The* title, you
idiot! The title of the magazine!'

It was the famous Volume 1, Number 1 of Unknown. *And I was in
it! Isaac Asimov can't make that statement.*

*But Isaac – and John, and Mr Lawlor (the head of Street & Smith)
and everybody else – said, 'It's the funniest story I ever read!'*

*Funny? After all Greenberg and I had suffered through? And the
millions of Jews under Hitler – were they funny, too?*

*I swore to prove otherwise. A year later, with 'Warm, Dark
Places', which John called 'the nastiest, most frightening story ever
written', I did.*

Greenberg did not deserve his surroundings. He was the first
fisherman of the season, which guaranteed him a fine catch; he sat in
a dry boat – one without a single leak – far out on a lake that was

134

ruffled only enough to agitate his artificial fly. The sun was warm, the air was cool; he sat comfortably on a cushion; he had brought a hearty lunch; and two bottles of beer hung over the stern in the cold water.

Any other man would have been soaked with joy to be fishing on such a splendid day. Normally, Greenberg himself would have been ecstatic, but instead of relaxing and waiting for a nibble, he was plagued by worries.

This short, slightly gross, definitely bald, eminently respectable businessman lived a gypsy life. During the summer he lived in a hotel with kitchen privileges in Rockaway; winters he lived in a hotel with kitchen privileges in Florida; and in both places he operated concessions. For years now, rain had fallen on schedule every week end, and there had been storms and floods on Decoration Day, July 4th and Labor Day. He did not love his life, but it was a way of making a living.

He closed his eyes and groaned. If he had only had a son instead of his Rosie! Then things would have been mighty different—

For one thing, a son could run the hot dog and hamburger griddle, Esther could draw beer, and he would make soft drinks. There would be small difference in the profits, Greenberg admitted to himself; but at least those profits could be put aside for old age, instead of toward a dowry for his miserably ugly, dumpy, pitifully eager Rosie.

'All right – so what do I care if she don't get married?' he had cried to his wife a thousand times 'I'll support her. Other men can set up boys in candy stores with soda fountains that have only two spigots. Why should I have to give a boy a regular International Casino?'

'May your tongue rot in your head, you no-good piker!' she would scream. 'It ain't right for a girl to be an old maid. If we have to die in the poorhouse, I'll get my poor Rosie a husband. Every penny we don't need for living goes to her dowry!'

Greenberg did not hate his daughter, nor did he blame her for his misfortunes; yet, because of her, he was fishing with a broken rod that he had to tape together.

That morning his wife opened her eyes and saw him packing his equipment. She instantly came awake. 'Go ahead!' she shrilled – speaking in a conversational tone was not one of her accomplishments – 'Go fishing, you loafer! Leave me here alone. I can connect the beer pipes and the gas for soda water. I can buy ice cream, frankfurters, rolls, sirup, and watch the gas and electric men at the same time. Go ahead – go fishing!'

'I ordered everything,' he mumbled soothingly. 'The gas and electric won't be turned on today. I only wanted to go fishing – it's my last chance. Tomorrow we open the concession. Tell the truth, Esther, can I go fishing after we open?'

'I don't care about that. Am I your wife or ain't I, that you should go ordering everything without asking me—'

He defended his actions. It was a tactical mistake. While she was still in bed, he should have picked up his equipment and left. By the time the argument got around to Rosie's dowry, she stood facing him.

'For myself I don't care,' she yelled. 'What kind of a monster are you that you can go fishing while your daughter eats her heart out? And on a day like this yet! You should only have to make supper and dress Rosie up. A lot you care that a nice boy is coming to supper tonight and maybe take Rosie out, you no-good father, you!'

From that point it was only one hot protest and a shrill curse to finding himself clutching half a broken rod, with the other half being flung at his head.

Now he sat in his beautifully dry boat on an excellent game lake far out on Long Island, desperately aware that any average fish might collapse his taped rod.

What else could he expect? He had missed his train; he had had to wait for the boathouse proprietor; his favorite dry fly was missing; and, since morning, not a fish had struck at the bait. Not a single fish!

And it was getting late. He had no more patience. He ripped the cap off a bottle of beer and drank it, in order to gain courage to change his fly for a less sporting bloodworm. It hurt him, but he wanted a fish.

The hook and the squirming worm sank. Before it came to rest, he felt a nibble. He sucked in his breath exultantly and snapped the hook deep into the fish's mouth. Sometimes, he thought philosophically, they just won't take artificial bait. He reeled in slowly.

'Oh, Lord,' he prayed, 'a dollar for charity – just don't let the rod bend in half where I taped it!'

It was sagging dangerously. He looked at it unhappily and raised his ante to five dollars; even at that price it looked impossible. He dipped his rod into the water, parallel with the line, to remove the strain. He was glad no one could see him do it. The line reeled in without a fight.

'Have I – God forbid! – got an eel or something not kosher?' he mumbled. 'A plague on you – why don't you fight?'

136

He did not really care what it was – even an eel – anything at all.

He pulled in a long, pointed, brimless green hat.

For a moment he glared at it. His mouth hardened. Then, viciously, he yanked the hat off the hook, threw it on the floor and trampled on it. He rubbed his hands together in anguish.

'All day I fish,' he wailed, 'two dollars for train fare, a dollar for a boat, a quarter for bait, a new rod I got to buy – and a five-dollar mortgage charity has got on me. For what? For you, you hat, you!'

Out in the water an extremely civil voice asked politely: 'May I have my hat, please?'

Greenberg glowered up. He saw a little man come swimming vigorously through the water toward him: small arms crossed with enormous dignity, vast ears on a pointed face propelling him quite rapidly and efficiently. With serious determination he drove through the water, and, at the starboard rail, his amazing ears kept him stationary while he looked gravely at Greenberg.

'You are stamping on my hat,' he pointed out without anger.

To Greenberg this was highly unimportant. 'With the ears you're swimming,' he grinned in a superior way. 'Do you look funny!'

'How else could I swim?' the little man asked politely.

'With the arms and legs, like a regular human being, of course.'

'But I am not a human being. I am a water gnome, a relative of the more common mining gnome. I cannot swim with my arms, because they must be crossed to give an appearance of dignity suitable to a water gnome; and my feet are used for writing and holding things. On the other hand, my ears are perfectly adapted for propulsion in water. Consequently, I employ them for that purpose. But please, my hat – there are several matters requiring my immediate attention, and I must not waste time.'

Greenberg's unpleasant attitude toward the remarkably civil gnome is easily understandable. He had found someone he could feel superior to, and, by insulting him, his depressed ego could expand. The water gnome certainly looked inoffensive enough, being only two feet tall.

'What you got that's so important to do, Big Ears?' he asked nastily.

Greenberg hoped the gnome would be offended. He was not, since his ears, to him, were perfectly normal, just as you would not be insulted if a member of a race of atrophied beings were to call you 'Big Muscles'. You might even feel flattered.

'I really must hurry,' the gnome said, almost anxiously. 'But if I have to answer your questions in order to get back my hat – we are engaged in restocking the Eastern waters with fish. Last year there was quite a drain. The bureau of fisheries is cooperating with us to some extent, but, of course, we cannot depend too much on them. Until the population rises to normal, every fish has instructions not to nibble.'

Greenberg allowed himself a smile, an annoyingly skeptical smile.

'My main work,' the gnome went on resignedly, 'is control of the rainfall over the Eastern seaboard. Our fact-finding committee, which is scientifically situated in the meteorological center of the continent, coordinates the rainfall needs of the entire continent; and when they determine the amount of rain needed in particular spots of the East, I make it rain to that extent. Now may I have my hat, please?'

Greenberg laughed coarsely. 'The first lie was big enough – about telling the fish not to bite. You make it rain like I'm President of the United States!' He bent toward the gnome slyly. 'How's about proof?'

'Certainly, if you insist.' The gnome raised his patient, triangular face toward a particularly clear blue spot in the sky, a trifle to one side of Greenberg. 'Watch that bit of the sky.'

Greenberg looked up humorously. Even when a small dark cloud rapidly formed in the previously clear spot, his grin remained broad. It could have been coincidental. But then large drops of undeniable rain fell over a twenty-foot circle; and Greenberg's mocking grin shrank and grew sour.

He glared hatred at the gnome, finally convinced. 'So you're the dirty crook who makes it rain on week ends!'

'Usually on week ends during the summer,' the gnome admitted. 'Ninety-two percent of water consumption is on weekdays. Obviously we must replace that water. The week ends, of course, are the logical time.'

'But, you thief!' Greenberg cried hysterically. 'You murderer! What do you care what you do to my concession with your rain! It ain't bad enough business would be rotten even without rain, you got to make floods!'

'I'm sorry,' the gnome replied, untouched by Greenberg's rhetoric. 'We do not create rainfall for the benefit of men. We are here to protect the fish.

'Now please give me my hat. I have wasted enough time, when I should be preparing the extremely heavy rain needed for this coming week end.'

Greenberg jumped to his feet in the unsteady boat. 'Rain this week end – when I can maybe make a profit for a change! A lot you care if you ruin business. May you and your fish die a horrible, lingering death.'

And he furiously ripped the green hat to pieces and hurled them at the gnome.

'I'm really sorry you did that,' the little fellow said calmly, his huge ears treading water without the slightest increase of pace to indicate his anger. 'We Little Folk have no tempers to lose. Nevertheless, occasionally we find it necessary to discipline certain of your people, in order to retain our dignity. I am not malignant; but, since you hate water and those who live in it, water and those who live in it will keep away from you.'

With his arms still folded in great dignity, the tiny water gnome flipped his vast ears and disappeared in a neat surface dive.

Greenberg glowered at the spreading circles of waves. He did not grasp the gnome's final restraining order; he did not even attempt to interpret it. Instead he glared angrily out of the corner of his eye at the phenomenal circle of rain that fell from a perfectly clear sky. The gnome must have remembered it at length, for a moment later the rain stopped. Like shutting off a faucet, Greenberg unwillingly thought.

'Good-by, week-end business,' he growled. 'If Esther finds out I got into an argument with the guy who makes it rain—'

He made an underhand cast, hoping for just one fish. The line flew out over the water; then the hook arched upward and came to rest several inches above the surface, hanging quite steadily and without support in the air.

'Well, go down in the water, damn you!' Greenberg said viciously, and he swished his rod back and forth to pull the hook down from its ridiculous levitation. It refused.

Muttering something incoherent about being hanged before he'd give in, Greenberg hurled his useless rod at the water. By this time he was not surprised when it hovered in the air above the lake. He merely glanced red-eyed at it, tossed out the remains of the gnome's hat, and snatched up the oars.

When he pulled back on them to row to land, they did not touch the water – naturally. Instead they flashed unimpeded through the air, and Greenberg tumbled into the bow.

'Aha!' he grated. 'Here's where the trouble begins.' He bent over the side. As he had suspected, the keel floated a remarkable distance above the lake.

By rowing against the air, he moved with maddening slowness toward shore, like a medieval conception of a flying machine. His main concern was that no one should see him in his humiliating position.

At the hotel he tried to sneak past the kitchen to the bathroom. He knew that Esther waited to curse him for fishing the day before opening, but more especially on the very day that a nice boy was coming to see her Rosie. If he could dress in a hurry, she might have less to say—

'Oh, there you are, you good-for-nothing!'

He froze to a halt.

'Look at you!' she screamed shrilly. 'Filthy – you stink from fish!'

'I didn't catch anything, darling,' he protested timidly.

'You stink anyhow. Go take a bath, may you drown in it! Get dressed in two minutes or less, and entertain the boy when he gets here. Hurry!'

He locked himself in, happy to escape her voice, started the water in the tub, and stripped from the waist up. A hot bath, he hoped, would rid him of his depressed feeling.

First, no fish; now, rain on week ends! What would Esther say – if she knew, of course. And, of course, he would not tell her.

'Let myself in for a lifetime of curses!' he sneered. 'Ha!'

He clamped a new blade into his razor, opened the tube of shaving cream, and stared objectively at the mirror. The dominant feature of the soft, chubby face that stared back was its ugly black stubble; but he set his stubborn chin and glowered. He really looked quite fierce and indomitable. Unfortunately, Esther never saw his face in that uncharacteristic pose, otherwise she would speak more softly.

'Herman Greenberg never gives in!' he whispered between savagely hardened lips. 'Rain on week ends, no fish – anything he wants; a lot I care! Believe me, he'll come crawling to me before I go to him.'

He gradually became aware that his shaving brush was not getting wet. When he looked down and saw the water dividing into streams that flowed around it, his determined face slipped and grew desperately anxious. He tried to trap the water – by catching it in his cupped hands, by creeping up on it from behind, as if it were some shy animal, and shoving his brush at it – but it broke and ran away from his touch. Then he jammed his palm against the faucet. Defeated, he heard it gurgle back down the pipe, probably as far as the main.

'What do I do now?' he groaned. 'Will Esther give it to me if I don't take a shave! But how? . . . I can't shave without water.'

Glumly, he shut off the bath, undressed and stepped into the tub. He lay down to soak. It took a moment of horrified stupor to realize that he was completely dry and that he lay in a waterless bathtub. The water, in one surge of revulsion, had swept out onto the floor.

'Herman, stop splashing!' his wife yelled. 'I just washed that floor. If I find one little puddle I'll murder you!'

Greenberg surveyed the instep-deep pool over the bathroom floor. 'Yes, my love,' he croaked unhappily.

With an inadequate washrag he chased the elusive water, hoping to mop it all up before it could seep through to the apartment below. His washrag remained dry, however, and he knew that the ceiling underneath was dripping. The water was still on the floor.

In despair, he sat on the edge of the bathtub. For some time he sat in silence. Then his wife banged on the door, urging him to come out. He started and dressed moodily.

When he sneaked out and shut the bathroom door tightly on the floor inside, he was extremely dirty and his face was raw where he had experimentally attempted to shave with a dry razor.

'Rosie!' he called in a hoarse whisper. 'Sh! Where's Mamma?'

His daughter sat on the studio couch and applied nail polish to her stubby fingers. 'You look terrible,' she said in a conversational tone. 'Aren't you going to shave?'

He recoiled at the sound of her voice, which, to him, roared out like a siren. 'Quiet, Rosie! Sh!' And for further emphasis, he shoved his lips out against a warning finger. He heard his wife striding heavily around the kitchen. 'Rosie,' he cooed, 'I'll give you a dollar if you'll mop up the water I spilled in the bathroom.'

'I can't, Papa,' she stated firmly. 'I'm all dressed.'

'Two dollars, Rosie – all right, two and a half, you blackmailer.'

He flinched when he heard her gasp in the bathroom; but, when she came out with soaked shoes, he fled downstairs. He wandered aimlessly toward the village.

Now he was in for it, he thought; screams from Esther, tears from Rosie – plus a new pair of shoes for Rosie and two and a half dollars. It would be worse, though, if he could not get rid of his whiskers—

Rubbing the tender spots where his dry razor had raked his face, he mused blankly at a drugstore window. He saw nothing to help him, but he went inside anyhow and stood hopefully at the drug counter. A face peered at him through a space scratched in the wall case mirror, and the druggist came out. A nice-looking, intelligent fellow, Greenberg saw at a glance.

'What you got for shaving that I can use without water?' he asked.

'Skin irritation, eh?' the pharmacist replied. 'I got something very good for that.'

'No. It's just— Well, I don't like to shave with water.'

The druggist seemed disappointed. 'Well, I got brushless shaving cream.' Then he brightened. 'But I got an electric razor – much better.'

'How much?' Greenberg asked cautiously.

'Only fifteen dollars, and it lasts a lifetime.'

'Give me the shaving cream,' Greenberg said coldly.

With the tactical science of a military expert, he walked around until some time after dark. Only then did he go back to the hotel, to wait outside. It was after seven, he was getting hungry, and the people who entered the hotel he knew as permanent summer guests. At last a stranger passed him and ran up the stairs.

Greenberg hesitated for a moment. The stranger was scarcely a boy, as Esther had definitely termed him, but Greenberg reasoned that her term was merely wish-fulfillment, and he jauntily ran up behind him.

He allowed a few minutes to pass, for the man to introduce himself and let Esther and Rosie don their company manners. Then, secure in the knowledge that there would be no scene until the guest left, he entered.

He waded through a hostile atmosphere, urbanely shook hands with Sammie Katz, who was a doctor – probably, Greenberg thought shrewdly, in search of an office – and excused himself.

In the bathroom he carefully read the directions for using brushless shaving cream. He felt less confident when he realized that he had to wash his face thoroughly with soap and water, but without benefit of either, he spread the cream on, patted it, and waited for his beard to soften. It did not, as he discovered while shaving. He wiped his face dry. The towel was sticky and black, with whiskers suspended in paste, and, for that, he knew, there would be more hell to pay. He shrugged resignedly. He would have to spend fifteen dollars for an electric razor after all; this foolishness was costing him a fortune!

That they were waiting for him before beginning supper, was, he knew, only a gesture for the sake of company. Without changing her hard, brilliant smile, Esther whispered: 'Wait! I'll get you later—'

He smiled back, his tortured, slashed face creasing painfully. All that could be changed by his being enormously pleasant to Rosie's young man. If he could slip Sammie a few dollars – more expense, he groaned – to take Rosie out, Esther would forgive everything.

He was too engaged in beaming and putting Sammie at ease to think of what would happen after he ate caviar canapes. Under other circumstances Greenberg would have been repulsed by Sammie's ultra professional waxed mustache – an offensively small, pointed thing – and his commercial attitude toward poor Rosie; but Greenberg regarded him as a potential savior.

'You open an office yet, Doctor Katz?'

'Not yet. You know how things are. Anyhow, call me Sammie.'

Greenberg recognized the gambit with satisfaction, since it seemed to please Esther so much. At one stroke Sammie had ingratiated himself and begun bargaining negotiations.

Without another word, Greenberg lifted his spoon to attack the soup. It would be easy to snare this eager doctor. A *doctor*! No wonder Esther and Rosie were so puffed with joy.

In the proper company way, he pushed his spoon away from him. The soup spilled onto the tablecloth.

'Not so hard, you dope,' Esther hissed.

He drew the spoon toward him. The soup leaped off it like a live thing and splashed over him – turning, just before contact, to fall on the floor. He gulped and pushed the bowl away. This time the soup poured over the side of the plate and lay in a huge puddle on the table.

'I didn't want any soup anyhow,' he said in a horrible attempt at levity. Lucky for him, he thought wildly, that Sammie was there to pacify Esther with his smooth college talk – not a bad fellow, Sammie, in spite of his mustache; he'd come in handy at times.

Greenberg lapsed into a paralysis of fear. He was thirsty after having eaten the caviar, which beats herring any time as a thirst raiser. But the knowledge that he could not touch water without having it recoil and perhaps spill made his thirst a monumental craving. He attacked the problem cunningly.

The others were talking rapidly and rather hysterically. He waited until his courage was equal to his thirst; then he leaned over the table with a glass in his hand. 'Sammie, do you mind – a little water, huh?'

Sammie poured from a pitcher while Esther watched for more of his tricks. It was to be expected, but still he was shocked when the water exploded out of the glass directly at Sammie's only suit.

'If you'll excuse me,' Sammie said angrily, 'I don't like to eat with lunatics.'

And he left, though Esther cried and begged him to stay. Rosie was too stunned to move. But when the door closed, Greenberg raised his agonized eyes to watch his wife stalk murderously toward him.

Greenberg stood on the boardwalk outside his concession and glared blearily at the peaceful, blue, highly unpleasant ocean. He wondered what would happen if he started at the edge of the water and strode out. He could probably walk right to Europe on dry land.

It was early – much too early for business – and he was tired. Neither he nor Esther had slept; and it was practically certain that the neighbors hadn't either. But above all he was incredibly thirsty.

In a spirit of experimentation, he mixed a soda. Of course its high water content made it slop onto the floor. For breakfast he had surreptitiously tried fruit juice and coffee, without success.

With his tongue dry to the point of furriness, he sat weakly on a boardwalk bench in front of his concession. It was Friday morning, which meant that the day was clear, with a promise of intense heat. Had it been Saturday, it naturally would have been raining.

'This year,' he moaned, 'I'll be wiped out. If I can't mix sodas, why should beer stay in a glass for me? I thought I could hire a boy for ten dollars a week to run the hot-dog griddle; I could make sodas, and Esther could draw beer. All I can do is make hot dogs, Esther can still draw beer; but twenty or maybe twenty-five a week I got to pay a sodaman. I won't even come out square – a fortune I'll lose!'

The situation really was desperate. Concessions depend on too many factors to be anything but capriciously profitable.

His throat was fiery and his soft brown eyes held a fierce glaze when the gas and electric were turned on, the beer pipes connected, the tank of carbon dioxide hitched to the pump, and the refrigerator started.

Gradually, the beach was filling with bathers. Greenberg writhed on his bench and envied them. They could swim and drink without having liquids draw away from them as if in horror. They were not thirsty—

And then he saw his first customers approach. His business experience was that morning customers buy only soft drinks. In a mad haste he put up the shutters and fled to the hotel.

'Esther!' he cried. 'I got to tell you. I can't stand it—'

Threateningly, his wife held her broom like a baseball bat. 'Go back to the concession, you crazy fool. Ain't you done enough already?'

He could not be hurt more than he had been. For once he did not cringe. 'You got to help me, Esther.'

'Why didn't you shave, you no-good bum? Is that any way—'

'That's what I got to tell you. Yesterday I got into an argument with a water gnome—'

'A what?' Esther looked at him suspiciously.

'A water gnome,' he babbled in a rush of words. 'A little man so high, with big ears that he swims with, and he makes it rain—'

'Herman!' she screamed. 'Stop that nonsense. You're crazy!'

Greenberg pounded his forehead with his fist. 'I *ain't* crazy. Look, Esther. Come with me into the kitchen.'

She followed him readily enough, but her attitude made him feel more helpless and alone than ever. With her fists on her plump hips and her feet set wide, she cautiously watched him try to fill a glass of water.

'Don't you see?' he wailed. 'It won't go in the glass. It spills all over. It runs away from me.'

She was puzzled. 'What happened to you?'

Brokenly, Greenberg told of his encounter with the water gnome, leaving out no single degrading detail. 'And now I can't touch water,' he ended. 'I can't drink it. I can't make sodas. On top of it all, I got such a thirst, it's killing me.'

Esther's reaction was instantaneous. She threw her arms around him, drew his head down to her shoulder, and patted him comfortingly as if he were a child. 'Herman, my poor Herman!' she breathed tenderly. 'What did we ever do to deserve such a curse?'

'What shall I do, Esther?' he cried hopelessly.

She held him at arm's length. 'You got to go to a doctor,' she said firmly. 'How long can you go without drinking? Without water you'll die. Maybe sometimes I am a little hard on you, but you know I love you—'

'I know, Mamma,' he sighed. 'But how can a doctor help me?'

'Am I a doctor that I should know? Go anyhow. What can you lose?'

He hesitated. 'I need fifteen dollars for an electric razor,' he said in a low, weak voice.

'So?' she replied. 'If you got to, you got to. Go, darling. I'll take care of the concession.'

Greenberg no longer felt deserted and alone. He walked almost confidently to a doctor's office. Manfully, he explained his symptoms. The doctor listened with professional sympathy, until Greenberg reached his description of the water gnome.

Then his eyes glittered and narrowed. 'I know just the thing for you, Mr. Greenberg,' he interrupted. 'Sit there until I come back.'

Greenberg sat quietly. He even permitted himself a surge of hope. But it seemed only a moment later that he was vaguely conscious of a siren screaming toward him; and then he was overwhelmed by the doctor and two interns who pounced on him and tried to squeeze him into a bag.

He resisted, of course. He was terrified enough to punch wildly. 'What are you doing to me?' he shrieked. 'Don't put that thing on me!'

'Easy now,' the doctor soothed. 'Everything will be all right.'

It was on that humiliating scene that the policeman, required by law to accompany public ambulances, appeared. 'What's up?' he asked.

'Don't stand there, you fathead,' an intern shouted. 'This man's crazy. Help us get him into this strait jacket.'

But the policeman approached indecisively. 'Take it easy, Mr. Greenberg. They ain't gonna hurt you while I'm here. What's all this about?'

'Mike!' Greenberg cried, and clung to his protector's sleeve. 'They think I'm crazy—'

'Of course he's crazy,' the doctor stated. 'He came in here with a fantastic yarn about a water gnome putting a curse on him.'

'What kind of a curse, Mr. Greenberg?' Mike asked cautiously.

'I got into an argument with the water gnome who makes it rain and takes care of the fish,' Greenberg blurted. 'I tore up his hat. Now he won't let water touch me. I can't drink, or anything—'

The doctor nodded. 'There you are. Absolutely insane.'

'Shut up.' For a long moment Mike stared curiously at Greenberg. Then: 'Did any of you scientists think of testing him? Here, Mr. Greenberg.' He poured water into a paper cup and held it out.

Greenberg moved to take it. The water backed up against the cup's far lip; when he took it in his hand, the water shot out into the air.

'Crazy, is he?' Mike asked with heavy irony. 'I guess you don't know there's things like gnomes and elves. Come with me, Mr. Greenberg.'

They went out together and walked toward the boardwalk. Greenberg told Mike the entire story and explained how, besides being so uncomfortable to him personally, it would ruin him financially.

'Well, doctors can't help you,' Mike said at length. 'What do they know about the Little Folk? And I can't say I blame you for sassing the gnome. You ain't Irish or you'd have spoke with more respect to him. Anyhow, you're thirsty. Can't you drink *anything*?'

'Not a thing,' Greenberg said mournfully.

They entered the concession. A single glance told Greenberg that business was very quiet, but even that could not lower his feelings more than they already were. Esther clutched him as soon as she saw them.

'Well?' she asked anxiously.

Greenberg shrugged in despair. 'Nothing. He thought I was crazy.'

Mike stared at the bar. Memory seemed to struggle behind his reflective eyes. 'Sure,' he said after a long pause. 'Did you try beer, Mr. Greenberg? When I was a boy my old mother told me all about elves and gnomes and the rest of the Little Folk. She knew them, all right. They don't touch alcohol, you know. Try drawing a glass of beer—'

Greenberg trudged obediently behind the bar and held a glass under the spigot. Suddenly his despondent face brightened. Beer creamed into the glass – and stayed there! Mike and Esther grinned at each other as Greenberg threw back his head and furiously drank.

'Mike!' he crowed. 'I'm saved. You got to drink with me!'

'Well—' Mike protested feebly.

By late afternoon, Esther had to close the concession and take her husband and Mike to the hotel.

The following day, being Saturday, brought a flood of rain. Greenberg nursed an imposing hang-over that was constantly aggravated by his having to drink beer in order to satisfy his recurring thirst. He thought of forbidden icebags and alkaline drinks in an agony of longing.

'I can't stand it!' he groaned. 'Beer for breakfast – phooey!'

'It's better than nothing,' Esther said fatalistically.

'So help me, I don't know if it is. But, darling, you ain't mad at me on account of Sammie, are you?'

She smiled gently. 'Poo! Talk dowry and he'll come back quick.'

'That's what I thought. But what am I going to do about my curse?'

Cheerfully, Mike furled an umbrella and strode in with a little old woman, whom he introduced as his mother. Greenberg enviously saw evidence of the effectiveness of icebags and alkaline drinks, for Mike had been just as high as he the day before.

'Mike told me about you and the gnome,' the old lady said. 'Now I

147

know the Little Folk well, and I don't hold you to blame for insulting him, seeing you never met a gnome before. But I suppose you want to get rid of your curse. Are you repentant?'

Greenberg shuddered. 'Beer for breakfast! Can you ask?'

'Well, just you go to this lake and give the gnome proof.'

'What kind of proof?' Greenberg asked eagerly.

'Bring him sugar. The Little Folk love the stuff—'

Greenberg beamed. 'Did you hear that, Esther? I'll get a barrel—'

'They love sugar, but they can't eat it,' the old lady broke in. 'It melts in water. You got to figure out a way so it won't. Then the little gentleman'll know you're repentant for real.'

'Aha!' Greenberg cried. 'I knew there was a catch!'

There was a sympathetic silence while his agitated mind attacked the problem from all angles. Then the old lady said in awe: 'The minute I saw your place I knew Mike had told the truth. I never seen a sight like it in my life – rain coming down, like the flood, everywhere else; but all around this place, in a big circle, it's dry as a bone!'

While Greenberg scarcely heard her, Mike nodded and Esther seemed peculiarly interested in the phenomenon. When he admitted defeat and came out of his reflected stupor, he was alone in the concession, with only a vague memory of Esther's saying she would not be back for several hours.

'What am I going to do?' he muttered. 'Sugar that won't melt—' He drew a glass of beer and drank it thoughtfully. 'Particular they got to be yet. Ain't it good enough if I bring simple sirup? That's sweet.'

He puttered about the place, looking for something to do. He could not polish the fountain or the bar, and the few frankfurters broiling on the griddle probably would go to waste. The floor had already been swept. So he sat uneasily and worried his problem.

'Monday, no matter what,' he resolved, 'I'll go to the lake. It don't pay to go tomorrow. I'll only catch a cold because it'll rain.'

At last Esther returned, smiling in a strange way. She was extremely gentle, tender and thoughtful; and for that he was appreciative. But that night and all day Sunday he understood the reason for her happiness.

She had spread word that, while it rained in every other place all over town, their concession was miraculously dry. So, besides a headache that made his body throb in rhythm to its vast pulse, Greenberg had to work like six men satisfying the crowd who mobbed the place to see the miracle and enjoy the dry warmth.

How much they took in will never be known. Greenberg made it a practice not to discuss such personal matters. But it is quite definite that not even in 1929 had he done so well over a single week end.

Very early Monday morning he was dressing quietly, not to disturb his wife. Esther, however, raised herself on her elbow and looked at him doubtfully.

'Herman,' she called softly, 'do you really have to go?'

He turned, puzzled. 'What do you mean – do I have to go?'

'Well—' she hesitated. Then: 'Couldn't you wait until the end of the season, Herman, darling?'

He staggered back a step, his face working in horror. 'What kind of an idea is that for my own wife to have?' he croaked. 'Beer I have to drink instead of water. How can I stand it? Do you think I *like* beer? I can't wash myself. Already people don't like to stand near me; and how will they act at the end of the season? I go around looking like a bum because my beard is too tough for an electric razor, and I'm all the time drunk – the first Greenberg to be a drunkard. I want to be respected—'

'I know, Herman, darling,' she sighed. 'But I thought for the sake of our Rosie— Such a business we've never done like we did this week end. If it rains every Saturday and Sunday, but not on our concession, we'll make a *fortune!*'

'Esther!' Herman cried, shocked. 'Doesn't my health mean anything?'

'Of course, darling. Only I thought maybe you could stand it for—'

He snatched his hat, tie and jacket, and slammed the door. Outside, though, he stood indeterminedly. He could hear his wife crying, and he realized that, if he succeeded in getting the gnome to remove the curse, he would forfeit an opportunity to make a great deal of money.

He finished dressing more slowly. Esther was right, to a certain extent. If he could tolerate his waterless condition—

'No!' he gritted decisively. 'Already my friends avoid me. It isn't right that a respectable man like me should always be drunk and not take a bath. So we'll make less money. Money isn't everything—'

And with great determination he went to the lake.

But that evening, before going home, Mike walked out of his way to stop in at the concession. He found Greenberg sitting on a chair, his head in his hands, and his body rocking slowly in anguish.

'What is it, Mr. Greenberg?' he asked gently.

Greenberg looked up. His eyes were dazed. 'Oh, you, Mike,' he said blankly. Then his gaze cleared, grew more intelligent, and he stood up and led Mike to the bar. Silently, they drank beer. 'I went to the lake today,' he said hollowly. 'I walked all around it, hollering like mad. The gnome didn't stick his head out of the water once.'

'I know.' Mike nodded sadly. 'They're busy all the time.'

Greenberg spread his hands imploringly. 'So what can I do? I can't write him a letter or send him a telegram; he ain't got a door to knock on or a bell for me to ring. How can I get him to come up and talk?'

His shoulders sagged. 'Here, Mike. Have a cigar. You been a real good friend, but I guess we're licked.'

They stood in an awkward silence. Finally Mike blurted: 'Real hot, today. A regular scorcher.'

'Yeah. Esther says business was pretty good, if it keeps up.'

Mike fumbled at the cellophane wrapper. Greenberg said: 'Anyhow, suppose I did talk to the gnome. What about the sugar?'

The silence dragged itself out, became intense and uncomfortable. Mike was distinctly embarrassed. His brusque nature was not adapted for comforting discouraged friends. With immense concentration he rolled the cigar between his fingers and listened for a rustle.

'Day like this's hell on cigars,' he mumbled, for the sake of conversation. 'Dries them like nobody's business. This one ain't, though.'

'Yeah,' Greenberg said abstractedly. 'Cellophane keeps them—'

They looked suddenly at each other, their faces clean of expression.

'Holy smoke!' Mike yelled.

'Cellophane on sugar!' Greenberg choked out.

'Yeah,' Mike whispered in awe. 'I'll switch my day off with Joe, and I'll go to the lake with you tomorrow. I'll call for you early.'

Greenberg pressed his hand, too strangled by emotion for speech. When Esther came to relieve him, he left her at the concession with only the inexperienced griddle boy to assist her, while he searched the village for cubes of sugar wrapped in cellophane.

The sun had scarcely risen when Mike reached the hotel, but Greenberg had long been dressed and stood on the porch waiting impatiently. Mike was genuinely anxious for his friend. Greenberg staggered along toward the station, his eyes almost crossed with the pain of a terrific hang-over.

They stopped at a cafeteria for breakfast. Mike ordered orange juice, bacon and eggs, and coffee half-and-half. When he heard the order, Greenberg had to gag down a lump in his throat.

'What'll you have?' the counterman asked.

Greenberg flushed. 'Beer,' he said hoarsely.

'You kidding me?' Greenberg shook his head, unable to speak. 'Want anything with it? Cereal, pie, toast '

'Just beer.' And he forced himself to swallow it. 'So help me,' he hissed at Mike, 'another beer for breakfast will kill me!'

'I know how it is,' Mike said around a mouthful of food.

On the train they attempted to make plans. But they were faced by a phenomenon that neither had encountered before, and so they got nowhere. They walked glumly to the lake, fully aware that they would have to employ the empirical method of discarding tactics that did not work.

'How about a boat?' Mike suggested.

'It won't stay in the water with me in it. And you can't row it.'

'Well, what'll we do then?'

Greenberg bit his lip and stared at the beautiful blue lake. There the gnome lived, so near to them. 'Go through the woods along the shore, and holler like hell. I'll go the opposite way. We'll pass each other and meet at the boathouse. If the gnome comes up, yell for me.'

'O.K.,' Mike said, not very confidently.

The lake was quite large and they walked slowly around it, pausing often to get the proper stance for particularly emphatic shouts. But two hours later, when they stood opposite each other with the full diameter of the lake between them, Greenberg heard Mike's hoarse voice: 'Hey, gnome!'

'Hey, gnome!' Greenberg yelled. 'Come on up!'

An hour later they crossed paths. They were tired, discouraged, and their throats burned; and only fishermen disturbed the lake's surface.

'The hell with this,' Mike said. 'It ain't doing any good. Let's go back to the boathouse.'

'What'll we do?' Greenberg rasped. 'I can't give up!'

They trudged back around the lake, shouting half-heartedly. At the boathouse, Greenberg had to admit that he was beaten. The boat house owner marched threateningly toward them.

'Why don't you maniacs get away from here?' he barked. 'What's the idea of hollering and scaring away the fish? The guys are sore—'

'We're not going to holler any more,' Greenberg said. 'It's no use.'

When they bought beer and Mike, on an impulse, hired a boat, the owner cooled off with amazing rapidity, and went off to unpack bait.

'What did you get a boat for?' Greenberg asked. 'I can't ride in it.'

'You're not going to. You're gonna walk.'

'Around the lake again?' Greenberg cried.

'Nope. Look, Mr. Greenberg. Maybe the gnome can't hear us through all that water. Gnomes ain't hardhearted. If he heard us and thought you were sorry, he'd take his curse off you in a jiffy.'

'Maybe.' Greenberg was not convinced. 'So where do I come in?'

'The way I figure it, some way or other you push water away, but the water pushes you away just as hard. Anyhow, I hope so. If it does, you can walk on the lake.' As he spoke, Mike had been lifting large stones and dumping them on the bottom of the boat. 'Give me a hand with these.'

Any activity, however useless, was better than none, Greenberg felt. He helped Mike fill the boat until just the gunwales were above water. Then Mike got in and shoved off.

'Come on,' Mike said. 'Try to walk on the water.'

Greenberg hesitated. 'Suppose I can't?'

'Nothing'll happen to you. You can't get wet, so you won't drown.'

The logic of Mike's statement reassured Greenberg. He stepped out boldly. He experienced a peculiar sense of accomplishment when the water hastily retreated under his feet into pressure bowls, and an unseen, powerful force buoyed him upright across the lake's surface. Though his footing was not too secure, with care he was able to walk quite swiftly.

'Now what?' he asked, almost happily.

Mike had kept pace with him in the boat. He shipped his oars and passed Greenberg a rock. 'We'll drop them all over the lake – make it damned noisy down there and upset the place. That'll get him up.'

They were more hopeful now, and their comments, 'Here's one that'll wake him,' and 'I'll hit him right on the noodle with this one,' served to cheer them still further. And less than half the rocks had been dropped when Greenberg halted, a boulder in his hands. Something inside him wrapped itself tightly around his heart and his jaw dropped.

Mike followed his awed, joyful gaze. To himself, Mike had to admit that the gnome, propelling himself through the water with his ears, arms folded in tremendous dignity, was a funny sight.

'Must you drop rocks and disturb us at our work?' the gnome asked.

Greenberg gulped. 'I'm sorry, Mr. Gnome,' he said nervously. 'I couldn't get you to come up by yelling.'

The gnome looked at him. 'Oh. You are the mortal who was disciplined. Why did you return?'

'To tell you that I'm sorry, and I won't insult you again.'

'Have you proof of your sincerity?' the gnome asked quietly.

Greenberg fished furiously in his pocket and brought out a handful of sugar wrapped in cellophane, which he tremblingly handed to the gnome.

'Ah, very clever, indeed,' the little man said, unwrapping a cube and popping it eagerly into his mouth. 'Long time since I've had some.'

A moment later Greenberg spluttered and floundered under the surface. Even if Mike had not caught his jacket and helped him up, he could almost have enjoyed the sensation of being able to drown.

HARPIST
Joe L. Hensley

'Harpist' is a story I fought with for a long time.

I think the first draft of it was finished in the late '70s. I let it sit for a time, didn't like what I read, and put it away. I had a book contract I needed to finish.

But the story haunted me. I came out of the limestone country in Indiana, and now I live in a small town on the Indiana-Kentucky border. The people in the story were all people I knew. Curly was like some of the musicians who used to play in my father's restaurant/beer garden when I was growing up; in the court where I'm a judge, I've met a dozen dozen Hickams. My brother is a professional musician, and once – long ago – I began to be.

So I kept going back to the story, changing it, polishing it. When it was done, I was more excited about it than anything I'd done for a long time. When I reread it now, it still gets to me and makes me want to write ten more as good as it is.

I am, most of the time, a circuit court judge presiding over two counties in southern Indiana. 'Harpist' is one of the few things I've done which make me glad I'm not a judge all the time.

B.C.: They were still a trinity after the accident at entry, but the Outer, to save the two, had to contract and partially burn. The Older and the Younger sought the Outer. The search was long and the years passed, but still they sang and searched.

A.D.: That year Curly was six, and he found a curiously shaped stone as he wandered the dry creek bed by the shack. Already he could pick out a tune, but suddenly he became better. And found his life.

Mike's Bar, at the end of the 1970s, was in a village in the Kentucky coalfields. The village was big enough for the bar, a general store, two churches, and a union hall. The bar drew trade mostly from dust-covered miners, and it could be a rough place on paydays. The outside was hewn logs. The inside was poorly lighted and always damp.

Curly, the man in the wheelchair, played electric guitar and sang in the bar nights. Sometimes, as on Saturdays, he had to turn the amplifier up high to make the crowd hear, but other nights it would get quiet when he played because he was still good. Sometimes he'd sing, and now and then he'd get them to join in singing, but mostly he played. His hands moved easily, his feet not at all. He had the gift. He could play anything he could put nimble fingers to: guitar, banjo, fiddle. He listened to himself as he played, forgetting his legs, sometimes even forgetting the drink beside him, intent only on the music. He was fifty-five years old, and his hair was only a fringe, so the name Curly was now a joke. The face below the hair had a perpetually astonished clown look, as if in shock at what life had done to its owner. He was thin and drank enormous amounts. Sometimes, late at night, he would be so intoxicated that he'd play only by instinct. Sometimes, afterward, he'd be sick from the effects of drinking and couldn't play well. Not playing made him sicker, so he drank to escape his own mediocrity. A circle. He no longer had any goal other than the music: to play it, to hear it. He had no friends other than those made anew each night. Days were for sodden sleeping. Only the nights had life.

Curly was coal country born, and he'd wandered back looking for a place to exist and drink and eventually die in the dark land of his childhood, a land of Indian ghosts and superstitions and childhood dreams, a bloody land of somber men, strikes, and guns. Sometimes he could recall bits of his childhood, when he'd played his first guitar, remember his thin, tubercular mother, remember the father who'd died young of black lung, remember the loveless relatives who'd passed him about like an unwanted football. It was the land itself and not the remnants of family that had drawn him back. It was a vague feeling that he should be here in coal country to die.

Curly knew a little about Hickam before the man came into the bar to see him – just some stories, not much. Hickam was a farmer-trader who'd made it rich, shrewdly buying and selling, cheating all the way, bluff and hard. Those who talked about him at all said Hickam was a strange one. He lived on the old Turner place now. They said he'd hauled in truckloads of equipment to the place, but not to mine it. The coal miners said darkly he was 'doing something' back there where the caves and the mounds were, something that had nothing to do with coal. The mounds were the last visible remains of the vanished Indians, who'd built a society to rival any present-day government before the star first appeared over Bethlehem.

Hickam was a known ravager of the mounds, an explorer of caves. If he did other things, none of the coal miners, tough as they were, ever ventured close enough to find out. The Turner place had always borne a bad name. Curly remembered that from childhood. No one went there.

Hickam came bouncing into the bar on one of Curly's better nights, when the feeling ran strong between head and hands, when the sounds from the guitar were more than good music. Hickam sat in the darkest corner of the room and listened and watched, drinking Jack Daniels and Coca-Cola instead of beer like most of the miners. Curly could see him singing and humming with the music now and then. Hickam sent a couple of Jacks to the podium with Jonce, the black bartender-owner, and Curly nodded his thanks. The bar seemed uneasy around Hickam, but no one started trouble. Curly thought Hickam could maybe have handled a lot of trouble anyway.

He returned a few nights later, during an off night in the week, when things weren't crowded.

Jonce sidled to the stand at Curly's intermission.

'Hickam wants to see you, man,' he said, his look unreadable. 'He'd like to buy you a drink and talk to you. I'll roll you on back.'

Curly was amiable. 'Sure, Jonce. What's he want?'

'You talk to him,' Jonce ordered.'What he says is okay with me. He owns this building. So please be nice.'

When Jonce had rolled him there Curly could see Hickam was younger than he'd thought, maybe low forties, and big, with arms like posts. His black eyes were slightly exophthalmic and very penetrating, the best point in a brutal face. Hickam examined Curly, and Curly felt like a bug under a microscope.

'You play damn good, Curly,' Hickam said. 'Can I buy you a drink?'

'Sure, Mr. Hickam.'

Hickam nodded at Jonce, who came running.

'Where'd you get that last song from?' Hickam asked.

'It was a variation that came to me. Winters. "Robinbird" stuff. It ain't really that original.' Hickam reminded Curly close up of a mean gunnery sergeant he'd once known, dead now, bones in Korea.

'I hear you used to be famous?' Hickam asked curiously. 'You was in Nashville. Made big records.'

Curly nodded emotionlessly. He had been famous within the

limitations of the trade. Not a headliner, but close. It seemed very long ago now.

'Jonce tells me you got bad blowed up in the K-War.'

Curly nodded again. The story was well known. Nothing worked under a line that began below his navel, nothing other than bowels and like that. Some things that did work he had no use for anymore. Karen had left him ten years back because of the drinking. At fifty-five, getting it together was too much trouble for too small a return. A woman always seemed to feel as if she were doing him a favor when they managed it.

'I maybe got a proposition for you,' Hickam said, leaning closer. He pointed at the raised podium where the silver-chased guitar and amp and speakers were. 'How loud can you rev that damned thing up?'

'Loud enough to clear this place,' Curly said, curious now. 'Soft enough to fill it,' he added.

'Good. That's real good. I need her loud. Forget about singing. I'd like to hire you for a few days, maybe even a week.'

'I work here every night but Sunday. We're closed Sundays.'

Hickam smiled. 'Sunday could be the first night. I talked with Mr. Jonce and it's okay with him for you to be out as long as I'd need you. I made him a deal. I'll pay you damn good over and above the deal.' He reached out a hand and covered one of Curly's.

Curly pulled his hand away, but Hickam only grinned.

'Ain't interested, Mr. Hickam,' Curly said, disliking the man. 'I don't need no place but here.'

'If I said the word there might not be a job here,' Hickam said carefully.

Curly shrugged. There were other places. The music was enough. There was always a place to play it.

Hickam watched him, frowning. 'I could pay you a lot more money than you get in here. Drinks and tips and eating money's all there is here. I know that.'

Curly looked down at his ruined legs and shook his head. 'Money ain't the all of it. I've got what I need.'

'I guess maybe you're afraid,' Hickam said, challenging him. 'You live in that wheelchair and you're afraid.' He looked around the room suspiciously. 'None of these black dust-covered bastards will come close to my place. It's that, ain't it? You've heard about my place and what I'm doing from someone?'

'I was born a few miles from here,' Curly said. 'I heard about the

Turner place lots of times. I remember that old man Turner's kids left early, and he died funny. I know his wife's in an asylum.'

'That's right, but nobody knows nothing about how it is now,' Hickam said, leaning closer, whispering scornfully. 'Whatever it is there, it makes music. That's why I want you. You can hear it real faint coming up out of that deep hole after it's dark. Put your ear close to the ground and you can hear it. You know "Dueling Banjos"? Kind of like that. Not that song, but the sound. Intricate.' He nodded. 'I went way back in the cave nearby. I couldn't hear it any better there, but there was a long wall I found with things painted on it. The first drawing showed something big and blazing that came down from the sky.' His eyes were intense. 'One picture showed all the trees down, another showed everything on fire: the trees, the grass, even the earth itself. Indian drawings, or maybe older than that. Other people have seen those drawings down the years. Them scientists from the state university wanted to come on the land and look around, but Turner wouldn't let them, and I ain't about to permit it. Turner told me once when I was drinking with him that only the sacred men of the five tribes was ever allowed on the place. Turner was afraid. He got old quick. So did his wife.'

Hickam fell silent and Curly waited.

'I ain't seen anything yet,' Hickam admitted. 'Listening to you gave me an idea. If you won't come then rent me your outfit. I'll try it alone.'

Curly had never heard about the music. All he could remember was that people had told him that Hickam's place had spooks on it and that it was a 'bad place', but good enough for Hickam. He searched in his pocket and fingered his stone. It was cold. The chain had broken years ago, but he still had the locket.

'What kind of music?' he asked, shaking his head at the rental offer. One didn't rent out what was an extension of self. But he was interested. He lifted his drink and finished it, waiting.

'You want to hear the music?' Hickam asked him cunningly. 'You got to come out there to hear it – it's simple.' He looked around the bar. 'Them in here will tell you not to do it. Will you come?'

Curly nodded, mildly interested, not caring much one way or the other.

'You'll need to bring along your guitar and stuff. I'll get it hauled back in for you. I got me a portable generator you can hook onto. Plenty of power.' He looked at Curly's empty glass. 'And there'll be plenty of good stuff.'

Curly smiled and nodded. 'Why not?' he asked softly.

Hickam sat unhearing, eyes shining with anticipation.

Curly touched the stone again. Sometimes in dreams he fancied it sang to him, strange songs about love and death. It seemed suddenly warmer to his touch. It did that now and then, changed temperatures.

The creek through the Turner place had run on down to Pa's place then. The stone might have come from upstream, from the mounds, rolling with the water, speckled blue, smooth to the touch.

Going home, he told it.

On Sunday morning Hickam came past in a big truck. He loaded Curly's equipment as if it were made of balsam and silk. Curly envied him his strong legs. Hickam caught him watching and grinned, his eyes obsidian. He hefted Curly into the cab and then drove the truck off the main highway after a way. They sought and found a secondary, gravel road, then a bumpy, rutted mud track, into trees so green they almost seemed blue. Once they were away from the main road the land was almost as it had been ten thousand years before. Curly held tight to the seat belt, his dead legs flopping. He felt clammy and nauseated from too much drinking. His canvas folding wheelchair in the back of the truck rattled against the amplifying equipment.

'Take it a little easier, Mr. Hickam. That stuff back there is delicate.'

'Oh? Sure.' Hickam got out a pint bottle and offered it. Curly accepted it gratefully and drank until he burned all the way down to where feeling ended. Hickam took a pull and put the bottle back in a hip pocket.

'You ever heard of Schliemann?' he asked expansively.

'Who?'

'Schliemann. Heinrich Schliemann. He discovered the ruins of Troy.' Hickam nodded to himself. 'I read about him in a book. I always wanted . . . Now maybe I got me a thing for myself. But it's alive, Curly. Something alive.'

Curly smiled and Hickam saw it.

'You wait,' he said darkly. 'You'll stop smiling.'

The cave was located in rough terrain. There was a complex of Indian mounds around it. At the front of the cave, near the entrance, there was a dry pond surrounded by bushes and trees, full of weeds now, except in the deepest part. A scum of water stood there.

Hickam pointed. 'That's the entrance down there. It's still spring muddy around it, and we'll have to be careful with the power lines, but I'll get you set up to play tonight.'

'And all I have to do is play?'

'Listen first, play after,' Hickam said seriously, nodding, not looking at Curly. 'See there near the front of the cave entrance? That's where I'm going to put you, close to the deep hole. That's where it lives. There's water starting maybe fifteen or twenty feet down the hole. Lord knows how deep it goes. Too deep to measure. I put a rope down it once, but I ran out of rope and hadn't hit bottom.'

'How much rope?' Curly felt a chill despite himself.

Hickam shrugged. 'A lot. All a winch could hold. I thought maybe it was hungry down there. I had me a whole hog on the end of my line, but it come back up untouched.'

Curly looked. The hole was maybe fifty feet across, curtained by trees and growth, curiously circular. The walls were smooth, and the hole was slightly separated from the old, dried pond. The hole entered the ground at a slight slant so that it angled back under the cave. Around its sides, as they drew nearer, Curly could see green plants flourishing in slick profusion.

Hickam smiled. 'I saw that hole and heard the sounds. And I've never seen plants around here exactly like the ones growing in that hole. I'm a curious man. I've run my way through two fortunes and a lot of women. I wondered what made the hole. And there's all the stories. Old man Turner thought he stuck me with something. I paid him too much money, but I'd have given more. And I knew there wasn't no coal here no matter how much he hinted. But I got me something nobody else has, and I own it free and clear.' He nodded, his eyes hooded and somehow lost. 'Now, we'll start out setting you up.' He handed Curly the bottle. 'There's more,' he said condescendingly, watching Curly drink.

First Curly listened. There was *something*. It was a queer sound. You had to fight to hear it, like lost whispers. Curly got out of the wheelchair and lay on the ground, putting his ear close to the rocky soil, smoothing a place. Just notes and only a hint of recognizable melody, but haunting. The stone in his pocket felt very warm when he touched it.

'Some nights it's louder,' Hickam said. They listened for a time longer while insects buzzed around them. They drank whiskey mixed with warm Cokes.

'You want to try to play some now that it's full dark?'

Curly nodded, and Hickam helped him back into the wheelchair.

It was the strangest concert Curly had ever played. An audience of one, and, in the distance, the hum of the gasoline powered generator. The moon was out, and Hickam hadn't erected any special lights. There was just one on a pole outside the cave entrance near the water-filled deep hole. Hickam himself had set up a camera behind a thicket of small trees about thirty yards from where Curly played.

Curly turned the volume up high. He played his own special version of 'Jim Bob', chording, picking, hands moving quicksilver. He moved to 'Greensleeves', and then to 'God's Fate', then mixed country western and gospel as he warmed to his own sounds. He no longer watched the edge of the deep hole after the first tunes, but was caught again for the thousand-thousandth time in his own music, not caring any longer about legs, about the wife who'd left him, or even the children he'd wanted but never had. He played, pausing only now and then to drink.

In the middle of 'Bodies' he realized that he and Hickam weren't alone. There was something, a something that moved and shone just at the rim of the deep hole, something playing softly with music, anticipating, weaving, joining, with a sound like none Curly had ever heard. It wasn't guitar or harp or banjo or anything human, but it was still in tune, catching instantly beats and changes. More like harp than anything else, Curly decided. With perhaps a little violin. But a harp.

He gave it his best, the sad and lonely 'Away Man, Away', and it came soaring and cavorting out over the top of the deep place. Curly nodded to it, not afraid. Nothing that made music could frighten him. The thing was big, and it spread its vaguely tentlike shape against the sky, with bright, moving lines that joined together, spinning and twirly, then apexed in blackness that was three feet in circumference at the top. No eyes, no features, but Curly knew it perceived him. For a while he thought the interaction of the bright lines produced its music, but then he became unsure. Perhaps the lines only spelled out rhythm, and the music welled from blackness. Its shape seemed vaguely familiar, as if he'd seen or dreamed it before.

It could make music. Lord, how it could make music. Curly had endured a lifetime of musicians who couldn't read, had no ear, no sense of timing, were happily off key, dragging, futile.

Not this. It could *fly*.

In the background, now and then, Curly could hear Hickam's busy camera snapping when there was a pause in the music.

All night Curly played in sweet companionship, forgetting Hickam, forgetting even the booze. Now and then he'd pause and wait a while for the being, which he now referred to in his own mind as the Harpist, to try a song on its own, but the Harpist would have none of that. It just hovered and outwaited Curly until Curly's fingers grew restless and began to move again. Curly cut the sound back to the place where he could hear the Harpist easily over the sounds of his own playing. It was better that way.

Near first light the Harpist grew restless. It moved to the edge of the deep hole and floated out over the water, airborne in some fashion that Curly could only envy. The bright, silvery lines seemed to flow more slowly, and Curly obliged with soft and simple songs, tiring also. Both of them were tired.

Before the sun began to peek the Harpist dropped back down below the edge of the deep hole and was gone. One moment it was there, the next, vanished.

Curly finished the last song alone. To leave a song unfinished wasn't in him.

Nearby he could hear Hickam chortling to himself, obviously happy.

'You did it – did it,' he called, smiling at Curly. 'Lord, Lord, the pictures I took. That pretty thing.' He nodded and smiled more, full for the moment of power and benevolence. 'I'm going to go in and develop them. I'll be back with food and more to drink. You stay here.' He gave Curly an oblique look. 'You know what it is?'

Curly shook his head. There was no place to begin, no reference point.

'A Harpist,' he said, smiling, still webbed in the music.

'Something from another world or time. Something out of legends. Lord knows how old it is. It could have been here for tens of thousands of years. What it came in surely dug that hole. A ship maybe. I want what we saw. I want the ship too. I'll need money to dig for that.'

'Want it?' Curly asked, alarmed.

'Capture it and show it to the world. Make me rich again.'

'Better to let them as wants come here and see it, if it will,' Curly said, remembering the sounds of the Harpist. 'Listen to it.'

'A rope wouldn't work, but maybe a net,' Hickam mused.

Curly shook his head. 'I ain't going to help with that.'

'You just play. You play and you drink. That's why I brought you, what you hired on for.' Hickam leaned darkly toward Curly, dwarfing him in size and strength. 'If you don't play it'll wind up bad for you. There won't be anything to drink, and I'll play myself.'

Curly looked away. He touched the old stone in his pocket for comfort. It seemed very warm to the touch. In a while Hickam left. Curly slept, with dreams.

When Hickam returned with food and the pictures Curly could tell the man had been drinking heavily.

He threw a bag of cold hamburgers at Curly and uncapped him a bottle of beer. He disgustedly dropped a mound of pictures in Curly's lap.

'Not one of them worth a damn,' he said angrily. 'All that high-priced camera picked up were some lines of light. Nothing like you and me saw.'

Curly looked at the pictures while he drank thirstily. In some of them faint lines of light, like distant summer lightning streaks, appeared against a background of trees and bushes. In others there was nothing except Curly and his wheelchair and guitar, somewhat distorted, as if photographed through a dark, wavery glass.

'I've got to capture it for me,' Hickam said morosely.

'Capturing it would be like trying to take its picture, Mr. Hickam. It ain't to be owned. It came up from somewhere to play along with me, but that's as close to this world as it'll ever get. I know that somehow. You think it's old, but I don't know. I done some thinking after you left. I think maybe it's here waiting for something, curious about us – me – nothing more. But I can play music so it's accepted me. Maybe messing with it could cause big trouble.'

Hickam gave him a scornful look. 'Who gives a damn what a crippled drunk like you thinks? You don't know anything. You had your chance once, your moment. Now give me a chance at mine. You play your pretty guitar and drink your whiskey. Leave the rest of it to me.'

'I ain't going to help, and I'll warn it if I can,' Curly said stubbornly. 'I'm telling you fairlike.'

'Do anything to mess me up, and I'll dump you into the deep hole, wheelchair and all,' Hickam warned ominously, his eyes bloodshot and angry.

Curly subsided, unchanged inside.

All day long Hickam drank and worked at something he wouldn't let Curly see. He hid his work behind the nearby trees, and the making of it brought back his smiles. Curly could tell it was being constructed of ropes and hooks and tire chains that Hickam carried from the bed of the big truck.

Curly sat quietly and waited. He longed for something to drink, but instinct kept him from asking, knowing Hickam would want to exact something in return for drink.

When darkness came Hickam rolled Curly to the edge of the deep hole. He hooked up the guitar to the generator, made sure it was on by touching the strings himself, and then retreated to his hiding place.

'Play!' he ordered hoarsely. 'Play, and I'll give you all you can drink, a barrel full, enough to drown in.'

Curly smiled gently at him and shook his head, not angry, but resolute, knowing it was wrong to try to capture the Harpist.

Hickam came striding back from his hiding place. He took the guitar from Curly's hands and put it on the ground. He slapped the crippled man strongly with heavy hands, again and again. Curly felt a rib give, teeth loosen. His nose trickled blood.

'I'm telling you the God's truth when I say I'll drop you in the water,' Hickam said, breathing hard. He watched Curly and suddenly his eyes widened. 'Maybe, halfway at least, that's what you want. To be out of it? To die?' He reached again with powerful hands and lifted Curly from his wheelchair. He carried him near the cave entrance and dropped him roughly there.

'Not yet for you,' he said. 'I told you once I could play and play I will. I'll bet I can play enough to get it up out of the water if only because it'll be curious about the different sound. I'll decide about you later.' He nodded. 'No one will miss you. Jonce will go along with what I tell him. I'll say you got drunk and fell into the water.' He nodded, intoxicated with liquor and plans. 'Sure.' He shambled away to his hiding place and returned with the device he'd fashioned. A cruel net of sorts, hooks and wires and tire chains and rope. He spread it near his feet, ready for casting. He sat down in Curly's wheelchair and picked up the guitar.

'Now, listen,' he ordered darkly at the air. 'You'd better listen.'

He played. It was clumsy and not good, but it was loud. His repertoire was limited, and he played the same songs over and over, played angrily, his face growing more and more sullen as the Harpist failed to appear.

'Damn you,' he cursed, meaning Curly and the deep hole, 'come up – come up!'

And finally, after Curly had decided it wouldn't come, that it was safe, the Harpist appeared, just visible at the edge of its pit. It came and forgave Hickam's harsh notes, forgave them with its own perfect, intricate harmony.

'Come up out of there,' Hickam screamed in total frustration.

Curley could see the Harpist rise a little higher, move out and away from the water, closer to Hickam. Close enough. Curly screamed a warning.

Hickam dropped the guitar. Curly winced in pain when it struck the ground. Hickam came like a great cat and picked up and cast his net in a fluid motion.

The black and silver thing drew in on itself, mewed and whined, struggled and subsided. Caught!

'Let it go,' Curly implored. 'It wasn't meant to be caged in something for you and me to look at.'

'Shut your double-damned mouth,' Hickam said triumphantly. 'I don't need you anymore. I'll finish with you when I get this thing good and hitched down.'

He pegged the net to the ground. The thing inside made noises not unlike a kitten, not moving much now, only the flickering 'arm' movements showing it still lived.

'It'll soon die in that net,' Curly called, realizing it.

Hickam threw a peg at him. It bounced off the rock wall nearby.

The Harpist drew itself into an even tighter ball. It made one huge, unmusical sound, so rending and terrifying that Curly hugged his chest with arms that had suddenly lost all warmth.

Up from the depths flew another Harpist. This one had arms of flashing light thick enough to blot away the pale glow of the moon. Its black apex was a dozen feet across. As Curly had believed the other Harpist might be young, he knew this one was old. It hovered over the deep hole momentarily, then up and away.

Hickam screamed and turned to run. The Harpist merged with him, enveloped him, released him. Hickam seemed suddenly smaller. He fell and lay without moving.

The big Harpist skirted the net, seemingly unable to figure it out, remove it. Inside the net it seemed to Curly that the small Harpist was becoming smaller.

Curly lunged forward on his strong hands. He dragged his body behind him, crawling toward the two Harpists. He could hear them pipping at each other, the sounds mixed together. When Curly reached the net the big one perceived him, and something reached out and touched him briefly, coldly, then withdrew.

Curly jerked out the pegs. He lifted a corner of the net and pushed it upward. The big one enveloped the emerging small Harpist and soared high into the air over the deep hole in triumph. Then, suddenly, both were gone without splash, without sound.

Curly crawled to Hickam. Nothing inside Hickam now moved, and the man's body was as cold as piled snow.

He lay beside Hickam and tried to figure what would now happen to him, not caring much. Perhaps he could start the truck and, with a weight on the accelerator and some luck, he could make the blacktop. They'd find him there. He shook his head. He'd paid no attention to trucks for a long time, and the smooth sides of the truck could defeat his entry, especially if Hickam had locked the vehicle. Fighting back revulsion he searched Hickam's pockets and came up with a chain and metal keys, but when he fingered them they felt light and funny and powdered away as he rubbed them.

He sighed in discouragement. He crawled to the truck and got up by rising from bumper to fender. He then hand-pushed on back to the cab. The doors were, as expected, locked.

He went back to the guitar. The generator still hummed. He picked up the guitar, got himself into position, and belted out an SOS signal on it, over and over, at highest volume. He kept it up until he was very tired and had lost interest, until it was near dawn. No one came. He didn't believe anyone would come. Maybe Jonce sometime, but not for a very long time. Maybe never. There was no one. People listened, but that was all.

After he'd given it up and let the guitar fall silent the small Harpist appeared at the edge of the hole. It rose and moved close to him, seemingly unafraid. Curly nodded at it and played a tune, but there was no response. Curly nodded again and put the guitar carefully on the ground, thinking that the Harpist might be curious. The Harpist inspected the instrument by moving over and around it, by letting the flashes caress the instrument. Sounds came from the amplifier, but the Harpist seemed uninterested in them. When it tired of the guitar it reached out and touched Curly. The touch was strange, but not unpleasant, cold and tingly. The delicate flashes played over Curly, moving here and there, pausing for a time at the scarred area. Then, perhaps as more interesting, the Harpist moved back to the guitar. Curly worried vaguely what might happen if the creature got cross-wise with the generator, so he unplugged the guitar. He pushed it toward the Harpist, the ultimate gift, expiation for whatever part he'd had in its capture.

166

'You take it,' he invited. 'If I get out I can get another. Maybe you can figure it out, learn from it.' He nodded at the Harpist and pushed the instrument insistently at it, hoping his meaning was clear.

The big Harpist blew up again from out of the deep hole, making the wind rise. It floated toward Curly. The two Harpists pipped at each other. The big one touched Curly much as the small one had, lingering here and there, exploring.

Curly pushed the guitar at it also.

When it was done the big one picked up the small Harpist in its flashing arms. It offered the guitar back to Curly and he shook his head and dragged himself backward, so that his intention couldn't be mistaken. The big Harpist bowed and made the guitar vanish inside its central blackness.

Curly touched his pocket, and the heat from the stone was almost enough to singe his fingers. It was one more thing to offer and give if they desired it.

He took it out and looked at it once again, shuffling it from hand to hand, a small creek stone shaped by someone or something a hundred or ten thousand years before. He put it down on the ground in front of him so that they could see it, then backed away again. They came to it, moving quickly, silver arms moving like windmills, obviously excited. They bowed to him, a solemn thing. The big one made the stone vanish, and Curly felt its loss, the last of childhood, the end of his mother. But whatever it had been it now seemed important to them. He was glad he'd found it – glad he'd given it.

At the deep hole the two stopped and played a duet for Curly, very strange and lovely, saying something in the music, so that Curly badly wanted the guitar back to reply. The big one brought out the stone and held it against the morning sky. It seemed larger to Curly. When that was done the Harpist waited by the deep hole, waited until Curly hoped he knew why they waited.

He crawled to them and held out his arms, and they moved over and through him. He felt himself swallowed gently into their joint blackness, fed through the stone, then on.

And then they were three and soon to be four and no more reason to hide and wait.

After that there were other things, but first there was a beginning and a knowing and loneliness was gone. And most of all, for Curly, there was now always music, a music that married harp and guitar.

BLUE VASE OF GHOSTS
Tanith Lee

I confess that every story I ever wrote is a favourite of mine – simply because each represents something unique to me. And so I am rather like the prince in the fable, who loved one girl for her bright eyes, another for her curling hair, a third because she had given him a drink of water when he was thirsty . . . so he married them all.

Unlike that prince, necessarily limited, I propose this one (aside from a fondness for it), since it has Lee-obsessive elements. The colours, for example, in which I splashed and swam. The parallel world, close-to-but-not-quite an historical place – indeed, here, two or three mingled – the kind of venue that pleases me. Lastly, a mind-theme I seem frequently to touch: the grim sameness of Utter Power.

There's a subsidiary reason I chose this, too. It's an example of me at my least trammelled. The story came from nowhere, in an hour, was written in a day, and with a sensation of continuous excitement. This is not unusual for me, it's how I most often do write. But when I step back, startled, and realize again the ecstasy writing is for me – I am always, always grateful.

1
Subyrus, the Magician

Above, the evening sky; dark blue, transparent and raining stars. Below, the evening-coloured land, also blue to the depths of its hills, its river-carven valley, blue to its horizon, where a dusting of gold freckles revealed the lights of the city of Vaim.

Between, a bare hillside with two objects on it: a curious stone pavilion and a frightened man.

The cause of the man's fear, evidently, was the pavilion, or what it signified. Nevertheless, he had advanced to the open door and was peering inside.

The entire landscape had assumed the romantic air of faint menace that attends twilight, all outlines darkening and melting in the mysterious smoke of dusk. The pavilion appeared no more sinister than everything else. About eight feet in height, with a flat roof set on five walls of rough-hewn slabs, its only truly occult area lay over the square step and through the square doormouth – a matched square of black shadow.

Until: 'I seek the Magician-Lord Subyrus,' the frightened man exclaimed aloud, and the black shadow vanished in an ominous brazen glare.

The man gasped. Not so much in fear, as in uneasy recognition of something expected. Nor did he cry out, turn to run or fall on his knees when, in the middle of the glare, there evolved an unnatural figure. It was a great toad, large as a dog and made of brass, which parted its jaws with a creaking of metal hinges, and asked: '*Who* seeks Subyrus, Master of the Ten Mechanicae?'

'My name is not important,' quavered the man. 'My mission is. Lord Subyrus is interested in purchasing rarities of magic. I bring him one.'

Galaxies glinted and wheeled in bulbous amphibian eyes.

'Very well,' the toad said. 'My maker hears. You are invited in. Enter.'

At which the whole floor of the pavilion rushed upwards, with the monster squatting impassively atop it. Revealed beneath was a sort of metal cage, big enough to contain a man. Into this cage all visitors must step, and the frightened visitor knew as much. Just as he had known of the hill, the pavilion, the glare of unseen lamps and the horrendous brazen guardian. For down the trade roads and throughout the river ports of Vaim, word of these wonders had spread, along with the news that Subyrus, Master of the Ten Mechanicae, would buy with gold objects of sorcery – providing they were fabulous, bizarre and, preferably, unique.

The visitor entered the cage, which was the second of the Ten Mechanicae (the toad being the first). The cage instantly plunged into the hollow hill.

His entrails seemingly left plastered to the pavilion roof by the rapid descent, the visitor clutched to himself the leather satchel he had brought, and thought alternately of riches and death.

Subyrus sat in a chair of green quartz in a hall hung with drapes the colours of charred roses and black panthers. A clear pink fire burned on the wide hearth that gave off the slight persuasive scent of strawberries. Subyrus studied the fire quietly with deep-lidded dark eyes. He had the face of a beautiful skull, long hands and a long leopardine body to concur with that image. The robe of murky murderous crimson threw into exotic relief his luminous and unblemished pallor, and the strange dull bronze of his long hair that seemed carved rather than combed.

When the cage dashed down into the hall and bounced on its cushioned buffers, throwing the occupant all awry, Subyrus looked up, unsmiling. He regarded the man who staggered from the cage clutching a satchel with none of the cruel arid expressions or gestures the man had obviously anticipated.

Subyrus' regard was compounded of pity, a vague inquiry, an intense drugged boredom.

It was, if anything, worse than sadism and savagery.

A melodramatic laugh and glimpse of wolf-fangs would have been somehow preferable to those opaque and disenchanted eyes.

'Well?' Subyrus said. Less a question than a plea – *Oh, for the love of the gods, interest me in something.* The plea of a man (if he were that alone) to whom other men were insects, and their deeds pages of a book to be turned and turned in the vain hope of a quickening.

The man with the satchel quailed.

'Magician-Lord – I had heard – you wished marvels to be brought to you that you might . . . acquire them.'

Subyrus sighed.

'You heard correctly. What then have you brought?'

'In this satchel, lordly one – something beyond—'

'Beyond what?' Subyrus' sombre eyes widened, but only with disbelief at the tedium this salesman was causing him. 'Beyond my wildest dreamings, perhaps you meant to say? I have no wild dreamings. I should welcome them.'

In a panic, the man with the satchel blurted something. The sort of overplay he might have used on an ordinary customer; it had become a habit with him to attempt startlement in order to gain the upper hand. But not here, where he should have left well alone.

'What did you say?' Subyrus asked.

'I said – I said—'

'Yes?'

'That the Lady Lunaria of Vaim – was wild dream enough.'

Now the satchel-man stood transfixed at his own idiocy, his very bones knocking together in wretched fright. Indeed, Subyrus had lost his mask of boredom, but it had been replaced merely by an appalling contempt.

'Have I become a laughing stock in Vaim?'

The query was idle, mild. Suddenly the man with the satchel realized the contempt of the magician was self-directed. The man slumped and answered, truthfully: 'No one would dare laugh, Magician-Lord, at anything of yours. The length of the river, men pale at your name. But the other thing – you can hardly blame them for envying you the Lady Lunaria.' He glanced up. Had he said the right words, at last? The magician did not respond. The frightened satchel-man had space to brood on the story then current in the city, that the Master of the Ten Mechanicae had taken for his mistress the most famous whore this side of the northern ocean, and that Lunaria Vaimian ruled Subyrus as if he were a toothless lion, ordering him to this and that, demanding costly gifts, setting him errands, and even in the matter of the bedchamber, herself saying when. Some claimed the story an invention of Lunaria's, a dangerous game she played with Subyrus' reputation. Others said that Subyrus himself had sent the fancy abroad to see if any dared mock him, so he might cut them down with his sorcery in some vicious and perverse fashion.

But the satchel-man had come over the mountain roads to Vaim. A stranger, he had never seen Lunaria for himself, nor, till tonight, the Magician-Lord.

'Well?' Subyrus said drowsily.

The satchel-man jumped in his skin.

'I suggest,' Subyrus said, 'you show me this rare treasure beyond wild dreamings. You may mention its origin and how you came by it. You may state its ability, if any, and demonstrate. You may then name your price. But, I beg you, no more sales patter.'

Shivering, the satchel-man undid the clasps and drew from the leather a padded bag. From the bag he produced a velvet box. In the box he revealed a sapphire glimmer wrapped in feathers. The feathers drifted to the floor as he lifted out a vase of blue crystal, about a foot in length, elongated of neck, with a broad base of oddly alternating swelling and tapering design. The castellated lip was sealed by a stopper that appeared to be a single rose-opal.

Prudently silent, and holding the vase before him like a talisman, the visitor approached Subyrus' chair.

'Charming,' said Subyrus. 'But what does it do?'

'My lord,' the satchel-man whispered, 'my lord – I can simply

recount what it is *supposed* to have done – and to do. I myself have
not the skill to test it.'

'Then you must tell me immediately how you came by it. Look at
me,' Subyrus added. His voice was all at once no longer indolent but
cool and terrible. Unwilling, but without choice, the satchel-man
raised his head. Subyrus was turning a great black ring, round and
round, on his finger. At first it was like a black snake darting in and
out, then like a black eye, opening and closing.

Subyrus sighed again, depressed at the ease with which most
human resistance could be overcome.

'Speak now.'

The satchel-man dutifully began.

Mesmerized by the black ring, he spoke honestly, without either
embroidery or omission.

2

The Satchel-Man's Tale

An itinerant scavenger by trade, the satchel-man had happened on a
remote town of the far north, and learned of a freakish enterprise
taking place in the vicinity. The tomb of an ancient king had been
located in the heart of one of the tall iron-blue crags that towered
above the town. Scholars of the town, fascinated by the tomb's
antiquity, had hired gangs of workmen to break into the inner
chamber and prise off the lid of the sarcophagus. At this event, the
satchel-man was a lurking bystander. He had made up to several of
the scholars in the hope of some arcane jewel dropping into his paws.
But in the end, all that had been uncovered were dust, stench, decay
and some brown grinning bones – clutched in the digits of which was
a vase of blue crystal stoppered with rose-opal.

The find being solitary, the scholars were obliged to offer it to the
town's Tyrant. He graciously accepted the vase, attempted to pull
out the opal stopper, failed, attempted to smash the vase in order to
release the stopper, failed, ordered various pounding devices to crush
the vase – which also failed – called for one of the scholars and
demanded he investigate the nature of the vase forthwith. This
scholar, who had leanings in the sorcerous direction, had also become the host of the parasitic satchel-man. The satchel-man had
spun some yarn of ill luck which the scholar, an unworldly in-

tellectual, credited. So the satchel-man was informed as to the scholar's magic assaults on the vase. Not that the satchel-man actually attended the rituals first hand (as, but for the mesmerism, he would have assured Subyrus he had). Yet he was advised of them over supper, when the fraught scholar complained of his unsuccess. Then late one night, as the satchel-man sprawled on a couch with his host's brandy pitcher, a fearsome yell echoed through the house. A second or so later, pale as steamed fish, the scholar stumbled into the room, and collapsed whimpering on the ground.

The satchel-man gallantly revived the scholar with some of his own brandy. The scholar spoke.

'It is a sorcery of the Brink, of the Abyss. More lethal than the sword, and more dreadful. In the hands of a Power what mischief could it not encompass? What mischief it *has* encompassed.'

'Have a little extra brandy,' said the satchel-man, torn between curiosity, avarice and nerves. 'Say more.'

The scholar drank deep, grew sozzled, and elaborated in such a way that the hairs bristled on the satchel-man's unclean neck.

Searching an antique book, the scholar had discovered an unusual spell of Opening. This he had performed, and the rose-opal had jumped free of the mouth of the vase. Such a whirling had then occurred inside it that the scholar had become alarmed. The crystal seemed full of milk on the boil and milky lather foamed in the opening of the castellated mouth. In consternation, the scholar had given vent to numerous rhetorical questions, such as: 'What shall I do?' and 'What in the world does this bubbling portend?' Finally he voiced a rhetorical question that utilised the name of the ancient king: 'What can King So-and-So have performed with such an artifact?'

Rhetorical questions do not expect answers. But to this question an answer came. No sooner was the king's name uttered than the frothing in the vase erupted outwards. A strand of this froth, proceeding higher than the rest from the vase's mouth, gradually solidified. Within the space of half a minute, there balanced in the atmosphere above the vase, deadly white but perfectly formed, the foot-high figure of a man, lavishly bearded and elaborately clad, a barbaric diadem on his head. With a minute sneer, this figure addressed the scholar:

'Normally, further ritual with greater accuracy is required. But since I was the last to enter, and since I have been within a mere four centuries, I respond to my name. Well, what do you wish, O absurd and gigantic fool?'

A dialogue then ensued which had to do with the scholar's astonishment and disbelief, and the white midget king's utter irritation at, and scorn of, the scholar.

In the course of this dialogue, however, the nature of the vase was specified.

A magician had made it, though when and how was unsure. Its purpose was original, providing the correct magic had been activated by rite and incantation. That done, whoever might die – or whoever might be slain – in the close neighbourhood of the vase, their soul would be sucked into the crystal and imprisoned there till the ending of time, or at least of time as mortal men know it. Since its creation, countless magicians, and others who had learned the relevant sorcery, had used the vase in this way, catching inside it the souls, or ghosts, of enemies, lovers and kindred for personal solace or entertainment. It might be reckoned (the king casually told the scholar) that seven thousand souls now inhabited the core of the vase. ('How is there room for so many?' the scholar cried. The king laughed. 'I am not bound to answer questions. Therefore, I will do no more than assure you that room there is, and to spare.') It appeared that whoever could name the vase-trapped ghosts by their exact appellations might call them forth. They might then reply to interrogation – but only if the fancy took them to do so.

The scholar, overwhelmed, dithered. At length the miniature being demanded leave to return into the vase, which the scholar had weakly granted. He had then flown downstairs to seek comfort from the satchel-man.

The satchel-man was not comforting. He was insistent. The scholar must summon the king's ghost up once again. Positively, the king would be able to tell them where the hoards of his treasure had been buried, for all kings left treasure hoards at death, if not in their tombs, then in some other spot. Was the scholar not a magus? He must recall the ghost and somehow coerce it into malleability, thereby unearthing incredible secrets of lore and (better) cash.

The scholar, convinced by the satchel-man's persistence and the dregs of the brandy, eventually resummoned the king's ghost. Nothing happened. The scholar and the satchel-man strenuously reiterated the summons. Still nothing. It seemed the ghost had been right in hinting that the ritual was important. He had obeyed on the first occasion because his had been the last and newest soul in the vase, but he had no need to obey further without proper incentive.

Then the scholar fell to philosophising and the satchel-man fell to cursing him. Presently the scholar turned the satchel-man out of his house. That night, while the scholar snored in brandy-pickled slumber, the satchel-man regained entry and stole the vase. It was not his first robbery, and his exit was swift from practice.

Thereafter he wandered, endeavouring to locate a mage who knew the correct magic to name, draw forth and browbeat the ghosts in the vase. Or even merely to draw out the rose-opal stopper with which the scholar had inconsiderately recorked it.

Months passed with the mission unaccomplished, and despair set in. Until the satchel-man caught word of the Magician-Lord Subyrus.

To begin with, the satchel-man may have indulged in a dream of enlisting Subyrus' aid, but rumour dissuaded him from this notion. In the long run, it seemed safer to sell the vase outright and be rid of the profitless item. If any mage alive could deal with the thing it was the Master of the Ten Mechanicae. And somehow the salesman did not think Subyrus would share his knowledge. To accept payment in gold seemed the wisest course.

The satchel-man came to himself and saw the fire on the wide hearth had changed. It was green now, and perfumed with apples. The fire must be the third of the Mechanicae.

Subyrus had not changed. Not at all.

'And your price?' he gently murmured. His eyes were nearly shut.

'Considering the treasure I forego in giving up the vase to your lordship—' The satchel-man meant to sound bold, succeeded in a whining tone.

'And considering you will never reach that treasure, as you have no power over the vase yourself,' Subyrus amended, and shut his eyes totally from weariness.

'Seven thousand vaimii,' stated the satchel-man querulously. 'One for each of the seven thousand ghosts in the vase.'

Subyrus' lids lifted. He stared at the satchel-man and the satchel-man felt his joints loosen in horror. Then Subyrus smiled. It was the smile of an old, old man, dying of ennui, his mood lightened for a split second by the antics of a beetle on the wall.

'That seems,' said Subyrus, 'quite reasonable.'

One hand moved lazily and the fourth of the Mechanicae manifested itself. It was a brazen chest which sprang from between the charred-rose draperies. Subyrus spoke to the chest, a compartment shot out and deposited a paralysing quantity of gold coins on the rugs at the satchel-man's feet.

'Seven thousand vaimii,' Subyrus said. 'Count them.'

'My lord, I would not suppose—'

'Count them,' repeated the magician, without emphasis.

Anxious not to offend, the satchel-man did as he was bid.

He was not a particularly far-sighted man. He did not realise how long it would take him.

A little over an hour later, fingers numb, eyes watering and spine unpleasantly locked, he slunk into the mechanical cage and was borne back to the surface. This time, his guts were left plastered to the lowermost floor of the hollow hill.

Musically clinking, and in terror lest he himself be robbed, the satchel-man limped hurriedly away through the starry and beautiful night.

3

Proving the Vase

The fire burned warmly black, and smelled of musk and ambergris. This was the aspect of the fire which Subyrus used to recall Lunaria to him. The idea of her threaded his muscles, his very bones, with an elusive excitement, not quite sexual, not quite pleasing, not quite explicable. In this mood, he did not even visualise Lunaria Vaimian as a woman, or as any sort of object. Abstract, her memory possessed him and folded him round with an intoxicating, though distant and scarcely recognisable, agony.

It was quite true that she, of the entire city of Vaim, defied him. She asked him continually for gifts, but she would not accept money or jewels. She wanted the benefits of his status as a magician. So he gave her a rose which endlessly bloomed, a bracelet which, at her command, would transmute to a serpent, gloves that changed colour and material, a ring that could detect the lies of others and whistle thinly, to their discomfort. He collected sorcerous trinkets and bought them for gold, to give to her. In response to these gifts, Lunaria Vaimian admitted Subyrus to her couch. But she also dallied with other men. Twice she had shut her doors to the Master of the Ten Mechanicae. Once, when he had smitten the doors wide, she had said to him: 'Do I anger you, lord? Kill me then. But if you lie with me against my will, I warn you, mighty Subyrus, it will be poor sport.'

On various occasions, she had publicly mocked him, struck him in the face, reviled his aptitude both for magic and love. Witnesses had trembled. Subyrus' inaction surprised and misled them.

They reckoned him besotted with a lovely harlot, and wondered at it, that he found her so indispensable he must accept her whims and never rebuke her for them. In fact, Lunaria *was* indispensable to the Magician-Lord, but not after the general interpretation.

Her skin was like that dark brown spice called cinnamon, her eyes the darker shade of malt. On this sombreness was superimposed a blanching of blonde hair, streaked gold by sunlight and artifice in equal measure. Beautiful she was, but not much more beautiful than several women who had cast themselves at the feet of Subyrus, abject and yielding. Indeed, the entire metropolis and hinterland of Vaim knew and surrendered to him. All-powerful and all-feared and, with women who beheld his handsomeness and guessed at his intellect, all-worshipped. All that, save by Lunaria. Hence, her value. She was the challenge he might otherwise find in no person or sphere. The natural and the supernatural he could control, but not her. She was not abject or easy. She did not yield. The exacerbation of her defiance quickened him and gave him a purpose, an excuse for his life, in which everything else might be won at a word.

But this self-analysis he concealed from himself with considerable cunning. He experienced only the pangs of her rejection and scorn, and winced as he savoured them like sour wine. Obsessed, he gazed at the vase of blue crystal, and pondered the toys of magic he had given her formerly.

The vase.

The stopper of rose-opal had already been removed by one of the spells of the Forax Foramen, a copy of which ancient book (there were but three copies on earth) was the property of Subyrus. At this spell, written in gold leaf on sheets of black bull's hide, Subyrus had barely glanced. His knowledge was vast and his sorcerous vocabulary extensive. The stopper leapt from the neck of the vase – Subyrus caught it and set it by. Inside the crystal there commenced the foaming and lathering which the scholar had described to the satchel-man.

At Subyrus' other hand lay a second tome. No exact copies of this book existed, for it was the task of each individual mage to compile his own version. The general title of such a compendium being Tabulas Mortem, Lists of the Dead.

From these lists Subyrus had selected seventy names, a hundredth portion of the number of souls to be trapped in the vase. They were accordingly names of those who had died in peculiar circumstances, and in an aura of shadows, such as might indicate the nearness at that time of the soul-snaring crystal and of someone who could operate its magic.

With each name there obtained attendant rituals of appeasement, summoning and other things that might apply when wishing to contact the dead. All were subtly different from each other, however similar-seeming to the uneducated eye.

The fire sank on the hearth now, paled and began to smell of incense and moist rank soil.

Subyrus had performed the correct ritual and called the first name. He omitted from it the five inflexions that would extend the summons beyond the world, since his intent was centred on the trapped ghosts of the vase. He had also discarded the name of the king from whose tomb the vase had been taken. Occult theory suggested that such a spirit, having been recently obedient to an inaccurate summons (such as the scholar's), could thereby increase its resistance to obeying any other summons for some while after. So the name Subyrus named was a fresh one. Nor, though the ritual was perfect, was it answered.

That soul, then, had never been encaged in the vase. Subyrus erased the name from his selection, and commenced the ritual for a second.

In Vaim it was midnight, and over the hill above the magician's subculum the configurations of midnight were jewelled out in stars.

Subyrus spoke the nineteenth name.

And was answered.

The moistureless foam-clouds gathered and overspilled the vase. White bubbles and curlicues expanded on the air. From their midst flowed up a slender strand unlike the rest, which proceeded to form a recognisable shape. Presently, a foot-high figurine balanced on the air, just over the castellated lip of the vase. It was a warrior, like an intricately sculptured chess piece, whose detail was intriguing on such a scale – the minute links of the mail, the chiselled cat that crouched on the helm, the sword like a woman's pin. And all of it matt white as chalk.

'I am here,' the warrior cried in bell-like miniature tones. 'What do you want of me?'

'Tell me how you came to be imprisoned in the crystal.'

'My city was at war with another. The enemy took me in a battle, and strove to gain, by torture, knowledge of a way our defences might be breached. When I would say nothing, a magician entered. He worked spells behind a screen. Then I was slain and my ghost sucked into the vase. Next moment, the magician summoned me forth, and they asked me again, and I told them everything.'

'So,' Subyrus remarked, 'what you would not betray as a man, you revealed carelessly once you were a spirit.'

'Exactly. Which was as the magician had foretold.'

'Why? Because you were embittered at your psychic capture?'

'Not at all. But once within, human things ceased to matter to me. Old loyalties of the world, its creeds, yearnings and antipathies — these foibles are as dreams to those of us who dwell in the vase.'

'Dwell? Is there room then, inside that little sphere, to dwell?'

'It would amaze you,' said the warrior.

'No. But you may describe it.'

'That is not normally one of the questions mortals ask when they summon us. They demand directions to our sepulchres, and ways to break in and come on our hoarded gold, or what hereditary defects afflict our line, in order they may harm our descendants. Or they command us to carry out deeds of malevolence, to creep in small hidden areas and steal for them, or to frighten the nervous by our appearance.'

'You have not replied to my question.'

'Nor can I. The interior of this tiny vase houses seven thousand souls. To explain its microcosmic structure in mortal terms, even to one of the mighty Magician-Lords, would be as impossible as to describe colour to the stone-blind or music to the stone-deaf.'

'But you are content,' said Subyrus.

The warrior laughed flamboyantly.

'I am.'

'You may return,' said Subyrus, and uttered the dismissing incantation.

Subyrus progressed to a twentieth name, a twenty-first, a twenty-second. The twenty-third answered. This time a white philosopher stood in the air, his head meekly bowed, his sequin eyes whitely gleaming with the arrogance of great learning.

'Tell me how you came to be imprisoned in the crystal.'

'A Tyrant acquired this vase and its spell. He feared me and the teachings I imparted to his people. I was burned alive, the spell activated, and my ghost entered the vase. Thereafter, the Tyrant would call me forth and try to force me to enact degrading tricks to titillate him. But though we who inhabit the vase must respond to a summons, we need not obey otherwise. The Tyrant waxed disappointed. He attempted to smash the vase. At length he went mad. The next man who called me forth wished only to hear my philosophies. But I related gibberish, which troubled him.'

'Describe the interior of the vase.'

'I refuse.'

'You understand, my arts are of the kind which can retain you here as long as I desire.'

'I understand. I pine, but still refuse.'

'Go then,' and Subyrus uttered again the dismissing incantation.

It was past three o'clock. Altogether, six white apparitions had evolved from the blue vase. Subyrus had reached the fortieth name selected from the Tabulas Mortem. He was almost too weary to speak it.

The atmosphere was feverish and heavy with rituals observed and magics pronounced. Subyrus' thin and beautiful hands shook slightly with fatigue, and his beautiful face had grown more skull-like. To these trivialities he was almost immune. Though exhaustion heightened his world-sated gravity.

He said the fortieth name, and the figure of a marvellous woman rose from the vase.

'Your death?' he asked her. She had been an empress in her day.

'My lover was slain. I had no wish to live. But the man who brought me poison brought also this vase under his cloak. When my soul was snared, he carried the vase to distant lands. He would call me up in the houses of lords, and bid me dance for his patrons. I did this, for it amused me. He received much gold. Then, one night, in a prince's palace, I lost interest in the jest. I would not dance, and the wretch was whipped. The prince appropriated the vase. When I begged leave to rest, the prince recited the incantation of dismissal, which the whipped man had revealed. Ironically, the prince was not comparably adept at the phrases of summoning, and could never draw me forth again.'

The woman smiled, and touched at the white hair which streamed about her white robe.

'Surely you miss the gorgeous mode of your earthly state?' Subyrus said.

'Not at all.'

180

'Your prison suits you then?'

'Wonderfully well.'

'Describe it.'

'Others have told me you asked a description of them.'

'None obliged me. Will you?'

But the woman only smiled.

Brooding, Subyrus effected her dismissal.

He pushed the further names aside, and taking up the stopper of rose-opal, replaced it in the vase. The fermentation stilled within.

Slowly, the fire reproduced the darkness and scents that recalled Lunaria for the magician.

The vase was proven – and ready. The promise of such a thing would flatter even Lunaria. She had had toys before. But this – perverse, oblique, its potential elusive but limitless – it resembled Lunaria herself.

As the brazen bell-clocks of Vaim struck the fourth hour of black morning, an iron bird with chalcedony eyes (fifth of the Mechanicae) flew to the balconied windows of Lunaria's house.

The house stood at the crest of a hanging garden, on the eastern bank of the river. Here Lunaria, honouring her name, made bright the dark, turning night into day with lamplight, singing, drums, harps and rattles. Her golden windows could be seen from miles off. 'There is Lunaria's house', insomniacs or late-abroad thieves would say, chuckling, envious and disturbed. An odour of flowers and roast meats and uncorked wines floated over the spot, and sometimes fire-crackers exploded, saffron, cinnebar and snow, above the roof and walls. But after sunrise the windows turned grey and the walls held silence, as if the house had burnt itself out during the night.

The iron bird rapped a pane with its beak.

Lunaria, heavy-eyed, opened her window. She was not astonished or dismayed. She had seen the bird before.

'My master asks when he may visit you.'

Lunaria frowned.

'He knows my fee: a gift.'

'He will pay.'

'Let it be something unheard of, and unsafe.'

'It is.'

'Tomorrow then. At sunset.'

4
Lunaria of Vaim

The sinking sun bobbed like a blazing boat on the river. Water and horizon had become a luminous scarlet stippled with copper and tangerine. A fraction higher than the tallest towers of Vaim, this holocaust gave way to a dense mulberry afterglow, next to a denser blue, and finally, in the east, a strange hollow black, littered by stars. Such a combination of colours and gems in the apparel of man or woman, or in any room of the house, would have been dubious. But in the infallible and faultless sky, were lovely beyond belief and almost beyond bearing.

Nevertheless, the sunset's beauty was lost on Subyrus, or, rather, alleviated, dulled. At a finger's snap almost, he could command the illusion of such a sunset, or, impossibly, a more glorious one. It could not therefore impress or stimulate him, even though he rode directly through its red and mulberry radiance, on the back of a dragon of brass. The sixth of the Mechanicae, the dragon was equipped with seat and jewelled harness, and with two enormous wings that beat regularly up and down in a noise of metal hinges and slashed air. It caught the last light, and glittered like a fleck of the sun itself. In Vaim, presumably, citizens pointed, between admiration and terror.

A servant beat frantically on the door of Lunaria's bedchamber.

'Lady – *he* is here!'

'Who?' Lunaria inquired sleepily from within.

'The Lord Subyrus,' cried the servant, plainly appalled at her forgetfulness.

On the terrace before the house, the dragon alighted. Subyrus stilled it with a single word of power. He stepped from the jewelled harness, and contemplated the length of the hanging garden. Trees precariously leaned over under their mass of unplucked fruit, the jets of fountains pierced shadowy basins that in turn overflowed into more shadowy depths beneath. Trellised night flowers were opening and giving up their scent. In Lunaria's garden no day flowers bloomed, and no man could walk. Sometimes the gardeners, crawling about the slanted cliff of the hanging garden to tend the growth and the water courses, fell to their deaths on the thoroughfare eighty feet below. The only entrance to the house was through a secret door at the garden's foot, of whose location Lunaria informed her clients. Or from the sky.

The servant ran out onto the terrace and cast himself on his knees.

'My lady is not yet ready – but she bids you enter.'

The servant was sallow with fear.

Subyrus stepped through the terrace doors, and beheld a richly clad man in maddened flight down a stairway.

Lunaria had kept one of her customers late in order that Subyrus should see him. This was but a variation on a theme she had played before.

Near the stair foot, about to rush to a new flight – for these stairs passed right the way to the interior side of the secret door – the customer paused, and looked up in a spasm of anguish.

'You have nothing to dread from me, sir,' Subyrus remarked. But the man went on with his escape, gabbling in distress.

'And I. Am I not to dread you?'

Subyrus moved about, and there Lunaria Vaimian stood, dressed in a vermilion gown that complemented one aspect of the sunset sky, her blonde hair powdered with crushed gilt.

She stared at Subyrus boldly. When he did not speak, she nodded contemptuously at the dining room.

'I am not proud,' she announced. 'I will take my fee at dinner. I am certain you will grant me that interim between my previous visitor and yourself.'

The red faded on gold salvers and crystal goblets. Lunaria was wealthy, and she had earned every vaimii.

They did not converse, she and her guest. Behind a screen, musicians performed love songs with wild and savage rhythms. Servitors came and went with skilfully prepared dishes. Lunaria selected morsels from many plates, but ate frugally. Subyrus touched nothing. Indeed, no one alive could remember ever having seen him eat, or raise more than a token cup to his lips. Occasionally, Lunaria talked, as if to a third person. For example:

'How solemn the magician is tonight. Though more solemn or less than when he came here before, I cannot say.'

Subyrus never took his eyes from her. He sat motionless, wonderful, awful, and quite frozen, like some exquisite graveyard moth, crucified by a pin.

'Are you dead?' Lunaria said to him at length. 'Come, do not grieve. I will always be yours, for a price.'

At that he stirred. He placed a casket on the table between them, murmured something. The casket was gone. The vase of blue crystal glimmered softly in the glow of the young candles.

Lunaria tapped the screen with a silver wand, and the musicians left off their music. In the quiet, they might be heard scrambling thankfully away into the house.

Lunaria and the magician were alone together, with sorcery.

'Well,' said Lunaria, 'there was a tale in the city today. A blue vase in which thousands of souls are trapped. Souls which can inform of fabulous treasures and unholy deeds of the past. Courtesans who will reveal wicked erotica from antique courts. Devotees of decadent sciences. Geniuses who will create new books and new inventions. If they can be correctly persuaded. Providing one can call them by name.'

'I could teach you the method,' Subyrus said.

'Teach me.'

'And so buy a night of your life?' Subyrus smiled. It was a melancholy though torpid smile. 'I mean to have more than that.'

'A week of nights, for such a gift,' Lunaria said swiftly. Her eyes were wide now. 'You shall have them.'

'Yes, I shall. And more than those.'

He had got up from his chair, and now walked round the table. He halted behind Lunaria's chair, and when she would have risen, lightly he rested his long fingers against her throat. She did not try to move again.

The scents of ambergis and musk flooded from her hair.

His obsession. The gnawing and only motive for his existence.

Obscuring from himself his true desire – the pang of her indifference, her challenge – he saw the road before him, the box in which he might lock her up. Physically, he had possessed her frequently. Such possession no longer mattered. Possession of mind, of emotion, of soul had become everything. The joy of actual possession, the intriguing misery of never being able actually to possess her again. And his fingers tightened about the contour of her neck.

She did not struggle.

'What will you do?' she whispered.

'Presently remove the stopper of the vase. It is already primed to receive another ghost. Whoever expires now in its close vicinity, will be drawn in. Into that microcosm where seven thousand dwell content. That enchanted world. They come forth haughtily and retreat gladly. It must be curious and fine. Perhaps you will be happy there.'

'I never knew you to lie, previously,' Lunaria said. 'You said the vase was a gift for me.'

'It is. It will be your new home. Your eternal home, I imagine.'

184

She relaxed in his grip and said no more. She remained some while like this, in a sort of limbo, before she was aware that his hands, rather than blotting out her consciousness, had unaccountably slackened.

Suddenly, to her bewilderment, Subyrus let her go.

He went away from her, about the table once more, and stopped, confronting the vase from a different vantage. An extraordinary expression had rearranged his face.

'Am I blind?' he said, so low she hardly made him out.

Youth, and of all things, panic, seemed swirling up from the darkened closets behind his eyes. And with those, an intoxication, such as Lunaria had witnessed in him the first night he had seen her, the first night she had refused him.

She rose and said sternly:

'Will you not finish murdering me, my lord?'

He glanced at her. She was startled. He viewed her with a novel and courteous indifference. Lunaria shrank. What an ultimate threat had not accomplished, this indifference could.

'I was mistaken,' he said. 'I have been too long gazing at leaves, and missed the tree.'

'No,' she said. 'Wait,' as he walked towards the terrace doors, where the bronze dragon grew vague and greenish on a damson twilight.

'Wait? No. There is no more need of waiting.'

The vase was in his hand. Sapphire flashed, and then went out as the dusk enclosed him.

The dragon heaved itself, with brass creakings, upright and abruptly aloft. Lunaria, rooted to the ground, watched Subyrus vanish into the sky over Vaim.

5

In Solitude

Somewhere in the hollow hill, a lion roared. It was a beast of jointed electrum, the seventh of the Mechanicae, activated and set loose by Subyrus on his return. Its task: to roam the chasm of the hill, a fierce guardian should any ever come there in the future, which was unlikely. It was unlikely because Subyrus, descending, had closed and sealed off the entrance to the hill by use of the eighth mechanism. The stone pavilion had folded and collapsed in unbroken and impenetrable slabs above the place. The periodic, inexhaustible roar of the lion from below was an added, really unnecessary deterrent.

And now Subyrus sat in his darkened hall, in his quartz chair. The fire did not burn. One lamp on a bronze tripod lit up the vase of blue crystal on a small table. The stopper lay beside it, and beside that a narrow phial with a fluid in it the colour of clear water.

Subyrus picked up the phial, uncorked, and leisurely drained it. It had the taste of wine and aloes. It was the most deadly of the six deadly poisons known on earth, but its nickname was Gentleness, for it slew without pain and in gradual, tactful, not unpleasant stages.

Subyrus rested in the chair, composed, and took the rose-opal stopper in his hand, and fixed his look on the vase.

He had exhausted the possibilities of the world long since. His intellect and his body, both were sick with the sparse fare they must subsist on. There was no height he might not scale at a step, no ocean he might not dredge at a blink. No learning he had not devoured, no game he had not played. Thus, it had needed a Lunaria to hold his horrified tedium in check, something so common and so ugly as a harlot's sneer to keep him vital and alive.

When the gate had opened, he had not seen it. He had nearly bypassed it altogether. He had sought a gift for Lunaria, then he had sought to trap her in the crystal, making her irrevocably his property and denying himself of her forever. Lunaria – he scarcely recalled her now.

Concentration on the minor issue had obscured the major. At the last instant, the truth had come to him, barely in time.

He had exhausted the world. Therefore he must find a second world of which he knew nothing. A world whose magic he had yet to learn, a world alien and unexplored, a world impossible to imagine – *the microcosm within the vase.*

Like a warm sleep, Gentleness stole over him. Primed to catch his ghost, the blue vase enigmatically waited. Perhaps nightmare crouched inside, perhaps a paradise. Even as the poison chilled it, Subyrus' blood raced with a heady excitement he had not felt for two decades and more.

In the shadows, a silver bell-clock struck a single dim note. It was the ninth of the Mechanicae, striking to mark the hour of the Magician-Lord's death.

And Subyrus sensed the moment of death come on him, as surely as he might gauge the supreme moment of love. He leaned forward to poise the rose-opal stopper above the lip of the vase. As the breath of life coursed from him, and the soul with it, unseen, was dashed into the trap of the crystal, the stopper dropped from his fingers to shut the gate behind him.

Subyrus, to whom existence had become mechanical, the tenth of his own Mechanicae, sat dead in his chair. And in the vase—

What?

Lunaria Vaimian had climbed the hill alone.

Below, at the hill's foot, uneasily, three or four attendants huddled about a gilded palanquin, dishevelled by cool winds and sombre fancies.

Lunaria wore black, and her bright hair was veiled in black. She regarded the fallen stone of the pavilion. Her eyes were angry.

'It is foolish for me,' she said, 'to chide you that you used me. Many have done so. Foolish also to desire to curse you, for you are proof against my ill-wishing as finally you were proof against my allure. But how I hate you, hate you as I love you, as I hated and I loved you from the beginning, knowing there was but one way by which to retain your interest in me; foreknowing that I should lose you in the end, whatever my tricks, and so I have.'

Leaves were blowing from woods in the wind, like yellow papers.

Lunaria watched them settle over the stone.

'A thousand falsehoods,' she said. 'A thousand pretences. Men I compelled to visit me (how afraid they were of the Magician-Lord), only that you might behold them. Gifts I demanded, poses I upheld. To mask my love. To keep your attention. And all, now, for nothing. I would have been your slave-ghost gladly. I would have let you slay me and bind me in the vase. I would have—'

The electrum lion roared somewhere beneath her feet in the hollow hill.

'There it is,' Lunaria muttered sullenly, 'the voice of my fury and my pain that will hurt me till I die; my despair, but more adequately expressed. I need say nothing while that other says it for me.'

And she went away down the hill through the blowing leaves and the blowing of her veil, and never spoke again as long as she lived.

'Blue Vase of Ghosts' by Tanith Lee, © 1983 by Charles de Lint. First published in *Dragonfields*, No. 4, 1983, and reprinted by permission of the author and the E.J. Carnell Literary Agency.

THE WIFE'S STORY
Ursula K. Le Guin

As science fiction is an intellectual kind of literature, much of it written by and for people not afraid of things of the mind, its characteristic failures are likely to be failures of feeling. Sometimes the feeling in sf is rationalized, and thereby trivialized; sometimes, more dangerously, it is cut off from intellect, not admitted to conscious thought, and so occurs as mindless sentimentality and/or blind hatred and blind fear. Recent films by Lucas and Spielberg exemplify these tendencies, in what I could wish was a definitive fashion.

One way to avoid actually having to use one's heart is to use ready-made, canned feeling – junkfood emotion – such as the horror, fascination, sexuality, etc. associated with such genuine archetypal themes as the Vampire and the Werewolf.

There is, however – as somebody remarked a long time ago – no such thing as a free lunch. Not even for Transylvanian noblemen.

I think the power of all animal/human stories can only come from a genuine identification with the animal, involving both knowledge and imagination. Writers trying to get a free lunch out of these great old themes, however, seem to know nothing and care nothing about the precarious, mysterious, complex existence of bats and wolves.

I knew less than I thought I knew when I wrote 'The Wife's Story', and my sociology is off on a couple of points, but I could not set it straight without bending the little tale all out of shape. So, to all readers who do take the trouble to know how our brothers and sisters live, I apologize for the liberties I have taken.

He was a good husband, a good father. I don't understand it. I don't believe in it. I don't believe that it happened. I saw it happen but it isn't true. It can't be. He was always gentle. If you'd have seen him playing with the children, anybody who saw him with the children would have known that there wasn't any bad in him, not one mean bone. When I first met him he was still living with his mother, over near Spring Lake, and I used to see them together, the mother and the sons, and think that any young fellow that was that nice with his family must be one worth knowing. Then one time when I was walking in the woods I met him by himself coming back from a hunting trip. He hadn't got any game at all, not so much as a field mouse, but he wasn't cast down about it. He was just larking along enjoying the morning air. That's one of the things I first loved about him. He didn't take things hard, he didn't grouch and whine when things didn't go his way. So we got to talking that day. And I guess things moved right along after that, because pretty soon he was over here pretty near all the time. And my sister said – see, my parents had moved out the year before and gone south, leaving us the place – my sister said, kind of teasing but serious, 'Well! If he's going to be here every day and half the night, I guess there isn't room for me!' And she moved out – just down the way. We've always been real close, her and me. That's the sort of thing doesn't ever change. I couldn't ever have got through this bad time without my sis.

Well, so he come to live here. And all I can say is, it was the happiest year of my life. He was just purely good to me. A hard worker and never lazy, and so big and fine-looking. Everybody looked up to him, you know, young as he was. Lodge Meeting nights, more and more often they had him to lead the singing. He had such a beautiful voice, and he'd lead off strong, and the others following and joining in, high voices and low. It brings the shivers on me now to think of it, hearing it, nights when I'd stayed home from meeting when the children was babies – the singing coming up through the trees there, and the moonlight, summer nights, the full moon shining. I'll never hear anything so beautiful. I'll never know a joy like that again.

It was the moon, that's what they say. It's the moon's fault, and the blood. It was in his father's blood. I never knew his father, and now I wonder what become of him. He was from up Whitewater way, and had no kin around here. I always thought he went back there, but now I don't know. There was some talk about him, tales, that come out after what happened to my husband. It's something runs in the blood, they say, and it may never come out, but if it does, it's the change of the moon that does it. Always it happens in the dark of the moon. When everybody's home and asleep. Something comes over the one that's got the curse in his blood, they say, and he gets up because he can't sleep, and goes out into the glaring sun, and goes off all alone – drawn to find those like him.

And it may be so, because my husband would do that. I'd half rouse and say, 'Where you going to?' and he'd say, 'Oh, hunting, be back this evening,' and it wasn't like him, even his voice was different. But I'd be so sleepy, and not wanting to wake the kids, and he was so good and responsible, it was no call of mine to go asking 'Why?' and 'Where?' and all like that.

So it happened that way maybe three times or four. He'd come back late, and worn out, and pretty near cross for one so sweet-tempered – not wanting to talk about it. I figured everybody got to bust out now and then, and nagging never helped anything. But it did begin to worry me. Not so much that he went, but that he come back so tired and strange. Even, he smelled strange. It made my hair stand up on end. I could not endure it and I said, 'What is that—those smells on you? All over you!' And he said, 'I don't know,' real short, and made like he was sleeping. But he went down when he thought I wasn't noticing, and washed and washed himself. But those smells stayed in his hair, and in our bed, for days.

And then the awful thing. I don't find it easy to tell about this. I want to cry when I have to bring it to my mind. Our youngest, the little one, my baby, she turned from her father. Just overnight. He come in and she got scared-looking, stiff, with her eyes wide, and then she begun to cry and try to hide behind me. She didn't yet talk plain but she was saying over and over, 'Make it go away! Make it go away!'

The look in his eyes, just for one moment, when he heard that. That's what I don't want ever to remember. That's what I can't forget. The look in his eyes looking at his own child.

I said to the child, 'Shame on you, what's got into you!' – scolding, but keeping her right up close to me at the same time, because I was frightened too. Frightened and shaking.

He looked away then and said something like, 'Guess she just waked up dreaming,' and passed it off that way. Or tried to. And so did I. And I got real mad with my baby when she kept on acting crazy scared of her own dad. But she couldn't help it and I couldn't change it.

He kept away that whole day. Because he knew, I guess. It was just beginning dark of the moon.

It was hot and close inside, and dark, and we'd all been asleep some while, when something woke me up. He wasn't there beside me. I heard a little stir in the passage, when I listened. So I got up, because I could bear it no longer. I went out into the passage, and it was light there, hard sunlight coming in from the door. And I saw him standing just outside, in the tall grass by the entrance. His head was hanging. Presently he sat down, like he felt weary, and looked down at his feet. I held still, inside, and watched — I didn't know what for.

And I saw what he saw. I saw the changing. In his feet, it was, first. They got long, each foot got longer, stretching out, the toes stretching out and the foot getting long, and fleshy, and white. And no hair on them.

The hair begun to come away all over his body. It was like his hair fried away in the sunlight and was gone. He was white all over, then, like a worm's skin. And he turned his face. It was changing while I looked. It got flatter and flatter, the mouth flat and wide, and the teeth grinning flat and dull, and the nose just a knob of flesh with nostril holes, and the ears gone, and the eyes gone blue — blue, with white rims around the blue — staring at me out of that flat, soft, white face.

He stood up then on two legs.

I saw him, I had to see him, my own dear love, turned into the hateful one.

I couldn't move, but as I crouched there in the passage staring out into the day I was trembling and shaking with a growl that burst out into a crazy, awful howling. A grief howl and a terror howl and a calling howl. And the others heard it, even sleeping, and woke up.

It stared and peered, that thing my husband had turned into, and shoved its face up to the entrance of our house. I was still bound by mortal fear, but behind me the children had waked up, and the baby was whimpering. The mother anger come into me then, and I snarled and crept forward.

The man thing looked around. It had no gun, like the ones from the man places do. But it picked up a heavy fallen tree branch in its long white foot, and shoved the end of that down into our house, at me. I snapped the end of it in my teeth and started to force my way out, because I knew the man would kill our children if it could. But my sister was already coming. I saw her running at the man with her head low and her mane high and her eyes yellow as the winter sun. It turned on her and raised up that branch to hit her. But I come out of the doorway, mad with the mother anger, and the others all were coming answering my call, the whole pack gathering, there in that blind glare and heat of the sun at noon.

The man looked round at us and yelled out loud, and brandished the branch it held. Then it broke and ran, heading for the cleared fields and plowlands, down the mountainside. It ran, on two legs, leaping and weaving, and we followed it.

I was last, because love still bound the anger and the fear in me. I was running when I saw them pull it down. My sister's teeth were in its throat. I got there and it was dead. The others were drawing back from the kill, because of the taste of the blood, and the smell. The younger ones were cowering and some crying, and my sister rubbed her mouth against her forelegs over and over to get rid of the taste. I went up close because I thought if the thing was dead the spell, the curse must be done, and my husband could come back – alive, or even dead, if I could only see him, my true love, in his true form, beautiful. But only the dead man lay there white and bloody. We drew back and back from it, and turned and ran, back up into the hills, back to the woods of the shadows and the twilight and the blessed dark.

THE HOUSE OF CTHULHU
Brian Lumley

Back in 1970-1, I had thoughts about breaking into the sword-and-sorcery markets, and attempted two or three short stories in that genre. There was nothing much wrong with them, but they somehow failed to satisfy me in the way that many of my Cthulhu Mythos tales and other short stories had. They lacked that frisson *– that delicious tingle down the spine – which distinguishes a really good tale from one which is merely satisfactory. I began to despair that I could not write S & S: I might eventually be mentioned (or acknowledged) alongside the great horror writers I so admired, but I would never find a place beside Robert E. Howard, Fritz Leiber, C.L. Moore, Henry Kuttner, etc. I was eager, in those days, and easily disillusioned. . . .*

On the other hand, there were ready markets for my horror stories, especially those set in the famous Cthulhu Mythos of H.P. Lovecraft. Hmm! Perhaps I had been too hasty. Perhaps – instead of rushing at S & S head-on, like a berserk barbarian – I should approach it rather more obliquely, through a medium in which I felt more truly at home.

Why not write a Mythos story set in a primal land of S & S? Why not set it way, way back – at the very dawn of time? After all, Cthulhu was here long before mere Man, wasn't he? And – with the one exception of Lovecraft's own 'Shadow Out of Time' – wouldn't that make mine the very 'first' Mythos tale? Yes, it would! And, since I was already being radical, why not give the story an anti-hero, using Cthulhu as the pivot? A tale of supernatural vengeance, with Cthulhu himself as the blunt instrument of revenge!

So I wrote 'The House of Cthulhu'.

The story was welcomed by Stuart Schiff for the American semi-prozine Whispers *– in fact, it was the first story in the very first issue of that magazine, which has since gone on from strength to strength. It was nominated for a World Fantasy Award. It was chosen for two year's-best collections,* Year's Best Horror *and* Year's Best Fantasy *–*

though, since DAW Books did both collections, it could only appear in one of them. In short, it very quickly became a firm favorite with both Mythos and S & S fans. And, of course, it also became a favorite of mine.

In the years since, this story has become the cornerstone of a whole volume of tales set in that same primal land at the dawn of time. Hopefully, by the time this book appears, Weirdbook Press in America will have published Tales of the Primal Land, in which ten more stories may be found – each with the same flavor, constructed of the same dark stone, as 'The House of Cthulhu'.

> Where weirdly angled ramparts loom,
> Gaunt sentinels whose shadows gloom
> Upon an undead hell-beast's tomb—
>   And gods and mortals fear to tread;
> Where gateways to forbidden spheres
> And times are closed, but monstrous fears
> Await the passing of strange years—
>   When that will wake which is not dead . . .

'Arlyeh' – a fragment from Teh Atht's Legends of the Olden Runes. As translated by Thelred Gustau from the Theem'hdra Manuscripts.

Now it happened aforetime that Zar-thule the Conqueror, who is called Reaver of Reavers, Seeker of Treasures and Sacker of Cities, swam out of the East with his dragonships; aye, even beneath the snapping sails of his dragonships. The wind was but lately turned favorable, and now the weary rowers nodded over their shipped oars while sleepy steersmen held the course. And there Zar-thule descried him in the sea the island Arlyeh, whereon loomed tall towers builded of black stones whose tortuous twinings were of angles all unknown and utterly beyond the ken of men. Aye, and this island was redly lit by the sun sinking down over its awesome black crags and burning behind the aeries and spires carved therefrom by other than human hands.

And though Zar-thule felt a great hunger and stood sore weary of the wide sea's expanse behind the lolling dragon's tail of his ship Redfire, and even though he gazed with red and rapacious eyes upon the black island, still he held off his reavers, bidding them that they ride at anchor well out to sea until the sun was deeply down and gone unto the Realm of Cthon; aye, even unto Cthon, who sits in silence to snare the sun in his net beyond the edge of the world. Indeed, such were Zar-thule's raiders as their deeds were best done by night, for then Gleeth the blind Moon God saw them not, nor heard in his celestial deafness the horrible cries which ever attended unto such deeds.

For notwithstanding his cruelty, which was beyond words, Zar-thule was no fool. He knew him that his wolves must rest before a whelming, that if the treasures of the House of Cthulhu were truly such as he imagined them – then that they must likewise be well guarded by fighting men who would not give them up easily. And his reavers were fatigued even as Zar-thule himself, so that he rested them all down behind the painted bucklers lining the decks, and furled him up the great dragon-dyed sails. And he set a watch that in the middle of the night he might be roused, when, rousing in turn the men of his twenty ships, he would sail in unto and sack the island of Arlyeh.

Far had Zar-thule's reavers rowed before the fair winds found them, aye, far from the rape of Yaht-Haal, the Silver City at the edge of the frostlands. Their provisions were all but eaten, their swords all oceanrot in rusting sheaths; but now they ate all of their remaining regimen and drank of the liquors thereof, and they cleansed and sharpened their dire blades before taking themselves into the arms of Shoosh, Goddess of the Still Slumbers. They well knew them, one and all, that soon they would be at the sack, each for himself and loot to that sword's wielder whose blade drank long and deep.

And Zar-thule had promised them great treasures from the House of Cthulhu, for back there in the sacked and seared city at the edge of the frostlands he had heard it from the bubbling, anguished lips of Voth Vehm, the name of the so-called 'forbidden' isle of Arlyeh. Voth Vehm, in the throes of terrible tortures, had called out the name of his brother-priest, Hath Vehm, who guarded the House of Cthulhu in Arlyeh. And even in the hour of his dying Voth Vehm had answered to Zar-thule's additional tortures, crying out that Arlyeh was indeed forbidden and held in thrall by the sleeping but yet dark and terrible god Cthulhu, the gate to whose House his brother-priest guarded.

Then had Zar-thule reasoned that Arlyeh must contain riches indeed, for he knew it was not meet that brother-priests betray one another; and aye, surely had Voth Vehm spoken exceedingly fearfully of this dark and terrible god Cthulhu only that he might thus divert Zar-thule's avarice from the ocean sanctuary of his brother-priest, Hath Vehm. Thus reckoned Zar-thule, even brooding on the dead and disfigured hierophant's words, until he bethought him to leave the sacked city. Then, with the flames leaping brightly and reflected in his red wake, Zar-thule put to sea in his dragonships. All loaded down with silver booty he put to sea, in search of Arlyeh and the treasures of the House of Cthulhu. And thus came he to this place.

Shortly before the midnight hour the watch roused Zar-thule up from the arms of Shoosh, aye, and all the freshened men of the dragonships; and then beneath Gleeth the blind Moon God's pitted silver face, seeing that the wind had fallen, they muffled their oars and dipped them deep and so closed in with the shoreline. A dozen fathoms from beaching, out rang Zar-thule's plunder cry, and his drummers took up a stern and steady beat by which the trained but yet rampageous reavers might advance to the sack.

Came the scrape of keel on grit, and down from his dragon's head leapt Zar-thule to the sullen shallow waters, and with him his captains and men, to wade ashore and stride the night-black strand and wave their swords . . . and all for naught! Lo, the island stood quiet and still and seemingly untended. . . .

Only now did the Sacker of Cities take note of this isle's truly awesome aspect. Black piles of tumbled masonry festooned with weeds from the tides rose up from the dark wet sand, and there seemed inherent in these gaunt and immemorial relics a foreboding not alone of bygone times; great crabs scuttled in and about the archaic ruins and gazed with stalked ruby eyes upon the intruders; even the small waves broke with an eery *hush, hush, hush* upon the sand and pebbles and primordial exuviae of crumbled yet seemingly sentient towers and tabernacles. The drummers faltered, paused and finally silence reigned.

Now many of them among these reavers recognized rare gods and supported strange superstitions, and Zar-thule knew this and had no liking for their silence. It was a silence that might yet yield mutiny!

'Hah!' quoth he, who worshipped neither god nor demon nor yet lent ear to the gaunts of night. 'See – the guards knew of our coming and are all fled to the far side of the island – or perhaps they gather ranks at the House of Cthulhu.' So saying, he formed him up his men into a body and advanced into the island.

And as they marched they passed them by other prehuman piles not yet ocean-sundered, striding through silent streets whose fantastic façades gave back the beat of the drummers in a strangely muted monotone.

And lo, mummied faces of coeval antiquity seemed to leer from the empty and oddly-angled towers and craggy spires, fleet ghouls that flitted from shadow to shadow apace with the marching men, until some of those hardened reavers grew sore afraid and begged them of Zar-thule, 'Master, let us get us gone from here, for it appears that there is no treasure, and this place is like unto no other. It stinks of death, aye even of death and of them that walk the shadowlands.'

But Zar-thule rounded on one who stood close to him muttering thus, crying, 'Coward! – Out on you!' Whereupon he lifted up his sword and hacked the trembling reaver in two parts, so that the sundered man screamed once before falling with twin thuds to the black earth. But now Zar-thule perceived that indeed many of his men were sore afraid, and so he had him torches lighted and brought up, and they pressed on quickly into the island.

There, beyond low dark hills, they came to a great gathering of queerly carved and monolithic edifices, all of the same confused angles and surfaces and all with the stench of the pit, aye, even the fetor of the very pit about them. And in the center of these malodorous megaliths there stood the greatest tower of them all, a massive menhir that loomed and leaned windowless to a great height, about which at its base squat pedestals bore likenesses of blackly carven krakens of terrifying aspect.

'Hah!' quoth Zar-thule. 'Plainly is this the House of Cthulhu, and see – its guards and priests have fled them all before us to escape the reaving!'

But a tremulous voice, old and mazed, answered from the shadows at the base of one great pedestal, saying, 'No one has fled, O reaver, for there are none here to flee, save me – and I cannot flee for I guard the gate against those who may utter The Words.'

At the sound of this old voice in the stillness the reavers started and peered nervously about at the leaping torch-cast shadows, but one stout captain stepped forward to drag from out of the dark an old, old man. And lo, seeing the mien of this mage, all the reavers fell back at once. For he bore upon his face and hands, aye, and upon all visible parts of him, a gray and furry lichen that seemed to crawl upon him even as he stood crooked and trembling in his great age!

'Who are you?' demanded Zar-thule, aghast at the sight of so hideous a spectacle of afflicted infirmity; even Zar-thule, aghast!

'I am Hath Vehm, brother-priest of Voth Vehm who serves the gods in the temples of Yaht-Haal; I am Hath Vehm, Keeper of the Gate at the House of Cthulhu, and I warn you that it is forbidden to touch me.' And he gloomed with rheumy eyes at the captain who held him, until that raider took away his hands.

'And I am Zar-thule the Conqueror,' quoth Zar-thule, less in awe now. 'Reaver of Reavers, Seeker of Treasures and Sacker of Cities. I have plundered Yaht-Haal, aye, plundered the Silver City and burned it low. And I have tortured Voth Vehm unto death. But in his dying, even with hot coals eating at his belly, he cried out a name. And it was *your* name! And he was truly a brother unto you, Hath Vehm, for he warned me of the terrible god Cthulhu and of this "forbidden" isle of Arlyeh. But I knew he lied, that he sought him only to protect a great and holy treasure and the brother-priest who guards it, doubtless with strange runes to frighten away the superstitious reavers! But Zar-thule is neither afraid nor credulous, old one. Here I stand and I say to you on your life that I'll know the way into this treasure house within the hour!'

And now, hearing their chief speak thus to the ancient priest of the island, and noting the old one's trembling infirmity and hideous disfigurement, Zar-thule's captains and men had taken heart. Some of them had gone about and about the beetling tower of obscure angles until they found a door. Now this door was great, tall, solid and in no way hidden from view; and yet at times it seemed very indistinct, as though misted and distant. It stood straight up in the wall of the House of Cthulhu, and yet looked as if to lean to one side . . . and then in one and the same moment to lean to the other! It bore leering, inhuman faces carven of its surface and horrid hieroglyphs, and these unknown characters seemed to writhe about the gorgon faces; and aye, those faces too, moved and grimaced in the light of the flickering torches.

The ancient Hath Vehm came to them where they gathered in wonder of the great door, saying: 'Aye, that is the gate of the House of Cthulhu, and I am its guardian.'

'So,' spake Zar-thule, who was also come there, 'and is there a key to this gate? I see no means of entry.'

'Aye, there is a key, but none such as you might readily imagine. It is not a key of metal, but of words . . .'

'Magic?' asked Zar-thule, undaunted. He had heard aforetime of similar thaumaturgies.

'Aye, magic!' agreed the Guardian of the Gate.

Zar-thule put the point of his sword to the old man's throat, observing as he did so the furry gray growth moving upon the elder's face and scrawny neck, saying: 'Then say those words now and let's have done!'

'Nay, I cannot say The Words—I am sworn to guard the gate that The Words are *never* spoken, neither by myself nor by any other who would foolishly or mistakenly open the House of Cthulhu. You may kill me—aye, even take my life with that very blade you now hold to my throat—but I will not utter The Words. . . .'

'And I say that you will—eventually!' quoth Zar-thule in an exceedingly cold voice, in a voice even as cold as the northern sleet. Whereupon he put down his sword and ordered two of his men to come forward, commanding that they take the ancient and tie him down to thonged pegs made fast in the ground. And they tied him down until he was spread out flat upon his back, not far from the great and oddly fashioned door in the wall of the House of Cthulhu.

Then a fire was lighted of dry shrubs and of driftwood fetched from the shore; and others of Zar-thule's reavers went out and trapped certain great nocturnal birds that knew not the power of flight; and yet others found a spring of brackish water and filled them up the waterskins. And soon tasteless but satisfying meat turned on the spits above a fire; and in the same fire sword-points glowed red, then white. And after Zar-thule and the captains and men had eaten their fill, then the Reaver of Reavers motioned to his torturers that they should attend to their task. These torturers had been trained by Zar-thule himself, so that they excelled in the arts of pincer and hot iron.

But then there came a diversion. For some little time a certain captain – his name was Cush-had, the man who first found the old priest in the shadow of the great pedestal and dragged him forth – had been peering most strangely at his hands in the firelight and rubbing them upon the hide of his jacket. Of a sudden he cursed and leapt to his feet, springing up from the remnants of his meal. He danced about in a frightened manner, beating wildly at the tumbled flat stones about with his hands.

Then of a sudden he stopped and cast sharp glances at his naked forearms. In the same second his eyes stood out in his face and he screamed as if he were pierced through and through with a keen blade; and he rushed to the fire and thrust his hands to its heart, even to his elbows. Then he drew his arms from the flames, staggering and moaning and calling upon certain trusted gods. And he tottered away into the night, his ruined arms steaming and dripping redly upon the ground.

Amazed, Zar-thule sent a man after Cush-had with a torch, and this man soon returned trembling with a very pale face in the firelight to tell how the madman had fallen or leapt to his death in a deep crevice. But before he fell there had been visible upon his face a creeping, furry grayness; and as he had fallen, aye, even as he crashed down to his death, he had screamed: 'Unclean . . . unclean . . . unclean!'

Then, all and all when they heard this, they remembered the old priest's words of warning when Cush-had dragged him out of hiding, and the way he had gloomed upon the unfortunate captain, and they looked at the ancient where he lay held fast to the earth. The two reavers whose task it had been to tie him down looked them one to the other with very wide eyes, their faces whitening perceptibly in the firelight, and they took up a quiet and secret examination of their persons; aye, even a *minute* examination. . . .

Zar-thule felt fear rising in his reavers like the east wind when it rises up fast and wild in the Desert of Sheb. He spat at the ground and lifted up his sword, crying: 'Listen to me! You are all superstitious cowards, all and all of you, with your old wives' tales and fears and mumbo-jumbo. What's there here to be frightened of? An old man, alone, on a black rock in the sea?'

'But I saw upon Cush-had's face—' began the man who had followed the demented captain.

'You only *thought* you saw something,' Zar-thule cut him off. 'It was only the flickering of your torch-fire and nothing more. Cush-had was a madman!'

'But—'

'Cush-had was a madman!' Zar-thule said again, and his voice turned very cold. 'Are you, too, insane? Is there room for you, too, at the bottom of that crevice?' But the man shrank back and said no more, and yet again Zar-thule called his torturers forward that they should be about their work.

The hours passed. . . .

Blind and coldly deaf Gleeth the old Moon God surely was, and yet perhaps he had sensed something of the agonized screams and the stench of roasting human flesh drifting up from Arlyeh that night. Certainly he seemed to sink down in the sky very quickly.

Now, however, the tattered and blackened figure stretched out upon the ground before the door in the wall of the House of Cthulhu was no longer strong enough to cry out loudly, and Zar-thule despaired for he saw that soon the priest of the island would sink into the last and longest of slumbers. And still The Words were not spoken. Too, the reaver king was perplexed by the ancient's stubborn refusal to admit that the door in the looming menhir concealed treasure; but in the end he put this down to the effect of certain vows Hath Vehm had no doubt taken in his inauguration to priesthood.

The torturers had not done their work well. They had been loath to touch the elder with anything but their hot swords; they *would* not – not even when threatened most direly – lay hands upon him, or approach him more closely than absolutely necessary to the application of their agonizing art. The two reavers responsible for tying the ancient down were dead, slain by former comrades upon whom they had inadvertently lain hands of friendship; and those they had touched, their slayers, they too were shunned by their companions and stood apart from the other reavers.

As the first gray light of dawn began to show behind the eastern sea, Zar-thule finally lost all patience and turned upon the dying priest in a veritable fury. He took up his sword, raising it over his head in two hands . . . and then Hath Vehm spoke:

'Wait!' he whispered, his voice a low, tortured croak. 'Wait, O reaver – I will say The Words.'

'What,' cried Zar-thule, lowering his blade. 'You will open the door?'

'Aye,' the cracked whisper came, 'I will open the Gate. But first, tell me: did you truly sack Yaht-Haal the Silver City? Did you truly raze it down with fire, and torture my brother-priest to death?'

'I did all that,' Zar-thule callously nodded.

'Then come you close,' Hath Vehm's voice sank low. 'Closer, O reaver king, that you may hear me in my final hour.'

Eagerly the Seeker of Treasures bent him down his ear to the lips of the ancient, kneeling down beside where he lay – and Hath Vehm immediately lifted up his head from the earth and spat upon Zar-thule!

Then, before the Sacker of Cities could think or make a move to wipe the slimy spittle from his brow, Hath Vehm said The Words. Aye, even in a loud and clear voice he said them – words of terrible import and alien cadence that only an adept might repeat – and at once there came a great rumble from the door in the beetling wall of weird angles.

Forgetting for the moment the tainted insult of the ancient priest, Zar-thule turned to see the huge and evilly carven door tremble and waver and then, by some unknown power, move or slide away until only a great black hole opened where it had been. And lo, in the early dawn light, the reaver horde pressed forward to seek them out the treasure with their eyes; aye, even to seek out the treasure beyond the open door. Likewise Zar-thule made to enter the House of Cthulhu, but again the dying hierophant cried out to him:

'Hold! There are more words, O reaver king!'

'More words?' Zar-thule turned with a frown. The old priest, his life quickly ebbing, grinned mirthlessly at the sight of the furry gray blemish that crawled upon the barbarian's forehead over his left eye.

'Aye, more words. Listen: long and long ago, when the world was very young, before Arlyeh and the House of Cthulhu were first sunken into the sea, wise elder gods devised a rune that should Cthulhu's House ever rise and be opened by foolish men, it might be sent down again – aye, and even Arlyeh itself sunken deep once more beneath the salt waters. *Now I say those other words!'*

Swiftly the king reaver leapt, his sword lifting, but ere that blade could fall Hath Vehm cried out those other strange and dreadful words; and lo, the whole island shook in the grip of a great earthquake. Now in awful anger Zar-thule's sword fell and hacked off the ancient's whistling and spurting head from his ravened body; but even as the head rolled free, so the island shook itself again, and the ground rumbled and began to break open.

From the open door in the House of Cthulhu, whereinto the host of greedy reavers had rushed to discover the treasure, there came loud and singularly hideous cries of fear and torment, and of a sudden an even more hideous stench. And now Zar-thule knew truly and truly indeed that there was no treasure.

Great ebony clouds gathered swiftly and livid lightning crashed; winds rose up that blew Zar-thule's long black hair over his face as he crouched in horror before the open door of the House of Cthulhu. Wide and wide were his eyes as he tried to peer beyond the reeking blackness of that nameless, ancient aperture – but a moment later he dropped his great sword to the ground and screamed; aye, even the Reaver of Reavers screamed.

For two of his wolves had appeared from out of the darkness, more in the manner of whipped puppies than true wolves, shrieking and babbling and scrambling frantically over the queer angles of the orifice's mouth . . . but they had emerged only to be snatched up and squashed like grapes by titanic tentacles that lashed after them from the dark depths beyond! And these rubbery appendages drew the crushed bodies back into the inky blackness, from which there instantly issued forth the most monstrously nauseating slobberings and suckings before the writhing members once more snaked forth into the dawn light. This time they caught at the edges of the opening, and from behind them pushed forward – *a face!*

Zar-thule gazed upon the enormously bloated visage of Cthulhu, and he screamed again as that terrible Being's awful eyes found him where he crouched – found him and lit with an hideous light.

The reaver king paused, frozen, petrified, for but a moment, and yet long enough that the ultimate horror of the thing framed in the titan threshold seared itself upon his brain forever. Then his legs found their strength. He turned and fled, speeding away and over the low black hills, and down to the shore and into his ship, which he somehow managed, even single-handed and in his frantic terror, to cast off. And all the time in his mind's eye there burned that fearful sight – the awful *Visage* and *Being* of Lord Cthulhu.

There had been the tentacles, springing from a greenly pulpy head about which they sprouted like lethiferous petals about the heart of an obscenely hybrid orchid, a scaled and amorphously elastic body of immense proportions, with clawed feet fore and hind; long narrow wings ill-fitting the horror that bore them in that it seemed patently impossible for *any* wings to lift so fantastic a bulk – and then there had been the eyes! Never before had Zar-thule seen such evil rampant and expressed as in the ultimately leering malignancy of Cthulhu's eyes!

And Cthulhu was not finished with Zar-thule, for even as the king reaver struggled madly with his sail the monster came across the low hills in the dawn light, slobbering and groping down to the very water's edge. Then, when Zar-thule saw against the morning the mountain that was Cthulhu, he went mad for a period; flinging himself from side to side of his ship so that he was like to fall into the sea, frothing at the mouth and babbling horribly in pitiful prayer – aye, even Zar-thule, whose lips never before uttered prayers – to certain benevolent gods of which he had heard. And it seems that these kind gods, if indeed they exist, must have heard him.

With a roar and a blast greater than any before, there came the final shattering that saved Zar-thule for a cruel future, and the entire island split asunder; even the bulk of Arlyeh breaking into many parts and settling into the sea. And with a piercing scream of frustrated rage and lust – a scream which Zar-thule heard with his mind as well as his ears – the monster Cthulhu sank Him down also with the island and His House beneath the frothing waves.

A great storm raged then such as might attend the end of the world. Banshee winds howled and demon waves crashed over and about Zar-thule's dragonship, and for two days he gibbered and moaned in the rolling, shuddering scuppers of crippled Redfire before the mighty storm wore itself out.

Eventually, close to starvation, the one-time Reaver of Reavers was discovered becalmed upon a flat sea not far from the fair strands of bright Theem'hdra; and then, in the spicy hold of a rich merchant's ship, he was borne in unto the wharves of the City of Klühn, Theem'hdra's capital.

With long oars he was prodded ashore, stumbling and weak and crying out in his horror of living – for he had gazed upon Cthulhu! The use of the oars had much to do with his appearance, for now Zar-thule was changed indeed, into something which in less tolerant parts of the world might certainly have expected to be burned. But the people of Klühn were kindly folk; they burned him not but lowered him in a basket into a deep dungeon cell with torches to light the place, and daily bread and water that he might live until his life was rightly done. And when he was recovered to partial health and sanity, learned men and physicians went to talk with him from above and ask him of his strange affliction, of which all and all stood in awe.

I, Teh Atht, was one of them that went to him, and that was how I came to hear this tale. And I know it to be true, for oft and again over the years I have heard of this Loathly Lord Cthulhu that seeped down from the stars when the world was an inchoate infant. There are legends and legends, aye, and one of them is that when times have passed and the stars are right Cthulhu shall slobber forth from His House in Arlyeh again, and the world shall tremble to His tread and erupt in madness at His touch.

I leave this record for men as yet unborn, a record and a warning: leave well enough alone, for that is not dead which deeply dreams, and while perhaps the submarine tides have removed forever the alien taint which touched Arlyeh – that symptom of Cthulhu, which loathsome familiar grew upon Hath Vehm and transferred itself upon certain of Zar-thule's reavers – Cthulhu himself yet lives and waits upon those who would set Him free. I know it is so. In dreams . . . I myself have heard His call!

And when dreams such as these come in the night to sour the sweet embrace of Shoosh, I wake and tremble and pace the crystal-paved floors of my rooms above the Bay of Klühn, until Cthon releases the sun from his net to rise again, and ever and ever I recall the aspect of Zar-thule as last I saw him in the flickering torchlight of his deep dungeon cell: a fumbling gray mushroom thing that moved not of its own volition but by reason of the parasite growth which lived upon and within it. . . .

'The House of Cthulhu' by Brian Lumley, © 1973 by Stuart David Schiff. Reprinted by permission of the author and the E.J. Carnell Literary Agency.

THE REAL SHAPE OF THE COAST
John Lutz

What sort of story can be classified as a fantasy? What sort of story can't?

Webster's defines fantasy as : 'Imagination. Fancy. A product of the imagination.' The definition of fiction from the same source is: 'Something (as a story) invented by the imagination.'

It is this nearness and narrowness of definition that causes me difficulty in choosing what I consider to be my favorite fantasy story.

Almost everything that is fantasy seems to overlap into other genres, making this kind of story rather elusive when it comes to categorization. Is a story involving Satan a fantasy, for instance, or is it occult? (Or is it neither? To those who firmly believe in fire and brimstone, it is simply a story about Satan.)

Most fantasy stories could also – and often more accurately – be described as occult, science-fiction or mystery stories. And defining these genres precisely is almost as difficult as defining fantasy. Almost, but not quite.

It soon becomes apparent that, in each genre, any definition used will close out many great stories, while most of the few stories that fit firmly into each genre also fit at least loosely under the heading of fantasy. It's easy to read a story and say, 'This is science fiction'. Or 'mystery', 'occult', 'detective', 'suspense', or even various combinations of these genres and subgenres. It is not so easy to read a story and say, 'This is not fantasy'.

What we have here is a grey area.

Not so surprising, since even 'reality' is difficult to make exempt from the definition of fantasy. People have fantasized that the Earth was flat, that they were burning real witches who just the night before had been cavorting as black cats, that the precise dance steps in the correct sequence would bring rain. . . .

It seems that a fantasy widely held becomes 'reality'. It seems that we are forever fantasizing, for the grey area is with us always.

Out of this shadowland, my favorite story by far is 'The Real

Shape of the Coast'. While it is clearly a detective story, it is also an allegory in which virtually all of the characters fantasize, and in which fantasies clash with each other and, finally, with 'reality'.

'The Real Shape of the Coast', too, is a denizen of the grey area. But where else would fantasy reside?

Where the slender peninsula crooks like a beckoning finger in the warm water, where the ocean waves crash in umbrellas of foam over the low-lying rocks to roll and ebb on the narrow white-sand beaches, there squats in a series of low rectangular buildings and patterns of high fences the State Institution for the Criminal Incurably Insane. There are twenty of the sharp-angled buildings, each rising bricked and hard out of sandy soil like an undeniable fact. Around each building is a ten-foot redwood fence topped by barbed wire, and these fences run to the sea's edge to continue as gossamer networks of barbed wire that stretch out to the rocks.

In each of the rectangular buildings live six men, and on days when the ocean is suitable for swimming it is part of their daily habit — indeed, part of their therapy — to go down to the beach and let the waves roll over them, or simply to lie in the purging sun and grow beautifully tan. Sometimes, just out of the grasping reach of the waves, the men might build things in the damp sand, but by evening those things would be gone. However, some very interesting things had been built in that sand.

The men in the rectangular buildings were not just marking time until their real death. In fact, the 'Incurably Insane' in the institution's name was something of a misnomer; it was just that there was an absolute minimum of hope for these men. They lived in clusters of six not only for security's sake, but so that they might form a more or less permanent sensitivity group — day-in, day-out group therapy, with occasional informal gatherings supervised by young Dr. Montaign. Here under the subtle and skilful probings of Dr. Montaign the men bared their lost souls — at least, some of them did.

Cottage D was soon to be the subject of Dr. Montaign's acute interest. In fact, he was to study the occurrences there for the next year and write a series of articles to be published in influential scientific journals.

The first sign that there was something wrong at Cottage D was when one of the patients, a Mr. Rolt, was found dead on the beach one evening. He was lying on his back near the water's edge, wearing only a pair of khaki trousers. At first glance it would seem that he'd had a drowning accident, only his mouth and much of his throat turned out to be stuffed with sand and with a myriad of tiny colorful shells.

Roger Logan, who had lived in Cottage D since being found guilty of murdering his wife three years before, sat quietly watching Dr. Montaign pace the room.

'This simply won't do,' the doctor was saying. 'One of you has done away with Mr. Rolt, and that is exactly the sort of thing we are in here to stop.'

'But it won't be investigated too thoroughly, will it?' Logan said softly. 'Like when a convicted murderer is killed in a prison.'

'May I remind you,' a patient named Kneehoff said in his clipped voice, 'that Mr. Rolt was not a murderer.' Kneehoff had been a successful businessman before his confinement, and now he made excellent leather wallets and sold them by mail order. He sat now at a small table with some old letters spread before him, as if he were a Chairman of the Board presiding over a meeting. 'I might add,' he said haughtily, 'that it's difficult to conduct business in an atmosphere such as this.'

'I didn't say Rolt was a murderer,' Logan said, 'but he is—was — supposed to be in here for the rest of his life. That fact is bound to impede justice.'

Kneehoff shrugged and shuffled through his letters. 'He was a man of little consequence – that is, compared to the heads of giant corporations.'

It was true that Mr. Rolt had been a butcher rather than a captain of industry, a butcher who had put things in the meat – some of them unmentionable. But then Kneehoff had merely run a chain of three dry-cleaning establishments.

'Perhaps you thought him inconsequential enough to murder,' William Sloan, who was in for pushing his young daughter out of a fortieth-story window, said to Kneehoff. 'You never did like Mr. Rolt.'

Kneehoff began to splutter. 'You're the killer here, Sloan! You and Logan!'

'I killed no one,' Logan said quickly.

Kneehoff grinned. 'You were proved guilty in a court of law—of killing your wife.'

'They didn't prove it to me. I should know whether or not I'm guilty!'

'I know your case,' Kneehoff said, gazing dispassionately at his old letters. 'You hit your wife over the head with a bottle of French Chablis wine, killing her immediately.'

'I warn you,' Logan said heatedly, 'implying that I struck my wife with a wine bottle—and French Chablis at that—is inviting a libel suit!'

Noticcably shaken, Kneehoff became quiet and seemed to lose himself in studying the papers before him. Logan had learned long ago how to deal with him; he knew that Kneehoff's 'company' could not stand a lawsuit.

'Justice must be done,' Logan went on. 'Mr. Rolt's murderer, a real murderer, must be caught and executed.'

'Isn't that a job for the police?' Dr. Montaign asked gently.

'The police!' Logan laughed. 'Look how they botched my case! No, this is a job for *us*. Living the rest of our lives with a murderer would be intolerable.'

'But what about Mr. Sloan?' Dr. Montaign asked. 'You're living with *him*.'

'His is a different case,' Logan snapped. 'Because they found him guilty doesn't mean he is guilty. He says he doesn't remember anything about it, doesn't he?'

'What's your angle?' Brandon, the unsuccessful mystery bomber, asked. 'You people have always got an angle, something in mind for yourselves. The only people you can really trust are the poor people.'

'My angle is justice,' Logan said firmly. 'We must have justice!'

'Justice for all the people!' Brandon suddenly shouted, rising to his feet. He glanced about angrily and then sat down again.

'Justice,' said old Mr. Heimer, who had been to other worlds and could listen to and hear metal, 'will take care of itself. It always does, no matter where.'

'They've been waiting a long time,' Brandon said, his jaw jutting out beneath his dark mustache. 'The poor people, I mean.'

'Have the police any clues?' Logan asked Dr. Montaign.

'They know what you know,' the doctor said calmly. 'Mr. Rolt was killed on the beach between nine fifteen and ten—when he shouldn't have been out of Cottage D.'

Mr. Heimer raised a thin speckled hand to his lips and chuckled feebly. 'Now, maybe that's justice.'

'You know the penalty for leaving the building during unauthorized hours,' Kneehoff said sternly to Mr. Heimer. 'Not death, but confinement to your room for two days. We must have the punishment fit the crime and we must obey the rules. Any operation must have rules in order to be successful.'

'That's exactly what I'm saying,' Logan said. 'The man who killed poor Mr. Rolt must be caught and put to death.'

'The authorities are investigating,' Dr. Montaign said soothingly.

'Like they investigated my case?' Logan said in a raised and angry voice. 'They won't bring the criminal to justice! And I tell you we must not have a murderer here in Compound D!'

'Cottage D,' Dr. Montaign corrected him.

'Perhaps Mr. Rolt was killed by something from the sea,' William Sloan said thoughtfully.

'No,' Brandon said, 'I heard the police say there was only a single set of footprints near the body and it led from and to the cottage. It's obviously the work of an inside subversive.'

'But what size footprints?' Logan asked.

'They weren't clear enough to determine the size,' Dr. Montaign said. 'They led to and from near the wooden stairs that come up to the rear yard, where the ground was too hard for footprints.'

'Perhaps they were Mr. Rolt's own footprints,' Sloan said.

Kneehoff grunted. 'Stupid! Mr. Rolt went to the beach, but he did not come back.'

'Well—' Dr. Montaign rose slowly and walked to the door. 'I must be going to some of the other cottages now.' He smiled at Logan. 'It's interesting that you're so concerned with justice,' he said. A gull screamed as the doctor went out.

The five remaining patients of Cottage D sat quietly after Dr. Montaign's exit. Logan watched Kneehoff gather up his letters and give their edges a neat sharp tap on the table top before slipping them into his shirt pocket. Brandon and Mr. Heimer seemed to be in deep thought, while Sloan was peering over Kneehoff's shoulder through the open window out to the rolling sea.

'It could be that none of us is safe,' Logan said suddenly. 'We must get to the bottom of this ourselves.'

'But we are at the bottom,' Mr. Heimer said pleasantly, 'all of us.'

Kneehoff snorted. 'Speak for yourself, old man.'

'It's the crime against the poor people that should be investigated,' Brandon said. 'If my bomb in the Statue of Liberty had gone off . . . And I used my whole week's vacation that year going to New York.'

'We'll conduct our own investigation,' Logan insisted, 'and we might as well start now. Everyone tell me what he knows about Mr. Rolt's murder.'

'Who put you in charge?' Kneehoff asked. 'And why should we investigate Rolt's murder?'

'Mr. Rolt was our friend,' Sloan said.

'Anyway,' Logan said, 'we must have an orderly investigation. Somebody has to be in charge.'

'I suppose you're right,' Kneehoff said. 'Yes, an orderly investigation.'

Information was exchanged, and it was determined that Mr. Rolt had said he was going to bed at 9.15, saying good night to Ollie, the attendant, in the TV lounge. Sloan and Brandon, the two other men in the lounge, remembered the time because the halfway commercial for 'Monsters of Main Street' was on, the one where the box of detergent soars through the air and snatches everyone's shirt. Then at ten o'clock, just when the news was coming on, Ollie had gone to check the beach and discovered Mr. Rolt's body.

'So,' Logan said, 'the approximate time of death has been established. And I was in my room with the door open. I doubt if Mr. Rolt could have passed in the hall to go outdoors without my noticing him, so we must hypothesize that he did go to his room at nine fifteen, and sometime between nine fifteen and ten he left through his window.'

'He knew the rules,' Kneehoff said. 'He wouldn't have just walked outside for everyone to see him.'

'True,' Logan conceded, 'but it's best not to take anything for granted.'

'True, true,' Mr. Heimer chuckled, 'take nothing for granted.'

'And where were *you* between nine and ten?' Logan asked.

'I was in Dr. Montaign's office,' Mr. Heimer said with a grin, 'Talking to the doctor about something I'd heard in the steel utility pole. I almost made him understand that all things metal are receivers, tuned to different frequencies, different worlds and vibrations.'

Kneehoff, who had once held two of his accountants prisoner for five days without food, laughed.

'And where were *you*?' Logan asked.

'In my office, going over my leather-goods vouchers,' Kneehoff said. Kneehoff's 'office' was his room, toward the opposite end of the hall from Logan's room.

'Now,' Logan said, 'we get to the matter of motive. Which of us had reason to kill Mr. Rolt?'

'I don't know,' Sloan said distantly. 'Who'd do such a thing fill Mr. Rolt's mouth with sand?'

'You were his closest acquaintance,' Brandon said to Logan. 'You always played chess with him. Who knows what you and he were plotting?'

'What about you?' Kneehoff said to Brandon. 'You tried to choke Mr. Rolt just last week.'

Brandon stood up angrily, his mustache bristling. 'That was the week *before* last!' He turned to Logan. 'And Rolt always beat Logan at chess—that's why Logan hated him.'

'He didn't *always* beat me at chess,' Logan said. 'And I didn't hate him. The only reason he beat me at chess sometimes was because he'd upset the board if he was losing.'

'You don't like to get beat at anything,' Brandon said, sitting down again. 'That's why you killed your wife, because she beat you at things. How middle-class, to kill someone because of that.'

'I didn't kill my wife,' Logan said patiently. 'And she didn't beat me at things. Though she was a pretty good business woman,' he added slowly, 'and a good tennis player.'

'What about Kneehoff?' Sloan asked. 'He was always threatening to kill Mr. Rolt.'

'Because he laughed at me!' Kneehoff spat out. 'Rolt was a braggart and a fool, always laughing at me because I have ambition and he didn't. He thought he was better at everything than anybody else —and you, Sloan—Rolt used to ridicule you and Heimer. There isn't one of us who didn't have motive to eliminate a piece of scum like Rolt.'

Logan was on his feet, almost screaming. 'I won't have you talk about the dead like that!'

'All I was saying,' Kneehoff said, smiling his superior smile at having upset Logan, 'was that it won't be easy for you to discover Rolt's murderer. He was a clever man, that murderer, cleverer than you.'

Logan refused to be baited. 'We'll see about that when I check the alibis,' he muttered, and he left the room to walk barefoot in the surf.

On the beach the next day Sloan asked the question they had all been wondering.

'What are we going to do with the murderer if we do catch him?' he asked, his eyes fixed on a distant ship that was just an irregularity on the horizon.

'We'll extract justice,' Logan said. 'We'll convict and execute him —eliminate him from our society!'

'Do you think we should?' Sloan asked.

'Of course we should!' Logan snapped. 'The authorities don't care who killed Mr. Rolt. The authorities are probably glad he's dead.'

'I don't agree that it's a sound move,' Kneehoff said, 'to execute the man. I move that we don't do that.'

'I don't hear anyone seconding you,' Logan said. 'It has to be the way I say if we are to maintain order here.'

Kneehoff thought a moment, then smiled. 'I agree we must maintain order at all costs,' he said. 'I withdraw my motion.'

'Motion, hell!' Brandon said. He spat into the sand. 'We ought to just find out who the killer is and liquidate him. No time for a motion—time for action!'

'Mr. Rolt would approve of that,' Sloan said, letting a handful of sand run through his fingers.

Ollie the attendant came down to the beach and stood there smiling, the sea breeze rippling his white uniform. The group on the beach broke up slowly and casually, each man idling away in a different direction.

Kicking the sun-warmed sand with his bare toes, Logan approached Ollie.

'Game of chess, Mr. Logan?' Ollie asked.

'Thanks, no,' Logan said. 'You found Mr. Rolt's body, didn't you, Ollie?'

'Right, Mr. Logan.'

'Mr. Rolt was probably killed while you and Sloan and Brandon were watching TV.'

'Probably,' Ollie agreed, his big face impassive.

'How come you left at ten o'clock to go down to the beach?'

Ollie turned to stare blankly at Logan with his flat eyes. 'You know I always check the beach at night, Mr. Logan. Sometimes the patients lose things.'

'Mr. Rolt sure lost something,' Logan said. 'Did the police ask you if Brandon and Sloan were in the TV room with you the whole time before the murder?'

'They did and I told them yes.' Ollie lit a cigarette with one of those transparent lighters that had a fishing fly in the fluid. 'You studying to be a detective, Mr. Logan?'

'No, no,' Logan laughed. 'I'm just interested in how the police work, after the way they messed up my case. Once they thought I was guilty I didn't have a chance.'

But Ollie was no longer listening. He had turned to look out at the ocean. 'Don't go out too far, Mr. Kneehoff!' he called, but Kneehoff pretended not to hear and began moving in the water parallel with the beach.

Logan walked away to join Mr. Heimer, who was standing in the surf with his pants rolled above his knees.

'Find out anything from Ollie?' Mr. Heimer asked, his body balancing slightly as the retreating sea pulled the sand and shells from beneath him.

'Some things,' Logan said, crossing his arms and enjoying the play of the cool surf about his legs. The two men – rather than the ocean – seemed to be moving as the tide swept in and out and shifted the sand beneath the sensitive soles of their bare feet. 'It's like the ocean,' Logan said, 'finding out who killed Mr. Rolt. The ocean works and works on the shore, washing in and out until only the sand and rock remain—the real shape of the coast. Wash the soil away and you have bare rock; wash the lies away and you have bare truth.'

'Not many can endure the truth,' Mr. Heimer said, stooping to let his hand drag in an incoming wave, 'even on other worlds.'

Logan raised his shoulders. 'Not many ever learn the truth,' he said, turning and walking through the wet sand toward the beach. Amid the onwash of the wide shallow wave he seemed to be moving backward, out to sea . . .

Two days later Logan talked to Dr. Montaign, catching him alone in the TV lounge when the doctor dropped by for one of his mid-day visits. The room was very quiet; even the ticking of the clock seemed slow, lazy, and out of rhythm.

'I was wondering, Doctor,' Logan said, 'about the night of Mr. Rolt's murder. Did Mr. Heimer stay very late in your office?'

'The police asked me that,' Dr. Montaign said with a smile. 'Mr. Heimer was in my office until ten o'clock, then I saw him come into this room and join Brandon and Sloan to watch the news.'

'Was Kneehoff with them?'

'Yes, Kneehoff was in his room.'

'I was in my room,' Logan said, 'with my door open to the hall, and I didn't see Mr. Rolt pass to go outdoors. So he must have gone out through his window. Maybe the police would like to know that.'

'I'll tell them for you,' Dr. Montaign said, 'but they know Mr. Rolt went out through his window because his only door was locked from the inside.' The doctor cocked his head at Logan, as was his habit. 'I wouldn't try to be a detective,' he said gently. He placed a smoothly manicured hand on Logan's shoulder. 'My advice is to forget about Mr. Rolt.'

'Like the police?' Logan said.

The hand patted Logan's shoulder soothingly.

After the doctor had left, Logan sat on the cool vinyl sofa and thought. Brandon, Sloan and Heimer were accounted for, and Kneehoff couldn't have left the building without Logan seeing him pass in the hall. The two men, murderer and victim, might have left together through Mr. Rolt's window – only that wouldn't explain the single set of fresh footprints to and from the body. And the police had found Mr. Rolt's footprints where he'd gone down to the beach farther from the cottage and then apparently walked up the beach through the surf to where his path and the path of the murderer crossed.

And then Logan saw the only remaining possibility – the only possible answer.

Ollie, the man who had discovered the body – Ollie alone had had the opportunity to kill! And after doing away with Mr. Rolt he must have noticed his footprints leading to and from the body; so at the wooden stairs he simply turned and walked back to the sea in another direction, then walked up the beach to make his 'discovery' and alert the doctor.

Motive? Logan smiled. Anyone could have had motive enough to kill the bragging and offensive Mr. Rolt. He had been an easy man to hate.

Logan left the TV room to join the other patients on the beach, careful not to glance at the distant white-uniformed figure of Ollie painting some deck chairs at the other end of the building.

'Tonight,' Logan told them dramatically, 'we'll meet in the conference room after Dr. Montaign leaves and I promise to tell you who the murderer is. Then we'll decide how best to remove him from our midst.'

'Only if he's guilty,' Kneehoff said. 'You must present convincing, positive evidence.'

'I have proof,' Logan said.

'Power to the people!' Brandon cried, leaping to his feet.

Laughing and shouting, they all ran like schoolboys into the waves.

The patients sat through their evening session with Dr. Montaign, answering questions mechanically and chattering irrelevantly, and Dr. Montaign sensed a certain tenseness and expectancy in them. Why were they anxious? Was it fear? Had Logan been harping to them about the murder? Why was Kneehoff not looking at his letters, and Sloan not gazing out the window?

'I told the police,' Dr. Montaign mentioned, 'that I didn't expect to walk up on any more bodies on the beach.'

'You?' Logan stiffened in his chair. 'I thought it was Ollie who found Mr. Rolt.'

'He did, really,' Dr. Montaign said, cocking his head. 'After Mr. Heimer left me I accompanied Ollie to check the beach so I could talk to him about some things. He was the one who saw the body first and ran ahead to find out what it was.'

'And it was Mr. Rolt, his mouth stuffed with sand,' Sloan murmured.

Logan's head seemed to be whirling. He had been so sure! Process of elimination. It had to be Ollie! Or were the two men, Ollie and Dr. Montaign, in it together? They had to be! But that was impossible! There had been only one set of footprints.

Kneehoff! It must have been Kneehoff all along! He must have made a secret appointment with Rolt on the beach and killed him. But Rolt had been walking alone until he met the killer, who was also alone! And *someone* had left the fresh footprints, the single set of footprints, to and from the body.

Kneehoff must have seen Rolt, slipped out through his window, intercepted him, and killed him. But Kneehoff's room didn't have a window! Only the two end rooms had windows, Rolt's room and Logan's room!

A single set of footprints – they could only be his own! *His own!*

Through a haze Logan saw Dr. Montaign glance at his watch, smile, say his goodbyes, and leave. The night breeze wafted through the wide open windows of the conference room with the hushing of the surf, the surf wearing away the land to bare rock.

'Now,' Kneehoff said to Logan, and the moon seemed to light his eyes, 'who exactly is our man? Who killed Mr. Rolt? And what is your evidence?'

Ollie found Logan's body the next morning, face down on the beach, the gentle lapping surf trying to claim him. Logan's head was turned and half buried and his broken limbs were twisted at strange angles, and around him the damp sand was beaten with, in addition to his own, four different sets of footprints.

THE SMALLEST DRAGONBOY
Anne McCaffrey

This story was written at the behest of Roger Elwood, and first appeared in Rand McNally's Science Fiction Tales *in 1973. At the time, I was trying to write a story involving a girl from a seahold, a girl named Menolly, but the yarn wouldn't write – so I turned to a boy of the Weyrs instead. Keevan, it was, who joggled my arm and asked, please, would I write about him?*

For Keevan's fortitude and courage I drew on my recollections of my younger brother, Kevin, who was afflicted with osteomyelitis at the age of thirteen. Keve spent months in full body casts and braces, showing the valor with which I have imbued my dragonboy.

The story has had great appeal, being reprinted for younger readers and used, in 1978, as the basis for a one-act play in Wisconsin. I have read it aloud to audiences from Liverpool, England to Fairbanks, Alaska.

I don't know what my brother Kevin thinks of it – but then he's not a great talker.

Although Keevan lengthened his walking stride as far as his legs would stretch, he couldn't quite keep up with the other candidates. He knew he would be teased again.

Just as he knew many things that his foster mother told him he ought not to know, Keevan knew that Beterli, the most senior of the boys, set that spanking pace just to embarrass him, the smallest dragonboy. Keevan would arrive, tail fork-end of the group, breathless, chest heaving, and maybe get a stern look from the instructing wing-second.

Dragonriders, even if they were still only hopeful candidates for the glowing eggs which were hardening on the hot sands of the Hatching Ground cavern, were expected to be punctual and prepared. Sloth was not tolerated by the Weyrleader of Benden Weyr. A good record was especially important now. It was very near hatching

217

time, when the baby dragons would crack their mottled shells, and stagger forth to choose their lifetime companions. The very thought of that glorious moment made Keevan's breath catch in his throat. To be chosen – to be a dragonrider! To sit astride the neck of a winged beast with jewelled eyes: to be his companion in good times and fighting extremes; to fly effortlessly over the lands of Pern! Or, thrillingly, *between* to any point anywhere on the world! Flying *between* was done on dragonback or not at all, and it was dangerous.

Keevan glanced upward, past the black mouths of the weyr caves in which grown dragons and their chosen riders lived, toward the Star Stones that crowned the ridge of the old volcano that was Benden Weyr. On the height, the blue watch dragon, his rider mounted on his neck, stretched the great transparent pinions that carried him on the winds of Pern to fight the evil Thread that fell at certain times from the skies. The many-faceted rainbow jewels of his eyes glistened fleetingly in the greeny sun. He folded his great wings to his back, and the watchpair resumed their statue-like pose of alertness.

Then the enticing view was obscured as Keevan passed into the Hatching Ground cavern. The sands underfoot were hot, even through heavy wher-hide boots. How the bootmaker had protested having to sew so small! Keevan was forced to wonder why being small was reprehensible. People were always calling him 'babe' and shooing him away as being 'too small' or 'too young' for this or that. Keevan was constantly working, twice as hard as any other boy his age, to prove himself capable. What if his muscles weren't as big as Beterli's? They were just as hard. And if he couldn't overpower anyone in a wrestling match, he could outdistance everyone in a footrace.

'Maybe if you run fast enough,' Beterli had jeered on the occasion when Keevan had been goaded to boast of his swiftness, 'you could catch a dragon. That's the only way you'll make a dragonrider!'

'You just wait and see, Beterli, you just wait,' Keevan had replied. He would have liked to wipe the contemptuous smile from Beterli's face, but the guy didn't fight fair even when a wingsecond was watching. 'No one knows what Impresses a dragon!'

'They've got to be able to *find* you first, babe!'

Yes, being the smallest candidate was not an enviable position. It was therefore imperative that Keevan Impress a dragon in his first hatching. That would wipe the smile off every face in the cavern, and accord him the respect due any dragonrider, even the smallest one.

Besides, no one knew exactly what Impressed the baby dragons as they struggled from their shells toward their lifetime partners.

'I like to believe that dragons see into a man's heart,' Keevan's foster mother, Mende, told him. 'If they find goodness, honesty, a flexible mind, patience, courage – and you've got that in quantity, dear Keevan – that's what dragons look for. I've seen many a well-grown lad left standing on the sands, Hatching Day, in favour of someone not so strong or tall or handsome. And if my memory serves me' – which it usually did: Mende knew every word of every Harper's tale worth telling, Keevan did not interrupt her to say so – 'I don't believe that F'lar, our Weyrleader, was all that tall when bronze Mnementh chose him. And Mnementh was the only bronze dragon of that hatching.'

Dreams of Impressing a bronze were beyond Keevan's boldest reflections, although that goal dominated the thoughts of every other hopeful candidate. Green dragons were small and fast and more numerous. There was more prestige to Impressing a blue or brown than a green. Being practical, Keevan seldom dreamed as high as a big fighting brown, like Canth, F'nor's fine fellow, the biggest brown on all Pern. But to fly a bronze? Bronzes were almost as big as the queen, and only they took the air when a queen flew at mating time. A bronze rider could aspire to become Weyrleader! Well, Keevan would console himself, brown riders could aspire to become wingseconds, and that wasn't bad. He'd even settle for a green dragon: they were small, but so was he. No matter! He simply had to Impress a dragon his first time in the Hatching Ground. Then no one in the Weyr would taunt him anymore for being so small.

Shells, Keevan thought now, but the sands are hot!

'Impression time is imminent, candidates,' the wingsecond was saying as everyone crowded respectfully close to him. 'See the extent of the striations on this promising egg?' The stretch marks *were* larger than yesterday.

Everyone leaned forward and nodded thoughtfully. That particular egg was the one Beterli had marked as his own, and no other candidate dared, on pain of being beaten by Beterli at his first opportunity, to approach it. The egg was marked by a large yellowish splotch in the shape of a dragon back-winging to land, talons outstretched to grasp the rock. Everyone knew that bronze eggs bore distinctive markings. And naturally, Beterli, who'd been presented at eight Impressions already and was the biggest of the candidates, had chosen it.

'I'd say that the great opening day is almost upon us,' the wingsecond went on, and then his face assumed a grave expression.

'As we well know, there are only forty eggs and seventy-two candidates. Some of you may be disappointed on the great day. That doesn't necessarily mean you aren't dragonrider material, just that *the* dragon for you hasn't been shelled. You'll have other hatchings, and it's no disgrace to be left behind an Impression or two. Or more.'

Keevan was positive that the wingsecond's eyes rested on Beterli, who'd been stood off at so many Impressions already. Keevan tried to squinch down so the wingsecond wouldn't notice him. Keevan had been reminded too often that he was eligible to be a candidate by one day only. He, of all the hopefuls, was most likely to be left standing on the great day. One more reason why he simply had to Impress at his first hatching.

'Now move about among the eggs,' the wingsecond said. 'Touch them. We don't know that it does any good, but it certainly doesn't do any harm.'

Some of the boys laughed nervously, but everyone immediately began to circulate among the eggs. Beterli stepped up officiously to 'his' egg, daring anyone to come near it. Keevan smiled, because he had already touched it – every inspection day, when the others were leaving the Hatching Ground and no one could see him crouch to stroke it.

Keevan had an egg he concentrated on, too, one drawn slightly to the far side of the others. The shell had a soft greenish-blue tinge with a faint creamy swirl design. The consensus was that this egg contained a mere green, so Keevan was rarely bothered by rivals. He was somewhat perturbed then to see Beterli wandering over to him.

'I don't know why you're allowed in this Impression, Keevan. There are enough of us without a babe,' Beterli said, shaking his head.

'I'm of age.' Keevan kept his voice level, telling himself not to be bothered by mere words.

'Yah!' Beterli made a show of standing on his toetips. 'You can't even see over an egg; Hatching Day, you better get in front or the dragons won't see you at all. 'Course, you could get run down that way in the mad scramble. Oh, I forget, you can run fast, can't you?'

'You'd better make sure a dragon sees *you*, this time, Beterli,' Keevan replied. 'You're almost overage, aren't you?'

Beterli flushed and took a step forward, hand half-raised. Keevan stood his ground, but if Beterli advanced one more step, he would call the wingsecond. No one fought on the Hatching Ground. Surely Beterli knew that much.

Fortunately, at that moment, the wingsecond called the boys together and led them from the Hatching Ground to start on evening chores. There were 'glows' to be replenished in the main kitchen caverns and sleeping cubicles, the major hallways, and the queen's apartment. Firestone sacks had to be filled against Thread attack, and black rock brought to the kitchen hearths. The boys fell to their chores, tantalized by the odours of roasting meat. The population of the Weyr began to assemble for the evening meal, and the dragonriders came in from the Feeding Ground on their sweep checks.

It was the time of day Keevan liked best: once the chores were done but before dinner was served, a fellow could often get close enough to the dragonriders to hear their talk. Tonight, Keevan's father, K'last, was at the main dragonriders' table. It puzzled Keevan how his father, a brown rider and a tall man, could *be* his father – because he, Keevan, was so small. It obviously puzzled K'last, too, when he deigned to notice his small son: 'In a few more Turns, you'll be as tall as I am – or taller!'

K'last was pouring Benden wine all around the table. The dragonriders were relaxing. There'd be no Thread attack for three more days, and they'd be in the mood to tell tales, better than Harper yarns, about impossible manoeuvres they'd done a-dragonback. When Thread attack was closer, their talk would change to a discussion of tactics or evasion, of going *between*, how long to suspend there until the burning but fragile Thread would freeze and crack and fall harmlessly off dragon and man. They would dispute the exact moment to feed firestone to the dragon so he'd have the best flame ready to sear Thread mid-air and render it harmless to ground – and man – below. There was such a lot to know and understand about being a dragonrider that sometimes Keevan was overwhelmed. How would he ever be able to remember everything he ought to know at the right moment? He couldn't dare ask such a question: this would only have given additional weight to the notion that he was too young yet to be a dragonrider.

'Having older candidates makes good sense,' L'vel was saying, as Keevan settled down near the table. 'Why waste four to five years of a dragon's fighting prime until his rider grows up enough to stand the rigours?' L'vel had Impressed a blue of Ramoth's first clutch. Most of the candidates thought L'vel was marvellous because he spoke up in front of the older riders, who awed them. 'That was well enough in the Interval when you didn't need to mount the full Weyr complement to fight Thread. But not now. Not with more eligible candidates than ever. Let the babes wait.'

'Any boy who is over twelve Turns has the right to stand in the Hatching Ground,' K'last replied, a slight smile on his face. He never argued or got angry. Keevan wished he were more like his father. And oh, how he wished he were a brown rider! 'Only a dragon – each particular dragon – knows what he wants in a rider. We certainly can't tell. Time and again the theorists,' K'last's smile deepened as his eyes swept those at the table, 'are surprised by dragon choice. *They* never seem to make mistakes, however.'

'Now, K'last, just look at the roster this Impression. Seventy-two boys and only forty eggs. Drop off the twelve youngest, and there's still a good field for the hatchlings to choose from. Shells! There are a couple of weyrlings unable to see over a wher egg much less a dragon! And years before they can ride Thread.'

'True enough, but the Weyr is scarcely under fighting strength, and if the youngest Impress, they'll be old enough to fight when the oldest of our current dragons go *between* from senility.'

'Half the Weyr-bred lads have already been through several Impressions,' one of the bronze riders said then. 'I'd say drop some of *them* off this time.'

'There's nothing wrong in presenting a clutch with as wide a choice as possible,' said the Weyrleader, who had joined the table with Lessa, the Weyrwoman.

'Has there ever been a case,' she said, smiling in her odd way at the riders, 'where a hatchling didn't choose?'

Her suggestion was almost heretical and drew astonished gasps from everyone, including the boys.

F'lar laughed. 'You say the most outrageous things, Lessa.'

'Well, *has* there ever been a case where a dragon didn't choose?'

'Can't say as I recall one,' K'last replied.

'Then we continue in this tradition,' Lessa said firmly, as if that ended the matter.

But it didn't. The argument ranged from one table to the other all through dinner, with some favouring a weeding out of the candidates to the most likely, lopping off those who were very young or who had had multiple opportunities to Impress. All the candidates were in a swivet, though such a departure from tradition would be to the advantage of many. As the evening progressed, more riders were favouring eliminating the youngest and those who'd passed four or more Impressions unchosen. Keevan felt he could bear such a dictum only if Beterli were also eliminated. But this seemed less likely than that Keevan would be turfed out, since the Weyr's need was for fighting dragons and riders.

By the time the evening meal was over, no decision had been reached, although the Weyrleader had promised to give the matter due consideration.

He might have slept on the problem, but few of the candidates did. Tempers were uncertain in the sleeping caverns next morning as the boys were routed out of their beds to carry water and black rock and cover the 'glows'. Twice Mende had to call Keevan to order for clumsiness.

'Whatever is the matter with you, boy?' she demanded in exasperation when he tippled black rock short of the bin and sooted up the hearth.

'They're going to keep me from this Impression.'

'What?' Mende stared at him. 'Who?'

'You heard them talking at dinner last night. They're going to turf the babes from the hatching.'

Mende regarded him a moment longer before touching his arm gently. 'There's lots of talk around a supper table, Keevan. And it cools as soon as the supper. I've heard the same nonsense before every hatching, but nothing is ever changed.'

'There's always a first time,' Keevan answered, copying one of her own phrases.

'That'll be enough of that, Keevan. Finish your job. If the clutch does hatch today, we'll need full rock bins for the feast, and you won't be around to do the filling. All my fosterlings make dragonriders.'

'The first time?' Keevan was bold enough to ask as he scooted off with the rock-barrow.

Perhaps, Keevan thought later, if he hadn't been on that chore just when Beterli was also fetching black rock, things might have turned out differently. But he had dutifully trundled the barrow to the outdoor bunker for another load just as Beterli arrived on a similar errand.

'Heard the news, babe?' Beterli asked. He was grinning from ear to ear, and he put an unnecessary emphasis on the final insulting word.

'The eggs are cracking?' Keevan all but dropped the loaded shovel. Several anxieties flicked through his mind then: he was black with rock dust – would he have time to wash before donning the white tunic of candidacy? And if the eggs were hatching, why hadn't the candidates been recalled by the wingsecond?

'Naw! Guess again!' Beterli was much too pleased with himself.

With a sinking heart, Keevan knew what the news must be, and he could only stare with intense desolation at the older boy.

'C'mon! Guess, babe!'

'I've no time for guessing games,' Keevan managed to say with indifference. He began to shovel black rock into the barrow as fast as he could.

'I said, guess.' Beterli grabbed the shovel.

'And I said I have no time for guessing games.'

Beterli wrenched the shovel from Keevan's hands.

'I'll have that shovel back, Beterli.' Keevan straightened up but he didn't come to Beterli's bulky shoulder. From somewhere, other boys appeared, some with barrows, some mysteriously alerted to the prospect of a confrontation among their numbers.

'Babes don't give orders to candidates around here, babe!'

Someone sniggered and Keevan, incredulous, knew that he must've been dropped from the candidacy.

He yanked the shovel from Beterli's loosened grasp. Snarling, the older boy tried to regain possession, but Keevan clung with all his strength to the handle, dragged back and forth as the stronger boy jerked the shovel about.

With a sudden, unexpected movement, Beterli rammed the handle into Keevan's chest, knocking him over the barrow handles. Keevan felt a sharp, painful jab behind his left ear, an unbearable pain in his left shin, and then a painless nothingness.

Mende's angry voice roused him, and startled, he tried to throw back the covers, thinking he'd overslept. But he couldn't move, so firmly was he tucked into his bed. And then the constriction of a bandage on his head and the dull sickishness in his leg brought back recent occurrences.

'Hatching?' he cried.

'No, lovey,' Mende said in a kind voice. Her hand was cool and gentle on his forehead. 'Though there's some as won't be at any hatching again.' Her voice took on a stern edge.

Keevan looked beyond her to see the Weyrwoman, who was frowning with irritation.

'Keevan, will you tell me what occurred at the black rock bunker?' asked Lessa in an even voice.

He remembered Beterli now and the quarrel over the shovel and . . . what had Mende said about some not being at any hatching? Much as he hated Beterli, he couldn't bring himself to tattle on Beterli and force him out of candidacy.

'Come, lad,' and a note of impatience crept into the Weyrwoman's voice. 'I merely want to know what happened from you, too. Mende said she sent you for black rock. Beterli – and every Weyrling in the cavern – seems to have been on the same errand. What happened?'

'Beterli took my shovel. I hadn't finished with it.'

'There's more than one shovel. What did he *say* to you?'

'He'd heard the news.'

'What news?' The Weyrwoman was suddenly amused.

'That . . . that . . . there'd been changes.'

'Is that what he said?'

'Not exactly.'

'What did he say? C'mon, lad, I've heard from everyone else, you know.'

'He said for me to guess the news.'

'And you fell for that old gag?' The Weyrwoman's irritation returned.

'Consider all the talk last night at supper, Lessa,' Mende said. 'Of course the boy would think he'd been eliminated.'

'In effect, he is, with a broken skull and leg.' Lessa touched his arm in a rare gesture of sympathy. 'Be that as it may, Keevan, you'll have other Impressions. Beterli will not. There are certain rules that must be observed by all candidates, and his conduct proves him unacceptable to the Weyr.'

She smiled at Mende and then left.

'I'm still a candidate?' Keevan asked urgently.

'Well, you are and you aren't, lovey,' his foster mother said. 'Is the numbweed working?' she asked, and when he nodded, she said, 'You must rest. I'll bring you some nice broth.'

At any other time in his life, Keevan would have relished such cosseting, but now he just lay there worrying. Beterli had been dismissed. Would the others think it was his fault? But everyone was there! Beterli provoked that fight. His worry increased, because although he heard excited comings and goings in the passageway, no one tweaked back the curtain across the sleeping alcove he shared with five other boys. Surely one of them would have to come in sometime. No, they were all avoiding him. And something else was wrong. Only he didn't know what.

Mende returned with broth and beachberry bread.

'Why doesn't anyone come see me, Mende? I haven't done anything wrong, have I? I didn't ask to have Beterli turfed out.'

Mende soothed him, saying everyone was busy with noontime

chores and no one was angry with him. They were giving him a chance to rest in quiet. The numbweed made him drowsy, and her words were fair enough. He permitted his fears to dissipate. Until he heard a hum. Actually, he felt it first, in the broken shin bone and his sore head. The hum began to grow. Two things registered suddenly in Keevan's groggy mind: the only white candidate's robe still on the pegs in the chamber was his; and the dragons hummed when a clutch was being laid or being hatched. Impression! And he was flat abed.

Bitter, bitter disappointment turned the warm broth sour in his belly. Even the small voice telling him that he'd have other opportunities failed to alleviate his crushing depression. *This* was the Impression that mattered! This was his chance to show *everyone*, from Mende to K'last to L'vel and even the Weyrleader that he, Keevan, was worthy of being a dragonrider.

He twisted in bed, fighting against the tears that threatened to choke him. Dragonmen don't cry! Dragonmen learn to live with pain.

Pain? The leg didn't actually pain him as he rolled about on his bedding. His head felt sort of stiff from the tightness of the bandage. He sat up, an effort in itself since the numbweed made exertion difficult. He touched the splintered leg; the knee was unhampered. He had no feeling in his bone, really. He swung himself carefully to the side of his bed and stood slowly. The room wanted to swim about him. He closed his eyes, which made the dizziness worse, and he had to clutch the wall.

Gingerly, he took a step. The broken leg dragged. It hurt in spite of the numbweed, but what was pain to a dragonman?

No one had said he couldn't go to the Impression. 'You are and you aren't,' were Mende's exact words.

Clinging to the wall, he jerked off his bedshirt. Stretching his arm to the utmost he jerked his white candidate's tunic from the peg. Jamming first one arm and then the other into the holes, he pulled it over his head. Too bad about the belt. He couldn't wait. He hobbled to the door, hung on to the curtain to steady himself. The weight on his leg was unwieldy. He wouldn't get very far without something to lean on. Down by the bathing pool was one of the long crooknecked poles used to retrieve clothes from the hot troughs. But it was down there, and he was on the level above. And there was no one nearby to come to his aid: everyone would be in the Hatching Ground right now, eagerly waiting for the first egg to crack.

The humming increased in volume and tempo, an urgency to which Keevan responded, knowing that his time was all too limited if he was to join the ranks of the hopeful boys standing around the cracking eggs. But if he hurried down the ramp, he'd fall flat on his face.

He could, of course, go flat on his rear end, the way crawling children did. He sat down, sending a jarring stab of pain through his leg and up to the wound on the back of his head. Gritting his teeth and blinking away tears, Keevan scrabbled down the ramp. He had to wait a moment at the bottom to catch his breath. He got to one knee, the injured leg straight out in front of him. Somehow, he managed to push himself erect, though the room seemed about to tip over his ears. It wasn't far to the crooked stick, but it seemed an age before he had it in his hand.

Then the humming stopped!

Keevan cried out and began to hobble frantically across the cavern, out to the bowl of the Weyr. Never had the distance between living caverns and the Hatching Ground seemed so great. Never had the Weyr been so breathlessly silent. It was as if the multitude of people and dragons watching the hatching held every breath in suspense. Not even the wind muttered down the steep sides of the bowl. The only sounds to break the stillness were Keevan's ragged gasps and the thump-thud of his stick on the hard-packed ground. Sometimes he had to hop twice on his good leg to maintain his balance. Twice he fell into the sand and had to pull himself up on the stick, his white tunic no longer spotless. Once he jarred himself so badly he couldn't get up immediately.

Then he heard the first exhalation of the crowd, the oohs, the muted cheer, the susurrus of excited whispers. An egg had cracked, and the dragon had chosen his rider. Desperation increased Keevan's hobble. Would he never reach the arching mouth of the Hatching Ground?

Another cheer and an excited spate of applause spurred Keevan to greater effort. If he didn't get there in moments, there'd be no unpaired hatchling left. Then he was actually staggering into the Hatching Ground, the sands hot on his bare feet.

No one noticed his entrance or his halting progress. And Keevan could see nothing but the backs of the white-robed candidates, seventy of them ringing the area around the egg. Then one side would surge forward or back and there'd be a cheer. Another dragon had been Impressed. Suddenly a large gap appeared in the white human wall, and Keevan had his first sight of the eggs. There didn't seem to be *any* left uncracked, and he could see the lucky boys standing beside wobble-legged dragons. He could hear the unmistakable plaintive crooning of hatchlings and their squawks of protest as they'd fall awkwardly in the sand.

Suddenly he wished that he hadn't left his bed, that he'd stayed away from the Hatching Ground. Now everyone would see his ignominious failure. So he scrambled as desperately to reach the shadowy walls of the Hatching Ground as he struggled to cross the bowl. He mustn't be seen.

He didn't notice, therefore, that the shifting group of boys remaining had begun to drift in his direction. The hard pace he had set himself and his cruel disappointment took their double toll of Keevan. He tripped and collapsed sobbing to the warm sands. He didn't see the consternation in the watching Weyrfolk above the Hatching Ground, nor did he hear the excited whispers of speculation. He didn't know that the Weyrleader and Weyrwoman had dropped to the arena and were making their way toward the knot of boys slowly moving in the direction of the entrance.

'Never seen anything like it,' the Weyrleader was saying. 'Only thirty-nine riders chosen. And the bronze trying to leave the Hatching Ground without making Impression.'

'A case in point of what I said last night,' the Weyrwoman replied, 'where a hatchling makes no choice because the right boy isn't there.'

'There's only Beterli and K'last's young one missing. And there's a full wing of likely boys to choose from . . .'

'None acceptable, apparently. Where is the creature going? He's not heading for the entrance after all. Oh, what have we there, in the shadows?'

Keevan heard with dismay the sound of voices nearing him. He tried to burrow into the sand. The mere thought of how he would be teased and taunted now was unbearable.

Don't worry! Please don't worry! The thought was urgent, but not his own.

Someone kicked sand over Keevan and butted roughly against him.

'Go away. Leave me alone!' he cried.

Why? was the injured-sounding question inserted into his mind. There was no voice, no tone, but the question was there, perfectly clear, in his head.

Incredulous, Keevan lifted his head and stared into the glowing jewelled eyes of a small bronze dragon. His wings were wet, the tips drooping in the sand. And he sagged in the middle on his unsteady legs, although he was making a great effort to keep erect.

Keevan dragged himself to his knees, oblivious of the pain in his leg. He wasn't even aware that he was ringed by the boys passed over, while thirty-one pairs of resentful eyes watched him Impress the dragon. The Weyrmen looked on, amused, and surprised at the draconic choice, which could not be forced. Could not be questioned. Could not be changed.

Why? asked the dragon again. *Don't you like me?* His eyes whirled with anxiety, and his tone was so piteous that Keevan staggered forward and threw his arms around the dragon's neck, stroking his eye ridges, patting the damp, soft hide, opening the fragile-looking wings to dry them, and wordlessly assuring the hatchling over and over again that he was the most perfect, most beautiful, most beloved dragon in the Weyr, in all the Weyrs of Pern.

'What's his name, K'van?' asked Lessa, smiling warmly at the new dragonrider. K'van stared up at her for a long moment. Lessa would know as soon as he did. Lessa was the only person who could 'receive' from all dragons, not only her own Ramoth. Then he gave her a radiant smile, recognizing the traditional shortening of his name that raised him forever to the rank of dragonrider.

My name is Heth, the dragon thought mildly, then hiccuped in sudden urgency. *I'm hungry.*

'Dragons are born hungry,' said Lessa, laughing. 'F'lar, give the boy a hand. He can barely manage his own legs, much less a dragon's.'

K'van remembered his stick and drew himself up. 'We'll be just fine, thank you.'

'You may be the smallest dragonrider ever, young K'van,' F'lar said, 'but you're one of the bravest!'

And Heth agreed! Pride and joy so leaped in both chests that K'van wondered if his heart would burst right out of his body. He looped an arm around Heth's neck and the pair, the smallest dragonboy and the hatchling who wouldn't choose anybody else, walked out of the Hatching Ground together forever.

CAVES IN CLIFFS
Josh Pachter

'To be, or not to be?' That was Hamlet's question. J. Alfred Prufrock tormented himself with more prosaic queries: 'Shall I part my hair behind? Do I dare to eat a peach?'

The question your editor finds himself faced with is even more mundane than Prufrock's – and certainly less poetic than either Eliot or Shakespeare: shall I take the liberty of including one of my own stories in this collection, or shall I restrict myself to being your humble compiler and editor?

You may have three guesses as to my final decision, and the first two don't count.

I wrote 'Caves in Cliffs' in the spring of 1983, while living in Umm al Hassam, a surburb of Manama, which is the capital city of the island-emirate of Bahrain. The original version of the story was half again as long as this published version: it began with a wonderful but irrelevant sequence in which Jack Farmer lectures to his students about interpersonal communication, then moved on to a terrific but irrelevant scene in which Farmer thinks about how great it is to work for the University of Maryland's European Division, then moved into a marvelous but irrelevant recapitulation of his recent experiences in Spain and his trip from there to Greece. Two thousand words, with nothing whatsoever happening! It was all very interesting stuff, but it had nothing to do with the story, really, and its only effect was to bog things down. So with tears in my eyes I cut it all away, and suddenly the story became a powerful one.

Some people have asked me if this tale is, perhaps, slightly autobiographical. I don't know where that idea can possibly have come from. I mean, just because I have taught interpersonal communication for the University of Maryland's European Division since early 1980, and just because one of my assignments was to the U.S. Air Force Station on Crete, and just because, while there, I paid a visit to Matala's famous caves in cliffs . . . does that make a story like this one autobiographical?

And just because one of the ways of saying 'farmer' in Holland *(where I lived before Bahrain) and Germany (where I now live, after Bahrain) is 'pachter' . . . I mean, seriously, haven't you people ever heard of a coincidence before?*

'That's it for tonight,' Jack Farmer told his class of enlisted men and lower-echelon officers and dependant wives and husbands. 'See you next week. Don't forget your journals are due.'

He put away his notes and attendance sheet, slung his leather totebag over his shoulder and left the classroom.

Another day, he sighed contentedly, as the door swung shut behind him; *another drachma.*

He was a term-appointed instructor in the University of Maryland's European Division, teaching three or four eight-week semesters a year on American military bases in England, West Germany, Holland, Spain and – now – Greece. It was an idyllic job, with small groups of dedicated, motivated students meeting four evenings a week for a couple of hours per session; the pay was adequate if not spectacular, the schedule was hard to beat, and the university paid his travel expenses from place to place. He was in his third year with the program, and he couldn't think of much else he would rather be doing with his life.

Humming merrily to himself, he walked out to his battered but trusty old Beetle and tossed his bag in the back seat and coaxed the engine to life.

He drove past the AFRTS station and the commissary and, with a wave to the gate guard, off the base. Two hundred yards down the road he turned off onto the narrow dirt trail that led to the beach, flicked on his brights and jounced forward slowly, playing his nightly game of connect-the-potholes.

Home, he checked the laundry for toothmarks – none; he'd hung it, for once, out of reach of the goats – pulled it from the line and let himself into his apartment.

Too warm for a fire, he decided. That was lucky, as he hadn't yet taken the time to go through the stack of driftwood he'd collected that afternoon to separate out the tarry pieces.

He kicked off his sandals, tossed his sweat-stained T-shirt at the bathroom hamper, poured himself a glass of the nameless local wine the neighbors kept plying him with, and spread out his roadmap on the living-room table.

231

It was Thursday night, and he had plans to make for the weekend that stretched langorously out before him.

His first weekend on Crete he'd stayed close to home, getting to know Iráklion on Friday and Saturday and paying what he'd expected-to-be a courtesy call to the what-he'd-expected-to-be-vastly-overrated Minoan ruins at Knossos on Sunday. Sir Arthur Evans' reconstruction had proven to be absolutely fascinating, though, and he'd wound up spending almost five hours there, then hurrying back to Iráklion to examine the Minoan relics in the archaeological museum while the images of the ancient city were still fresh in his mind. Then, on Monday morning, he'd gone up to the Plains of Lassíthi – and he would never forget that one awesome moment of cresting the final mountain peak to see, spread out beneath him, the incredible, other-worldly sight of 10,000 snow-white windmills spinning gently in the breeze.

The second weekend he'd headed west, to the charming fishing centers of Réthymnon and Khaniá, to drink beer and eat fresh squid and chatter away the days with French and Dutch tourists around the similar, yet individual, harbors.

The third weekend he'd gone east, skirting the ritzy resort town of Ágios Nikólaos and arrowing straight out to Vai, where he'd lain on cool sands under the shade of Europe's only palm forest.

Iráklion, Knossos and Lassíthi in the north, Réthymnon and Khaniá to the west, Vai to the east.

This weekend, then, it was time to take off for the south.

He pored over his map, examining the long stretch of Crete's southern coast carefully and waiting for inspiration to strike.

Halfway across the island, next to a village called Matala, a red star and a number appeared on the map, indicating the location of a sight worth seeing. He checked the reference guide on the reverse of the sheet, and by the corresponding number he found one short phrase, three simple words: 'Caves in cliffs.'

Caves in cliffs, he thought happily. *Of course!*

'*Matala*', Jack Farmer decided, before he had been there half an hour, *must be Greek for 'Shangri-la'*.

He had arrived early that afternoon, following a leisurely drive south across the waist of Crete, with stops only for lunch and a quick look around the ruins at Phaestos.

The village of Matala was practically nonexistent: a square, a single street, another square. But the first square was ringed with charming outdoor cafés, and the street was covered over with a cloth awning to keep out the burning sun and lined with colorful vegetable stalls and tasteful souvenir stands and displays of local crafts, and around the second, smaller square were three delightful *tavernas*, each decorated with hanging fishnets and outrageous murals of mythological creatures of the sea – and the whole was set on a rise overlooking a crescent of immaculate, deserted beach, and the shimmering mystery of the Mediterranean stretching all the way to Africa, and, of course, the cliffs.

One cliff, really, rising from the far end of the beach, a powerful structure of bright tan stone studded amazingly with row upon row of tiny black mouths, hundreds of them, reaching from 20 feet above the surface of the water up to the very top of the cliff: the caves.

No one he asked seemed to know how long they had been there, whether they were entirely manmade or if, originally, nature had had a hand in their construction. But he found out that, when the Aquarian Age had dawned, back in the '60s, an avalanche of backpacking, guitar-playing, pot-smoking hippies had discovered Matala's 'caves in cliffs', had enlarged them and extended them and covered their walls with mindblowing psychedelic design, had turned the hive of individual stone compartments into a commune which drew converts from all over Europe and as far away as the United States. Some of the flower children had stayed only a few weeks before rolling up their sleeping-bags and moving on; many had been there for months, though, and even years, until the complaints about nudity and drugs reached the ears of the Greek government at last, and the cavedwellers were evicted and a chain-link fence put up between the beach and the cliff.

And Matala had gone back to sleep, and was sleeping still, a slumbering lassitude set apart from the rest of the world, untroubled by progress or current events or change. The toothless old women dressed in shapeless black, mourning long-dead fathers and brothers, husbands and sons. The old men let their hair and beards grow wild, and sat around the quiet cafés alone or in pairs, sipping silently at their tumblers of fiery *ouzo*. They sold vegetables to each other and trivia to the occasional tourists. They tended their gardens and goats and chickens and children, and their little girls grew older and dressed in black when someone died, and their little boys aged and let their hair and beards grow wild. . . .

Jack Farmer fell in love with the village at first sight. He found a room at a *domatia* above one of the cafés, dined on *souvlakia* and fried potatoes and a huge farmer's salad rich with black olives and salty *feta* cheese, then carried a bottle of oily yellow *retsina* down to the beach to sit crosslegged on the sand and watch the long arms of what Homer had called 'the wine-red sea' draw the flaming sunset down into its loving embrace. . . .

It was early the next morning that he saw them.

He was back on the beach, armed for a day of ray-catching with suntan lotion, coco mat and dogeared copy of Kazantsakis' *Report to Greco*.

A sudden noise from the cliff startled him, and he looked up, shading his eyes with his book.

High above him, only three levels from the top of the cliff, two figures stood on a ledge near one of cave mouths. They were too far away and the sun was too bright for him to see them clearly: all he could make out was a woman with long brown hair and a brief dress of some dark material, and a bearded man, a head taller than his companion, naked except for a pair of shorts of the same dark fabric.

Leftover hippies, he chuckled to himself. *Somebody forgot to tell them the party's been over for years.*

But then the tall man raised his arm and Jack saw that he was holding a club in his fist and waving it menacingly. The woman screamed, a shrill, piercing cry which ripped through the stillness of the morning. The man swung his weapon with terrible force and she jumped back, trying desperately to avoid the murderous blow. She was too slow, though, and it caught her on the shoulder and flung her against the stone face of the cliff.

Jack stared wide-eyed at the scene unfolding above him, shocked motionless as the woman sank to her knees, sobbing. The man in dark shorts pointed angrily at the nearest cave opening, and she crawled brokenly towards it and disappeared into the blackness. The man watched her go, then shouldered his club and stormed off along the ledge, around a protruding boulder and out of sight.

Jack turned in a dazed circle and looked around him. He was the only person on the beach at that hour. No one else had seen what had happened. No one else had heard that poor woman's scream or witnessed the viciousness of the blow she had taken.

He found himself shaking with fury at the cold-blooded cruelty of the bearded hippie. 'Damn him!' he said aloud, spitting out the words as if they were soaked in bile. 'Damn him!'

He tossed his book to the sand and set off for the cliff at a run. The chain-link fence barely slowed him down: he hoisted himself over it and dropped to the other side in seconds. There was a narrow switchback path up to the first level of caves, and from there crude flights of stone steps connected each level with the one above it.

Halfway up the cliff he stumbled and fell, scraping his palms on the warm, jagged rocks. A dizzying distance below him, the waves rolled in sedately to wash the golden sands of the beach. There was movement in the village – an old woman pushing a cart towards the street of vegetable stalls, a café proprietor setting out tables and chairs on his wide terrace – but he was blind to the charm of the scene. He pushed himself away from the stone and continued up the face of the cliff.

He reached what he was sure was the level where he had seen them, and dashed recklessly along the narrow ledge; uncertain which of the caves she had crawled into, he peered eagerly into each of them as he came to it.

But except for the faded colors daubed on their walls, dying reminders of the long-ago tenancy of the flower children, each of the shadowy vaults he checked seemed empty.

He almost missed her. He saw nothing in the cave at first, but the faintest movement in the darkness caught his eye as he turned to go on, and he stuck his head inside again to be sure.

She was lying huddled at the rear of the cave, her back to him, legs drawn up protectively and thin arms hugging her bare and dusty knees. She was trembling with pain and fear, and an almost animal despair came from somewhere deep in her throat.

Jack approached her softly and laid a reassuring hand on her shoulder.

She jerked away from his touch with a cry, pressed herself tightly against the stone wall behind her. Unlike the other caves Jack had passed, the walls here were unpainted, barren.

He moved several paces backward, out of the personal space he had invaded. 'It's alright,' he soothed her. 'I'm here to help you.'

At the sound of his voice, her eyes went wide; they shone vibrantly, catlike, in the dark. She said something Jack didn't catch, and stepped toward him hesitantly. He stood where he was and let her come to him.

As she neared, he found that he could see her more clearly. Her face was puffy with crying, her long brown hair hung limp and uncombed down her back, a vivid bruise purpled her shoulder where the club had caught her. She was young – 20, perhaps, 23 or 24 at most – but her skin was older, baked rough and dry by the sun. She was not pretty, not at all, yet there was something about her, some strange magnetism which attracted Jack strongly.

Her lips were her best feature, perfectly bowed, full and moist and parted in wonder. In slow-motion, she raised a hand to his face and ran her fingers gently across his smoothly-shaven jaw. Her feline eyes glittered luminously, compellingly.

'My name is Jack,' he told her, swallowing away a sudden thirst. 'What's yours?'

She looked a question at him, touched a fingertip to his lips, did not answer.

'Do you speak English?' he asked. 'What's your name?' He reached into his memory for the bits and pieces of language he had picked up in his travels. *'To ono masou, parakalo?'* he tried, beginning with phrasebook Greek. *'Como te llama? Comment vous appelez-vous? Wie ist Ihr Name? Hoe heet jij?'*

She stared at him blankly, curiously, silent.

'Are you okay?' said Jack. 'Can you speak? Do you understand me?'

She looked down – shyly, he thought – and her gaze came to rest on his bathing trunks. She made a surprised noise and took the cloth between her thumb and forefinger and felt it. When she looked up at him again, he saw confusion and awe written together on her face.

For the first time, he looked closely at the dress she was wearing. It was not made of fabric, as he had thought when he saw it from the beach. It was fur, coarse brown fur, skinned from some animal he had not yet spotted on the island. It was not stitched together, the garment, but simply draped around her body and tied with a length of vine.

'Who – who *are* you?' Jack asked her nervously, the words prickly in his throat. 'What are you doing here? Why don't you speak?'

And then his own eyes widened and he gaped, stunned, around the cave. 'The walls!' he cried. 'They're painted, everywhere else! Why aren't they painted in here?'

She smiled at him, and murmured something unintelligible.

He whirled about, frightened now, and rushed to the mouth of the cave. He looked out and down, saw the deserted beach and brooding sea – and froze.

Matala!

The village!

It was gone!

Where the sleepy hamlet had been – squares and street, low buildings and unhurried inhabitants – there was nothing to be seen but forest, dense, impenetrable greenery and the chatter of a million birds.

'Where am I?' he screamed. 'What *is* this place?'

And then the man in the dark shorts was there, not five feet away from him on the ledge. Incongruously, the first thing Jack noticed about him was that it was not a pair of shorts he was wearing, after all, but a coarse fur loincloth that divided his bronzed torso from his thick, muscular legs.

Only then did he register the two enormous fists clenched tightly about the butt end of the wooden club, and the savage fury etched coldly across the primitive countenance.

With a moan of fear, he flung himself backwards into the cave. The brute came after him, growling angrily and swinging his club with dreadful force. Jack backed away from the steady advance, staring in petrified fascination at the scything motion of the weapon, until he bumped up against the rear wall of the cave and could go no further.

'Stay away from me!' he shrieked, his mind drenched in panic. 'Stay away!'

There was an evil, animal grin on the bearded face, and the man drew back his club and came closer—

And, from nowhere, the strange young woman threw herself frantically at the creature's back, knocking him off-balance and sending his heavy club flying.

Jack jumped for it automatically, got his hands on it and spun to face his attacker. The man in the loincloth had already scrambled to his feet, but he had forgotten about Jack for the moment. His powerful hands balled, his broad chest heaving, he was after the woman now, snarling with frustrated rage.

As he moved slowly towards her, Jack crept up behind him and hoisted the club high above his head. He brought it down with every ounce of strength in his body, felt it connect solidly and heard the creature's skull split open with one sickening crack.

Rippling muscles sagged, fisted fingers splayed wide, violent energy dissipated as if it had never been – and the tall man crumpled to the floor of the cave like a marionette whose strings had abruptly been severed.

Sobbing, screaming, Jack struck the fallen figure again and again, battered the broken head till all that remained was a shapeless mass of pulp and bone and blood.

At last he stopped, gasping hoarsely for breath. Hot tears stung his eyes as he saw what he had done. He felt the rough wood of the club chafing his raw, blistered hands, and threw it away from him with a cry of revulsion. He remembered the woman and how she had saved him, and turned around to look for her.

She wasn't there.

Must have run outside, he thought dazedly, and stumbled after her, half wanting to make sure that she was safe and half just to get away from the terrible thing on the cave floor.

Out on the ledge, she was nowhere to be seen.

But Matala was there, spread out peacefully below him, and a knot of figures were standing on the beach, staring up at him and pointing.

It never happened! Jack thought wildly. *It wasn't real!*

But when he spun around and peered back into the dimness of the cave behind him, the lifeless body that lay there on the floor was real.

And when he clutched his arms to his chest to stop the shivering, the wine-red blood that stained them was real.

And when he gazed down over the ledge to the beach and saw two uniformed policemen clambering over the chain-link fence and climbing rapidly towards him up the face of the cliff, he knew that they, too, were very, very real. . . .

THE BROKEN HOOP
Pamela Sargent

This story speaks for itself. Anything I could add has been said before, though that doesn't mean it shouldn't be said again. The United States, along with every other country in its hemisphere, has committed genocide on its indigenous peoples. Perhaps the US has been subtler than most, for there are nearly as many Indians now as there were when the first settlers arrived on her shores, but all native American cultures have been wounded and many no longer exist. Indians have the shortest lifespans of any Americans, and some of the highest rates of alcoholism and suicide. Sacred lands have been scarred by digging for resources, graveyards have been robbed for artifacts. Craig Strete, an American Indian writer of fantasy, says that the Indians have already experienced an alien invasion.

'The Broken Hoop' took me ten years to write. When I first began the story, I didn't have the ability to tell it properly, and I finally had to put the manuscript aside. Years later, I saw the problems more clearly: the story was rife with the grinding of axes (though they were axes which needed to be ground, and still do), and was embedded in unnecessary details I had researched and couldn't bear to cut.

It is here, rewritten, as it finally appeared in Twilight Zone *Magazine. I chose it for this anthology because, of all my fantasy stories, it was the most difficult to write, and also because it refused to let me go until I had told it to the best of my ability.*

There are other worlds. Perhaps there is one in which my people rule the forests of the northeast, and there may even be one in which white men and red men walk together as friends.

I am too old now to make my way to the hill. When I was younger and stronger, I would walk there often and strain my ears trying to hear the sounds of warriors on the plains or the stomping of buffalo herds. But last night, as I slept, I saw Little Deer, a cloak of buffalo hide over his shoulders, his hair white; he did not speak. It was then that I knew his spirit had left his body.

Once, I believed that it was God's will that we remain in our own worlds in order to atone for the consequences of our actions. Now I know that He can show some of us His mercy.

I am Mohawk, but I never knew my parents. Perhaps I would have died if the Lemaîtres had not taken me into their home.

I learned most of what I knew about my people from two women. One was Sister Jeanne at school, who taught me shame. From her I learned that my tribe had been murderers, pagans, eaters of human flesh. One of the tales she told was of Father Isaac Jogues, tortured to death by my people when he tried to tell them of Christ's teachings. The other woman was an old servant in the Lemaîtres' kitchen; Nawisga told me legends of a proud people who ruled the forests and called me little Manaho, after a princess who died for her lover. From her I learned something quite different.

Even as a child, I had visions. As I gazed out my window, the houses of Montréal would vanish, melting into the trees; a glowing hoop would beckon. I might have stepped through it then, but already I had learned to doubt. Such visions were delusions; to accept them meant losing reality. Maman and Père Lemaître had shown me that. Soon, I no longer saw the woodlands, and felt no loss. I was content to become what the Lemaîtres wanted me to be.

When I was eighteen, Père Lemaître died. Maman Lemaître had always been gentle; when her brother Henri arrived to manage her affairs, I saw that her gentleness was only passivity. There would no longer be a place for me; Henri had made that clear. She did not fight him.

I could stay in that house no longer. Late one night, I left, taking a few coins and small pieces of jewelry Père Lemaître had given me, and shed my last tears for the Lemaîtres and the life I had known during that journey.

I stayed in a small rooming house in Buffalo throughout the winter of 1889, trying to decide what to do. As the snow swirled outside, I heard voices in the wind, and imagined that they were calling to me. But I clung to my sanity; illusions could not help me.

In the early spring, a man named Gus Yeager came to the boarding house and took a room down the hall. He was in his forties and had a thick, gray-streaked beard. I suspected that he had things to hide; he was a yarn-spinner who could talk for hours and yet say little. He took a liking to me and finally confided that he was going west to sell patent medicines. He needed a partner. I was almost out of money by then and welcomed the chance he offered me.

I became Manaho, the Indian princess, whose arcane arts had supposedly created the medicine, a harmless mixture of alcohol and herbs. I wore a costume Gus had purchased from an old Seneca, and stood on the back of our wagon while Gus sold his bottles: 'Look at Princess Manaho here, and what this miracle medicine has done for her – almost forty, but she drinks a bottle every day and looks like a girl, never been sick a day in her life.' There were enough foolish people who believed him for us to make a little money.

We stopped in small towns, dusty places that had narrow roads covered with horse manure and wooden buildings that creaked as the wind whistled by. I remember only browns and grays in those towns; we had left the green trees and red brick of Pennsylvania and northern Ohio behind us. Occasionally we stopped at a farm; I remember men with hatchet faces, women with stooped shoulders and hands as gnarled and twisted as the leafless limbs of trees, children with eyes as empty and gray as the sky.

Sometimes, as we rode in our wagon, Gus would take out a bottle of Princess Manaho's Miracle Medicine and begin to sing songs between swallows. He would get drunk quickly. He was happy only then; often, he was silent and morose. We slept in old rooming houses infested with insects, in barns, often under trees. Some towns would welcome us as a diversion; we would leave others hastily, knowing we were targets of suspicion.

Occasionally, as we went farther west, I would see other Indians. I had little to do with them, but would watch them from a distance, noting their shabby clothes and weather-worn faces. I had little in common with such people; I could read and speak both French and English. I could have been a lady. At times, the townsfolk would look from one of them to me, as if making a comparison of some sort, and I would feel uncomfortable, almost affronted.

We came to a town in Dakota. But instead of moving on, we stayed for several days. Gus began to change, and spent more time in saloons.

One night, he came to my room and pounded on the door. I let him in quickly, afraid he would wake everyone else in the boarding house. He closed the door, then threw himself at me, pushing me against the wall as he fumbled at my nightdress. I was repelled by the smell of sweat and whiskey, his harsh beard and warm breath. I struggled with him as quietly as I could, and at last pushed him away. Weakened by drink and the struggle, he collapsed across my bed; soon he was snoring. I sat with him all night, afraid to move.

Gus said nothing next morning as we prepared to leave. We rode for most of the day while he drank; this time, he did not sing. That afternoon, he threw me off the wagon. By the time I was able to get to my feet, Gus was riding off; dust billowed from the wheels. I ran after him, screaming. He did not stop.

I was alone on the plain. I had no money, no food and water. I could walk back to the town, but what would become of me there? My mind was slipping; as the sky darkened, I thought I saw a ring glow near me.

The wind died; the world became silent. In the distance, someone was walking along the road toward me. As the figure drew nearer, I saw that it was a woman. Her face was coppery, and her hair black; she wore a long yellow robe and a necklace of small blue feathers.

Approaching, she took my hand, but did not speak. Somehow I sensed that I was safe with her. We walked together for a while; the moon rose and lighted our way. 'What shall I do?' I said at last. 'Where is the nearest town? Can you help me?'

She did not answer, but instead held my arm more tightly; her eyes pleaded with me. I said, 'I have no money, no place to go.' She shook her head slowly, then released me and stepped back.

The sudden light almost blinded me. The sun was high overhead, but the woman's face was shadowed. She held out her hand, beckoning to me. A ring shone around her, and then she was gone.

I turned, trembling with fear. I was standing outside another drab, clapboard town; my clothes were covered with dust. I had imagined it all as I walked through the night; somehow my mind had conjured up a comforting vision. I had dreamed as I walked; that was the only possible explanation. I refused to believe that I was mad. In that way, I denied the woman.

I walked into the town and saw a man riding toward the stable in a wagon. He was dressed in a long black robe – a priest. I ran to him; he stopped and waited for me to speak.

'Father,' I cried out. 'Let me speak to you.'

His kind brown eyes gazed down at me. He was a short, stocky man whose face had been darkened by the sun and lined by prairie winds. 'What is it, my child?' He peered at me more closely. 'Are you from the reservation here?'

'No. My name is Catherine Lemaître, I come from the east. My companion abandoned me, and I have no money.'

'I cannot help you, then. I have little money to give you.'

'I do not ask for charity.' I had sold enough worthless medicine with Gus to know what to say to this priest. I kept my hands on his seat so that he could not move without pushing me away. 'I was sent to school, I can read and write and do figures. I want work, a place to stay. I am a Catholic, Father.' I reached into my pocket and removed the rosary I had kept, but rarely used. 'Surely there is something I can do.'

He was silent for a few moments. 'Get in, child,' he said at last. I climbed up next to him.

His name was Father Morel and he had been sent by his superiors to help the Indians living in the area, most of whom were Sioux. He had a mission near the reservation and often traveled to the homes of the Indians to tell them about Christ. He had been promised an assistant who had never arrived. He could offer me little, but he needed a teacher, someone who could teach children to read and write.

I had arrived at Father Morel's mission in the autumn. My duties, besides teaching, were cooking meals and keeping the small wooden house next to the chapel clean. Father Morel taught catechism, but I was responsible for the other subjects. Winter arrived, a harsh, cold winter with winds that bit at my face. As the drifts grew higher, fewer of the Sioux children came to school. The ones who did sat silently on the benches, huddling in their heavy coverings, while I built a fire in the wood-burner.

The children irritated me with their passivity, their lack of interest. They sat, uncomplaining, while I wrote words or figures on my slate board or read to them from one of Father Morel's books. A little girl named White Cow Sees, baptized Joan, was the only one who showed interest. She would ask to hear stories about the saints, and the other children, mostly boys, would nod mutely in agreement.

I was never sure how much any of them understood. Few of them spoke much English, although White Cow Sees and a little boy named Whirlwind Chaser, baptized Joseph, managed to become fairly fluent in it. Whirlwind Chaser was particularly fond of hearing about Saint Sebastian. At last I discovered that he saw Saint

Sebastian as a great warrior, shot with arrows by an enemy tribe; he insisted on thinking that Sebastian had returned from the other world to avenge himself.

I lost most of them in the spring to the warmer days. White Cow Sees still came, and a few of the boys, but the rest had vanished. There was little food that spring and the Indians seemed to be waiting for something.

I went into town as often as possible to get supplies, and avoided the Indians on the reservation. They were silent people, never showing emotion; they seemed both hostile and indifferent. I was irritated by their mixture of pride and despair, saw them as unkempt and dirty, and did not understand why they refused to do anything that might better their lot.

I began to view the children in the same way. There was always an unpleasant odor about them, and their quiet refusal to learn was more irritating to me than pranks and childish foolishness would have been. I became less patient with them, subjecting them to spelling drills, to long columns of addition, to lectures on their ignorance. When they looked away from me in humiliation, I refused to see.

I met Little Deer at the beginning of summer. He had come to see Father Morel, arriving while the children and I were at Mass. He looked at me with suspicion as we left the chapel.

I let the children go early that day, watching as they walked toward their homes. White Cow Sees trailed behind the boys, trying to get their attention.

'You.' I turned and saw the Indian who had come to see Father Morel. He was a tall man, somewhat paler than the Sioux I had seen. He wore a necklace of deer bones around his neck; his hair was in long, dark braids. His nose, instead of being large and prominent, was small and straight. 'You are the teacher?'

'Yes, I am Catherine Lemaître.' I said it coldly.

'Some call me John Wells, some call me Little Deer. My mother's cousin has come here, a boy named Whirlwind Chaser.'

'He stays away now. I have not seen him since winter.'

'What can you teach him?'

'More than you can.'

'You teach him Wasichu foolishness,' he said. 'I have heard of you and have seen you in the town talking to white men. You think you will make them forget who you are, but you are wrong.'

'You have no right to speak to me that way.' I began to walk away, but he followed me.

'My father was a Wasichu, a trader,' Little Deer went on. 'My mother is a Minneconjou. I lived with the Wasichu, I learned their speech and I can write my name and read some words. My mother returned here to her people when I was small. You wear the clothes of a Wasichu woman and stay with the Black Robe, but he tells me you are not his woman.'

'Priests have no women. And you should tell Whirlwind Chaser to return to school. White men rule here now. Learning their ways is all that can help you.'

'I have seen their ways. The Wasichus are mad. They hate the earth. A man cannot live that way.'

I said, 'They are stronger than you.'

'You are only a foolish woman and know nothing. You teach our children to forget their fathers. You think you are a Wasichu, but to them you are only a silly woman they have deceived.'

'Why do you come here and speak to Father Morel?'

'He is foolish, but a good man. I tell him of troubles, of those who wish to see him. It is too bad he is not a braver man. He would beat your madness out of you.'

I strode away from Little Deer, refusing to look back, sure that I would see only scorn on his face. But when I glanced out my window, I saw that he was smiling as he rode away.

The children stayed away from school in the autumn. There were more soldiers in town and around the reservation and I discovered that few Indians had been seen at trading posts. I refused to worry. A young corporal I had met in town had visited me a few times, telling me of his home in Minnesota. Soon, I prayed, he would speak to me, and I could leave with him and forget the reservation.

Then Little Deer returned. I was sweeping dust from the porch, and directed him to the small room where Father Morel was reading. He shook his head. 'It is you I wish to see.'

'About what? Are you people planning another uprising? You will die for it—there are many soldiers here.'

'The Christ has returned to us.'

I clutched my broom. 'You are mad.'

'Two of our men have seen him. They traveled west to where the Fish Eaters—the Paiutes—live. The Christ appeared to them there. He is named Wovoka and he is not a white man as I have thought.

245

He was killed by the Wasichus on the cross long ago, but now he has returned to save us.'

'That is blasphemy.'

'I hear it is true. He will give us back our land, he will raise all our dead and return our land to us. The Wasichus will be swept away.'

'No!' I shouted.

Little Deer was looking past me, as if seeing something else beyond. 'I have heard,' he went on, 'that Wovoka bears the scars of crucifixion. He has told us we must dance so that we are not forgotten when the resurrection takes place and the Wasichus disappear.'

'If you believe that, Little Deer, you will believe anything.'

'Listen to me!' Frightened, I stepped back. 'A man named Eagle Wing Stretches told me he saw his dead father when he danced. I was dancing with him and in my mind I saw the sacred tree flower, I saw the hoop joined once again. I understood again nature's circle in which we are the earth's children, and are nourished by her until as old men we become like children again and return to the earth. Yet I knew that all I saw was in my thoughts, that my mind spoke to me, but I did not truly see. I danced until my feet were light, but I could not see. Eagle Wing Stretches was at my side and he gave a great cry and then fell to the ground as if dead. Later, he told me he had seen his father in the other world, and that his father had said they would soon be together.'

'But you saw nothing yourself.'

'But I have. I saw the other world when I was a boy.'

I leaned against my broom, looking away from his wild eyes.

'I saw it long ago, in the Moon of Falling Leaves. My friends were talking of the Wasichus and how we would drive them off when we were men. I grew sad and climbed up a mountain near our camp to be alone. In my heart, I believed that we would never drive off the Wasichus, for they were many and I knew their madness well—I learned it from my father and his friends. It was that mountain there I climbed.'

He pointed and I saw a small mountain on the horizon. 'I was alone,' Little Deer continued. 'Then I heard the sound of buffalo hooves and I looked down the mountain, but I saw no buffalo there. Above me, a great circle glowed, brighter than the yellow metal called gold.'

'No,' I said softly.

He looked at me and read my face. 'You have seen it, too.'

'No,' I said after a few moments.

'You have. I see that you have. You can step through the circle, and yet you deny it. I looked through the circle, and saw the buffalo, and warriors riding at their side. I wanted to step through and join them, but fear held me back. Then the vision vanished.' He leaned forward and clutched my shoulders. 'I will tell you what I think. There is another world near ours, where there are no Wasichus and my people are free. On that mountain, there is a pathway that leads to it. I will dance there, and I will find it again. I told my story to a medicine man named High Shirt and he says that we must dance on the mountain—he believes that I saw Wovoka's vision.'

'You will find nothing.' But I remembered the circle, and the robed woman, and the woods that had replaced Montréal. I wanted to believe Little Deer.

'Come with me, Catherine. I have been sick since I first saw you— my mind cannot leave you even when I dance. Your heart is bitter and you bear the seeds of the Wasichu madness and I know that I should choose another, but it is you I want.'

I shrank from him, seeing myself in dirty hides inside a tepee as we pretended that our delusions were real. I would not tie my life to that of an ignorant half-breed. But before I could speak, he had left the porch, muttering, 'I will wait', and was on his horse.

On a cold night in December, I stared at Little Deer's mountain from my window.

I was alone. Father Morel was with the Indians, trying again to tell them that their visions were false. The ghost dancing had spread and the soldiers would act soon.

Horses whinnied outside. Buttoning my dress, I hurried downstairs, wondering who could be visiting at this late hour. The door swung open; three dark shapes stood on the porch. I opened my mouth to scream and then saw that one of the men was Little Deer.

'Catherine, will you come with me now?' I managed to shake my head. 'Then I must take you. I have little time.' Before I could move, he grabbed me; one of his companions bound my arms quickly and threw a buffalo robe over my shoulders. As I struggled, Little Deer dragged me outside.

He got on his horse behind me and we rode through the night. Snowflakes melted on my face. 'You will be sorry for this,' I said. 'Someone will come after you.'

'It will soon be snowing and there will be no tracks. And no one will follow an Indian woman who decided to run off and join her people.'

'You are not my people.' I pulled at my bonds. 'Do you think this will make me care for you? I will only hate you more.'

'You will see the other world, and travel to it. There is little time left – I feel it.'

We rode on until we came to a small group of houses which were little more than tree branches slung together. We stopped and Little Deer murmured a few words to his companions before getting off his horse.

'High Shirt is here,' he said. 'A little girl is sick. We will wait for him.' He helped me off the horse and I swung at him with my bound arms, striking him in the chest. He pulled out his knife and I thought he would kill me; instead, he cut the ropes, freeing my hands.

'You do not understand,' he said. 'I wish only to have you with me when we pass into the next world. I thought if I came for you, you would understand. Sometimes one must show a woman these things or she will think you are only filled with words.' He sighed. 'There is my horse. I will not force you to stay if your heart holds only hate for me.'

I was about to leave. But before I could act, a cry came from the house nearest to us. Little Deer went to the entrance and I followed him. An old man came out and said, 'The child is dead.'

I looked inside the hovel. A fire was burning on the dirt floor and I saw a man and woman huddled over a small body. The light flickered over the child's face. It was White Cow Sees.

The best one was gone, the cleverest. She might have found her way out of this place. I wept bitterly. I do not know how long I stood there, weeping, before Little Deer led me away.

A few days after the death of White Cow Sees, we learned that the great chief Sitting Bull had been shot by soldiers. Little Deer had placed me in the keeping of one of his companions, Rattling Hawk. He lived with his wife, Red Eagle Woman, in a hovel not far from Little Deer's mountain. I spent most of my days helping their three children search for firewood; I was still mourning White Cow Sees and felt unable to act. Often Rattling Hawk and Red Eagle Woman would dance with others and I would watch them whirl through the snow.

After the death of Sitting Bull, I was afraid that there would be an uprising. Instead, the Indians only danced more, as if Wovoka's promise would be fulfilled. Little Deer withdrew to a sweat lodge with Rattling Hawk, and I did not see him for three days.

During this time, I began to see colored lights shine from the mountain, each light a spear thrown at heaven; the air around me would feel electric. But when daylight came, the lights would disappear. I had heard of magnetism while with the Lemaîtres. Little Deer had only mistaken natural forces for a sign; now he sat with men in an enclosure, pouring water over hot stones. I promised myself that I would tell him I wanted to go back to the mission.

But when Little Deer and High Shirt emerged from the lodge, they walked past me without a word and headed for the mountain. Little Deer was in a trance, his face gaunt from the days without food and his eyes already filled with visions. I went back to Rattling Hawk's home to wait. I had to leave soon; I had seen soldiers from a distance the day before, and did not want to die with these people.

Little Deer came to me that afternoon. Before I could speak, he motioned for silence. His eyes stared past me and I shivered in my blanket, waiting.

'High Shirt said that the spirits would be with us today. We climbed up and waited by the place where I saw the other world. High Shirt sang a song of the sacred tree and then the tree was before us and we both saw it.'

'You thought you saw it,' I said. 'One would see anything after days without food in a sweat lodge.'

He held up his hand, palm toward me. 'We saw it inside the yellow circle. The circle grew larger and we saw four maidens near it dressed in fine dresses with eagle feathers on their brows, and with them four horses, one black, one chestnut, one white, and one gray, and on the horses four warriors painted with yellow streaks like lightning. Their tepees were around them in a circle and we saw their people, fat with good living and smiling as the maidens danced. Their chief came forward and I saw a yellow circle painted on his forehead. He lifted his arms, and then he spoke: Bring your people here, for I see you are lean and have sad faces. Bring them here, for I see your people traveling a black road of misery. Bring them here, and they will dance with us, but it must be soon, for our medicine men say the circle will soon be gone. He spoke with our speech. Then the circle vanished, and High Shirt leaped up and we saw that the snow where the circle had been was melted. He ran to tell our people. I came to you.'

'So you will go and dance,' I said, 'and wait for the world which will never come. I have seen—' He took my arm, but I would say no more. He released me.

'It was a true vision,' he said quietly. 'It was not Wovoka's vision, but it was a true one. The Black Robe told me that God is merciful, but I thought He was merciful only to Wasichus. Now I think that he has given us a road to a good world and has smiled upon us at last.'

'I am leaving, Little Deer. I will not freeze on that mountain with you or wait for the soldiers to kill me.'

'No, Catherine—you will come. You will see this world with me.' He led me to Rattling Hawk's home.

We climbed up that evening. Rattling Hawk and his family came, and High Shirt brought fifteen people. The rest had chosen to stay behind. 'Your own people do not believe you,' I said scornfully to Little Deer as we climbed. 'See how few there are. The others will dance down there and wait for Wovoka to sweep away the white men. They are too lazy to climb up here.'

He glanced at me; there was pain in his eyes. I regretted my harsh words. It came to me that out of all the men I had known, only Little Deer had looked into my mind and seen me as I was. At that moment, I knew that I could have been happy with him in a different world.

We climbed until High Shirt told us to stop. Two of the women built a fire and I sat near it as the others danced around us.

'Dance with us, Catherine,' said Little Deer. I shook my head and he danced near me, feet pounding the ground, arms churning at his sides. I wondered how long they would dance, waiting for the vision. Little Deer seemed transformed; he was a chief, leading his people. My foot tapped as he danced. He had seen me as I was, but I had not truly seen him; I had looked at him with the eyes of the white woman, and my mind had clothed him in white words – 'half-breed', 'illiterate', 'insane', '*sauvage*'.

I fed some wood to the fire, then looked up at the sky. The forces of magnetism were at work again. A rainbow of lights flickered, while the stars shone on steadily in their places.

Suddenly the stars shifted.

I cried out. The stars moved again. New constellations appeared, a cluster of stars above me, a long loop on the horizon. Little Deer danced to me and I heard the voice of High Shirt chanting nearby.

I huddled closer to the fire. Little Deer pounded the ground, his arms cutting the air like scythes. He spun around and became an eagle, soaring over me, ready to seize me with his talons. The stars began to flash, disappearing and then reappearing. One of the women gave a cry. The dancers seemed to flicker.

I leaped up, terrified. Little Deer swirled around me, spinning faster and faster. Then he disappeared.

I spun around. He was on the other side of the fire, still dancing; then he was at my side again. I tried to run toward him; he was behind me. A group of dancers circled me, winking on and off.

'Catherine!' Little Deer's voice surrounded me, thundering through the night. His voice blended with the chants of High Shirt until my ears throbbed with pain.

I fled from the circle of dancers and fell across a snow-covered rock. 'Catherine!' the voice cried again. The dark shapes dancing around the fire grew dimmer. A wind swept past me, and the dancers vanished.

I stood up quickly. And then I saw the vision.

A golden circle glowed in front of me; I saw green grass and a circle of tepees. Children danced around a fire. Then I saw High Shirt and the others, dancing slowly with another group of Indians, weaving a pattern around a small tree. The circle grew larger; Little Deer stood inside it, holding his arms out to me.

I had only to step through the circle to be with him. My feet carried me forward; I held out my hand and whispered his name.

Then I hesitated. My mind chattered to me – I was sharing a delusion. The dancers would dance until they dropped, and then would freeze on the mountain, too exhausted to climb down. Their desperation had made them mad. If I stepped inside the circle, I would be lost to the irrationality that had always been dormant inside me. I had to save myself.

The circle wavered and dimmed. I saw the other world as if through water, and the circle vanished. I cried out in triumph; my reason had won. But as I looked around at the melted snow, I saw that I was alone.

I waited on the mountain until it grew too cold for me there, then climbed down to Rattling Hawk's empty home before going back up the mountain next day. I do not know for how many days I did this. At last I realized that the yellow circle I had seen would not reappear. In my sorrow, I felt that part of me had vanished with the circle, and imagined that my soul had joined Little Deer. I never saw the glowing hoop again.

I rode back to the mission a few days after Christmas through a blizzard, uncaring about whether I lived or died. There, Father Morel told me that the soldiers had acted at last, killing a band of dancing Indians near Wounded Knee, and I knew that the dancing and any hope these people had were over.

I was back in the white man's world, a prisoner of the world to come.

'The Broken Hoop' by Pamela Sargent, copyright © 1982 by TZ Publications, Inc. Originally published in *Twilight Zone Magazine*. Reprinted by permission of the author and the author's agent, Joseph Elder.

DANCERS IN THE TIME-FLUX
Robert Silverberg

In 1969 I wrote a strange novel called Son of Man *— a rich, lush book about the far future, in which a man of the twentieth century finds himself set down without explanation in a world where humanity has evolved into a dozen or more successor species, all inhabiting the Earth at once. It was a joy to write — an intoxicating experience — and it has had a small but intense following since its first publication.*

From time to time, I toyed with the idea of returning to the world of Son of Man *for other stories, but never found the occasion until I was invited to contribute to an anthology of fantasy sometime in 1981. The notion struck me then of dropping another human being down into that world — not a twentieth-century man, this time, but someone from an earlier era. For my protagonist I borrowed Olivier van Noort, a very unheroic hero, a not very effective admiral who nevertheless managed to carry out one of the earliest circumnavigations of the world during the great era of Dutch maritime ventures. (I had previously written about Olivier and five other circumnavigators in a nonfiction book called* The Longest Voyage, *which dates from about the same time as* Son of Man.*)*

Returning to the world of Son of Man, *fourteen years later, proved to be an odd experience — fascinating, and yet without the sense of momentum that inventing that world in the first place had provided.*

I may yet write further stories of Olivier van Noort in the far future, and indeed I began one not long after the first (though I set it aside for other projects). But perhaps it would be better to set all my legs forward, like van Noort, and attempt other voyages instead.

We'll see.

Under a warm golden wind from the west, Bhengarn the Traveler moves steadily onward toward distant Crystal Pond, his appointed place of metamorphosis. The season is late. The swollen scarlet sun clings close to the southern hills. Bhengarn's body – a compact silvery tube supported by a dozen pairs of sturdy three-jointed legs – throbs with the need for transformation. And yet the Traveler is unhurried. He has been bound on this journey for many hundreds of years. He has traced across the face of the world a glistening trail that zigzags from zone to zone, from continent to continent, and even now still glimmers behind him with a cold brilliance like a thread of bright metal stitching the planet's haunches. For the past decade he has patiently circled Crystal Pond at the outer end of a radial arm one tenth the diameter of the Earth in length; now, at the prompting of some interior signal, he has begun to spiral inward upon it.

The path immediately before him is bleak. To his left is a district covered by furry green fog; to his right is a region of pale crimson grass sharp as spikes and sputtering with a sinister hostile hiss; straight ahead a roadbed of black clinkers and ashen crusts leads down a shallow slope to the Plain of Teeth, where menacing porcelaneous outcroppings make the wayfarer's task a taxing one. But such obstacles mean little to Bhengarn. He is a Traveler, after all. His body is superbly designed to carry him through all difficulties. And in his journeys he has been in places far worse than this.

Elegantly he descends the pathway of slag and cinders. His many feet are tough as annealed metal, sensitive as the most alert antennae. He tests each point in the road for stability and support, and scans the thick layer of ashes for concealed enemies. In this way he moves easily and swiftly toward the plain, holding his long abdomen safely above the cutting edges of the cold volcanic matter over which he walks.

As he enters the Plain of Teeth he sees a new annoyance: an Eater commands the gateway to the plain. Of all the forms of human life – and the Traveler has encountered virtually all of them in his wanderings, Eaters, Destroyers, Skimmers, Interceders, and the others – Eaters seem to him the most tiresome, mere noisy monsters. Whatever philosophical underpinnings form the rationale of their bizarre way of life are of no interest to him. He is wearied by their bluster and offended by their gross appetites.

All the same he must get past this one to reach his destination. The huge creature stands straddling the path with one great meaty leg at each edge and the thick fleshy tail propping it from behind. Its steely claws are exposed, its fangs gleam, driblets of blood from recent victims stain its hard reptilian hide. Its chilly inquisitive eyes, glowing with demonic intelligence, track Bhengarn as the Traveler draws near.

The Eater emits a boastful roar and brandishes its many teeth.

'You block my way,' Bhengarn declares.

'You state the obvious,' the Eater replies.

'I have no desire for an encounter with you. But my destiny draws me toward Crystal Pond, which lies beyond you.'

'For you,' says the Eater, 'nothing lies beyond me. Your destiny has brought you to a termination today. We will collaborate, you and I, in the transformation of your component molecules.'

From the spiracles along his sides the Traveler releases a thick blue sigh of boredom. 'The only transformation that waits for me is the one I will undertake at Crystal Pond. You and I have no transaction. Stand aside.'

The Eater roars again. He rocks slightly on his gigantic claws and swishes his vast saurian tail from side to side. These are the preliminaries to an attack, but in a kind of ponderous courtesy he seems to be offering Bhengarn the opportunity to scuttle back up the ashstrewn slope.

Bhengarn says, 'Will you yield place?'

'I am an instrument of destiny.'

'You are a disagreeable boastful ignoramus,' says Bhengarn calmly, and consumes half a week's energy driving the scimitars of his spirit to the roots of the world. It is not a wasted expense of soul, for the ground trembles, the sky grows dark, the hill behind him creaks and groans, the wind turns purplish and frosty. There is a dull droning sound which the Traveler knows is the song of the time-flux, an unpredictable force that often is liberated at such moments. Despite that, Bhengarn will not relent. Beneath the Eater's splayed claws the fabric of the road ripples. Sour smells rise from sudden crevasses. The enormous beast utters a yipping cry of rage and lashes his tail vehemently against the ground. He sways; he nearly topples; he calls out to Bhengarn to cease his onslaught, but the Traveler knows better than to settle for a half-measure. Even more fiercely he presses against the Eater's bulky form.

'This is unfair,' the Eater wheezes. 'My goal is the same as yours: to serve the forces of necessity.'

'Serve them by eating someone else today,' answers Bhengarn curtly, and with a final expenditure of force shoves the Eater to an awkward untenable position that causes it to crash down onto its side. The downed beast, moaning, rakes the air with his claws but does not arise, and as Bhengarn moves briskly past the Eater he observes that fine transparent threads, implacable as stone, have shot forth from a patch of swamp beside the road and are rapidly binding the fallen Eater in an unbreakable net. The Eater howls. Glancing back, Bhengarn notices the threads already cutting their way through the Eater's thick scales like tiny streams of acid. 'So, then,' Bhengarn says, without malice, 'the forces of necessity will be gratified today after all, but not by me. The Eater is to be eaten. It seems that this day *I* prove to be the instrument of destiny.' And without another backward look he passes quickly onward into the plain. The sky regains its ruddy color, the wind becomes mild once more, the Earth is still. But a release of the time-flux is never without consequences, and as the Traveler trundles forward he perceives some new creature of unfamiliar form staggering through the mists ahead, confused and lost, lurching between the shining lethal formations of the Plain of Teeth in seeming ignorance of the perils they hold. The creature is upright, two-legged, hairy, of archaic appearance. Bhengarn, approaching it, recognizes it finally as a primordial human, swept millions of years past its own true moment.

'Have some care,' Bhengarn calls. 'Those teeth can bite!'

'Who spoke?' the archaic creature demands, whirling about in alarm.

'I am Bhengarn the Traveler. I suspect I am responsible for your presence here.'

'Where are you? I see no one! Are you a devil?'

'I am a Traveler, and I am right in front of your nose.'

The ancient human notices Bhengarn, apparently for the first time, and leaps back, gasping. 'Serpent!' he cries. 'Serpent with legs! Worm! Devil!' Wildly he seizes rocks and hurls them at the Traveler, who deflects them easily enough, turning each into a rhythmic juncture of gold and green that hovers, twanging softly, along an arc between the other and himself. The archaic one lifts an immense boulder, but as he hoists it to drop it on Bhengarn he overbalances and his arm flies backward, grazing one of the sleek teeth behind him. At once the tooth releases a turquoise flare and the man's arm vanishes to the elbow. He sinks to his knees, whimpering, staring bewilderedly at the stump and at the Traveler before him.

Bhengarn says, 'You are in the Plain of Teeth, and any contact with these mineral formations is likely to be unfortunate, as I attempted to warn you.'

He slides himself into the other's soul for an instant, pushing his way past thick encrusted stalagmites and stalactites of anger, fear, outraged pride, pain, disorientation, and arrogance, and discovers

256

himself to be in the presence of one Olivier van Noort of Utrecht, former tavernkeeper at Rotterdam, commander of the voyage of circumnavigation that set forth from Holland on the second day of July, 1598 and traveled the entire belly of the world, a man of exceedingly strong stomach and bold temperament, who has experienced much, having gorged on the meat of penguins at Cape Virgines and the isle called Pantagoms, having hunted beasts not unlike stags and buffaloes and ostriches in the cold lands by Magellan's Strait, having encountered whales and parrots and trees whose bark had the bite of pepper, having had strife with the noisome Portugals in Guinea and Brazil, having entered into the South Sea on a day of divers storms, thunders, and lightnings, having taken ships of the Spaniards in Valparaiso and slain many Indians, having voyaged thence to the Isles of Ladrones or Thieves, where the natives bartered bananas, coconuts, and roots for old pieces of iron, overturning their canoes in their greed for metal, having suffered a bloody flux in Manila of eating palmitos, having captured vessels of China laden with rice and lead, having traded with folk on a ship of the Japans, whose men make themselves bald except a tuft left in the hinder part of the head, and wield swords which would, with one stroke, cut through three men, having traded also with the barebreasted women of Borneo, bold and impudent and shrewd, who carry iron-pointed javelins and sharp darts, and having after great privation and the loss of three of his four ships and all but 45 of his 248 men, many of them executed by him or marooned on remote islands for their mutinies but a good number murdered by the treacheries of savage enemies, come again to Rotterdam on the 26th of August in 1601, bearing little in the way of salable goods to show for his hardships and calamities. None of this has any meaning to Bhengarn the Traveler except in the broadest sense, which is to say that he recognizes in Olivier van Noort a stubborn and difficult man who has conceived and executed a journey of mingled heroism and foolishness that spanned vast distances, and so they are brothers, of a sort, however millions of years apart. As a fraternal gesture Bhengarn restores the newcomer's arm. That appears to be as bewildering to the other as was its sudden loss. He squeezes it, moves it cautiously back and forth, scoops up a handful of pebbles with it. 'This is Hell, then,' he mutters, 'and you are a demon of Satan.'

'I am Bhengarn the Traveler, bound toward Crystal Pond, and I think that I conjured you by accident out of your proper place in time while seeking to thwart that monster.' Bhengarn indicates the fallen

Eater, now half dissolved. The other, who evidently had not looked that way before, makes a harsh choking sound at the sight of the giant creature, which still struggles sluggishly. Bhengarn says, 'The time-flux has seized you and taken you far from home, and there will be no going back for you. I offer regrets.'

'You offer regrets? A worm with legs offers regrets! Do I dream this, or am I truly dead and gone to Hell?'

'Neither one.'

'In all my sailing round the world I never saw a place so strange as this, or the likes of you, or of that creature over yonder. Am I to be tortured, demon?'

'You are not where you think you are.'

'Is this not Hell?'

'This is the world of reality.'

'How far are we, then, from Holland?'

'I am unable to calculate it,' Bhengarn answers. 'A long way, that's certain. Will you accompany me toward Crystal Pond, or shall we part here?'

Olivier van Noort is silent a moment. Then he says, 'Better the company of demons than none at all, in such a place. Tell me straight, demon: am I to be punished here? I see hellfire on the horizon. I will find the rivers of fire, snow, toads, and black water, will I not? And the place where sinners are pronged on hooks jutting from blazing wheels? The ladders of red-hot iron, eh? The wicked broiling on coals? And the Arch-Traitor himself, sunk in ice to his chest—he must be near, is he not?' He shivers. 'The fountains of poison. The wild boars of Lucifer. The aloes biting bare flesh, the dry winds of the abyss— when will I see them?'

'Look there,' says Bhengarn. Beyond the Plain of Teeth a column of black flame rises into the heavens, and in it dance creatures of a hundred sorts, melting, swirling, coupling, fading. A chain of staring lidless eyes spans the sky. Looping whorls of green light writhe on the mountaintops. 'Is that what you expect? You will find whatever you expect here.'

'And yet you say this is not Hell?'

'I tell you again, it is the true world, the same into which you were born long ago.'

'And is this Brazil, or the Indies, or some part of Africa?'

'Those names mean little to me.'

'Then we are in the Terra Australis,' says van Noort. 'It must be. A land where worms have legs and speak good Dutch, and rocks can

258

bite, and arms once lost can sprout anew—yes, it must surely be the Terra Australis, or else the land of Prester John. Eh? Is Prester John your king?' van Noort laughs. He seems to be emerging from his bewilderment. 'Tell me the name of this land, creature, so I may claim it for the United Provinces, if ever I see Holland again.'

'It has no name.'

'No name! No name! What foolishness! I never found a place whose folk had no name for it, not even in the endless South Sea. But I will name it, then. Let this province be called New Utrecht, eh? And all this land, from here to the shores of the South Sea, I annex hereby to the United Provinces in the name of the States-General. You be my witness, creature. Later I will draw up documents. You say I am not dead?'

'Not dead, not dead at all. But far from home. Come, walk beside me, and touch nothing. This is troublesome territory.'

'This is strange and ghostly territory,' says van Noort. 'I would paint it, if I could, and then let Mynheer Brueghel look to his fame, and old Bosch as well. Such sights! Were you a prince before you were transformed?'

'I have not yet been transformed,' says Bhengarn. 'That awaits me at the Crystal Pond.' The road through the plain now trends slightly uphill; they are advancing into the farther side of the basin. A pale yellow tint comes into the sky. The path here is prickly with little many-faceted insects whose hard sharp bodies assail the Dutchman's bare tender feet. Cursing, he hops in wild leaps, bringing him dangerously close to outcroppings of teeth, and Bhengarn, in sympathy, fashions stout gray boots for him. Olivier van Noort grins. He gestures toward his bare middle, and Bhengarn clothes him in a shapeless gray robe.

'Like a monk, is how I look!' van Noort cries. 'Well, well, a monk in Hell! But you say this is not Hell. And what kind of creature are you, creature?'

'A human being,' says Bhengarn, 'of the Traveler sort.'

'A human being!' van Noort booms. He leaps across a brook of sparkling bubbling violet-hued water and waits on the far side as Bhengarn trudges through it. 'A human under an enchantment, I would venture.'

'This is my natural form. Humankind has not worn your guise since long before the falling of the Moon. The Eater you saw was human. Do you see, on yonder eastern hill, a company of Destroyers turning the forest to rubble? They are human.'

'The wolves on two legs up there?'

'Those, yes. And there are others you will see. Awaiters, Breathers, Skimmers—'

'These are mere noises to me, creature. What is human? A Dutchman is human! A Portugal is human! Even a Chinese, a black, a Japonder with a shaven head. But those beasts on yon hill? Or a creature with more legs than I have whiskers? No, Traveler, no! You flatter yourself. Do you happen to know, Traveler, how it is that I am here? I was in Amsterdam, to speak before the Lords Seventeen and the Company in general, to ask for ships to bring pepper from the Moluccas, but they said they would choose Joris van Spilbergen in my place—do you know van Spilbergen? I think him much over-praised—and then all went dizzy, as though I had taken too much beer with my gin—and then—then—ah, this is a dream, is it not, Traveler? At this moment I sleep in Amsterdam. I am too old for such drinking. Yet never have I had a dream so real as this, and so strange. Tell me: when you walk, do you move the legs on the right side first, or the left?' He does not wait for a reply. 'If you are human, Traveler, are you also a Christian, then?'

Bhengarn searches in van Noort's mind for the meaning of that, finds something approximate, and says, 'I make no such claim.'

'Good. Good. There are limits to my credulity. How far is this Crystal Pond?'

'We have covered most of the distance. If I proceed at a steady pace I will come shortly to the land of smoking holes, and not far beyond that is the approach to the Wall of Ice, which will demand a difficult but not impossible ascent, and just on the far side of that I will find the vale that contains Crystal Pond, where the beginning of the next phase of my life will occur.' They are walking now through a zone of sparkling rubbery cones of a bright vermilion color, from which small green Stangarones emerge in quick succession to chant their one-note melodies. The flavor of a heavy musk hangs in the air. Night is beginning to fall. Bhengarn says, 'Are you tired?'

'Just a little.'

'It is not my custom to travel by night. Does this campsite suit you?' Bhengarn indicates a broad circular depression bordered by tiny volcanic fumaroles. The ground here is warm and spongy, moist, bare of vegetation. Bhengarn extends an excavator claw and pulls free a strip of it, which he hands to van Noort, indicating that he should eat. The Dutchman tentatively nibbles. Bhengarn helps himself to some also. Van Noort, kneeling, presses his knuckles against the ground, makes it yield, mutters to himself, shakes his head, rips off another strip and chews it in wonder. Bhengarn says, 'You find the world much changed, do you not?'

'Beyond all understanding, in fact.'

'Our finest artists have worked on it since time immemorial, making it more lively, more diverting. We think it is a great success. Do you agree?'

He does not answer. He is staring bleakly at the sky, suddenly dark and jeweled with blazing stars. Bhengarn realizes that he is searching for patterns, navigators' signs. Van Noort frowns, turns round and round to take in the full circuit of the heavens, bites his lip, finally lets out a low groaning sigh and says, 'I recognize nothing. Nothing. This is not the northern sky, this is not the southern sky, this is not any sky I can understand.' Quietly he begins to weep. After a time he says somberly, 'I was not the most adept of navigators, but I knew something, at least. And I look at this sky and I feel like a helpless babe. All the stars have changed places. Now I see how lost I am, how far from anything I ever knew, and once it gave me great pleasure to sail under strange skies, but not now, not here, because these skies frighten me and this land of demons offers me no peace. I have never wept, do you know that, creature, never, not once in my life! But Holland—my house, my tavern, my church, my sons, my pipe—where is Holland? Where is everything I knew? The skies above Magellan's Strait were not the thousandth part so strange as this.' A harsh heavy sob escapes him, and he turns away, huddling into himself.

Compassion floods Bhengarn for this miserable wanderer. To ease van Noort's pain he summons fantasies for him, dredging images from the reservoirs of the ancient man's spirit and hurling them against the sky, building a cathedral of fire in the heavens, and a royal palace, and a great armada of ships with bellying sails and the Dutch flag fluttering, and the watery boulevards of busy Amsterdam and the quiet streets of little Haarlem, and more. He paints for van Noort the stars in their former courses, the Centaur, the Swan, the Bear, the Twins. He restores the fallen Moon to its place and by its cold light creates a landscape of time lost and gone, with avenues of heavy-boughed oaks and maples, and drifts of brilliant red and yellow tulips blazing beneath them, and golden roses arching in great bowers over the thick newly-mowed lawn. He creates fields of ripe wheat, and haystacks high as barns, and harvesters toiling in the hot sultry afternoon. He gives van Noort the aroma of the Sunday feast and the scent of good Dutch gin and the sweet dense fumes of his long clay pipe. The Dutchman nods and murmurs and clasps his hands, and gradually his sorrow ebbs and his weeping ceases, and he drifts off into a deep and easy slumber. The images fade. Bhengarn, who rarely sleeps, keeps watch until first light comes and a flock of fingerwinged birds passes overhead, shouting shrilly, jesting and swooping.

Van Noort is calm and quiet in the morning. He feeds again on the spongy soil and drinks from a clear emerald rivulet and they move onward toward Crystal Pond. Bhengarn is pleased to have his company. There is something crude and coarse about the Dutchman, perhaps even more so than another of his era might be, but Bhengarn finds that unimportant. He has always preferred companions of any sort to the solitary march, in his centuries of going to and fro upon the Earth. He has traveled with Skimmers and Destroyers, and once a ponderous Ruminant, and even on several occasions visitors from other worlds who have come to sample the wonders of Earth. At least twice Bhengarn has had as his traveling companion a castaway of the time-flux from some prehistoric era, though not so prehistoric as van Noort's. And now it has befallen him that he will go to the end of his journey with this rough hairy being from the dawn of humanity's day. So be it. So be it.

Van Noort says, breaking a long silence as they cross a plateau of quivering gelatinous stuff, 'Were you a man or a woman before the sorcery gave you this present shape?'

'I have always had this form.'

'No. Impossible. You say you are human, you speak my language—'

'Actually, you speak *my* language,' says Bhengarn.

'As you wish. If you are human you must once have looked like me. Can it be otherwise? Were you born a thing of silvery scales and many legs? I will not believe that.'

'Born?' says Bhengarn, puzzled.

'Is this word unknown to you?'

'Born,' the Traveler repeats. 'I think I see the concept. To *begin,* to *enter,* to *acquire one's shape*—'

'Born,' says van Noort in exasperation. 'To come from the womb. To hatch, to sprout, to drop. Everything alive has to be born!'

'No,' Bhengarn says mildly. 'Not any longer.'

'You talk nonsense,' van Noort snaps, and scours his throat angrily and spits. His spittle strikes a node of assonance and blossoms into a dazzling mound of green and scarlet jewels. 'Rubies,' he murmurs. 'Emeralds. I could puke pearls, I suppose.' He kicks at the pile of gems and scatters them; they dissolve into spurts of moist pink air. The Dutchman gives himself over to a sullen brooding. Bhengarn does not transgress on the other's taciturnity; he is content to march forward in his steady plodding way, saying nothing.

Three Skimmers appear, prancing, leaping. They are heading to the south. The slender golden-green creatures salute the wayfarers with pulsations of their great red eyes. Van Noort, halting, glares at them and says hoarsely to Bhengarn, 'These are human beings, too?'

'Indeed.'

'Natives of this realm?'

'Natives of this era,' says Bhengarn. 'The latest form, the newest thing, graceful, supple, purposeless.' The Skimmers laugh and transform themselves into shining streaks of light and soar aloft like a trio of auroral rays. Bhengarn says, 'Do they seem beautiful to you?'

'They seem like minions of Satan,' says the Dutchman sourly. He scowls. 'When I awaken I pray I remember none of this. For if I do, I will tell the tale to Willem and Jan and Piet, and they will think I have lost my senses, and mock me. Tell me I dream, creature. Tell me I lie drunk in an inn in Amsterdam.'

'It is not so,' Bhengarn says gently.

'Very well. Very well. I have come to a land where every living thing is a demon or a monster. That is no worse, I suppose, than a land where everyone speaks Japanese and worships stones. It is a world of wonders, and I have seen more than my share. Tell me, creature, do you have cities in this land?'

'Not for millions of years.'

'Then where do the people live?'

'Why, they live where they find themselves! Last night we lived where the ground was food. Tonight we will settle by the Wall of Ice. And tomorrow—'

'Tomorrow,' van Noort says, 'we will have dinner with the Grand Diabolus and dance in the Witches' Sabbath. I am prepared, just as I was prepared to sup with the penguin-eating folk of the Cape, that stood six cubits high. I will be surprised by nothing.' He laughs. 'I am hungry, creature. Shall I tear up the earth again and stuff it down?'

'Not here. Try those fruits.'

Luminous spheres dangle from a tree of golden limbs. Van Noort plucks one, tries it unhesitatingly, claps his hands, takes three more. Then he pulls a whole cluster free, and offers one to Bhengarn, who refuses.

'Not hungry?' the Dutchman asks.

'I take my food in other ways.'

'Yes, you breathe it in from flowers as you crawl along, eh? Tell me, Traveler: to what end is your journey? To discover new lands? To fulfill some pledge? To confound your enemies? I doubt it is any of these.'

'I travel out of simple necessity, because it is what my kind does, and for no special purpose.'

'A humble wanderer, then, like the mendicant monks who serve the Lord by taking to the highways?'

'Something like that.'

'Do you ever cease your wanderings?'

'Never yet. But cessation is coming. At Crystal Pond I will become my utter opposite, and enter the Awaiter tribe, and be made immobile and contemplative. I will root myself like a vegetable, after my metamorphosis.'

Van Noort offers no comment on that. After a time he says, 'I knew a man of your kind once. Jan Huygen van Linschoten of Haarlem, who roamed the world because the world was there to roam, and spent his years in the India of the Portugals and wrote it all down in a great vast book, and when he had done that went off to Novaya Zemlya with Barents to find the chilly way to the Indies, and I think would have sailed to the Moon if he could find the pilot to guide him. I spoke with him once. My own travels took me farther than Linschoten, do you know? I saw Borneo and Java and the world's hinder side, and the thick Sargasso Sea. But I went with a purpose other than my own amusement or the gathering of strange lore, which was to buy pepper and cloves, and gather Spanish gold, and win my fame and comfort. Was that so wrong, Traveler? Was I so unworthy?' Van Noort chuckles. 'Perhaps I was, for I brought home neither spices nor gold nor most of my men, but only the fame of having sailed around the world. I think I understand you, Traveler. The spices go into a cask of meat and are eaten and gone; the gold is only yellow metal; but so long as there are Dutchmen, no one will forget that Olivier van Noort, the tavernkeeper of Rotterdam, strung a line around the middle of the world. So long as there are Dutchmen.' He laughs. 'It is folly to travel for profit. I will travel for wisdom from now on. What do you say, Traveler? Do you applaud me?'

'I think you are already on the proper path,' says Bhengarn. 'But look, look there: the Wall of Ice.'

Van Noort gasps. They have come around a low headland and are confronted abruptly by a barrier of pure white light, as radiant as a mirror at noon, that spans the horizon from east to west and rises skyward like an enormous palisade filling half the heavens. Bhengarn studies it with respect and admiration. He has known for hundreds of years that he must ascend this wall if he is to reach Crystal Pond, and that the wall is formidable; but he has seen no need before now to contemplate the actualities of the problem, and now he sees that they are significant.

'Are we to ascend that?' van Noort asks.

'I must. But here, I think, we shall have to part company.'

'The throne of Lucifer must lie beyond that icy rampart.'

'I know nothing of that,' says Bhengarn, 'but certainly Crystal Pond is on the farther side, and there is no other way to reach it but to climb the wall. We will camp tonight at its base, and in the morning I will begin my climb.'

'Is such a climb possible?'

'It will have to be,' Bhengarn replies.

'Ah. You will turn yourself to a puff of light like those others we met, and shoot over the top like some meteor. Eh?'

'I must climb,' says Bhengarn, 'using one limb after another, and taking care not to lose my grip. There is no magical way of making this ascent.' He sweeps aside fallen branches of a glowing blue-limbed shrub to make a campsite for them. To van Noort he says, 'Before I begin the ascent tomorrow, I will instruct you in the perils of the world, for your protection on your future wanderings. I hold myself responsible for your presence here and I would not have you harmed once you have left my side.'

Van Noort says, 'I am not yet planning to leave your side. I mean to climb that wall alongside you, Traveler.'

'It will not be possible for you.'

'I will make it possible. That wall excites my spirit. I will conquer it as I conquered the storms of the Strait and the fevers of the Sargasso. I feel I should go with you to Crystal Pond, and pay my farewells to you there, for it will bring me luck to mark the beginning of my solitary journey by witnessing the end of yours. What do you say?'

'I say wait until the morning,' Bhengarn answers, 'and see the wall at close range, before you commit yourself to such mighty resolutions.'

During the night a silent lightstorm plays overhead; twisting turbulent spears of blue and green and violet radiance clash in the throbbing sky, and an undulation of the atmosphere sends alternating waves of hot and cool air racing down from the Wall of Ice. The time-flux blows, and frantic figures out of forgotten eras are swept by now far aloft, limbs churning desperately, eyes rigid with astonishment. Van Noort sleeps through it all, though from time to time he stirs and mutters and clenches his fists. Bhengarn ponders his obligations to the Dutchman, and by the coming of the sharp blood-hued dawn he has arrived at an idea. Together they advance to the edge of the Wall; together they stare upward at that vast vertical field of shining whiteness, smooth as stone. Hesitantly van Noort touches it with his fingertip, and hisses at the coldness of it. He turns his back to it, paces, folds and unfolds his arms.

He says finally, 'No man of woman born could achieve the summit of that wall. But is there not some magic you could work, Traveler, that would enable me to make the ascent?'

'There is one. But I think you would not like it.'

'Speak.'

'I could transform you – for a short time, only a short time, no longer than the time it takes to climb the wall – into a being of the Traveler form. Thus we could ascend together.'

Van Noort's eyes travel quickly over Bhengarn's body – the long tubular serpentine thorax, the tapering tail, the multitude of powerful little legs – and a look of shock and dismay and loathing comes over his face for an instant, but just an instant. He frowns. He tugs at his heavy lower lip.

Bhengarn says, 'I will take no offense if you refuse.'

'Do it.'

'You may be displeased.'

'Do it! The morning is growing old. We have much climbing to do. Change me, Traveler. Change me quickly.' A shadow of doubt crosses van Noort's features. 'You will change me back, once we reach the top?'

'It will happen of its own accord. I have no power to make a permanent transformation.'

'Then do what you can, and do it now!'

'Very well,' says Bhengarn, and the Traveler, summoning his fullest force, drains metamorphic energies from the planets and the stars and a passing comet, and focuses them and hurls them at the Dutchman, and there is a buzzing and a droning and a shimmering and when it is done a second Traveler stands at the foot of the Wall of Ice.

Van Noort seems thunderstruck. He says nothing; he does not move; only after a long time does he carefully lift his frontmost left limb and swing it forward a short way and put it down. Then the one opposite it; then several of the middle limbs; then, growing more adept, he manages to move his entire body, adopting a curious wriggling style, and in another moment he appears to be in control. 'This is passing strange,' he remarks at length. 'And yet it is almost like being in my own body, except that everything has been changed. You are a mighty wizard, Traveler. Can you show me now how to make the ascent?'

'Are you ready so soon?'

'I am ready,' van Noort says.

So Bhengarn demonstrates, approaching the wall, bringing his penetrator claws into play, driving them like pitons into the ice, hauling himself up a short distance, extending the claws, driving them in, pulling upward. He has never climbed ice before, though he has faced all other difficulties the world has to offer, but the climb, though strenuous, seems manageable enough. He halts after a few minutes and watches as van Noort, clumsy but determined in his altered body, imitates him, scratching and scraping at the ice as he pulls himself up the face until they are side by side. 'It is easy,' van Noort says.

And so it is, for a time, and then it is less easy, for now they hang high above the valley and the midday sun has melted the surface of the wall just enough to make it slick and slippery, and a terrible cold from within the mass of ice seeps outward into the climbers, and even though a Traveler's body is a wondrous machine fit to endure anything, this is close to the limit. Once Bhengarn loses his purchase, but van Noort deftly claps a claw to the middle of his spine to hold him firmly until he has dug in again; and not much later the same happens to van Noort, and Bhengarn grasps him. As the day wanes they are so far above the ground that they can barely make out the treetops below, and yet the top of the wall is too high to see. Together they excavate a ledge, burrowing inward to rest in a chilly nook, and at dawn they begin again, Bhengarn's sinuous body winding upward over the rim of their little cave and van Noort following with less agility. Upward and upward they climb, never pausing and saying little, through a day of warmth and soft perfumed breezes and through a night of storms and falling stars, and then through a day of turquoise rain, and through another day and a night and a day and then they are at the top, looking out across the broad unending field of ferns and bright blossoms that covers the summit's flat surface, and as they move inward from the rim van Noort lets out a cry and stumbles forward, for he has resumed his ancient form. He drops to his knees and sits there panting, stunned, looking in confusion at his fingernails, at his knuckles, at the hair on the backs of his hands, as though he has never seen such things before. 'Passing strange,' he says softly.

'You are a born Traveler,' Bhengarn tells him.

They rest a time, feeding on the sparkling four-winged fruits that sprout in that garden above the ice. Bhengarn feels an immense calmness now that the climax of his peregrination is upon him. Never has he questioned the purpose of being a Traveler, nor has he had regret that destiny gave him that form, yet now he is quite willing to yield it up.

'How far to Crystal Pond?' van Noort asks.

'It is just over there,' says Bhengarn.

'Shall we go to it now?'

'Approach it with great care,' the Traveler warns. 'It is a place of extraordinary power.'

They go forward; a path opens for them in the swaying grasses and low fleshy-leaved plants; within minutes they stand at the edge of a perfectly circular body of water of unfathomable depth and of a clarity so complete that the reflections of the sun can plainly be seen on the white sands of its infinitely distant bed. Bhengarn moves to the edge and peers in, and is pervaded by a sense of fulfillment and finality.

Van Noort says, 'What will become of you here?'

'Observe,' says Bhengarn.

He enters Crystal Pond and swims serenely toward the farther shore, an enterprise quickly enough accomplished. But before he has reached the midpoint of the pond a tolling sound is heard in the air, as of bells of the most pure quality, striking notes without harmonic overtones. Sudden ecstasy engulfs him as he becomes aware of the beginning of his transformation: his body flows and streams in the flux of life, his limbs fuse, his soul expands. By the time he comes forth on the edge of the pond he has become something else, a great cone of passive flesh, which is able to drag itself no more than five or six times its own length from the water, and then sinks down on the sandy surface of the ground and begins the process of digging itself in. Here the Awaiter Bhengarn will settle, and here he will live for centuries of centuries, motionless, all but timeless, considering the primary truths of being. Already he is gliding into the earth.

Van Noort gapes at him from the other side of the pond.

'Is this what you sought?' the Dutchman asks.

'Yes.'

'I wish you farewell and Godspeed, then!' van Noort cries.

'And you—what will become of you?'

Van Noort laughs. 'Have no fears for me! I see my destiny unfolding!'

Bhengarn, nestled now deep in the ground, enwombed by the earth, immobile, established already in his new life, watches as van Noort strides boldly to the water's edge. Only slowly, for an Awaiter's mind is less agile than a Traveler's, does Bhengarn comprehend what is to happen.

Van Noort says, 'I've found my vocation again. But if I'm to travel, I must be equipped for traveling!'

He enters the pond, swimming in broad awkward splashing strokes, and once again the pure tolling sound is evoked, a delicate carillon of crystalline transparent tone, and there is sudden brilliance in the pond as van Noort sprouts the shining scales of a Traveler, and the jointed limbs, and the strong thick tail. He scuttles out on the far side wholly transformed.

'Farewell!' van Noort cries joyously.

'Farewell,' murmurs Bhengarn the Awaiter, peering out from the place of his long repose as Olivier van Noort, all his legs ablaze with new energy, strides away vigorously to begin his second circumnavigation of the globe.

AMENDS, A TALE OF THE SUN KINGS

Nancy Springer

The novelist writes the same book over and over again, someone has said, and I know that every fantasy novel I have written has, in a sense, been the same as the first one, The Silver Sun, *the story of Hal and Alan, the Sun Kings. For the rest of my life, I may dream of them and write of them. Names change, departures are made, characters grow into lives of their own, but the same themes remain: the oddling befriended, the outcast made king, high king or sacred king, his very difference, otherness, loneliness being that which lends him power.*

'Amends' is a tale of the Sun Kings, with another element – friendship – added. It is a sort of vignette, from the same fantasy ambiance as all of my Isle novels – The White Hart, The Silver Sun, The Sable Moon *and, most recently,* The Golden Swan *– but not included in any of them. It is a vignette of the Sun Kings' wandering years. Hal and Alan met many dangers during those years, as Hal slowly marshalled his forces and grew into his power and his king-ship. For a long time, he found it hard to accept that he would always be a stranger. His elfin name, Mireldeyn, embodies his essential strangeness: it means 'elf-man'. It is his true-name. Speaking it, he taps his innermost strength, the power of his elfin blood, and he cannot possibly tell an untruth. Speaking it, he suffers, for he affirms his own hated fate.*

This is the only short tale of the Sun Kings yet written, but I think that there are many more such tales, of Hal and Alan and of the lives they touched during those wandering years. Yet as much as this is a story of the Sun Kings, I think it is, perhaps, even more the story of another youth, Ward, who is frightened and angry and sometimes petty in the presence of godlike greatness – very much as you and I might be.

The procession wound through streets lined with cheering people. Hal and Alan, the Sun Kings, had returned to their court city of

Laueroc after a month's journey. The news had flown; everyone had turned out to greet them.

They rode at the head of their retainers. They made no showy cavalcade; the Kings shunned ostentation at any time, and that day their plain clothing was travel-stained. But their horses were beautiful, they themselves beautiful and well loved, the circlets, silver and gold, riding high on their youthful heads. The crowd cheered them wildly. Alan grinned and hailed people he knew. Hal, more restrained as always, glanced about him. Petitioners waited at the castle gates, shouting like the rest. One face among the many caught his searching eye, the one that did not cry out a greeting, that looked back at him white and still. Hal pulled his steed to a halt as memory took hold of him. Vision, rather, seen through eyes not his own . . .

Ward shivered in a winterbound cottage darkened by early dusk, snow blowing in through the cracks death-white and a fiercer storm coming on. They were all sick, lying abed, mother and the boys and the small sister, everyone except himself and the useless old man his father. Not much to eat, nothing to burn except the innards of the cottage itself. They would destroy their home from within, feed it to the fire as the fever fed at their vitals; they would die. The youth rose, gave to the small blaze the three-legged stool he had been sitting on – and then came the knock at the door.

'Open it, Ward,' said his father numbly from his place by the hearth.

'Who could it be except lordsmen?' the young man flared in reply. 'Let them knock.'

The father rose stiffly and went to the door himself, undid the string latch. The door swung open with a bang, blown aside by the wind. No lordsmen stood there. Instead, there in the white whirl of snow stood two youths, hoods back in defiance of the cold, their cloaks whipping about them. Ward stared. They looked no older than himself, and yet far older. Behind them loomed dark, leggy shapes – their horses. Horses! He resented them already.

'Your hospitality, Goodman, or we are likely to perish in this smother.' It was the grave-faced one who spoke, as much in command as in request. Ward noticed his gray eyes, curiously intense. Noticed them from all the way across the room.

'To be sure, you are welcome,' replied his father courteously, 'though we've little enough to offer you.'

Hot anger flamed up in Ward, warming him as the fire could not.

What would these strangers care if they ate everything and left his family destitute? He stepped forward, fists clenched, but no one looked at him.

'Did I see a cowshed yonder?' the second youth asked. He was blond and held his mouth in a faintly humorous half smile.

'Ay. Naught in it.'

'I'll put the horses there, then.' The two of them swung into motion in the manner of men who have long been accustomed to each other's ways of doing things, wordlessly. In a moment a knobby pile of bundles and gear had grown on the doorstep, the blond youth had led the horses into the gathering darkness and the other had stepped inside, swinging his pack.

'I am Hal,' he said quietly, 'and my brother's name is Alan.'

'Worth, they call me,' the goodman introduced himself, 'and yon is my eldest, Ward, and the wife Embla, and the younger ones. . . .' His tired voice faltered away.

'And all sick with fever,' Hal muttered. He dropped his pack and strode straight across the room, kneeling and feeling at the woman's forehead with a delicate fingertip touch.

'Let her alone!' Ward shouted, startled. Most folk would have shied away.

Hal did not move. 'Put on some water to boil,' he said absently. 'We'll make her a broth, some tea—'

'There's nothing except potatoes and old turnips!'

'Ward!' his father reproved him.

Hal got up and crossed to his pack, loosened the fastening. He drew out a sack of oats and one of maslin flour and a chunk of meat wrapped in the raw deerhide. Alan blundered in at the door, shouldering an enormous bundle of firewood. He grinned at the goodman, who was staring at him open-mouthed.

'We try not to come visiting emptyhanded,' he said, easing his load to the earthen floor. Hal had shoved the foodstuffs aside and was rooting impatiently in the recesses of his pack.

'Alan, see if you can't get some water started. I can't find my agrimony – oh, there it is.'

Alan stood still. 'Sickness,' he murmured, looking across the room to where a sufferer stirred and trembled.

'Ay. Where's a pot? By the mothers, must I do everything myself?'

'I will take care of it,' Worth said unexpectedly. He dipped the water from a covered bucket. A half-fearful hope enlivened his face, made it look years younger. Ward stirred from his stance in the middle of the floor and sullenly sat on it, idle. He felt hateful, and guilty at his own anger. These two had brought help, but he could not like them any the better for it, not when they made him feel foolish. He almost wished they had been brigands after all.

His ill humor kept him from enjoying the food much, though it was the best he had eaten in months. Real meat, venison! Hal made a rich, good soup with a sort of bread in it for strength. He spooned off the broth and fed it to the invalids. He and Alan did not eat much. By the time everyone was done it was late, very dark, and the fire was dying to a flicker. Alan rose, yawning, and set about fastening a blanket over the worst portion of the wall. It blew and billowed as if there were no wall at all.

'What a wind,' he grumbled. 'Listen to it, would you!'

Moans and howls sounded overhead. Something sobbed just above the rafters. Worth gasped and dropped with a clatter the pan he was washing.

'That's no wind,' he stammered. 'Black Nick is on the wild hunt tonight, him and his red-eared hounds, come to take souls as lords take deer, the mothers help us!' The words caught in his throat.

'He shall not have them,' Hal said flatly. He took a seat by the little girl who lay and whimpered on her cot by the wall. 'Get that fire going.'

Worth numbly obeyed, his face twitching. Ward could not move; he felt frozen. Something was mewling and wailing around the eaves. 'It sounds like babies,' he whispered.

'The souls that run before,' Hal said sternly. 'Pay no attention. I tell you, he shall not have these.'

'How do you propose to prevent him?' Alan asked, almost as if it were possible.

'It is fear that draws him here like a scent, the fear and despair – feel them in the room, here, almost as solid as the night? I have felt them since I entered. Fire and warm food weren't enough.'

A high-pitched distant yelping sound, overhead, where it had no right to be – wild geese, Ward thought. But it was not the season for wild geese.

'We have no elfin balm,' said Alan.

'I know. You think I haven't longed – well. Let me try it with the plinset.'

Alan handed over the instrument in its leather case. Hal took it out carefully, warm gleaming of well-loved wood. . . . Music was a rare occurrence. A chant or a few sung words flung to the wind might be all a person heard from one year to the next. When Hal struck a soft chord, it was as much a sound of wonder and delight as the hunt was a sound of terror.

'Lint in the bell,' Hal murmured. He sang the song of the blue flax flowers and the summer sun. Alan joined in on the choruses, tuning his voice a triad away, lending resonance. The sound of music shut out for the listeners the weird noises without; the room filled with the glow of imagined sunlight. Hal went on at once to another song, this one about heartsease and the flower of that name.

He defied the powers of winter and death – but only as an embrace defies hatred. Some of his songs were full of valor and glorious folly, some witty, some of them sad, but all were very much alive, all warm. The bedridden folk stopped their shivering and moaning. Even the fire seemed to glow more steadily and bright.

The children settled one by one into peaceful slumber, and then the mother, and then Ward, leaning his head against the wall where he sat by himself in the farthest corner. He was aware for a while of Hal's playing, and then he swam like a trout to a deeper place, so he thought. . . . Then he had a strange and vivid dream.

It seemed to him that the door burst open with a freezing blast of air. And there in the black entry of night stood a specter, eight feet tall, a skull for head and branching from the skull two great forked horns. Hal rose to face it, his plinset in his hands.

'You shall not have them, Arawn,' he said.

Arawn was the black rider's name in the western tongue. His shadow loomed huge upon the wall. At his shoulder nodded the gaunt head of his pale, luminous horse, and around his heels crowded the red-eared hounds, uneasily whining.

'How can you defy me?' Though the giant spoke hollowly through his naked, clacking teeth, he seemed amused.

'I defy you with mortal defiance,' said Hal. 'The spirit that has always defied you. Take your leave.'

'Why, you poor fool,' Black Nick boomed, 'don't you know it is no use? Poor silly hero – give way, now, before I take you as well. I suppose next you will be offering yourself in their stead.'

'Nay. You are to have none of us this night.' Hal stood taut but firm.

'And who are you, that you think you can deny me my rightful game?' All amusement had vanished from the spectral hunter's voice.

'I am Hal, son of Gwynllian, heir to Torre and Taran and the Blessed Kings of Welas, Star Son, Son of the Mothers, Very King.'

'No court has hailed you,' Black Nick mocked.

'The time is not yet. The gypsies hail me, and the elves, and the spirits of the dead.'

'Yours is a mighty magic,' the prince of darkness said, 'but not mighty enough to halt me. Give way.' Towering, he took a step forward. Hal trembled, struggling within himself, forcing himself to say yet one more thing.

'I am Mireldeyn,' he whispered, 'and I bid you begone.'

Black Nick stopped where he stood.

'Well,' he said, in a voice impersonal and oddly gentle. 'Well. You know then that there is a price to pay.'

'I pay with every breath.'

The specter gave a nod, perhaps a sort of bow, his spreading antlers scraping against the rafters. Then he turned and vanished in a single stride. The door banged behind him, and it seemed to Ward that Hal went limp and nearly fell, that Alan appeared from somewhere, caught hold of him to support him. What happened after that he could not tell, for he was asleep. Was he not asleep?

When he got up in the morning Hal was lying near the fire in a sleep that was almost a swoon. Alan was quietly cooking oatmeal, and Ward's mother was sitting up in her bed, staring at the strangers. The children lay sleeping peacefully, and so did Worth. Ward stumbled over to his mother's bedside.

'Are – are you all right?' he stammered, unbelieving.

'I seem to be much better.' Embla turned her puzzled eyes on her son. 'What has happened, Ward? I remember music, the sweetest of music—'

'Nothing. Nothing has happened.' Ward shook his head vehemently, shaking off memory, shaking off shreds of dream.

Snow still fell heavily, but the wind calmed. The snow ceased to seem an enemy, became an insulating downy comforter that sealed them, cocoon-like, from all harm. Alan trudged outside and returned with firewood and more meat from the haunch he had hung behind the cowshed. The snow was his veil; no lordsmen would threaten. Alan made stew, and the children sat up and ate it, all three of them, while Worth moved from one to the other to his wife in restless joy. Hal still lay in a stupor. Alan hauled and heaved him into a bed and he hardly stirred.

'Will he be all right?' Worth asked anxiously.

'Ay, he is just – tired. He was up all night – nursing them,' Alan said awkwardly. 'Herbs—'

'And something more,' Worth stated with a keen glance.

Ward thought of his father as a coward because he quietly met the demands of the lordsmen who kept him constantly poor. Surely the old man did not mean – no. It was too frightening. It was just a dream. Even though Alan seemed more strained and anxious than he had any reason to be.

In midafternoon Alan made an abrupt gesture and went over to wake Hal, took him in his arms, pulled him up against his powerful chest. 'Hal!' he called him, but Hal's head hung limp; there was no response. Alan spoke very softly in his ear: 'Mireldeyn.' Ward stood near enough to hear the word. Hal's eyes fluttered open and he made a dry sobbing sound.

'All right,' Alan murmured. 'It's all right. Wake up. Please.' He helped Hal to sit up on his own. And to Ward's astonishment and chagrin, his father went and knelt by the bed.

'Lord,' said Worth huskily, 'they are better, they will be well. A thousand thanks—' Hal gave him the ghost of a smile.

'Never mind that,' he said. 'You have turnips. Would you get me one? I ought to eat.'

'A turnip!' Worth protested. 'Lord, there is meat.'

'I get meat all the time. You take the meat. I'll take a turnip.'

They spent the evening gathered around the hearth, all of them, even the little ones, talking and talking in a sort of celebration. It was family talk, tales of good times or funny times, touching only lightly on the hardships, the grinding difficulty of life under greedy lord and evil king. Ward sat scowling in their midst, full of rebellion. How could they prattle so? Saved, for what? Brutish slavery, he thought. Hal did not sing. He sat quietly, looking pale, and when the rest of them went to sleep he paced about, the hollows of his cheeks and eyes looking huge in the dim light. Ward, half-wakeful, was aware of his pacing, aware that Alan kept him company and whispered with him from time to time. He chose not to be aware that they spoke of the specter, and Mireldeyn, and the price that must be paid, the loneliness.

The next day Embla was up and about for a while. The snow stopped. Toward evening Hal and Alan packed their things, planning to be off in the morning. They sat by the fire for an hour and went early to bed. That night everyone slept.

Everyone except Ward. When the fire had died down from embers to ashes he slipped from his bed and crept softly to the piles of gear near the door, opened a pack. In the shaft of moonlight that wavered through the single window he examined the contents—

'Ward!' It was his father, whispering. 'What are you doing?'

'Digging carrots!' he whispered back hotly. He rummaged in the pack, muttering to himself. 'Here we are to sit, starving, and likely they have gold, booty, who knows what.'

'Are you mad?' his father gasped. 'Are you my son? You would thieve from those who befriended us?'

Ward made no reply. He drew from the pack a burnished helm and stared at it in the moonlight. There were old songs about a sunset king who would rid Isle of the oppressors; Ward discounted them. But he admired the helm. It shone with the subtle glow of rare silver.

'There,' he breathed.

'Put it back!' hissed Worth.

'Nay, indeed. I plan to feed my brothers and sister if you will not.' Ward reached for Hal's sword. Worth restrained him.

'You will get yourself killed!' he cried, forgetting silence. 'If I did not submit to the lord's demands we would all be dead!' His wife stirred, and he lowered his voice again. 'Put that helm back. What, boy, do you think they will tamely let you have it?'

Ward shook off his father's grip. 'They are outlaws,' he said impatiently. 'They have no recourse.'

'No recourse!' Worth choked, then laughed heartily and silently, a rare event for him and one his son could least stand, to be laughed at. 'Do you mean to tell me you have not noticed Hal's power?' he gasped. 'You cannot face him and prevail.'

Anger and frustration rushed through Ward – the interfering old man! He struck out at his father with the hand that clutched the silver helm, knocking Worth sideways with a metallic thud. The next instant he was himself flung backwards, landing hard on the dirt floor. Hal's hands pinned him there, and he lay frozen, unable to move, stunned by the blazing wrath in those moonlit eyes; he had never seen such flashing fury. Hal panted with rage, and yet when he spoke he spoke evenly. 'Now, listen,' he said. The phrase was a command. 'I will lie and watch you filch from my pack, and if there were any coin in there I'd let you have it. I would have given it to you before now. And I will lie and watch you finger my helm. But I will not lie and watch you strike your father. That you do at your peril.'

Worth was standing behind Hal, pale. 'Don't hurt him, Lord,' he begged, and Ward realized with a sudden pang that Worth's fear was all for his worthless son.

Hal got up and in the same effortless motion he lifted Ward

upright, grasping him by the shoulders, shaking him. 'If I had a father like yours,' he said intensely, 'if I had ever had a loving father, even for a day—'

'Hush, Hal.' Alan stood beside him. 'You'll wake the little one.'

He released Ward and turned away from him. 'Let's go.'

'In the middle of the night?' Alan asked mildly.

'Ay, so much the better. The wind is up again; it will cover our traces before dawn. Let's go.' He turned to the goodman. 'The deer is hanging in the brush behind the cowshed, frozen. Eat it or trade the meat for what you need.'

'What can I give you for thanks?' asked Worth. 'I owe you so much. . . .'

'Your loyalty. You will know what to do when the time comes.'

Now Hal was King, Sunset King. Worth had helped make him so. And now he had encountered Ward again. The youth stared back at him, white-faced, and he had seen himself through those frightened eyes.

Hal vaulted down off his elfin steed, waved his retainers onward and strode to where Ward stood, took his limp hand in welcome. The youth trembled under that touch.

'Ward! I can't believe it!' Alan stood by Hal's side, warmth and concern in his voice. 'What brings you to Laueroc? Nothing wrong, I hope?'

The youth lifted his lowered eyes, incredulous. They were greeting him as old friends! His lips moved, but he could not produce an answer.

'Is your father all right?' Alan asked worriedly.

'Fine!' Ward stammered. 'He lost an arm in the fighting—' He looked down again. His so-called coward of a father had led the assault on the lord's stronghold while he, Ward, had trembled in line, missed his aim—

'But he is all right without it?' Hal asked.

Ward nodded.

'Of course, he would be,' said Hal. 'He has that quiet courage. How are your mother and the little ones?'

'Fine.' Ward managed the one word and no more. He faced his King whom he had wronged, his King who had swept away the lordsmen like dirt off the land. His head swam and he could not meet those gray eyes. 'Lord,' he whispered, 'please kill me and have it done with.'

'Mothers, what am I to do with him?' Hal appealed. 'Ward, can't you tell I mean you no harm?'

'Bring him in,' Alan said. 'This is going to take a while.' At a soft glance from Hal he smiled and went in himself, to his castle chamber, his lady and his supper. Hal led Ward and the horses to the stable. He rubbed his steed dry with a cloth while Ward watched in wonder. How one so kingly could care for his own

'Surely you don't really want me to kill you, Ward?' Hal remarked. 'What is the matter? Why have you come to see me?'

'I – Lord, I am so ashamed. I must make amends somehow.'

'Why? That row we had?' Hal paused as he pulled down fodder, looked at the youth. 'It was nothing. We can forget it, we have both grown since then. Alan tells me that everyone hates his father at one time or another, that it is part of the love.'

Ward winced. He had lately left his father with a harvest to get in, all for no better reason than his own uneasy ache. 'I feel as if I've done nothing right in all my life,' he said.

Hal snorted, blanketing a horse. 'Let go of shame for a while, Ward, and think! Turn and face the thing that is chasing you.'

The youth stood stiff with fear again. 'But that's just it,' he whispered. 'The shame.'

'Not a certain dream in the night?'

Ward shook and sweated as if the fever had hold of him at last. 'I knew it was real,' he said hoarsely.

'I gave you strong herbs,' Hal said. 'You should have been fast asleep. You should never have seen.'

'I was a coward, I would not move to help you—'

'Help me!' Hal exclaimed. 'Even Alan could not help me much that night. I could scarcely help myself. I could scarcely stand.'

'I am a coward!' Words burst out of Ward. 'I saw your power, you defeated Death himself, you are – you are a wizard, or a god, I don't know what you are, you saved us all and I hated you for it, I am such a wretch! I am terrified of you, I wish you would strike me so I could hate you—' Ward covered his quivering face with his hands. 'Liege, help me,' he choked.

Incredibly, he felt arms around him. 'It is all right, truly it is,' said Hal softly. 'Those were dark days, dark years. You were filled with bitterness, and I – after that night with Arawn I was so tired I had no patience, no strength to befriend you. I must always struggle to befriend. Your fear is the price Arawn mentioned, the price I pay.'

Ward stopped trembling and glanced up, startled. Hal nodded at him, his face bleak, his gray eyes unnaturally bright.

'It is not just you. . . . Ward, whatever gave you the notion that you are a coward, that you do nothing right? You are here, are you not? Here, inches from me? Why?'

'Amends . . .'

'Then you are honorable as well as brave.' With a small smile Hal released him. 'There is no need for amends. Just seeing you here is enough.'

'It is not enough,' said Ward with a daring that surprised him. 'Lord, there must be something I can do.'

'A penance?' Hal grumbled. 'No need.' But Ward did not hear; a thought had taken hold of him.

'You say my fear – people's fear – is the price you pay for – being what you are?'

Hal only nodded, watching him.

The youth felt as if he was risking his life. All wary instincts made him feel that way. Nevertheless, he squared his shoulders, straightened himself with a long indrawn breath and met the bright gray eyes. It had to be done, even if he should die for his temerity—

'Why, then, Liege, if it pleases you, I for one will no longer be afraid,' he said, unwavering. And he saw with delight that for once in his life he had done something exactly, ineffably right. Joy touched those shining eyes.

'Amends are made,' Hal said.

'Amends, A Tale of the Sun Kings' by Nancy Springer, copyright © 1983 by Mercury Press, Inc. Originally published in *The Magazine of Fantasy & Science Fiction*. Reprinted by permission of the author and the author's agent, Virginia Kidd.

SING A LAST SONG OF VALDESE
Karl Edward Wagner

Readers often ask writers: 'Where do you get your ideas?' In most instances, the writer cannot begin to find an answer. In the case of 'Sing a Last Song of Valdese', though, I can say exactly where I got the idea – or, at least, the inspiration. It was while I was sitting in Manly Wade Wellman's cabin in the North Carolina mountains, drinking moonshine whiskey and listening to Obray Ramsey pick his banjo and sing those eerie old mountain ballads.

For about twenty-five years, now, I have been writing novels and stories about Kane, a damned immortal wanderer based upon Cain of the Bible. While most modern fantasy characters have their origins in the work of Robert E. Howard or J.R.R. Tolkien, Kane is a throwback to the hero-villains of the eighteenth- and early nineteenth-century Gothic romances; he owes far more to Maturin's Melmoth or Goethe's Faust than to Conan the Barbarian.

Kane has always been the subject for my experimentation within the heroic-fantasy genre; the book Night Winds, *in which 'Sing a Last Song of Valdese' appears, is a collection of my experimental themes and treatments.*

This was the first Kane story to be anthologized: it was selected for The Year's Best Horror Stories: Series V *by Gerald W. Page, my predecessor as editor of that series.*

I would not be doing you a favor by saying anything further before you read the story.

1

The Girl Beneath the Oak

'Reverence! Hold up a moment!'

The burly priest drew rein in a swirl of autumn leaves. Calloused fingers touched the plain hilt of the sword strapped to his saddle as his cowled head bent in the direction of her call.

Raven-black hair twining in the autumn wind, the girl stepped out from the gnarled oaks that shouldered the mountain trail. Bright black eyes smiled up at him from her wide-browed, strong-boned face. Her mouth was wide as well, and smiled.

'You ride fast this evening, reverence.'

'Because the shadows grow deeper, and I have a good way to ride to reach the inn ahead.' His voice was impatient.

'There's an inn not more than a mile from here.' She swayed closer, and he saw how her full figure swelled against her long-skirted dress.

The priest followed the gesture. Just ahead the trail forked, the left winding alongside the mountain river, the right cutting along the base of the ridge. While the river road bore signs of regular travel, the other trail showed an aspect of disuse. Toward this the girl was pointing.

'That trail leads toward Rader,' he told her, shifting in his saddle. 'My business is in Carrasahl.

'Besides,' he added, 'I was told the inn near the fork of the road had long been abandoned. Few have cause to travel to Rader since the wool fair was shifted south to Enseljos.'

'The old inn has lately been reopened.'

'That may be. But my path lies to Carrasahl.'

She pouted. 'I was hoping you might carry me with you to the inn yonder.'

'Climb up and I'll take you to the inn on the Carrasahl road.'

'But my path lies to Rader.'

The priest shrugged thick shoulders, beneath his cassock. 'Then you'd best be going.'

'But reverence,' her voice pleaded. 'It will be dark long before I reach the inn, and I'm afraid to walk this trail at night. Won't you take me there on your horse? It won't take you far from your way, and you can lodge the night there just as well.'

Shadows were lengthening, merging into dusk along the foot of the ridges. The declining sun shed only a dusty rubrous haze across the hilltops, highlighting tall hardwoods already fired by autumn's touch. Streaked with mist, the valleys beyond were swallowed in twilight.

Night was fast overtaking him, the rider saw. He recalled the warnings of villagers miles behind, who for his blessing had given him food and sour wine. They had answered his questions concerning the road ahead, then warned him to keep to the trail if night caught him and on no account make camp by himself. The priest had not been certain whether they warned him of robbers or some darker threat.

His horse stamped impatiently.

'I could make it worth your while to ride out of your way.'

About to ride off, he glanced back down at her. Her smile was impish. Hidden by the cowl, his face could not be read.

She touched the ties of her embroidered bodice. 'I would see that you had a most pleasant stay at Vald's Cove Inn, reverence.' There was witchery in her voice. The bodice loosened, parted across her breasts.

'Though I can't see your face, I can see there's a man beneath that priest's cassock. Would you like to enjoy a mountain flower tonight? You'll remember her sweetness when you grow old in some musty temple.'

Her breasts were firm and well shaped. Against their whiteness the tan flesh of her nipples matched the color of the swirling oak leaves.

Whatever his interest in her, the priest carried gold beneath his robe. The girl's eagerness to draw him onto a little-frequented trail aroused deep suspicion.

'The lure of wanton flesh is nothing to a priest of Thoem,' he intoned.

'Then bugger yourself!' she spat, and lunged with a shrill scream for his horse's face. Sharp claws raked blood across his nose.

Already nervous, the horse screamed and reared. Caught by surprise, the priest lost his stirrups. Cassock flapping about his limbs, he scrambled for balance, then was thrown from the terrified mount. He fell heavily, somehow landing half on his feet, and cursed as his ankle turned under him.

The rearing horse bolted down the trail, took the right fork toward Rader, and disappeared. With mocking laughter, the girl ran after.

Limping badly, the priest stumbled after her, cursing with blasphemous invective. But the darkness quickly swallowed the flash of her white legs, though her laughter taunted him invisibly still.

2

The Inn by the Side of the Road

The lights of the inn were smoky yellow through the thick, leaded panes. The night winds caught the smoke and smell of horses, drove it down the road to Rader, so that the priest came upon the inn all at once.

He noted the many horses tethered in the outlying stables. There were a number of travellers at the inn tonight, and it seemed less likely that the girl meant to lead him into a trap. Or had her confederates lain in wait along the trail, probably they were content to steal his horse and gear. The priest swore angrily, decided he had been too suspicious.

His ankle stabbed with pain, but at least it bore his weight. His boots had probably prevented worse injury. He damned the voluminous grey cassock as it flapped about his trousered legs. It was slitted front and back from ankle to midthigh, and while that enabled him to straddle a horse, he blamed the clumsy garment for his fall.

The two-storey square log structure was a welcome sight. The autumn night grew chill; mist flowed like waves across the ridges. A night spent in the open would be uncomfortable at best. Worse, he had been warned of danger, and his sword was strapped to his saddle somewhere in the darkened hills.

A sign hung over the door: Vald's Cove Inn. The carving seemed of recent work, the priest noted as he climbed up to the door. The latch was not out, though the hour was not late. Hearing voices within, he knocked loudly.

He was about to knock a third time, when the door was opened. Light and voices and the smell of warmth spilled out into the night.

A narrow, beardless face frowned out at him from the half-open doorway. 'Who . . . what do you want . . . reverence?' His voice was thin and nervous, and he spoke in half-whisper.

'Food and lodging,' the priest rumbled impatiently. 'This *is* an inn, I believe.'

'I'm sorry. There's no more room. You'll have to go elsewhere.' He made to close the door.

The priest's huge fist checked him. 'Are you a fool? Where is the innkeeper?' he demanded, suspicious at the man's show of anxious confusion.

'I'm master here,' the other snapped in annoyance. 'I'm sorry, reverence. I've no more room, and you'll have to—'

'Look, damn you!' The priest's bulk shouldered onto the threshold. 'My horse threw me, and I've hobbled for miles already to get here. Now I'll have food and lodging if it's no more than floor space near the fire!'

The skeletal innkeeper did not quail before the bigger man. His narrow jaw clamped in anger; he clenched his black-gloved hands.

'What is this, man?' demanded a voice from within. 'Do I hear you denying lodging to a brother servant of Thoem! What manner of innkeeper are you?'

The innkeeper started, then cringed effusively. 'Forgive me, eminence. I only meant that my accommodations were not sufficient for one of his reverence's—'

'Let him in, you idiot! Turn away a priest of Thoem, would you! I see it's true how sadly you mountain folk have fallen in your respect for the true god! Let him in, do you hear?'

The priest pushed past the suddenly solicitous innkeeper. 'Thank you, eminence. The manners of these folk are pitiable.'

There were several people in the common room of the inn. Seated alone at one of several small tables was a tall, thin man whose scarlet cassock identified him as an abbot in the priesthood of Thoem. Like the priest, his face was hidden by the cowled garment. He waved to the other man with a finely groomed, blue-veined hand.

'Come join me by the fire and have some wine,' he invited. 'I see you're limping somewhat. Did I hear you say your horse threw you? That's bad luck. Our host must send his servants out to find it. Are you badly hurt?'

'Thoem saved me from serious harm, eminence, though I'd rather not walk another mile on it tonight.'

'I'm certain. More wine, innkeeper! And hurry with that roast! Would you starve your guests? Sit down here, please. Have we met? I am Passlo, on my way in the service of Thoem to take charge of the abbey at Rader.'

'A pleasure to meet you, Eminent Passlo.' The priest touched hands as he seated himself. 'I am Callistratis, journeying in the service of Thoem to Carrasahl. I've heard the abbey at Rader has fallen to the Dualists in these evil times.'

The abbot scowled. 'Certain rumors have reached us in the South. Word that there are certain rebel priests in the northern provinces who would contend that Thoem and Vaul are but dual expressions of the same deity. No doubt these heretics consider it prudent to align themselves with the god of these northern barbarians, now that the empire drifts into civil war.'

The priest poured wine and drank hunched forward so that his lips were hidden in the shadow of his cowl. 'I have heard such attempts to vindicate the Dualist heresy. It may be that our errands are the same, Eminent Passlo.'

'Well, Revered Callistratis, that doesn't surprise me. I'd sensed immediately that there was a presence about you that argued for more than the simple priest. But I'll not intrude further on one whose mission requires that he travel incognito. But tell me, though, how would you deal with the Dualists?'

'By the prescribed formula for any heresy. They should all suffer impalement, their bodies left for night beasts and carrion birds.'

The abbot clapped him on the shoulder. 'Splendid, Revered Callistratis! We are of one accord! It pleases me to know that those who believe unswervingly in Thoem's sacred precepts have not all passed from the priesthood! I foresee a pleasant evening of theological discussion.'

'Come, revered gentlemen, don't judge too harshly. After all, there is precedent for Dualism in the history of your priesthood.'

A short, stocky gentleman with a fine grey beard looked gravely at the priests. He straightened from the fire where he had stooped to light his pipe. A silver medallion embossed with a university seal depended from a chain about his thick neck.

'Precedent?' the abbot snapped.

The short man nodded through a puff of smoke. 'Yes. I refer to the dogma formalized under the reign of King Halbros I that Thro'ellet and Tloluvin are but dual identities of the evil principle. No one in the days of the monarchy considered such doctrine heretical, although ancient beliefs plainly ascribe separate identities to those demonlords.'

The abbot paused to consider. 'An interesting point,' he conceded grudgingly, 'although the manifold embodiments of evil are certainly acknowledged by our doctrine. Nonetheless, your argument does not hold in this instance, for there is but one true cosmic principle of good, whom true believers worship as Thoem. May I inquire, sir . . . ?'

The grey-bearded gentleman blew smoke in a flourish. 'I am Claesna, of the Imperial University at Chrosanthe. Your proposal of theological debate caught my ear, eminence. The prospect of intelligent discussion promises salvation from what I had previously feared would be a dull evening in a backwoods tavern. May I join you?'

'Claesna?' The abbot's tone was surprise. 'Yes, I've heard a great deal of you, sir. Please join us! Why does a scholar of your high renown pass through these dismal mountains?'

Claensna smiled acknowledgment. 'I'm headed for Rader myself, actually. I've heard of certain inscriptions on what are said to be prehuman ruins near there. If so, I'd like to copy them for study and comparison with others that I've seen.'

'So it's true that you plan to supplement Nentali's *Interpretation of Elder Glyphics?*' suggested the grey-cowled priest.

Claesna lifted a bushy eyebrow. '*Supplant*, not *supplement*, Revered Callistratis. Well, I see you are an extraordinarily well-informed man yourself. This *does* promise to be an illuminating evening.'

'Oh, please, learned gentlemen,' mimicked a sneering voice from the corner. 'Don't bore us all to death with such learned discussions.'

'Shut up, Hef!' A gruff voice cut him off. 'You'll find a neater death than boredom when we get to Rader!'

The other made an obscene reply. An open fist slapped on flesh, then sounded the clash of chains, subdued cursing.

'Ranvyas, you son of a pox-eaten whore, you busted that tooth half out of my head. Takes guts for a pissant bounty hunter like you to bust a man all chained up.'

'You had an even chance before the chains went on, Hef,' growled Ranvyas. 'And you won't need that tooth once I get you to Rader.'

'We'll see, Ranvyas. Oh, we'll see, won't we? There was other smart bastards all set to count their bounty money, but ain't one of them lived to touch a coin of it.'

Claesna indicated the two men in the near corner. One was a tall, lantern-jawed swordsman with iron-grey hair who wore the green tunic of a ranger. The other, his prisoner, was a wiry man with pinched face and stained yellow beard, whose blue eyes seemed startlingly innocent for one weighed down with wrist and leg irons.

'That's Mad Hef over there, whose black fame ought to be known even to you, revered sirs. Looks harmless enough, though I doubt all the prayers of your priesthood could cleanse his soul of the deeds he's committed here in the mountains. They were talking about it before you came in. The ranger finally tracked him to the cave where he laired, and if he succeeds where so many other brave men have failed, the public executioner at Rader is due for a strenuous afternoon.'

From the rooms above came the echoing moan of a woman in agony.

The priest started from his chair, then halted half-crouched when none of the room's other occupants seemed to pay heed.

Again the cry of pain ripped through the panelled hallway above, down the narrow log stairway. A door slammed at the foot of the stairs, muffled the outcry.

Two other travellers exchanged glances. One, grotesquely fat, shrugged and continued to devour an apple pastry. His smaller companion shuddered and buried his chinless face in his hands.

'Pray Thoem, make her stop!' he moaned.

The fat man wiped his slobbery lips and reached for another pastry. 'Drink more wine, Dordron. Good for the nerves.'

Passlo's hand pulled at the priest's arm. 'Don't be alarmed, Revered Callistratis. The merchant's young wife is giving birth upstairs. No one thought to mention it. As you see, the father is untroubled. Only his brother seems a bit shaken.'

'The fat blob is a half-wit!' sneered Claesna. 'I judge his mind is rotten with pox. I pity his wife, poor child. If our host hadn't sent a serving girl to stay with her, these swine would certainly have left her to labor alone.'

'The mystery of birth,' quoted the abbot, 'where pain is joyful duty.'

Now the innkeeper moved among them, setting before each guest a wooden trencher and a loaf of black bread. Behind him walked a swarthy, bristle-bearded dwarf, the first servant the priest had noted in the inn. His squat, powerful arms carried a great platter of roast meat, which he presented to each guest that he might serve himself as he desired. The fat merchant growled impatiently when the dwarf halted first before the abbot and his two table companions.

'Please, Jarcos!' his brother begged. 'Don't offend these revered sirs!'

Hef giggled. 'Don't eat it all now! Save a nice hefty bone for poor toothless Hef!'

From overhead the screams, distant through the thick boards, sounded now at closer intervals.

The innkeeper smiled nervously and wrung his black-gloved

hands. 'I'll bring out more wine, Bodger,' he told the dwarf. 'Bring out your mandolin and play for them.'

The dwarf grinned and scuttled into the back rooms. He cavorted out again in a moment, wearing a flop-brim hat with a feather and carrying a black-stained mandolin. His strangely pointed fingers struck the strings like dagger tips, and he began to caper about the room, singing comic ballads in a bullfrog voice.

The moans from upstairs continued monotonously, and soon the travellers forgot to listen to them, or to notice when they ceased.

3

'Do You Know the Song of Valdese?'

'Then, just as the hunter spun around at the sound, the werewolf leaped down from the roof of his cabin! He clawed for the silver dagger at his belt, but the sheath was empty! Too late he remembered the old man's warning! And as he died, he saw that the beast at his throat had the sun-colored eyes of his wife!'

Claesna leaned back against his chair and blew smoke at the listeners circled about the fire.

'Bravo!' squealed Jarcos, the fat merchant. 'Oh, that was good! Do you mean that the werewolf was really his wife, then?'

Claesna did not deign to reply, instead nodded acceptance of the others' applause.

The meal was a scattering of picked bones and cheese rinds. The autumn night tightened its chill around the inn, where inside the travellers shared the companionship of wine and a warm fire. The hour grew late, but no one yet sought his bed. Pulling chairs in a rough circle about the glowing hearth, they had listened to the ballads of Bodger the dwarf, and as the night wore on someone had suggested that each tell a story.

'The mountains of Halbrosn seem haunted with all manner of inhuman fiends,' Dordron remarked with a shiver. 'Jarcos, why did you insist we make this journey to Rader? You know the wool market there has been dead for years.'

'My astrologer agreed this was a wise venture. Let me worry about our business, little brother.' Jarcos contrived to shape his rolls of chins into a resolute expression.

'Not only "inhuman fiends" to watch for,' Ranvyas commented, jerking a gnarled thumb toward his prisoner. 'Up until two days ago there was Mad Hef here. Thoem knows how many poor travellers he's waylaid and murdered. Had a favorite trick of crawling out onto the road all covered with blood and moaning he was one of Mad Hef's victims. Too damn many good-hearted folks left their bones in the rocks for the mice to nest in. And I'd as soon forget if I could some of the things I seen back in that cave where he was laired.'

Hef snickered and shook his chains against the post. 'Got a special niche for your skull there, Ranvyas dear. Old man like you should've brought help along, 'stead of trying to sneak after me all alone. You're just too brave for your—'

Ranvyas raised his fist; Hef broke off in an angry mutter.

'There have been human monsters in these mountains worse than this carrion-eater,' the abbot said.

'Oh? Do you know this region, eminence?' asked the innkeeper, who had joined them at the fire.

'Only from my learning. I dare say that the old provinces of the Halbros kings have figured so prominently in our history and literature that all of us know some tale of their mountains—though we are all strangers here.'

He glanced around at the others. 'Perhaps you observed the stone ruins that crest the ridge along the gap ahead. Quite striking against the sunset, I thought. That was the fortress from which Kane held these mountains in thrall for a hundred years. He ruled the land with a bloody fist, exacted tribute from all who passed through, fought back every expedition led against him. Some say he had made a pact with the forces of evil by which they granted him eternal youth and victory in return for the innocent blood he sacrificed each dark of the moon.

'For a while he aided Halbros-Serrantho in the imperial wars, but even the great emperor sickened of Kane's depravity and finally used the combined armies of the new empire to pull the tyrant's citadel down on his head. They say his evil ghost haunts the ruins to this day.'

'A tale somewhat garbled by popular superstition,' Claesna remarked. 'Actually the legend of Kane has far darker implications. His name, I have observed, reappears in all ages and all lands. The literature of the occult recurrently alludes to him. In fact, there is an ancient compendium of prehuman glyphics that Kane is said to have authored. If it exists, I'd give a fortune to read it.'

'A rather long-lived villain, this Kane,' said Passlo drily.

'Some occult authors contend that Kane was one of the first true men, damned to eternal wandering for some dark act of rebellion against mankind's creator.'

'I doubt Thoem would have damned a blasphemer to immortality,' scoffed the abbot. 'Doubtless his legend appeals to certain evil types who take his name for their own.'

'Then they steal his physical appearance, as well,' Claesna countered. 'Legend describes him as a man of powerful build, seemingly a warrior in his prime years. His hair is red and he is left-handed.'

'So are many others.'

'But his eyes are his mark. The eyes of Kane are blue, and in them glows the mad gaze of a ruthless killer. No man may look into Kane's eyes and not know him.'

Ranvyas started. 'There's talk of an assassin who's behind these murders that are pushing the empire into civil war. Said to be an outlander brought in by Eypurin to remove those who oppose his false claim to the throne. His name is reportedly Kane, and what little is known of him answers to your description. Did this Kane die in the fall of his citadel?'

Passlo looked startled. 'Why, of course . . . I suppose. Yes, he must have. That was centuries ago, man!'

'I had been warned against staying the night in the open,' suggested the priest. 'While nothing definite was said, I can see that these mountains have more sinister legends than the road has turns.'

'That's so, Revered Callistratis,' affirmed the ranger, running a hand over his short-cropped hair. 'You say you lost your horse on the trail? Lucky for you you didn't meet Valdese while you was limping along in the dark.'

'Valdese?'

'A lamia, reverence,' explained the innkeeper. 'A most beautiful spectre, Valdese is—and most malevolent. Legend says she haunts the mountain trails at night. Entices travellers into her arms and leaves them bloodless beneath the moon.'

Suddenly it had grown very quiet. Leaves rustled against the frosted windowpanes.

The innkeeper sensed the unease of his guests. 'Had you not heard that legend, gentlemen? But I forget—you're strangers here, all of you. Still I thought you must have heard her song. Do you know the Song of Valdese?'

He raised a black-gloved hand. 'Come out, Bodger. Sing Valdese's song for our guests.'

The dwarf scuttled out of the shadow with his mandolin. Bowing to his audience, he began to sing, his voice comic no longer.

In the dark hills of Halbros' land,
There dwelled a lovely maid—
The brightest flower, the rarest jewel,
Shone dull in Valdese's hand.

Her father's inn stood beside the road,
Great was his wealth of gold—
But the choicest treasure of the land,
Was the heart of fair Valdese.

Then came brash suitors to her door,
Six bright and bold young men—
Said they had come to win the hand,
Of the maiden called Valdese.

'Sirs,' she said, 'don't think me cruel,
For I love another youth—
He must be gone for seven long years,
To study in a hidden school.'

And when she told them the suitors laughed,
'Oh, your beauty is not for him—
Choose instead from one of our band,
And not some wizard's fool.'

Then came her lover in a cloak of grey,
Returning from the hidden school—
Said, 'I've been gone these seven long years,
Now I've come for the love of Valdese.'

'Oh no,' swore the suitors in jealousy,
'You'll not steal our prize'—
And with cruel knives they took his life,
And the heart of Valdese after.

Now Valdese lies in the cold, cold ground,
And her spirit haunts these hills—
But her lover was sworn in the Grey Lord's name,
To serve seven times seven years.

'That's terrifying!' breathed Dordron, when the dwarf stopped singing. 'So uncanny an ending, that last verse!'

'Perhaps the last verse hasn't been written,' the innkeeper suggested. 'Bodger, see how things are upstairs. It's grown strangely quiet up there.'

'Well, at least we servants of Thoem have nothing to fear from lamiae!' muttered the abbot stoutly. 'Do we not, Revered Callistratis?'

'To be certain, eminence,' the priest assured him. 'Thoem protects his servants from all creatures of evil.'

Passlo suddenly drew a crystal-hilted dagger from the folds of his cassock. 'And for added protection in these shadow-haunted hills I carry with me this sacred blade. It was shaped from star-metal by priests long dead, and the runes on its blade give it power over evil's foul servants.' He did not add that he had stolen the blade from the abbey vaults.

'Seven years in a hidden school,' mused the priest. 'That can only mean one thing.'

Claesna nodded. 'He was apprenticed to the cult of the Seven Nameless—and sworn to the Grey Lord.'

'Thoem grant that we someday see the extinction of that black cult of devil worshippers!' growled Passlo.

'The cult is far older than your own religion,' Claesna informed him. 'And it isn't devil worship, strictly speaking.'

'Well, they're devils they worship!' Jarcos said shrilly.

'No. The Seven Nameless are elder gods. Or "proto-gods", more accurately, since they exist beyond the ordered universe of good and evil forces. Their realm is one of timeless chaos, a limbo of unformed creation and ultimate dissolution—opposite forces that somehow exist simultaneously.'

Claesna preened his beard. 'Their entire worship is structured on the energy of opposing systems. Little is known of the cult, since its devotees worship in secret. New initiates must study seven years in a "hidden school" to master the secret powers of the cult; then each is sworn to one of the Seven for the space of forty-nine years. The names of the Seven are secret, for should the uninitiate utter them he would evoke the god without having power over him. A rather hideous fate, it's said. Korjonos was sworn to the Grey Lord, who is the most feared of the Seven.'

'Korjonos? Was that the young wizard's name?' the priest inquired.

Claesna bit his pipestem testily. 'Yes, I believe so. After all, the ballad was based on true events. Happened a century ago, I believe.'

'Not at all,' corrected the innkeeper. 'Not quite fifty years ago. And very near here.'

'Indeed?' Dordron's voice was strained.

'In fact, at this very inn.'

The eyes of the travellers bored back into their host's smiling face.

'Why, yes. But I forgot you gentlemen are strangers here. Would you like to know the story behind Valdese's song?'

No one spoke. He went on as if there were no tension in the room.

'Valdese and Korjonos were childhood lovers. She was the daughter of one of the richest men in Halbrosn, while he was the son of a servant at his inn. They were both barely past ten when Korjonos was orphaned. Penniless, he left the inn to study at a hidden school and vowed to return for her in seven years, with the wealth and power that his wisdom would bring him.

'Valdese waited for him. But there were others. Six coarse young louts from the settlements close by. They lusted for her beauty, and more for the gold she would inherit. Valdese would not have them, but they argued and waited, for the time was near when Korjonos had promised to return.

'And after seven years he did return. To their brutish anger, Valdese's love for the young wizard had not diminished with time. They were married that night at her father's inn.

'But hate was black in the hearts of her rejected suitors, and they drank long into the night.'

A log burst apart in a shower of sparks, cast light over the circle of nervous faces.

'The guests were gone; her father they slew with the few others who were there. They took his gold, and they dragged the lovers from their wedding chamber.

'They hung Korjonos between two trees. Valdese they threw to the ground.

'"He'll not curse us," said one, and they cut out his tongue.

'"He'll not cast spells against us," said another; and they cut off his hands.

'"Nor seek to follow after us," and they cut off his feet.

'Then they cut away his manhood and told her, "He's not fit to lie with."'

'And they cut away his face and told her, "He's not fit to look at."'

'But they spared him his eyes so that he might watch what they did to her, and they spared him his ears so he might listen to her screams.'

'When they were finished . . . she died. Korjonos they left hanging. Then they divided the gold and fled, each choosing a separate path to follow. And while the infamy of their deed shamed the land, not one of them was ever punished.'

'Korjonos?' asked the priest.

'Did not die. He was sworn to the Grey Lord for seven times seven years, and death could not claim him. His familiar demon cut him down and carried him away. And the rage of the sorcerer waited years upon painful years for fitting vengeance to transpire.'

A chair crashed as Claesna leaped to his feet. 'Gods! Don't you see? It's been near fifty years, and our faces and names were otherwise! But I thought several of your faces seemed familiar to me! Don't deny it! It's no coincidence that all six of us have returned to this inn tonight! Sorcery has drawn us here! But who . . . ?'

The innkeeper smiled in secret mirth as their startled voices shouted in protest. He crossed over to in front of the fire. Still smiling, he peeled off the black gloves.

And they saw what manner of hands were grafted to his wrists.

With these hands he dug at the flesh of his face.

The smiling lips peeled away with the rest, and they saw the noseless horror that had been a face, saw the black reptilian tongue that lashed between broken teeth.

They sat frozen in shock. The dwarf entered unnoticed, a tiny corpse in his hairy hands.

'Stillborn, master,' he snickered, holding by its heels the blue-skinned infant. 'Strangled by her cord, and the mother died giving forth.' He stepped into the center of their circle.

Then the chill of the autumn night bore down upon them, a chill greater than that of any natural darkness.

'Seven years times seven,' hissed Korjonos. 'So long have I plotted for this. I've shaped your lives from the day of your crime, let you fatten like cattle, let you live for the day when you would pay as no man has ever paid!

'Callistratis,' he called aside, 'this isn't for you! I don't know how you came here, but go now if you still can.'

Faces set in fear, they stared at the wizard. Invisible bonds held them in their places about the circle.

Korjonos chanted and gestured. 'Holy man, evil man. Wise man, fool. Brave man, coward. Six corners of the heptagon, and I, a dead man who lives, make the seventh. Contradicting opposites that invoke the chaos lords – and the final paradox is the focus of the spell: an innocent soul who has never lived, a damned soul who can never die!

'Seven times seven years have passed, and when the Grey Lord comes for me, you six shall follow into his realm!'

Suddenly Ranvyas sprang to life. 'The dagger!'

The abbot stared dumbly, then fumbled at his cassock. He seemed to move at a dreamlike pace.

Hissing in rage, Korjonos rushed into the incantation.

Passlo clumsily extended the dagger, but the ranger was faster.

Tearing the dagger from Passlo's trembling fingers, he hurled it at the grinning dwarf.

Bodger shrieked and dropped the stillborn infant. Reeking smoke boiled from his chest where the crystal hilt protruded. He reeled, seemed to sag inward upon himself, like a collapsing coat of mail. Then there was only a charred greasy smear, a pile of filthy clothes – and a hairy spider that scurried away to vanish through a chink in the wall.

'Well done, Ranvyas!' Claesna gasped shakily. 'You've slain his familiar, and the spell is shattered!'

He sneered at the wizard. 'Unless, of course, you've another "damned soul who cannot die" who can complete your incantation.'

Korjonos's bowed shoulders signalled his defeat.

'Let's get out of here!' blubbered Jarcos. His brother was weeping mindlessly.

'Not until we slay the wizard,' growled Ranvyas.

'And set me free,' Hef advised. 'I don't think you'll want me to tell them in Rader about my five old comrades.'

'Thoem! It's cold!' chattered Passlo. 'And what's wrong with the light in here?'

The priest broke into their circle and bent over the pile of seared clothing. They thought he meant to retrieve the enchanted dagger, but when he straightened he held the stillborn child in his left hand.

His cowl fell back. They saw his red hair.

They saw his eyes.

'Kane!' screamed Claesna.

Korjonos shouted out syllables that formed another name.

Hands went for futile swordhilts, but already the room was heavy with the sweet dust stench of ancient decay.

At the doorway behind them the bolt snapped with rust; boards rotted and sagged, crumbled into powdery dissolution. They stared in dread understanding. In the threshold stood a tall figure in a tattered cloak of grey.

Kane turned his face.

And the Grey Lord lifted his mask.

Kane shook the darkness from his mind. He started to come to his feet, then almost fell because he already stood.

He was standing in the gutted interior of a log building. The floor overhead had collapsed, as had the roof, and he could see stars in the night sky. Small trees snagged up through the rotting debris. The inn had been abandoned for many years.

The air was musty with decay. He stumbled for the doorway, thought he heard the snap of dry bones beneath his boots. Outside he breathed raggedly and glanced again at the sky.

The mist crawled in wild patterns across the stars. And Kane saw a wraithlike figure of grey, his cloak flapping in the night winds. Behind him seemed to follow seven more wraiths, dragging their feet as if they would not follow.

Then another phantom. A girl in a long dress, racing after. She caught the seventh follower by the hand. Strained, then drew him away. The Grey Lord and those who must follow vanished into the night skies. The girl and her lover fell back in an embrace – then melted as one into the mist.

Kane's horse was waiting outside the ruined inn. Kane was not surprised, for he had recognized the girl in the mist. His heels touched the horse's flanks, and Kane vanished into the mist as well.

'Sing a Last Song of Valdese' by Karl Edward Wagner, copyright © 1976 by the Nemedian Chronicles. Originally published in *Chacal 1*. Reprinted by permission of the author and the author's agent, the E.J. Carnell Literary Agency.

THE FATHER OF THE BRIDE
Connie Willis

When I was a child, fairy tales were my favorite stories. They have been criticized a good deal recently. Child psychologists have worried about the grisly violence in fairy tales, and have discreetly removed some of the gorier parts. Feminists have furiously attacked what they see as sexual stereotyping, and have replaced the traditional stories with their own versions. An assortment of people have decided that stories about princesses and forests have nothing to say to today's democratic, urban children, and have filled the library shelves with stories about traffic lights and street vendors.

I think all these people have forgotten – or never knew – what it was about the fairy tale they loved. Fairy tales are not stories about killing or about sexual roles or even about princesses and forests – they are stories about us. They are set in ancient times and faraway places and they speak of people who never existed, so that we can see ourselves *more clearly.*

And sometimes, as I hope happens in 'The Father of the Bride', they have something important to say . . .

I should be happy. Everyone tells me so: my wife, my daughter, my brave new son-in-law. This is the happily ever after for which we have waited all these long years. But I fear we have waited far too long, and now it is too late to be happy.

My wife tries to jolly me out of this dark mood. 'The roads are better,' she says. 'There is a new bridge at the ford.'

'The better for armies to pass along, burning and killing,' I answer. There are English already in Crécy, a story I would not believe at first, and they are carrying weapons I never heard of – a bow as tall as a man, a *ribaud* that spits black smoke and sudden death.

'You never liked the forest at our gates,' she says. 'Or the wolves.'

'Nor do I like the town. And there are still wolves at our gates,' I say. 'Merchants and pedlars.'

'They bring you the cinnamon and pepper for your food.'

'That give me the bellyache.'

'And medicines for the bellyache,' she says, smiling to herself. She is embroidering on a piece of linen. Do women still do that, sitting with their heads bent forward over their work, pulling the fine stitches taut with their white hands? I do not think so. Embroidered cloth can be bought by the length in the town, I suppose. What cannot be bought in that town? Beauty, perhaps. Repose. I have seen nothing of either in this new world.

'This is a beautiful coat,' said the insolent tailor they sent me to. Nothing would do but that I have a new coat for the wedding. The tailor shouted in my ear through all the fitting and did not once call me 'my lord'. 'A beautiful coat. Brocade. From the east.'

'Gaudy, you mean,' I said, but he did not hear me. How could he? The water mill runs night and day, sawing the forest into shops, houses, bridges. Soon the whole world will be town. 'The coat is too short,' I shouted at him. It showed what God intended decent men to hide.

'You are old-fashioned,' he said. 'Turn around.'

The coat is too short. I am cold all the time. 'Where are the servants?' I say to my wife. 'I want a fire.'

She looks up from her sewing as if she knows the answer will grieve me. 'Gone,' she says. 'We are getting new ones from the town.'

'Gone? Where?' I say, but I know already. Hardly awake, the cooks ran off to be bakers; the chamberlains, burghers; the pages, soldiers. 'I shall catch my death of cold in this coat.'

'The pedlars have medicines for chills,' she says, and looks sideways at me to make me smile.

'It is all so changed,' I say, frowning instead. 'There is nothing about this world that I like.'

'Our daughter has a husband and a kingdom,' she says. 'She did not prick her finger on a spindle and die that terrible day.'

'No,' I say, and have to smile after all. She is so beautiful, so happy with her prince. She would not have minded sleeping a thousand years so long as he kissed her awake. She thinks the forest parted when he rode to find her, and I do not tell her it was not she he came to find, but land for his fields, land for his new town, land to clear and settle and tax. He was as surprised as any of his woodsmen to find us drowsing here. But he seems to love her, and there is no denying he is a brave young man. He moves through this strange time as if it held no terrors. Perhaps the forest does part for him. Or perhaps he has only chopped it down.

Only a little remains to the east and even it is not so dark as before, so full of guarding briars. I went into it one day, looking, or so I said to myself, for the good fairy who saved my daughter, though she had never lived in that part of the forest. I found myself instead near the tower of the old fairy, who by her spite brought us all to this pass.

'I have come to ask a question,' I shouted into the silence of the trees. 'Why did you hate us so? What had we done to you that you should have come to our christening bearing curses?' There was no answer. 'Had you outlived your time so that you hated all things new, even my infant daughter?' Silence. 'Do you hate us still?'

In the answering silence I thought I could hear the town, builders and rumbling wheels. As I came nearer, I saw that the tower had been knocked down, the stones heaped into piles and carted away. I followed the tracks of the wheels and came to a sunny clearing and to men in a holy habit I did not recognize. They told me they are Cistercians (Are there new saints as well? is everything new?) and that they are using the stones to build a church.

'Are you not afraid of the fairy who lived in this tower?' I asked them.

'Old man,' said one of them, clapping his hand to my shoulder, 'there are no fairies. Only God and his angels.'

So I came away with the answer to my question after all. We have outlived our old enemy, and the only curse upon us is the cruel spell of time.

'We have lived through the worst of our days,' my wife says, trying to comfort me.

'I hope so,' I say, looking out the window of my castle onto the town, the fields beyond, the sea, onto a world without forests or wolves or fairies, a world with who knows what terrors to replace them? 'I hope so.'

'There is not a spinning wheel in all the kingdom,' she says tearfully. 'Not even in the town.' She has pricked her finger on her embroidery. There are drops of blood on the linen. 'I have not seen a single spinning wheel.'

'Of course not,' I say, and pat her shoulder.

There is at least no danger from that direction. What need have we of spinning wheels when every ship brings velvets, silks, cloth of gold? And perhaps other cargoes, not so welcome. English soldiers from the west. And from the east, tales of a black spell that kills men where they stand and moves like a curse toward France. Perhaps the old fairy is not dead after all, but only biding her time in some darker forest to the east.

I have dozed off. My wife comes to wake me for yet another feast. I grumble and turn on my side. 'You're tired,' she says kindly. 'Go back to sleep.'

Would that I could.

'The Father of the Bride' by Connie Willis, copyright © 1982 by TZ Publications, Inc. Reprinted by permission of the author.

KEVIN MALONE
Gene Wolfe

Four or five years ago, the city of Chicago boasted a minute organization called the Windy Writers Club. Algis Budrys, George R.R. Martin and Alex and Phyllis Eisenstein all belonged; so did I, and so did Chuck Ott and E. Michael Blake, two talented young writers who have since become playwrights almost exclusively.

The Windy's procedure was pretty simple. Some hardworking member (usually Phyllis or Chuck) would collect the manuscripts to be discussed at the next meeting, make xerox copies and mail them to the other members to be read in advance. We'd meet in each other's homes and, after an hour or so of soft drinks, potato chips and shop talk, discuss the stories, tackling them alphabetically by title.

The topic of dream stories came up at one of these sessions, and although most of us had heard of such stories (which began, I suppose, with Jacob's ladder), none of us had ever written one.

As it happens, I am a prolific and vivid dreamer. The psychologists say all of us are, though some of us cannot remember our dreams upon awakening. I can usually recall mine, and often remember three or four from a single night. Some are pleasant. Some are frightening. Some are heartbreaking (as when I dream, as I sometimes do, that my parents are alive again). Most are simply strange.

With only minor exceptions, dreams lack all the essentials of a story: one sees an odd person or hears, perhaps, an odd remark, and knows — though one can never say how — it to be of vast significance. My mother used to dream that she could fly, and awake convinced, for a moment or two, that she recalled the method; I am sometimes six or eight hours in shaking off some wild conviction born in a dream.

A week or so after that Windy Writers meeting, I dreamed the story you are about to read.

Marcella and I were married in April. I lost my position with Ketterly, Bruce & Drake in June, and by August we were desperate.

We kept the apartment – I think we both felt that if we lowered our standards there would be no chance to raise them again – but the rent tore at our small savings. All during July I had tried to get a job at another brokerage firm, and by August I was calling fraternity brothers I had not seen since graduation, and expressing an entire willingness to work in whatever businesses their fathers owned. One of them, I think, must have mailed us the advertisment.

Attractive young couple, well educated and well connected, will receive free housing, generous living allowance for minimal services.

There was a telephone number, which I omit for reasons that will become clear.

I showed the clipping to Marcella, who was lying with her cocktail shaker on the chaise-longue. She said, 'Why not?' and I dialed the number.

The telephone buzzed in my ear, paused, and buzzed again. I allowed myself to go limp in my chair. It seemed absurd to call at all; for the advertisement to have reached us that day, it must have appeared no later than yesterday morning. If the position were worth having—

'The Pines.'

I pulled myself together. 'You placed a classified ad. For an attractive couple, well educated and the rest of it.'

'I did not, sir. However, I believe my master did. I am Priest, the butler.'

I looked at Marcella, but her eyes were closed. 'Do you know, Priest, if the opening has been filled?'

'I think not, sir. May I ask your age?'

I told him. At his request, I also told him Marcella's (she was two years younger than I), and gave him the names of the schools we had attended, described our appearance, and mentioned that my grandfather had been a governor of Virginia, and that Marcella's uncle had been ambassador to France. I did not tell him that my father had shot himself rather than face bankruptcy, or that Marcella's family had disowned her – but I suspect he guessed well enough what our situation was.

'You will forgive me, sir, for asking so many questions. We are almost a half day's drive, and I would not wish you to be disappointed.'

I told him that I appreciated that, and we set a date – Tuesday of the next week – on which Marcella and I were to come out for an interview with 'the master'. Priest had hung up before I realized that I had failed to learn his employer's name.

During the teens and twenties some very wealthy people had designed estates in imitation of the palaces of the Italian Renaissance. The Pines was one of them, and better preserved than most – the fountain in the courtyard still played, the marbles were clean and unyellowed, and if no red-robed cardinal descended the steps to a carriage blazoned with the Borgia arms, one felt that he had only just gone. No doubt the place had originally been called *La Capana* or *Il Eremitaggio*.

A serious-looking man in dark livery opened the door for us. For a moment he stared at us across the threshold. 'Very well,' he said.

'I beg your pardon?'

'I said that you are looking very well.' He nodded to each of us in turn, and stood aside. 'Sir. Madame. I am Priest.'

'Will your master be able to see us?'

For a moment some exiled expression – it might have been amusement – seemed to tug at his solemn face. 'The music room, perhaps, sir?'

I said I was sure that would be satisfactory, and followed him. The music room held a Steinway, a harp, and a dozen or so comfortable chairs; it overlooked a rose garden in which old remontant varieties were beginning that second season that is more opulent though less generous than the first. A kneeling gardener was weeding one of the beds.

'This is a wonderful house,' Marcella said. 'I really didn't think there was anything like it left. I told him you'd have a John Collins – all right? You were looking at the roses.'

'Perhaps we ought to get the job first.'

'I can't call him back now, and if we don't get it, at least we'll have had the drinks.'

I nodded to that. In five minutes they arrived, and we drank them and smoked cigarettes we found in a humidor – English cigarettes of strong Turkish tobacco. A maid came, and said that Mr. Priest would be much obliged if we would let him know when we would dine. I told her that we would eat whenever it was convenient, and she dropped a little curtsy and withdrew.

'At least,' Marcella commented, 'he's making us comfortable while we wait.'

Dinner was lamb in aspic, and a salad, with a maid – another maid – and footman to serve while Priest stood by to see that it was done properly. We ate at either side of a small table on a terrace overlooking another garden, where antique statues faded to white glimmerings as the sun set.

Priest came forward to light the candles. 'Will you require me after dinner, sir?'

'Will your employer require us; that's the question.'

'Bateman can show you to your room, sir, when you are ready to retire. Julia will see to madame.'

I looked at the footman, who was carrying in fruit on a tray.

'No, sir. That is Carter. Bateman is your man.'

'And Julia,' Marcella put in, 'is my maid, I suppose?'

'Precisely.' Priest gave an almost inaudible cough. 'Perhaps, sir – and madame – you might find this useful.' He drew a photograph from an inner pocket and handed it to me.

It was a black and white snapshot, somewhat dogeared. Two dozen people, most of them in livery of one kind or another, stood in brilliant sunshine on the steps at the front of the house, men behind women. There were names in India ink across the bottom of the picture: James Sutton, Edna De Buck, Lloyd Bateman . . .

'Our staff, sir.'

I said, 'Thank you, Priest. No, you needn't stay tonight.'

The next morning Bateman shaved me in bed. He did it very well, using a straight razor and scented soap applied with a brush. I had heard of such things – I think my grandfather's valet may have shaved him like that before the First World War – but I had never guessed that anyone kept up the tradition. Bateman did, and I found I enjoyed it. When he had dressed me, he asked if I would breakfast in my room.

'I doubt it,' I said. 'Do you know my wife's plans?'

'I think it likely she will be on the South Terrace, sir. Julia said something to that effect as I was bringing in your water.'

'I'll join her then.'

'Of course, sir.' He hesitated.

'I don't think I'll require a guide, but you might tell my wife I'll be with her in ten minutes or so.'

Bateman repeated his, 'Of course, sir,' and went out. The truth was that I wanted to assure myself that everything I had carried in the pockets of my old suit – car keys, wallet, and so on – had been transferred to the new one he had laid out for me; and I did not want to insult him, if I could prevent it, by doing it in front of him.

Everything was where it should be, and I had a clean handkerchief in place of my own only slightly soiled one. I pulled it out to look at (Irish linen) and a flutter of green came with it – two bills, both fifties.

Over eggs Benedict I complimented Marcella on her new dress, and asked if she had noticed where it had been made.

'Rowe's. It's a little shop on Fifth Avenue.'

'You know it, then. Nothing unusual?'

She answered, 'No, nothing unusual,' more quickly than she should have, and I knew that there had been money in her new clothes too, and that she did not intend to tell me about it.

'We'll be going home after this. I wonder if they'll want me to give this jacket back.'

'Going home?' She did not look up from her plate. 'Why? And who are "they"?'

'Whoever owns this house.'

'Yesterday you called him *he*. You said Priest talked about *the master*, so that seemed logical enough. Today you're afraid to deal with even presumptive masculinity.'

I said nothing.

'You think he spent the night in my room – they separated us, and you thought that was why, and you just waited there – was it under a sheet? – for me to scream or something. And I didn't.'

'I was hoping you had, and I hadn't heard you.'

'Nothing happened, dammit! I went to bed and went to sleep; but as for going home, you're out of your mind. Can't you see we've got the job? Whoever he is – wherever he is – he likes us. We're going to stay here and live like human beings, at least for a while.'

And so we did. That day we stayed on from hour to hour. After that, from day to day; and at last from week to week. I felt like Klipspringer, the man who was Jay Gatsby's guest for so long that he had no other home – except that Klipspringer, presumably, saw Gatsby from time to time, and no doubt made agreeable conversation, and perhaps even played the piano for him. Our Gatsby was absent. I do not mean that we avoided him, or that he avoided us; there were no rooms we were forbidden to enter, and no times when the servants seemed eager that we should play golf or swim or go riding. Before the good weather ended, we had two couples up for a weekend; and when Bette Windgassen asked if Marcella had inherited the place, and then if we were renting it, Marcella said, 'Oh, do you like it?' in such a way that they left, I think, convinced that it was ours, or as good as ours.

And so it was. We went away when we chose, which was seldom, and returned when we chose, quickly. We ate on the various terraces and balconies, and in the big, formal dining room, and in our own bedrooms. We rode the horses, and drove the Mercedes and the cranky, appealing old Jaguar as though they were our own. We did everything, in fact, except buy the groceries and pay the taxes and the servants; but someone else was doing that; and every morning I found one hundred dollars in the pockets of my clean clothes. If summer had lasted for ever, perhaps I would still be there.

The poplars lost their leaves in one October week; at the end of it I fell asleep listening to the hum of the pump that emptied the swimming pool. When the rain came, Marcella turned sour and drank too much. One evening I made the mistake of putting my arm about her shoulders as we sat before the fire in the trophy room.

'Get your filthy hands off me,' she said. 'I don't belong to you. Priest, look here. He hasn't said an intelligent word to me all day or done a decent thing, and now he wants to paw me all night.'

Priest pretended, of course, that he had not heard her.

'Look over here! Damn it, you're a human being, aren't you?'

He did not ignore that. 'Yes, madame, I am a human being.'

'I'll say you are. You're more a man than he is. This is your place, and you're keeping us for pets – is it me you want? Or him? You sent us the ad, didn't you? He thinks you go into my room at night, or he says he does. Maybe you really come to his – is that it?'

Priest did not answer. I said, 'For God's sake, Marcella.'

'Even if you're old, Priest, I think you're too much of a man for that.' She stood up, tottering on her long legs and holding onto the stonework of the fireplace. 'If you want me, take me. If this house is yours, you can have me. We'll send him to Vegas – or throw him on the dump.'

In a much softer tone than he usually used, Priest said, 'I don't want either of you, madame.'

I stood up then, and caught him by the shoulders. I had been drinking, too, though only half or a quarter as much as Marcella; but I think it was more than that – it was the accumulated frustration of all the days since Jim Bruce told me I was finished. I outweighed

Priest by at least forty pounds, and I was twenty years younger. I said: 'I want to know.'

'Release me, sir, please.'

'I want to know who it is; I want to know now. Do you see that fire? Tell me, Priest, or I swear I'll throw you in it.'

His face tightened at that. 'Yes,' he whispered, and I let go of his shoulders. 'It was not the lady, sir. It was you. I want that understood this time.'

'What the hell are you talking about?'

'I'm not doing this because of what she said.'

'You aren't the master, are you? For God's sake tell the truth.'

'I have always told the truth, sir. No, I am not the master. Do you remember the picture I gave you?'

I nodded.

'You discarded it. I took the liberty, sir, of rescuing it from the wastecan in your bedroom. I have it here.' He reached into his coat and pulled it out, just as he had on the first day, and handed it to me.

'It's one of these? One of the servants?'

Priest nodded and pointed with an impeccably manicured fore-finger to the figure at the extreme right of the second row. The name beneath it was *Kevin Malone*.

'Him?'

Silently, Priest nodded again.

I had examined the picture on the night he had given it to me, but I had never paid special attention to that particular half-inch-high image. The person it represented might have been a gardener, a man of middle age, short and perhaps stocky. A soft, sweat-stained hat cast a shadow on his face.

'I want to see him.' I looked toward Marcella, still leaning against the stonework of the mantel. 'We want to see him.'

'Are you certain, sir?'

'Damn you, get him!'

Priest remained where he was, staring at me; I was so furious that I think I might have seized him as I had threatened and pushed him into the fire.

Then the French windows opened, and there came a gust of wind. For an instant I think I expected a ghost, or some turbulent elemental spirit. I felt that pricking at the neck that comes when one reads Poe alone at night.

The man I had seen in the picture stepped into the room. He was a small and very ordinary man in worn khaki, but he left the windows wide behind him, so that the night entered with him, and remained in the room for as long as we talked.

'You own this house,' I said. 'You're Kevin Malone.'

He shook his head. 'I am Kevin Malone – this house owns me.'

Marcella was standing straighter now, drunk, yet still at that stage of drunkenness in which she was conscious of her condition and could compensate for it. 'It owns me too,' she said, and walking almost normally she crossed the room to the baronial chair Malone had chosen, and managed to sit down at his feet.

'My father was the man-of-all-work here. My mother was the parlor maid. I grew up here, washing the cars and raking leaves out of the fountains. Do you follow me? Where did you grow up?'

I shrugged. 'Various places. Richmond, New York, three years in Paris. Until I was sent off to school we lived in hotels, mostly.'

'You see, then. You can understand.' Malone smiled for a moment. 'You're still recreating the life you had as a child, or trying to. Isn't that right? None of us can be happy any other way, and few of us even want to try.'

'Thomas Wolfe said you can't go home again,' I ventured.

'That's right, you can't go home. There's one place where we can never go – haven't you thought of that? We can dive to the bottom of the sea and some day NASA will fly us to the stars, and I have known men to plunge into the past – or the future – and drown. But there's one place where we can't go. We can't go where we are already. We can't go home, because our minds, and our hearts, and our immortal souls are already there.'

Not knowing what to say, I nodded, and that seemed to satisfy him. Priest looked as calm as ever, but he made no move to shut the windows, and I sensed that he was somehow afraid.

'I was put into an orphanage when I was twelve, but I never forgot The Pines. I used to tell the other kids about it, and it got bigger and better every year; but I knew what I said could never equal the reality.'

He shifted in his seat, and the slight movement of his legs sent Marcella sprawling, passed out. She retained a certain grace still; I have always understood that it is the reward of studying ballet as a child.

Malone continued to talk. 'They'll tell you it's no longer possible for a poor boy with a second-rate education to make a fortune. Well, it takes luck; but I had it. It also takes the willingness to risk it all. I had that, too, because I knew that for me anything under a fortune was nothing. I had to be able to buy this place – to come back and buy The Pines, and staff it and maintain it. That's what I wanted, and nothing less would make any difference.'

'You're to be congratulated,' I said. 'But why . . .'

He laughed. It was a deep laugh, but there was no humor in it. 'Why don't I wear a tie and eat my supper at the end of the big table? I tried it. I tried it for nearly a year, and every night I dreamed of home. That wasn't home, you see, wasn't The Pines. Home is three rooms above the stables. I live there now. I live at home, as a man should.'

'It seems to me that it would have been a great deal simpler for you to have applied for the job you fill now.'

Malone shook his head impatiently. 'That wouldn't have done it at all. I had to have control. That's something I learned in business – to have control. Another owner would have wanted to change things, and maybe he would even have sold out to a subdivider. No. Besides, when I was a boy this estate belonged to a fashionable young couple. Suppose a man of my age had bought it? Or a young woman, some whore.' His mouth tightened, then relaxed. 'You and your wife were ideal. Now I'll have to get somebody else, that's all. You can stay the night, if you like. I'll have you driven into the city tomorrow morning.'

I ventured, 'You needed us as stage properties, then. I'd be willing to stay on those terms.'

Malone shook his head again. 'That's out of the question. I don't need props, I need actors. In business I've put on little shows for the competition, if you know what I mean, and sometimes even for my own people. And I've learned that the only actors who can really do justice to their parts are the ones who don't know what they are.'

'Really—' I began.

He cut me off with a look, and for a few seconds we stared at one another. Something terrible lived behind those eyes.

Frightened despite all reason could tell me, I said, 'I understand,' and stood up. There seemed to be nothing else to do. 'I'm glad, at least, that you don't hate us. With your childhood it would be quite natural if you did. Will you explain things to Marcella in the morning? She'll throw herself at you, no matter what I say.'

He nodded absently.

'May I ask one question more? I wondered why you had to leave and go into the orphanage. Did your parents die or lose their places?'

Malone said, 'Didn't you tell him, Priest? It's the local legend. I thought everyone knew.'

The butler cleared his throat. 'The elder Mr. Malone – he was the stableman here, sir, though it was before my time. He murdered Betty Malone, who was one of the maids. Or at least he was thought to have, sir. They never found the body, and it's possible he was accused falsely.'

'Buried her on the estate,' Malone said. 'They found bloody rags and the hammer, and he hanged himself in the stable.'

'I'm sorry . . . I didn't mean to pry.'

The wind whipped the drapes like wine-red flags. They knocked over a vase and Priest winced, but Malone did not seem to notice. 'She was twenty years younger and a tramp,' he said. 'Those things happen.'

I said, 'Yes, I know they do,' and went up to bed.

I do not know where Marcella slept. Perhaps there on the carpet, perhaps in the room that had been hers, perhaps even in Malone's servants' flat over the stables. I breakfasted alone on the terrace, then – without Bateman's assistance – packed my bags.

I saw her only once more. She was wearing a black silk dress; there were circles under her eyes and her head must have been throbbing, but her hand was steady. As I walked out of the house, she was going over the Sèvres with a peacock-feather duster. We did not speak.

I have sometimes wondered if I was wholly wrong in anticipating a ghost when the French windows opened. How did Malone know the time had come for him to appear?

Of course I have looked up the newspaper reports of the murder. All the old papers are on microfilm at the library, and I have a great deal of time.

There is no mention of a child. In fact, I get the impression that the identical surnames of the murderer and his victim were coincidental. *Malone* is a common enough one, and there were a good many Irish servants then.

Sometimes I wonder if it is possible for a man – even a rich man – to be possessed, and not to know it.